Ultraviolet

Elise Noble

Published by Undercover Publishing Limited

Copyright © 2017 Elise Noble

ISBN: 978-1-910954-47-8

Edited by Amanda Ann Larson

Cover art by Abigail Sins

www.undercover-publishing.com

www.elise-noble.com

Let the fire inside you burn brighter than the fire around you.

PROLOGUE

I HAVE NO name. That died years ago, along with my soul, my hopes, and my dreams. Now all that's left is a body and a number. Some say seven's lucky, but it sure didn't work out that way for me.

Once, there were ten of us. Three died young, and sometimes when I looked back on how I became what I did, I wondered what happened to the other six. Out of our little group, two girls, eight boys, I'd been the smallest. Not surprising, really, considering I was only twelve and the next youngest was fourteen. We were together for three years before we were scattered, like seeds from a dandelion, to all the corners of the world to do our masters' bidding.

I used to wonder how things would have turned out if fate hadn't picked me that night. Well, not so much fate, but Pyotr, the janitor at the orphanage where I'd lived since the age of four. There was a reason Pyotr chose to work at the Vladivostok Home for Girls, and it had nothing to do with the generous wages or the luxurious living conditions and everything to do with the abundance of helpless young flesh available to him, no questions asked, no problems.

Only that night, nineteen years ago, I made my first big mistake. I caused a problem.

I don't remember everything that happened, but I

remember enough. Some parts are crystal clear, and I'm grateful my mind blurred out the rest.

I do recall that it was the middle of winter, and I couldn't sleep because the cold had seeped into my bones. The heating, meagre though it was, had been turned off hours before and the thin blanket that covered me wasn't enough to stop me from shivering. I lay on a threadbare mattress, just one in a row of six on that side of the dormitory. All but one of the other beds were occupied. Tatiana had disappeared a few days previously, and none of us knew where she'd gone.

That night, the light of the full moon glinted on the metal handle as the door swung open. There was no sound apart from the breathing of the girls sleeping around me because, like a good Boy Scout, Pyotr had oiled the hinges.

The edge of my bed dipped as he sat down on it, and when I started to scream, he put his bony hand over my mouth. I could hardly breathe. The smell of engine oil and cigarettes from his filthy palm invaded my nostrils, and I gagged, bile rising in my throat.

Then he grabbed me by the arm and forced me to walk in front of him, all the way to his room in the basement. I didn't understand what was going to happen, but I knew it would be painful. The other girls had told me how much it stung, and when they cried, he laughed and made it hurt more. I didn't want it to hurt.

Pyotr unzipped his pants, and his fetid breath made me want to vomit as he forced his lips onto mine. A cluster of wiry hairs sprouting from the mole next to his nose tickled my face. Funny how you remember the small things, isn't it? I squirmed on the lumpy mattress as he pushed me onto his bed, the dim light on his bedside table illuminating the few yellowed teeth he had left.

Then the blackness came.

I remember walking down the corridor in a daze, covered in Pyotr's blood, knowing that I had to clean myself up or I'd be in trouble. A flash of his body lying on the bed. Then I cried as I scrubbed myself in the grimy shower cubicle all the girls shared, blackened with years of mould and dirt. Until that day, I didn't know how blood could stick. How it could embed itself under your fingernails and stain your skin. The water in the shower ran pink, mixed with my tears.

The next day, I thought it had been a bad dream. Over breakfast, I kept glancing at the door, waiting for Pyotr to walk in and show his foul temper by shouting at us for some imagined misdemeanour. But of course, he didn't. Then the police came, their faces fierce and yet solemn at the same time, I watched through the railings at the top of the stairs as the staff were called into Matron's office, one at a time, to answer their questions. Each time a worker left, they looked as scared as I felt.

It wasn't until two days later that they came for me. The little bitch in the bed next to mine told Matron who Pyotr had chosen, and they found my bloody nightshirt wadded up in the back of my locker, hidden under my thick winter coat.

Matron fetched me with two big policemen standing behind her, and I waited for the lash of her tongue. That was the usual punishment for disobedience, along with a beating with whatever she happened to have in her hand and no food for several days, sometimes even a week.

But when she walked into the communal room where I was mopping the floor, she didn't have anger in her eyes. It was something else. Fear.

That day, I left the Vladivostok Home for Girls. Left the city entirely. At first, I didn't know where I'd been taken, but if not for all the ice, I'd have said it was hell.

The military base was in the middle of nowhere, surrounded by trees as far as the eyes could see. Miles and miles of forest. Larch, spruce, fir, and pine. Apart from some mountains in the distance, that was all there was, and despite the vast space, it somehow felt claustrophobic.

The guards spoke Russian, and snow lay on the ground for most of the year, so I knew I hadn't left the country, but whether I was in the north or the south, the east or the west, I couldn't say. The only way in or out was by plane, or occasionally helicopter. I was a prisoner.

That was where he trained me. The man who burrowed into my psyche and peeled away my fears, layer by layer, until the only thing left that scared me was him. The man who taught me to gain a mark's confidence with a coquettish smile, or strike terror into his heart with a well-timed glare.

"It's all in the eyes," he used to tell me.

The man who showed me how to kill with everything from my bare hands, to a knife, to a scarf, to a gun, to a bottle, to a shoe, to an umbrella, to a fucking rocket launcher.

It was where I became Seven.

Seven of Ten.

CHAPTER 1

I SAT ON my bed, fidgeting from one butt cheek to the other. A bead of sweat popped out on my chest and ran between my breasts, and I rubbed it away with my sweater. Fuck. I closed my eyes for a second and let out a steady breath. This nervousness wasn't something I felt often, but then again, it wasn't often I tried to break out of a maximum-security military base guarded by a legion of Russian special forces and hundreds of miles from anywhere. And I'd never before attempted something so stupid with a two-year-old child in tow.

I looked down at her, nestled against my side, and for the thousandth time asked myself whether I was crazy enough to go through with what I was planning. In sleep, with her tiny hand curled into mine, her beautiful face showed none of the tension usually present. Tension no child should ever have to suffer. I knew the answer was yes.

It was the only chance, for both of us. It had taken years to come along, and I'd probably be dead before this sort of opportunity arose again. Then what would happen to my daughter? She'd be left alone with the monster who'd brought us here in the first place.

With that as the alternative, death seemed like the better option.

I ran through the plan in my head one more time.

Until earlier today, when I overheard a group of the guards talking, I hadn't been sure it was feasible. But when I ran through the logistics in my head, I decided the time window was just large enough that it could work. Not only did the guards have a potential distraction from Elizabeth and friends, the radio system had been malfunctioning all day, which meant they couldn't call for backup. But there was no room for error on my part.

Boots sounded on the concrete outside my cell, and I forced my shoulders to relax in case an overly vigilant guard peered through the bars. That box, twenty feet by eighteen of stark white paint and industrial carpet, had been my home for the past three years. I wouldn't miss it.

Deep breaths, Seven. I was as ready as I could be. I mean, it wasn't as if I had a lot to pack. Just an extra pair of contact lenses and my daughter's favourite toy, a fluffy rabbit she'd named Twixy after one of the more humane guards snuck her an American chocolate bar a month or so ago. As nothing was supposed to go in or out of our cell without prior approval, the poor sod hadn't lasted long. A week later, I'd stood on my bed, watching through the bars as the general executed him in the courtyard for some perceived indiscretion. At least the *mudak* had done his own dirty work that day. Most of the time that fell to me.

Gently, I lay my daughter on the bed as I stood up and bounced on my toes. No noise. Good—I hadn't left anything loose in the pockets of the lightweight cargo pants I wore. A few stretches helped me to relax, and as I sat back down, the sense of calm I'd felt many times over the years settled through me. I wasn't a woman anymore, not a mother or even a human being. I was a bitch, pure and simple. He'd trained me that way.

I glanced at my watch again and took one last look around my prison. No, nothing else worth taking. The matte black Rolex I wore was the only thing of value I was allowed, probably because I couldn't kill anybody with it. The thirty-thousand-dollar watch had been a thirtieth birthday gift from the general a year ago. By then, our relations had soured to the point that I spent my birthday dinner with my ankles shackled to the floor while his staff served up a five-course feast complete with a fucking string quartet playing in the background. I'd refused to speak to him, and when we'd finished our coffee, the drugs he'd stirred into it kicked in, and he delivered me back to my cell to sleep it off. I know what you're thinking—why did he bother? Because he could. With the general, everything was about control.

With that thought, I undid the strap. The bastard had probably put a tracking device inside. I'd already checked Twixy thoroughly, which was why he only had one ear now.

Another minute ticked by.

Please, let this work. According to the handful of books on child development I'd had access to, Tabitha was smart for her age, but would she keep to the plan? I'd always preferred to work alone because I never trusted a partner not to screw things up, but when my accomplice was two-and-a-half years old? Had I lost my damn mind?

No, General Zacharov had stolen it, and this was my only chance to get it back.

I pressed a kiss to Tabby's forehead, waking her up,

then put a finger to my lips.

"Stay still," I whispered. "Okay?"

She stared up at me with her big brown eyes—her father's eyes, not mine—and nodded.

It was time.

I took a deep breath and laid my beautiful little girl on the cold floor of our prison. She closed her eyes, a tiny smile on her lips. A smile that I mirrored. Yes, that was my daughter.

"Help! I need help!" I injected enough panic into my voice to make the guard stationed outside come right away rather than waiting until half-time.

He stomped up to the bars and peered through, his face screwed up in disgust.

"What do you want? I'm missing the football game."

I waved over to where Tabby lay flat by the bed. "She just fell on the floor. I don't think she's breathing!"

Outwardly, I projected the fear of a mother with everything to lose, but inside I willed myself to remain calm as I studied every twitch of the bastard's face, every movement of his hands. Did I look panicked enough? I was going for scared but not hysterical. No man wanted to deal with a hysterical female.

I increased the pitch of my voice slightly. "Help her. Please, you've got to help her!"

My fists wanted to clench, but I grabbed the bars instead. *Please, Tabby, don't move. Keep your eyes closed.* I'd practised this over and over with her, always at night while the guards were lax, but training a toddler to keep still was almost as difficult as teaching a new conscript to think first then shoot.

The guard glanced through the doorway at the TV

screen as it dissolved into static for a few seconds then looked back at Tabby.

"I'll call for the doctor."

He acted like he was doing me a favour, and I wasn't sure whether his lack of compassion was passed down from his parents or instilled by the general.

Either way, his suggestion wouldn't work. "The doctor's on the other side of the base." I collapsed to my knees beside Tabby and forced the tears to match my broken voice. "She'll die before he gets here. Please, I need help with CPR. If she dies, I can't go on without her."

He knew that. They all did. From the procedures the general had put in place, anyone with half a brain could work out that he used Tabby to control me. Without her alive, I had nothing to lose but the general did.

If anything happened to my daughter, the young guard in front of me would have to explain to General Zacharov why he no longer had his favourite assassin under his thumb to do his dirty work. And the general was definitely the type to shoot the messenger.

A step backwards, a step forwards. I could see the indecision on the guard's face and in his movements as I pretended to give my daughter mouth-to-mouth.

"Stay still, Tabby," I whispered.

Come on, open the door. I willed the guard to make the right decision. Well, the right one for me. He knew as well as I did Dr. Kurkov would take at least ten minutes to arrive, and that was a long time to go without a heartbeat. I knew what was going through his mind—he was weighing up the general's wrath against the harmless-looking woman before him. Sure, he'd heard the stories about me, legends, if you like, but in the three years I'd been in this room, neither he nor any of the other guards had seen for themselves why General Zacharov insisted they follow his security procedures to the letter around me.

Patience? It was one of the few things I had left, and I knew how to use it to my advantage. Zacharov had taught me well in that respect.

The rules were strict. When I came back from a job, I was drugged, stripped naked, and searched. Everywhere. Before I woke up, they threw me back into my cell, and only once the door was securely locked did they fetch Tabby and put her into the small room next door. Then the door between the rooms opened, and she came through to join me. Eleven times over the past two and a half years I'd woken from a groggy sleep, aching from work I was no longer fit enough to do, violated by the guards' rough fingers, to find my daughter curled up against my side.

And every time I saw the fear etched into her face, my resolve to kill each and every one of those fuckers intensified a little more.

But how? When I went out on a job, the procedure was reversed. I wasn't allowed to leave my cell with Tabby, ever, and everything that came in had to be approved by the general and checked by three separate guards, just in case I'd managed to corrupt a couple of them. I wasn't even allowed a fucking pencil, and my cutlery was the cheap plastic kind that snapped if I tried to eat anything of substance.

Guards sat in an ante-room twenty-four-seven, with checks done at irregular intervals just to keep me on my toes, and even left to my own devices, there wasn't much I could do with a foam mattress and a beanbag chair.

My new best friends became patience and revenge.

I didn't cause trouble, I didn't talk back, and apart from the occasions I was alone with the general, I never challenged an instruction.

Tick tock, tick tock. The second hand on my overpriced watch swept around tirelessly.

Today's guard was young, new. Yevgeny. Yevgeny liked football, ran three miles every morning, and had a weakness for his mama's chicken pie. But I didn't care about any of that. All I cared about was how much pressure it would take before his neck snapped like a dry twig.

Yevgeny chewed his bottom lip as he considered his options.

I thought back to the man I'd lost, Tabby's father, and the events that led me to this hellhole, and let out a quiet sob. "She's going to die," I whispered.

Mind made up, Yevgeny eyed me warily as he reached for the lever that opened my door.

"You stay seated."

His hand touched the pistol on his hip in an unconscious gesture. Nervous, and so he should be.

"Please, just hurry."

The door slid to the side with a muffled thunk, and Yevgeny scurried across the room and knelt next to me. Tabby twitched as his shadow loomed over her, and I willed her not to move. We were so damn close.

"I'll do the chest compressions," Yevgeny said.

My daughter's beautiful face was the last thing he ever saw. He may have been bigger than me, but I'd discovered many years ago that it didn't take much more effort to break a big man's neck than a small man's. It was all about the angle.

However, it did take more effort to drag him over to our bed and squash him under the blankets.

Tabby opened her eyes as I stood back to admire my handiwork. Yes, anyone taking a quick glance would assume we were asleep. They didn't get paid enough to check properly.

I'd liberated Yevgeny's pistol before I tucked him into bed, and now I stuck it into my waistband. Its cool bulk comforted me, although all hell would break loose if I fired it.

"You did well, sweetie," I whispered to Tabby, and her eyes flicked to the lump on the bed.

Damn the fucking general for putting me into this position. No child should have to witness their mother kill a man.

The sound of a shampoo commercial drifted over from the ancient television as I hefted Tabby onto my left hip, leaving my right hand free for my weapon. The two hours I spent working out every day meant I'd kept some of my strength, even if my operational effectiveness was somewhat rusty.

"We're going to take a little walk, okay, *katyonak*?" I'd nicknamed Tabby *kitten* when she was a baby because her name reminded me of the old tabby cat we'd had when I was her age. "You remember our game? We stay quiet, yes?"

She nodded, and I hoped she understood. Luckily, she'd never been a chatty child, probably because she didn't have anybody to talk to but me and Olga, the old battle axe who took care of her when I was forced to work.

Extra sweater, extra socks, a blanket... I bundled my daughter up, ready for the cold. At the beginning of October, temperatures in southern Siberia hovered around zero. Another month and I wouldn't even attempt this.

"Ready?" I asked, more to myself than her.

She looked up at me, eyes soft. She may have got her father's facial features, but her personality was all mine, and she set her tiny jaw as she curled her fingers into the collar of the jacket I'd just put on.

The TV was back to football as we slipped out the door, and I closed the cell door behind us. A quick check around the guard's room garnered me a chocolate bar and a metal pen. Useful—I could take a man's eye out with that. So far, so good. Now for the second part of my plan, the part that wasn't so much a plan as a prayer.

On a normal day, even if I escaped from my cell, I'd have no way to get off Base 13. The nearest city, Tayshet, was a four-hour drive away, and despite the base's isolation, General Zacharov's paranoia meant the perimeter of what had become his own private playground was well-guarded. Supplies and personnel went in and out by plane.

Sure, there were jeeps used for transport within the base, but even if I could sneak out in one, I didn't rate my chances on the rutted road that led to civilisation. The general's helicopter was loaded with a 30mm automatic cannon plus twelve anti-tank missiles, and he knew how to use them. For years, I'd fantasised about stealing a plane, but the rigorously maintained counter-air defences and Zacharov's twitchy trigger finger ensured I wouldn't get far.

But today? Today was different.

Because for the past four days, a team of international weapons inspectors had been touring the base, part of the Russian president's attempt to appease NATO following a small hiccup with a bunch of terrorists and an escaped super virus. Far from being worried, Zacharov had been his usual arrogant self as he'd told me about it over dinner a couple of weeks back—him on one side of the bars, eating veal orlov off a bone china plate, me on the other with the same meal and disposable utensils.

"More wine, Seven?"

"Fuck you."

He leaned back in his seat and sighed. "That attitude is why we can't have a proper meal together anymore. It saddens me."

"You're the one who locked us up like animals."

"Only when you got a crazy notion to quit in your head. I didn't spend sixteen years training you so you could play housewife with some American dropout."

"Well, you got your wish when you had him killed, didn't you?"

"I've told you many times, that was an accident."

Accident, my ass. Like his apartment just happened to explode. I stabbed at a piece of veal with my fork, and two of the plastic tines snapped. Zacharov passed me another through the bars, and I resisted the temptation to break his fingers.

"You need to eat, *tigryonak*." Little tiger. He'd been calling me that for years. "I have another job for you in a few weeks, after the inspection team has been through. Those fools," he added under his breath.

"What's happening with that, anyway?"

"The American president is stamping his feet again, and our ministers are prostituting themselves to please him. But no matter, they can look all they want. They won't find anything."

"You've moved the weapons?"

"No need. They're hidden well enough. They want Likho, and it's in the same place as it's always been." His face clouded over as he sprinkled more salt on his dinner. "But if I ever catch the traitor who told of its existence..."

I maintained my impassive mask as I forked up slimy mushrooms, but inside I was laughing. Me. I'd told the Americans about Likho. Back when I wasn't tethered by my daughter, I'd given up a number of Zacharov's secrets to the other side, although it took them forever to act on the information.

"Whoever it was is probably dead, anyway. Your staff don't have a long life expectancy."

"That's because most of them are imbeciles. But you, Seven, you're the one with talent. You shouldn't let it go to waste."

He locked me in a cell for most of my life, and *I* was the one wasting my talent? I bit back a snarky comment and chewed so hard I risked cracking a tooth. The general didn't tolerate sarcasm well, or humour in any form, and I'd long since dialled mine back. His recruits could literally laugh themselves to death.

Anyhow, as Zacharov foretold, the inspection team hadn't got lucky. He'd played the congenial host, showing them around all the areas he wanted guests to see and evading their questions while plying them with lies.

"Idiots!" he'd told me the night before last. "They

couldn't find their own *zad* with two hands and a map."

I'd heard the guards talking too. Those guys gossiped worse than mothers at a school yard. The inspection team consisted of twelve people—six inspectors and six bodyguards. The bodyguards did nothing but stand around, and the inspectors did nothing but ask stupid and pointless questions. Apart from one of them, it seemed. Elizabeth was a woman with an extremely ample chest who not only asked stupid and pointless questions, she tripped over a lot and provided the guards with a source of entertainment too. And they didn't get much of that on Base 13, believe me.

And today, when Yevgeny relieved Igor, they'd lamented her imminent departure. The inspectors would be flying out at eight o'clock this evening, one hour from now.

CHAPTER 2

I PLUCKED YEVGENY'S black woollen cap off the table and pulled it down over my own head. My hair might have been the colour of the night, but I didn't want it shining in the lights that illuminated the base between the hours of dusk and dawn. He'd left a half-drunk glass of water too, and I spilled some on the floor then rubbed the dirty paste over my face.

With the grey woollen blanket covering Tabby, we'd blend into the shadows. We had to—this was all or nothing. Either we'd escape, or we'd be dead.

The corridor that led from our basement prison lay silent as one of Zacharov's makeshift graveyards as we stole along it. Years of practice meant I didn't make a sound as I walked. Outside, I took in my first breath of fresh air in almost three months as we hunkered down behind a storage shed, watching as the inspection team loaded the last of their equipment into the six jeeps waiting to drive them over to the runway. That trip would take almost ten minutes. Base 13 was a sprawling scar on the Siberian landscape. As I'd come to expect, the team's bodyguards stood around, hands in pockets, while Russian conscripts sullenly carried all the bags and boxes.

Fifteen metres away, a woman wearing a black parka trimmed with rainbow fur around the hood stood talking to a group of guards. Impractical and tasteless at the same time—that could only be Elizabeth.

She reached out to Vlad, a sadistic bastard if there ever was one, and squeezed his bicep. "Ooh, Vlad. Your muscles are so big. Do you go to the gym every day?"

Oh, please.

Vlad laughed, the deep sound like a train rumbling through a tunnel, and placed his hand over hers. "No, Elizavet. I do lots of fighting and shoot the big guns."

"So tough! I wish the men in California were as strong as you."

She grinned up at him, and I swear the asshole blushed. Still, when the only female company for two hundred miles came via the porn channel, it wasn't surprising half of the guards had hard-ons.

"Your American men, they are weak. Russians, we are real men."

Vlad launched into a rambling monologue about combat training and the wars he'd fought in while Elizabeth lapped up every word. Most of what Vlad said was bullshit. Elizabeth's bodyguard was standing next to her, and his eyes had glazed over.

Vlad had barely closed his mouth when Elizabeth started up again, and her saccharine tones made me wish for earplugs. "Vlad, could you do me a teensy favour and fetch my cases from my room? They're really heavy, but I'm sure you'll hardly notice the weight."

"Of course, Miss Elizavet. It would be my pleasure."

Don't make me throw up. Still, I had to thank her, because Vlad and the other muscle-bound waste of space with him trailed Elizabeth and her bodyguard back to the building that had served as their guest quarters, and that meant the coast was clear.

As their voices receded into the darkness, I scuttled from my hiding place and ran to the nearest jeep. The trunk was stacked with equipment, but there was enough room at the side of it for Tabby and me to fit. I'd pulled the edge of a tarpaulin over the pair of us by the time they returned a few minutes later.

Vlad threw a bag on top of us, and I shielded Tabby's head, waiting for another hit.

"That car's kind of full, don't you think?" Elizabeth screeched. "I don't want the *pirozhki* Yulia made me getting squashed." Another car door opened. "There's plenty of space in this one."

Pirozhki? Good grief, she was taking home food as a souvenir? Vlad retreated, and thumps echoed as he shoved the rest of her luggage into the next car.

"Would you mind if I took a couple of photos?" Elizabeth asked. "The girls back home will never believe how cute you guys all are otherwise."

Mumbles of agreement came, followed by Elizabeth's instructions of "left a bit...right a bit... closer." Then a squeal. "Ooh, here's Oleg."

Wonderful, Zacharov was here, and it seemed he and the bimbo were on first-name terms. How did somebody with so few brain cells ever qualify as a weapons inspector in the first place? The general must have been celebrating from the moment she turned up.

His footsteps sounded near the car, slow and measured. I could pick them out anywhere. Please, don't look inside.

"Did you get everything you needed, Miss Elizabeth?"

"I think so, and it was so kind of you to show us

around personally. Can I just get a picture with you? I've never been to Russia before, and this whole trip's been quite an adventure."

"Of course."

I heard the amusement in his voice, but I figured I'd be smiling too if an inspection team had just failed to find the bunkers where all my good weapons were hidden.

Finally, the squawking stopped, and the suspension dipped as people climbed into the vehicle. One, two, three, four times. Four occupants. Who was on board with us?

A Russian driver—I heard him talking to a colleague out of the window. Something about lining the vodka up for when they got back. And... Elizabeth. I got Elizabeth. Fantastic.

"Could you turn the heating up?" she asked. "It's freezing in here."

Then we were off, and I forced my heart to remain steady as I counted down the ten minutes to freedom or... No, I didn't want to think about it because that meant Tabby would have no life either.

Elizabeth frayed my last nerve as she rattled on with a constant stream of drivel about how much snow there was, how big the tanks were, how exciting her whole entire trip had been, how strange the food tasted, and on, and on, and on. If I was the guy driving, I'd have been tempted to test my gun on her. For sure, I could have found some way to write it off as an accident.

Just as I had that thought, I got the shock of my life, and I wasn't an easy person to shock, believe me. I'd been there, done that, and got the T-shirt and battle scars to prove it. But when Elizabeth's hand snaked over the back of the seat and dropped a phone into my hand, I'll admit it nearly gave me a heart attack.

The screen was lit up, and as she carried on with her ceaseless chatter, I read what she'd typed.

I take it you're not along for a joyride?

What the fuck? She knew I was there? Why didn't she say anything? Even now she was talking as if nothing had happened, and unless my ears deceived me, she'd just asked the driver whether there were any sabre-toothed tigers in these parts.

I couldn't ignore her. Her arm was hanging over the seat, fingers twitching for my answer. I didn't have a clue what her game was, but I had to play along. I kept my reply vague and put the phone back into her waiting hand.

There is nothing joyous about this place.

A few seconds later, as the bodyguard next to her patiently explained that sabre-toothed tigers had been extinct for millions of years, she handed the phone back.

Our plane is waiting. Are you coming with us?

I typed out the only answer I could.

Yes.

I waited longer for her next message as the jeep wove around a series of hangars near the runway.

I'll distract them while you get on board. Hide in the bedroom at the back.

Well, it seemed I'd found an unlikely ally. I had no idea what she wanted or why she was helping us, but as long as we got out of this godforsaken hellhole, I'd deal with that later.

Tabby and I slid forwards as the driver braked

roughly to a halt, and cold air rushed in as the doors opened one after another. The stink of Vlad's body odour washed over me as he wrenched up the lid of the trunk and began heaving the equipment out onto the tarmac. Whatever Elizabeth was planning, she needed to fucking hurry up about it. One more case and our hiding place would be revealed.

"Aaah! My ankle! I think I might have broken it."

Vlad's deep voice sounded from a little further away. "Poor Elizavet. Did you slip?"

"Yes, on the ice. Could you help me up?" A sharp intake of breath. "It really hurts."

I peered out from under the tarpaulin and saw Elizabeth sitting on the ground a car length away with the guards gathered around. The only person facing me was her bodyguard, and he remained impassive as I gathered Tabby up and slipped out of the trunk. Elizabeth let out an anguished wail as I ran to the plane, then she burst into tears as I hurried up the stairs. The bedroom. She'd said to hide in the bedroom. It wasn't big, just a double bed with a nightstand each side plus a narrow closet big enough to fit Tabby. I yanked open the door and evicted a flight case then tucked her into the bottom.

"Stay quiet, *katyonak*, okay?" I touched a finger to my lips.

"Yes, mama."

I covered her with the blanket as best I could, then crawled into the space along the far side of the bed. If somebody walked around it, I couldn't be more obvious, but a cursory glance through the door wouldn't reveal my hiding place. Russian voices sounded from the cabin, and I held my breath. Just a few minutes more, that was all we needed, but if they discovered Yevgeny's body in my cell before that, the general would unleash hell.

Footsteps came closer, closer, right up to the bed. A shadow loomed over, and Elizabeth's bodyguard looked down at me.

"Shhh." He put a finger to his lips then dropped a pile of coats over the top of me. I burrowed into them, tucking my legs against my stomach.

Outside, Elizabeth arrived in the main cabin, no doubt assisted by Vlad and his minions.

"I can't believe you carried me up the steps so easily. I know you said you were strong, but that was something else. Do you think I might be able to get some ice for my ankle?"

Sure, he could just scoop some up from outside.

Every second of the wait seemed to last an hour, but finally the Russian voices faded away, and the engines roared into life. Slowly, so slowly, the plane began to move.

When the wheels left the tarmac, the crushing weight on my chest lifted with them. I may have been penniless with nothing but the clothes on my back, but I had my daughter, and she was worth everything to me. As the plane flew towards an unknown destination, I found myself wanting to live for the first time in three years.

CHAPTER 3

FIVE MINUTES PASSED, then ten, before footsteps came into the bedroom and the coats over me were lifted away. Elizabeth looked down at me, hands on her hips and one eyebrow raised.

"Okay, this had better be good. I'm dying to know why we just helped you to escape from General Fuckwit and his merry band of assholes."

The first thing I noticed was that her West Coast accent had vanished, replaced by clipped English tones. The second thing was that she wasn't Elizabeth anymore. Well, she was, but not the giggling, irritating, simpering Elizabeth who'd been there a quarter of an hour ago. This Elizabeth was calm, self-assured, and perfectly composed. I met her gaze, and she held my eyes with an unforgiving stare.

I fought to keep my face blank as a groan rose in my throat. Fuck. I'd fallen right into the trap I'd set for others so many times before. I'd taken Elizabeth at face value and grossly underestimated her. Inwardly, I cursed first myself and then Zacharov. Three years in that hole had dulled my senses, which was why I found myself trapped on a plane at ten thousand feet with a woman who very much reminded me of the person I'd been before my prison sentence began.

I didn't take my eyes off her as I reached for my

gun, praying it was loaded with ammunition that wouldn't go through the plane as well as her head should I need to fire it. In a situation like this, I'd want MagSafe, which would fragment on impact, making a nice mess of the target while leaving everything behind it untouched. Oh, who was I kidding? Yevgeny had probably never even heard of MagSafe.

"Don't even think about it."

Dammit, I'd blinked, and now she had a gun in her hand. A Walther P88.

"And I know what's going through your mind," she said. "Yes, it's loaded with MagSafe, and no, I won't miss."

"Shit." The word escaped my lips as I laid my head back. Out of the fucking frying pan and straight into hell, part two.

"Oh, for crying out loud. Get up."

She motioned to the bed with the barrel of the gun as I calculated angles and distances. Could I take her down safely? She stepped back a pace. No. I couldn't.

She sighed. "I'm not going to shoot you, but I know you've got a weapon of some sort on you, and I'd rather you didn't use it."

If the situation was reversed, I wouldn't choose to fire at that point, so I got to my knees, careful to keep my hands in view. The last thing I wanted was for Tabby to end up in the middle of a gunfight.

"What have you got?" Elizabeth asked.

I shrugged. At this point in time, it didn't matter. "A Makarov."

She laughed. "There's a reason why they're cheap."

"Beggars can't be choosers."

"I guess not. Give me the mag, eject the round in

the chamber, and I'll put mine away."

I released the magazine while the gun was aimed at the floor and tossed it in her direction. She caught it without looking and tucked her Walther behind her back. I did the same with the Makarov. Even without the ammunition, I could use it to do a significant amount of damage to a normal person, but I had a feeling Elizabeth was anything but normal.

A muffled "Mama" sounded from the closet, and our eyes flicked in that direction.

"Do you mind?" I asked.

"Be my guest."

I had to turn my back on Elizabeth to get Tabby, which caused my throat to tighten, but I made the effort to smile as I picked my daughter up and hugged her tightly against me. "It's okay, *katyonak*," I whispered, hating that I had to lie to her.

When I straightened, Elizabeth was leaning against the wall by the door, a less aggressive stance than before. I followed her lead and sat on the edge of the bed with Tabby cradled on my lap.

"You want something to eat?" Elizabeth asked. She smiled at Tabby, and the knot in my stomach loosened just a little.

Tabby looked back and forth between Elizabeth and me, eyes wide. The only other woman she'd seen was Olga, whose position as Tabby's de facto nanny while I went away on jobs always bothered me since it was obvious she hated kids. And now here was this smiling brunette, and Tabby's confusion was written all over her face.

"Are you hungry?" I asked her.

She nodded and rubbed her stomach.

"And you?" Elizabeth asked.

"Yes, please."

She stuck two fingers in her mouth and whistled, and a few seconds later, her bodyguard cracked the door open.

"You summoned?"

"I did."

He pushed the door all the way open and peered in. "Oh, good. You haven't killed each other yet. Did you want something other than my presence?"

"Be a babe and bring some food, would you?"

"Any preferences?"

"As long as it's not that Russian shit I've been eating all week, I don't care."

"Not a fan of the *pirozhki*, then?" I asked.

"Every time I took a bite, a rock gave up its soul."

The guy raised an eyebrow at me, and I was momentarily at a loss. I couldn't remember the last time somebody asked for my preference on anything. Actually, I could. Three years and one month ago, when Tabby's father took me out for what was to be our last meal together. Nothing expensive, just steak and chips at an American-style diner in Moscow, but because it was with him, the steak tasted like the best I'd ever eaten.

Stop it, Seven. I couldn't dwell on the past. Sam Jessop was nothing more than a memory now, a ghost whose image grew fainter with every passing day. Tabby was the only thing left of him, and I needed to get a grip for her sake.

"I'll eat anything."

When the bodyguard left, Elizabeth sat on the bed and scooted back until she was sitting on one pillow.

"What was that about?"

I clutched Tabby tighter. "What was what about?"

"You disappeared there."

"It was nothing." I didn't mean to snap, but I couldn't help it.

"Fine, be like that. And you still haven't answered my first question."

What question? Oh, right. Why was I escaping from Base 13? "Let's just say General Zacharov and I no longer see eye to eye."

"That's all you're gonna give me?"

"What else do you want?"

"Are you defecting?"

"No, I'm quitting."

"Quitting what?"

"My previous life."

"Which is...?"

"You don't give up, do you?"

She grinned. "It's one of my better qualities."

"I worked for Zacharov, on...various projects. But over the last few years, he's been more and more difficult to get along with, and the only other way to leave his employment would have been feet first. But I have a daughter now."

"What about her father? Will he come after her?"

I understood her real question—did Tabby's father work at Base 13? "Her father is dead."

"I'm sorry."

The door opened again, and the bodyguard came back with an armful of packets. "Sorry, it's all pre-processed junk until we land. You want coffee?"

"You already know my answer," Elizabeth said.

I nodded. "Please."

"Milk? Sugar?"

"Neither."

Tabby's eyes lit up at the sight of all the colourful snacks, and I helped her to open a bag of cookies. She tried to stuff a whole one into her mouth and crumbs went everywhere.

"Sorry. She doesn't often get sweet things."

Elizabeth smiled faintly. "Don't worry. It's not my plane, anyway. The UN can pick up the valet bill."

I opened a bag of chips and helped myself to a soda. The food was far from gourmet, but compared to the fish and potatoes Olga served up for almost every meal, it tasted like a little piece of heaven.

The bodyguard came back again with two plastic mugs, one for me and one for Elizabeth. I blew the steam away from mine and took a sip, relishing the burn as the coffee slid down my throat. My cell was so far from the kitchen, all my meals got served lukewarm, and although I had a heater, it had barely taken the edge off the Siberian winter. I'd spent the last three years freezing. Tabby had never felt the sun on her face, and the vitamin D tablets we took daily were no substitute for spending time outdoors.

In those three years, I hadn't dared to make any plans for the future. Doing so would have felt like tempting fate. But now I needed to think about the logistics, and I knew one thing—our final destination would be hot.

"Where are we going?" I asked Elizabeth.

She took a sip of her coffee. "Switzerland first to drop off the weapons inspectors, then the United States. Take your pick—Geneva or Virginia."

I noticed she didn't class herself among them. "So

you're not a weapons inspector?"

Her shrill American accent came back. "No, I was the comic relief."

"What were you doing at the base?"

"A favour."

"Is that all you're going to give me?" I echoed her earlier words back to her.

She paused, considering her words. "General Zacharov has upset a few people."

It wasn't a proper answer, but I couldn't blame her for being evasive, not when she barely knew me. "General Zacharov has the finesse of a bull."

She wrinkled her nose. "And Vlad smelled like one."

"I'm not sure he ever takes a bath."

"It wasn't just him. There's a serious personal hygiene problem on Base 13."

"You didn't seem to mind when you were posing for pictures with them earlier."

"I needed photos for my report, and it was easier to get them to pose than rely on a lapel camera. Those often come out blurry."

"Good call, *suka*." I called her a bitch without thinking, and from me, it was meant as a compliment.

She took it as one. "Thanks. I do try."

I knew at that moment I'd met a kindred spirit. My first genuine smile in years crept onto my face, and Elizabeth grinned back.

Russians had a saying, "To smile with no reason is the sign of a fool," but today, I had a reason.

Then the door opened, and the bodyguard held out a phone. "Lizzie, James is on the line."

She made a face. "I've got to take this. It'll probably be a long one. You should get some rest."

Once the door closed behind her, I realised she was right. All the adrenaline had seeped out of me and been replaced by a gnawing tiredness, as so often happened after a job.

But even exhaustion couldn't mask the tingle of elation growing inside me. The hard part was over. We'd left Base 13, and now we had the choice of Switzerland or the United States to disappear in. It wasn't a difficult decision. My English was better than my German and my French, so I'd be more comfortable in America. Plus, Tabby's father had come from Massachusetts, and although it wasn't a great basis for such an important decision, I wanted Tabby to see the country he'd called home.

With Elizabeth back in the main cabin, I rummaged through the bedroom for anything that might be useful. The closet held a few items of women's clothing, and I quickly pulled on a soft purple sweater under my own black polo neck so it wouldn't show, as well as rolling up a pair of leggings and stuffing them into my jacket pocket.

The flight case was mostly empty, but I found a blank legal pad and a pen that would come in useful before hitting the jackpot in the nightstand drawer. A knife glinted up at me, and not just any knife. The Emerson CQC-6 was my tactical knife of choice, designed for one purpose: killing people. Elizabeth's? I pocketed it, hoping it wouldn't come in handy later. I didn't need that kind of drama in my life anymore.

Blood stained my soul.

I'd hoped to find cash, but apart from a stray nickel under the bed, I came up empty. I'd need to steal money when we landed. No, my days of dancing on the wrong side of the law weren't over yet.

Without my watch, I didn't know for sure how long we had until the plane landed in Geneva, but I guessed at two or three hours. Elizabeth was right—I needed to sleep. But first I wanted to write a letter, a thank you, if you like.

Beside me, Tabby yawned, and I cleared the mess of food packets out of the way and tucked her under the blanket.

"Sleep, *katyonak*."

Her forehead felt so soft as I pressed my lips against her skin.

As she snuggled against me, safe at last, I leaned against the wall and began to write.

Chapter 4

THROUGH A HAZE of sleep, I felt something soft hit my shoulder. The knife was in my hand as I sat bolt upright, an automatic reflex.

Elizabeth laughed at me from the doorway, and I followed her gaze to the toilet roll lying on the bed.

"Why did you throw that at me?"

"Because I needed to wake you up, and I don't have a death wish."

She must have recognised the knife as hers, but she didn't say anything as I folded it up and put it back in my pocket. "Are we landing soon?"

"We're at ten thousand feet, just waiting for a slot. You want another coffee?"

"I wouldn't say no."

By the time she came back with two mugs and took a seat on the edge of the bed, I'd woken up properly. "What's the plan? Shall we hide again while the weapons inspectors get off?"

"You're eight hours behind. We're about to touch down in Virginia."

We were what? I never slept for longer than five hours. Even as a child, I'd broken my sleep into smaller chunks, and as an adult, I liked to check my surroundings at regular intervals. And now Elizabeth was telling me I'd slept for half a day?

"What if I'd wanted to stay in Switzerland?"

"You didn't. The Swiss haven't been too keen on foreigners lately, and less than half of women work so it would have been harder to blend in. Plus, it's bloody cold."

I peered out the window, where the lights of a large city twinkled below. Rows of car headlights moved in unison along the highway. "Whereabouts in Virginia?"

"Richmond. The state capital," she added unnecessarily, because I already knew that.

I might never have been there, but I'd had a detailed knowledge of geography hammered into me as a teenager. Quite literally, at one point. I thought back to the day I'd dared to disagree with my teacher over the dialect spoken in a particular part of Iraq. I was right, but that didn't stop him from slamming my head against the desk.

His was a tasteful funeral. A horse-drawn hearse, if I recalled correctly.

I was drawn out of my thoughts by Elizabeth snapping her fingers at me. "Earth to... What is your name, anyway? You zoned out again."

I had to stop doing that. "Seven."

"Seven what?"

"It's my name. Seven."

"Did your mother run out of inspiration after the first six?"

"Something like that."

She rolled her eyes. "Well, Seven, what's your plan?"

Yeah, my plan. I really, really needed to come up with one of those. Elizabeth took my silence for the lack of forethought that it was.

"I didn't think so. Fuck, what happened to you in that place? Did they lobotomise you or something?" She didn't wait for me to answer, not that I would have. "It's a good thing one of us has a brain that still functions. Get some decent clothes out of the wardrobe. Something should fit. You look like a ninja, and that's only going to draw attention. I'll be back in five."

She closed the door behind her, and I shook my head. Before my incarceration, nobody ever spoke to me like that. They were all too afraid of getting a bullet through their head. But coming from Elizabeth...her attitude spoke more of camaraderie than anything else. And I shouldn't have liked that as much as I did.

With free rein to choose my clothes, I ditched the cargo pants and picked out a pair of jeans instead. The soft blue denim moulded to me perfectly, much to my surprise. It seemed that under our bulky winter clothes, Elizabeth and I were the same size. A black turtleneck and the purple sweater I'd borrowed earlier completed the outfit, and I stuffed my own clothes into a nylon bag I found on the top shelf, together with a few more garments from Elizabeth's collection. Well, she had said to help myself.

Turned out we had the same size feet too, and I swapped my fur-lined boots for a pair of black sneakers then put my down jacket back over the top just as Elizabeth came back.

"Better. The jeans look nicer on you than they do on me. The colour makes me look washed out." She rolled her eyes again. "Good grief, listen to me. I sound like my assistant. He's the one who's into all that fashion bullshit."

She'd changed as well, I noticed. The rainbow-hued

monstrosity of a coat had disappeared in favour of a pantsuit that fitted so well it had to be made-to-measure.

"I usually wear black." It matched my soul.

"Maybe now you can try a little colour occasionally."

"Maybe." I sat back on the bed, my last moment of calm before a new adventure began. "Did you find what you were looking for at Base 13?"

"Some of it, but not the main prize."

"Likho?"

"You know about the virus?"

"I know enough to wish it didn't exist. Zacharov told me you were looking for it."

"He's got it, we know he has." A hint of frustration crept into her voice. "But I only had four nights to explore, and I couldn't find it."

"Here." I passed over the yellow sheets I'd torn from the legal pad, and her eyebrows rose as she scanned my notes and the rough map I'd drawn.

"He hid Likho under our fucking visitor quarters? That sick bastard."

"The entrance to the lab is in the basement. Last time I went there, the main facility had been sealed off. There was an accident. He left the bodies where they were and bricked up the whole damn lot, but there's one storage room left open, and that's where Likho is, along with the rest of his biological weapons. Trust me when I say you don't want to go down there without wearing a hazmat suit. When he needs something, he sends a conscript and shoots them afterwards."

"Charming."

"Zacharov is a monster."

"He is. I don't suppose you fancy telling me what else he's got hidden away on the base?"

"I can't. One secret, and he can't know for sure that I told you. If I spill them all, he'll hunt me to the ends of the earth." Perhaps he would anyway.

"We can protect you."

"I don't want to live like that anymore. I'll always be looking over my shoulder, but if I have to monitor every other direction too, I might as well have no life at all."

Elizabeth squeezed the top of my arm, and I jumped like I'd been burned. Only Sam had ever touched me that way, and a dull ache radiated out from the hole in my chest.

"I get it, I do. You want Zacharov to forget about you, but from what I've seen of him, I'm not sure he's the type to let things go."

He wasn't. Yes, for the most part he was cold and calculating, but he also had a vindictive streak running below the surface, and he could hold a grudge for years. *Years.* When I was thirteen, a young sergeant reported the then major general for brutality during an interrogation. Five years later, one chilly October day, that same sergeant killed himself. At least, that was what the official report said. I hadn't seen many suicides where the victim cut off their own head and placed it on their chest.

"Watch and learn, Seven," Zacharov had told me as he decapitated the poor bastard with barely a drop of blood spilled. The key was not to cut too deep before the heart stopped beating, apparently.

A shiver ran through me. I wouldn't be safe until Zacharov was dead, but I couldn't hide in a bunker forever. I needed to be careful, but I also needed to give Tabby a chance at normality, otherwise what would have been the point in escaping?

"You're right. He'll never forget me, but making him angry isn't the answer."

She drew a couple of objects out of her pocket and threw them in my direction, one after the other. First my gun magazine then a roll of money.

I held up the magazine. "Aren't you taking a chance, giving this back?"

"If you wanted to kill me, you'd have done it already."

"Even with the knife, it would have been difficult."

"I'm not talking about today."

What? "We've met before?"

A faint smile. "Maybe."

Her demeanour said not to push, but I was intrigued. "Thanks for the money too."

"Call it a down payment."

A down payment for what? Before I could ask, there was a bump as the wheels hit the tarmac. Tabby's eyes popped open, and I rushed to gather her up in my arms.

"What, Mama?"

"That was the airplane landing."

"Where?"

"We're in America now." And we were halfway to being free.

For the first time since Sam's death, I felt a flicker of happiness.

"I can find you a place to stay, if you want," Elizabeth offered.

For a moment, I was tempted. A roof over my head,

even if it was only for a day or two, would save me from having to strike out on my own straight away. But a little voice at the back of my mind niggled at me. What if it was a trap? I still didn't understand Elizabeth's motives in helping me, what her goal was, or who she worked for. But if there was one thing in my mind I had no doubt over, it was that Elizabeth was dangerous.

No, I'd go it alone, but as the plane ground to a halt next to a hangar, I figured I'd try a bluff of my own first.

"A place to stay would be good, but I don't want to put you to any trouble."

For a second, she looked surprised, but her mask quickly slammed back on. "It's no trouble."

"Just for a few days."

"Right. I need to go straight to a meeting, but I'll have someone take you to an apartment. You can stay there as long as you like."

"Thanks. For everything."

"Thanks for Likho." She dug in her pocket and handed me a card with a printed number, nothing else. "Here, take this. Call me if you have any problems." She got halfway to the door before she turned back and winked. "Or if you want a job."

"I told you; I quit."

"Yeah, I tried that once too. Lasted three months before I was bored out of my mind. Don't lose my number."

Before I could say another word, she left.

CHAPTER 5

ELIZABETH'S CASH PAID for a cheap motel room in a small town an hour's bus ride from Richmond. It claimed to have two stars, and some joker had drawn a minus sign in front of them, which seemed quite appropriate. But when I'd handed over an extra twenty bucks, the greasy lump behind the reception desk had dropped a key on the counter without asking for any of my details then gone back to the can of beer he'd left on the arm of the stained recliner he appeared to live in.

I hated having to take Tabby into that room for our first night of freedom. Every piece of furniture was filthy or broken, and the odour of stale cigarettes clung to the walls. I spread out my coat on the bed for Tabby to sit on while I set about unpacking the groceries I'd picked up on the way. Lucky I hadn't banked on having any cooking facilities, because the wires hanging out the back of the one-ring hotplate were an invitation for the fire brigade to visit. Probably the only people desperate enough to use it tended to cook crack rather than SpaghettiOs. Sandwiches it was, then.

I used Elizabeth's knife to butter the bread and slice the cheese, and even those simple actions felt strange, unfamiliar. In the last three years, the only time I'd used a knife was to kill a British politician on holiday in Tunisia, and I hadn't cooked a meal since my days with

Sam. We used to take it in turns—one night in his apartment then one in mine.

"You want ham as well, *katyonak*?"

"Yes."

Tabby tucked into the picnic I'd assembled, remembering to offer a square of chocolate to Twixy, who'd survived the journey in my coat pocket. She'd probably be happy living on that junk forever. I needed to remember to buy some fruit tomorrow, vegetables too. Carrots, peppers, cauliflower. No celery because that was the devil's food.

While my daughter ate, I took stock of the situation. Thanks to our unlikely rescuer, I had just over two thousand dollars, but that wouldn't last forever. I needed money, and I had two options—steal it or earn it. I preferred to go the legitimate route. With a child in tow, I couldn't afford to get into trouble with the police, and as I wasn't operating at full capacity right now, I was liable to do something stupid. Not only that, my karma had to be at an all-time low, and I needed to atone for some of the shit I'd done at Zacharov's behest.

But my priority was to survive. My daughter needed me.

Sleep didn't come easily. Not because we were in a new place, or because of nerves, but because the couple in the next room spent the entire night having an argument. By the time they'd threatened to kill each other for the fourth time, I was on the verge of picking up my gun, knocking on their door, and offering to save them the trouble.

As I buried my head under the pillow, I felt a pang of regret for turning down Elizabeth's offer. I was ninety percent sure it was genuine, and if the car she'd had pick us up was anything to go by, the apartment she'd offered to provide would have been considerably more luxurious than the dump we were in.

When I'd knocked out the driver of the Bentley limousine, I'd taken care not to scratch the interior, and after I'd hefted him into the trunk, I'd left it parked in a good area so nobody stole the wheels.

Having Tabby in tow had been a little awkward.

"Mama, why are you putting the man in the dark?"

"We're playing hide and seek, *katyonak*. It's just a game."

"Can I play?"

"We'll play later; I promise."

Just not around here. The shadows of the peeling wallpaper were long in the moonlight filtering through the gap in the drapes. Any potential hiding places would be filled with needles, or vomit, or worse. This was the armpit of America.

I'd travelled to the United States several times before, always alone and always for work. Los Angeles, Tuscaloosa, Houston, New Orleans, Atlanta, and half a dozen times to New York. Back then, Zacharov's resources had allowed me to stay in comfortable hotels, and his support network helped me to stay hidden. But now I was alone.

As I lay there, my thoughts strayed back to Sam. He'd grown up in Boston but spent a few years in New York before he moved to Moscow. We'd talked about taking a trip back to his hometown someday, but it wasn't to be.

I hadn't been looking for a relationship or even a one-night stand when Sam walked into the office I was working in one fateful Friday afternoon. Zacharov had installed me there to look for a leak. The import and export company was a front for smuggling old Soviet armaments out of the country, and he wanted to know who was letting his secrets slip out. I'd only been there for a week when Sam turned up, tool bag in hand, to service the copy machine.

"Would you like coffee?" I asked.

As receptionist, it was my job to greet guests and make them comfortable, and the office was quiet that day.

"Love one. Milk, no sugar. I'm Sam, by the way. Sam Jessop."

His Russian was fluent, but he spoke with an accent, and when he grasped my hand in greeting, electricity crackled across my skin.

"Zhenya. You're American?"

"Yes, but I've lived here for six years now."

"You moved all the way to Moscow to fix copy machines?"

He straightened up and fixed me with amber-flecked brown eyes. "Don't knock it. There's good money in copiers."

"Sorry, I didn't mean to..." The last thing I wanted to do was insult him, but his smile had jumbled my thoughts.

"You can fix it by bringing me a cookie with that coffee."

While the filter machine whirred away, I ran to the bakery three doors up and bought spice cookies and *ptichie moloko*, the chocolate-covered marshmallow that was my weakness when I was in my mother country. What was I doing? Had I lost my mind? I knew better than to get involved with a man, but from the moment I met him, Sam had a way of making me cast my reservations aside in favour of satisfying my craving for him and his...okay, the sex was good. Better than good.

In between answering the phone, greeting guests, and snooping through the boss's computer when he went home early, I spent the afternoon chatting to Sam while he changed parts in all three of the office copiers. By the time he'd finished, I knew he was born in the United States to an American father and Russian mother, his hobbies included playing the guitar and tinkering with his motorbike, and he'd adopted a dog called Vaska because he felt sorry for him sitting on the street every morning. And when he asked me to meet him for dinner that night, I'd agreed.

Our first date, if you could call it that, had been a disaster. We were having burgers and beer at the American-style diner near the office when the fire alarm went off, and we got evacuated into the street.

"Think it's a drill?" Sam asked.

I groaned as a plume of smoke rose from the back of the restaurant. "I don't think so. Good thing we finished most of our food."

"You didn't get dessert. I owe you something sweet for the cakes earlier."

As flames licked up the outside of the building, I leaned over and whispered in his ear. "You're my something sweet, Sam."

It was official—I'd gone insane.

Rather than go our separate ways, we began walking. Hand in hand at first, but by the time we'd gone past the Kremlin and a mile or two along the Moskva River, Sam's arm was wrapped firmly around my shoulders, and my right hand had found its way into his back pocket. And yes, he worked out. That ass starred in my dreams every night for weeks. We didn't talk about anything heavy, just the city, events in the news, sports, the food we liked. It didn't matter what Sam said, as long as I got to listen to his voice. I loved his accent, and when I confessed I spoke English, we chatted in a mix of both languages.

Midnight came, the temperature dropped, and the time came to go home.

"I'll walk you back to your apartment," Sam said, hugging me tighter to his side. "It's not safe for a lady to be out on her own at this time."

Oh, if only he knew.

But I wasn't about to argue, not if it gave me a few more precious moments with him. I'd expected to get his number when we got to my door, but what I actually got was his lips, plus his tongue and a hint of teeth. Fire flared inside me, and I may have hooked a leg around his calf as I kissed him back.

"I should go," he said, breathless, when we'd finally pulled apart.

"You should."

Then I unlocked my door and dragged him inside.

It was a good thing the next day was a Saturday because neither of us got any sleep that night. We didn't venture out of bed until the next afternoon, when hunger got the better of us and we'd run out of condoms, and by then, my world had shifted on its damn axis.

From that day on, it became our custom to meet each evening after work. Mostly we stayed in, but occasionally we'd grab a back table at the Red Star bar near Sam's apartment and drink and dance until the early hours. For the first time in my life I was having fun, and back then, Zacharov had held me on a long leash.

I worked in the day, digging out details of my boss's misdemeanours, of which there were plenty, and reporting them back to Zacharov. But in the evening, nothing else existed except Sam and Zhenya, or Zhen, as he called me. Then later, "my Zhen."

Because after two weeks, I knew I was his. I'd never be anybody else's. Every time I saw him, I got that light, heady feeling that only love could bring. And he was mine. He told me so.

But even as we grew more serious, worries about the future gnawed away at me. Zacharov wouldn't approve of us. A Russian spy having a relationship with an American citizen? I may as well have lined myself up in front of the firing squad and told them to shoot.

But I couldn't give Sam up. When I was with him, he drove away my loneliness, my memories, and the shit that came with my job. I was just a normal girl who'd fallen for a normal guy.

Then one evening, I arrived home while Sam was working late. My arms were laden with groceries, and as I kicked the door shut behind me, the sound of a hammer cocking made me drop the whole lot.

"What are you playing at, Seven?" Zacharov stalked through the kitchen door and stopped six feet away with his revolver aimed at my head. "Sloppy. Where's your gun?"

"Uh, I..."

Nausea climbed my throat, one rusty claw at a time.

"It's in the closet, and it should be in your fucking

hand."

"Everything's quiet. I'm not in any danger here. I thought—"

"You've got a pistol pointed at your head. I assure you, you're in danger."

"I'm sorry, I—"

"Shut up! On your knees."

I knelt before him as he paced the hallway, his expression black.

"You've been stupid, Seven. I trained you better than this."

I stayed quiet.

"Cavorting with some American pig and not even one who can offer us anything. A diplomat or an oligarch, I could have understood, but a copier engineer? You're a dirty whore, Seven. You've lost all your self-respect." He sighed, and his gleaming boots paused in front of me. "Now, here's how it's going to go."

An hour later, Zacharov listened from the lounge as I told Sam I didn't love him anymore. Sam pleaded and cajoled while I kept Zacharov's threat to kill both of us if I didn't break it off at the forefront of my mind. Hunt us to the ends of the earth; that was what he'd promised to do.

"You're talking bullshit, Zhen. I don't know what happened between last night and this evening, but you're lying."

"I'm not. This won't work between us, Sam. It's been fun, but it was never going to be more than that."

He placed a hand over my traitorous heart, whose rapid tattoo betrayed the blank mask I wore.

"Your heart says you're lying." He took my hand

and placed it over his own chest, where his pulse raced with mine. "*My* heart says you're lying. And I'm not giving up. I belong to you, and I'll never stop reminding you of that."

"Please, Sam, don't..."

He leaned his forehead onto mine. "I love you. I always will."

I pushed him out of the door, and my heart broke in two as I closed it behind him. It remained broken to this day.

"Good girl," Zacharov said. "Tomorrow, we kill your boss then we go home."

I was numb as I helped Zacharov to stage the man's accidental death in the early hours of the morning, and by evening, I was back at Base 13. Back then I'd had a luxurious room in Zacharov's personal residence, not a cell. But it might as well have been a prison.

The sickness didn't start until two weeks later, and the first time I threw up, I knew it wasn't a simple virus I'd caught. I couldn't get a pregnancy test on the base, but my tender breasts and tiredness confirmed it even before I missed a period. I knew my own body, and now it had an unexpected guest.

And that changed everything.

I needed Sam. My child needed a father. And that meant I had to leave Russia, and I needed to convince Sam to come with me. I knew I'd be asking for a lot, for him to give up the business he'd worked so hard to build up, especially once I told him the story that I'd come up with—that a jealous ex-boyfriend was threatening both our lives. I didn't have anything to offer him but myself and our baby, but this was Sam, my Sam, and I hoped he'd choose a new life with us. If we left, Seven would die, her secrets would be buried, and there would only be Zhenya.

Except Zacharov got to him first.

The day Sam died, I did too. I was numb as Zacharov stuck the syringe into my thigh, and when I woke up in the cell that was to become my home for the next three years, there was only a shell of me left. Zhenya had died, not Seven, and even though I wanted to finish the job, I couldn't. Not while there was a tiny piece of Sam growing inside me.

Only to Zacharov, Tabitha wasn't a little girl, a miracle born out of a love that would never die. She was leverage.

I was Zacharov's weapon, a deadly marionette who danced at his will.

He was the puppet master, and Tabby was the string between us.

I'd spent every moment since then trying to find a way out, and after three years of dreaming, here we were in America. Land of the free, home of the brave.

I was both.

CHAPTER 6

A WEEK LATER, I tugged on my vintage-style pink dress in the back room of Rick's Diner. It was a size too small, and the skirt was more suitable for working on a street corner than serving food. Still, the job paid in cash, and as long as I showed cleavage, Rick-the-pervert was happy to turn a blind eye to pesky things like my lack of social security number.

My name badge proclaimed me to be Brandy, with a squirly tail on the "y." The pervert had given me the choice between Brandy, Mandy, or Sandy. Apparently, the customers ordered more food from waitresses whose names ended in "ee."

"You'll get yourself more tips as well, little lady," he'd said, patting me on the bottom.

That had nearly got him castrated, but by thinking of Tabby, I'd managed to hold back. Besides, Brandy was as good a name as any for the moment.

Working the night shift had two advantages. Firstly, Rick wasn't there. He always got drunk by nine, and his wife shovelled him into his truck and drove him home to sleep it off. Secondly, I could bring Tabby with me to sleep in the back room. Farrah, the cook, did the same with her little boy.

At four, Rhys was a year and a half older than Tabby and a brat when he was awake. Farrah tended to give in to his demands, and since I'd worked at the diner, the kid had thrown enough tantrums to make a pop diva blush. Thankfully, tonight he'd fallen asleep after his juice carton and given us all some peace.

"Brandy, can you take this out to the guy with the checked shirt?"

Farrah, or Cindy, if you went by her name badge, shoved a plate heaving with grease through the hatch.

Ah, the "Special," with extra sausages. That heart attack waiting to happen belonged to cowboy number four, a delightful specimen who made Jabba the Hut look attractive.

"Here you go, honey."

I'd got my American accent down to a tee. My aptitude for languages meant I spoke six fluently, and I was passable in a couple more.

He patted me on the ass and handed me a dime. "Put Sinatra on the jukebox, would ya?"

The diner was fifties-style, just like my outfit. Actually, not so much of the "style," just fifties. The cracked vinyl seats in the booths lining one side of the room looked as if they'd been installed when Dwight D Eisenhower was president.

I gave Jabba a fake smile and walked past the guys lined up on stools at the counter to the old jukebox against the far wall. It looked like an original. A glutton for punishment, I picked out "Come Fly with Me" and fought back the tears that prickled at my eyes as Sinatra's voice drifted from the speakers. Memories of dancing with Sam in his apartment flooded my mind. A few days before he died, he'd made us his specialty of beef stroganoff, put this song on his stereo, and held me close as he pretended to sing. And now, as I listened to the lyrics, I wondered if he'd been trying to tell me something.

"Brandy, you want something to eat?" Farrah called.

Did I mention another perk of the job? Staff got as much free food as they could eat. Just looking at the mountains of bacon and eggs and fried potatoes made me want to gag, and after every shift, I scrubbed myself in the shower to try and get rid of the smell of rancid fat that clung to my skin.

"I'm good, thanks."

"I'm taking my break. Holler if you need anything."

Before I could get back to the register, cowboy number three raised his hand. "Got any more catsup?"

Yes, it promised to be a long night.

In contrast, the week since I'd arrived in Virginia had flown by. Between finding a job, buying the necessities, learning my way around the area, and looking for somewhere to live, I'd been rushed off my feet.

The accommodation situation still wasn't sorted. The three apartments I'd found within my price range weren't anywhere I'd want my child to stay, so we were still stuck in a low-rent motel that rented most of its rooms by the hour. But because of that, the cops tended to do a lap of the parking lot a couple of times a night, which meant the real criminals gave it a wide berth.

I'd bought an economy-sized bottle of bleach and scrubbed the place from top to bottom. The cheap panties I'd found under the bed suggested that somebody had once had a more enjoyable time in there than me. By the time I'd finished, the place was habitable, and Tabby had claimed the rickety table in the corner for the colouring books and dolls I'd bought her. One of Rick's order pads shoved under the dodgy leg stopped it from wobbling too much. Colouring was a new thing for her since she hadn't been allowed pencils back in Russia, and she spent every waking moment scribbling away, making up for lost time. With every shaky line she drew, I cursed Zacharov and the time he'd stolen from us.

That room was never going to be the Ritz, but it was a home of sorts, and it had something the Ritz couldn't offer: love. I thought back to my last trip to the Ritz in Paris, almost six years ago now. Back then, if anybody had suggested I'd become a mother, I'd have laughed.

Zacharov had wanted me with him that weekend to attend a party. While he schmoozed in the ballroom, I'd been busy liberating a Rembrandt from its frame in an upstairs bedroom. Not because Zacharov wanted the painting, you understand, but because the owner was causing problems with a business deal and Zacharov wanted to apply some pressure. Leverage. It was all about the leverage. And yeah, I guess I could add art thief to my résumé.

In our penthouse suite, I'd been waited on by my own butler and eaten the finest food Paris had to offer, but for all its opulence, the hotel remained cold and impersonal. Or maybe that was me.

Before I met Sam, before he taught me how to feel, I was a tool, not a person. A living, breathing weapon.

Need a high-ranking foreign dignitary to die quietly in his sleep? Call Seven. How about a politician who doesn't quite share the same views as your side? I'd take care of it. Or a business rival cutting your share of the profits? Consider him gone.

But now I had Tabby. That little piece of me and Sam who made me smile in the mornings, laugh all day, and fall asleep exhausted at night. Because of her, that shitty motel room was filled with sunshine.

And because of her, I was currently serving up yet another refill of coffee to a long-distance trucker with wandering hands, smiling through gritted teeth as thoughts of chopping those hands right off flitted through my mind.

I had a knife stuffed into my bra. Just a simple cut at the right angle, a bit of pressure, and his wrist would pop clean apart.

Then I pictured Tabby sleeping in the back room, sighed, and asked, "Anything else, honey?"

"Not unless you're on the menu."

I stepped back out of his reach, shaking my head to clear my wayward thoughts. My job now was to be a waitress and a mother. I shouldn't even be considering the removal of body parts.

After four more hours of tedium, my shift finally ended, and I carried a sleeping Tabby out to the car for the ten-minute drive back to the motel. Speaking of cars, I needed to sort out a legal one. I'd borrowed the battered Honda from a long-term parking lot and changed the plates, but sooner or later the owner was going to notice it was missing.

But for now, I craved sleep. Welcome to my new life.

Dull, but tolerable.

At least until the next night.

It started off like any other evening. Tabby was curled up under a blanket next to Rhys, Farrah was grumbling about Rhys's no good father and his inability to keep a job for longer than two weeks, and I was tugging down my skirt and mentally dissecting the brown-haired asshole on the stool closest to the door. He'd drunk nine cups of coffee already and he would. Not. Shut. Up.

The bell over the door tinkled, and I glanced over at the newcomer, desperate for some respite from the yap, yap, yapping, but my relief was short-lived when I saw the pistol he was carrying.

Skinny guy, late twenties, maybe. He ran his fingers through his greasy hair, sweeping it away from his face to reveal a row of oozing scabs running along his jawline, then his hand jerked out to push one of the salt shakers next to the register back into line. Dude couldn't stop shaking. A tweaker.

"Gimme the money. Quick!"

Beside me, Mr. Coffee raised his arms in the air, and a dark stain spread across the front of his pants as fear won the battle of bladder vs. beverage. A gasp sounded from behind as Farrah came out of the kitchen to see what the commotion was about.

Wonderful. Now I had an audience.

I moved slowly towards the register, careful to keep my hands in sight. "You got a bag?"

"Find one. Find one!"

The tweaker's finger hovered over the trigger as I reached for a paper bag, the kind we used for takeout. Why me? Why couldn't I come to work, do my crappy job, then go home again without having to deal with drama? To be honest, I didn't really care whether he stole the cash or not. It wasn't my money. No, it was more the principle of the matter. Nobody walked into a room, threatened me with a gun, then walked out without consequences.

"Hurry up. Hurry up. Hurry up."

I took the cash out of the register, one handful at a time, while he reached out for the salt shakers again.

Then I froze.

"Mama?" Tabby stood in the back doorway, rubbing sleep from her eyes.

Time slowed as the muzzle swung in her direction, but I vaulted the counter and one well-aimed kick knocked the gun away from Tabby as the tweaker's finger squeezed the trigger. My ears rang as the bullet embedded itself into the ceiling. Another second, another kick, and blood spilled from his mouth, followed by a couple of teeth and an anguished wail. But the noise didn't last long. The gun was in my hand now, and when the butt connected with his temple, he dropped to the floor.

Brandy died that night. Coffee-guy had called the cops while I was trussing the tweaker up like a bitch with a bondage fetish, and I didn't want to answer their questions. By the time sirens sounded in the distance, I had Tabby in the backseat of the Honda, and we were on our way to a new town before the sun came up.

So much for the American dream.

CHAPTER 7

"FARRAH, COULD YOU take a bunch of flowers around to my wife? I need to work late again."

Another day, another town, another name. I'd borrowed Farrah's social security number and was now the proud owner of my own office cubicle. Working as a secretary to the boss of a lingerie company wasn't my dream job either, but it was a step up from serving up all-day breakfasts with a fake smile.

"Of course, Mr. Dobson."

Although, my new boss did give Rick a run for his money in the pervert stakes. While Rick was quite open about his appreciation of the female form, Mr. Dobson hid his proclivities behind closed doors and a veneer of respectability. I'd only worked at Love Your Curves for two weeks, and I already knew that if a model wanted to be in the catalogue, she had to get down on her knees.

But my colleagues were friendly, there was on-site day care, and I earned enough to rent a small apartment. So I took thirty dollars out of the petty cash tin and went to the florist. Which flowers should I buy? Lilies again? Or tulips? A single, perfect red rose by the register caught my attention, and I clenched my fists at my sides, feeling Zacharov's thorns dig in. Sam used to buy me a red rose every Friday, the anniversary of the day we met, because the colour reminded him of my lips.

Fuck it, the mixed bunch of flowers would do—I couldn't stay in the shop any longer.

Mrs. Dobson was thrilled with them, anyway. "They're beautiful. Now, I must find a vase. Would you like to stop in for a coffee?"

"I'd better get back to work."

Making small talk while her husband was banging at least one wannabe model over his office desk would be awkward.

"Tell Frank thank you, won't you? He's always so thoughtful."

"I sure will."

If only he was thoughtful enough to clean the cum stains off the notes he wanted me to type up tomorrow, I'd be grateful.

Back in the office, I bumped into Sara as I picked up Tabby from day care. She had a daughter the same age, and she'd gone out of her way to make me feel welcome in the office. Bringing me a coffee, showing me around the building, those little things that had never happened in my previous line of work.

"Are you coming to Vibe with us on Friday night?"

"What's Vibe?"

"A bar in town. Steve's coming. You know he likes you, right?"

"I'm not sure about that." Yes, he'd stopped by to chat a few times, but I'd done nothing to encourage him.

"Ooh, I am. I overheard him talking to Clive by the water cooler. He said he likes a girl who isn't too eager."

"Oh."

"He's a nice guy, honestly. And he hasn't dated anybody since he split from his ex months ago, and they only broke up because she cheated on him." Sara got a faraway look in her eyes. "He's a wounded soul."

She was probably right. Steve was handsome in a preppy kind of way, and whenever he hung around to talk to me, Charlene in accounts threw dirty looks in my direction. If I was a normal girl, I'd have fluffed up my hair, put on a pair of heels, and pranced out for cocktails. But I wasn't.

"I need to look after Tabby on Friday night."

"You can share my sitter. She doesn't charge the earth, and she's super reliable."

Leave Tabby with a stranger? Maybe one day I'd feel safe enough to do that, but this week was too soon. "My sister's stopping by on her way upstate on Saturday, and I promised her we'd go out and do something fun." I forced a laugh. "Better avoid that hangover."

"Okay, next time?"

"Sure." At least I'd had a warning to think up a new excuse.

The lady who ran the day care centre led Tabby over with Sara's daughter, and I stifled a groan. They were both covered in lime green paint, and Tabby had playdough stuck in her hair.

"Sorry," the girl said. "I only took my eyes off them for a second, and, well…"

"It doesn't matter."

In truth, I couldn't be upset. After Tabby's years of isolation, I'd worried about her making friends, but she became more talkative by the day, and if a little mess was the price for her happiness, I'd willingly pay it. I could put her straight in the shower when we got home.

Home. We had a home now, albeit a tiny one. A friend of Sara's rented the apartment to us at a decent price, and the good neighbourhood made up for its size. Better still, it was within walking distance of Love Your Curves as well as the mall, which meant I hadn't needed to steal a car this week.

Slowly, life was becoming more normal.

"Farrah, you want to get lunch with us?"

Steve's head poked over the top of my cubicle with his trademark grin.

Today was Monday. I'd declined his offer every day last week, and I couldn't be antisocial my whole life. "Just give me two minutes to send this email."

I adjusted my glasses and looked back at the screen. No, I didn't need the glasses or the contact lenses I wore under them, but they made a decent disguise.

I tagged onto the back of the group walking towards the elevator, and Steve slowed to walk with me. "You like Italian? Gino's serves the best cannoli. Unless you're watching your weight. Not that you need to watch your weight. I mean, you look great as you are. Not that I've been looking or anything..." He trailed off. "I think I'll stop talking now."

I laughed in spite of myself. "The cannoli sounds great."

Steve really wasn't a bad guy, but when he gave me those little sideways glances, I felt nothing but regret. Regret that it wasn't Sam walking by my side. How could I replace the one man I'd ever loved when I hadn't yet been able to grieve for him properly?

For years, I'd wanted to say a proper goodbye, but I didn't even know where he was buried. Was his grave in Russia? Or did his family take him back to America? I had no idea where to start looking. Funnily enough, our pasts weren't something we'd spent a lot of time talking about. I'd certainly never volunteered information on mine, because the truth was out of the question and I felt guilty for every lie I told him. Sam had said his parents were still alive and that he had an old college buddy he thought of as a brother. That was all. He'd never told me their names, and I bet there were a few Jessops in Boston.

"How about pizza? You like pizza?" Steve asked, pulling me out of my thoughts.

"Yeah, I like pizza too."

Gino himself looked more like an accountant than a chef, but he waved us all towards two tables by the window.

"We come here every Monday," Sara said. "It makes returning to work after the weekend a bit less depressing."

The novelty of having an office job hadn't worn off for me yet, but I smiled and nodded, anyway. I'd spent the weekend exploring Raleigh with Tabby, and she'd tried flying a kite for the first time, with limited success. I wasn't much better at it than she was, but we'd had fun. And I began to think about the future— creating a proper identity, enrolling Tabby in kindergarten, buying more smart clothes. Things had changed so much in the last three weeks.

"What's good?" I asked Steve.

"Everything. But the Panino Tirolese is my favourite."

"I'll try that, then."

I even smiled. There we go, making an effort.

Steve was right about the food—the smoked ham and gorgonzola melted in my mouth, and I wondered whether it was practical to buy all my meals from there. Hmm, only if I started exercising again. Zacharov had made me work out in the third room of my underground prison for two hours every morning, and since I'd got to America, I'd given the finger to the sadistic Russian bastard and sat on my ass all day.

Perhaps it was time to buy a pair of running shoes.

My phone rang as I took my first mouthful of cannoli, and the sweet pastry was quickly soured by the panicked voice of the day care manager.

"Tabby's a little sick."

I dropped the fork on my plate. "Sick? What do you mean, sick?"

"Like, she just threw up. I'm sure it's just a bug or something, but..."

"On my way."

I threw a twenty-dollar bill on the table, and I was jogging out of the door before Gino could offer to box up the sorry remains of my lunch.

"Where are you going?"

I turned to find Steve following. "Tabby's not feeling well, so I'm going to pick her up."

"Shit. Well, I'll keep you company."

When we got to day care, I found "a little sick" meant my daughter had thrown up three times, and now she was sitting on her own clutching her stomach while the other kids talked behind their hands.

"What happened?" I asked.

"It came on real sudden. One minute she was drinking juice, and the next, bleurgh."

I felt Tabby's forehead. Hot. "I'm taking her to the hospital."

"I'll give you a ride," Steve offered. "You don't think she'll throw up in my car, do you?"

"I'm not sure there's much left inside her," the day care lady said.

Tabby's cheek was clammy as I pressed my lips against it. "It's okay, sweetie." Then to Steve, "Is your car close?"

"Right outside. I got in early this morning."

How long would a cab take to arrive? Too long when my daughter was ill. "Are you sure you don't mind driving us?"

He shrugged. "Dobson's off on a lingerie shoot this afternoon. He won't even notice we're gone."

Steve held the door open while the day care manager rushed up with Tabby's coat and her little pink lunch bag. "I hope she feels better tomorrow."

So did I.

As Steve wove through traffic, Tabby shivered in my arms despite her raised temperature, and I stroked her hair while cursing poor hygiene and kids who touched everything. Tabby's immune system was probably lacking, seeing as she'd rarely come into contact with anyone but me. Hopefully, it would prove to be nothing, but I wasn't about to take any chances, even though we didn't have health insurance. I still had most of Elizabeth's money stashed in my purse for emergencies, and I'd say this qualified.

By the time Steve pulled up outside the ER, I was in

a worse state than Tabby. Crazy, huh? I could stay rock steady while I shot a rebel leader through the head at a thousand yards, but give me a sick child and my hands shook.

The lady at the desk frowned when I told her I didn't have insurance, but she grudgingly agreed to get a doctor while I made up the details to go on her forms. Name, address, date of birth—it was all a work of fiction.

After a quarter of an hour, Steve strolled in, twirling his BMW keys on one finger. "Parking was tricky."

"You don't have to wait."

"What sort of guy would I be if I left you on your own?"

Dammit, if he wasn't careful, I might actually start to like him. Another twenty minutes passed as I paced with Tabby in my arms, then a doctor in scrubs came out, tired looking, with a stethoscope draped around his neck. "What's wrong with this little lady?"

"She was sick a couple of times, and her stomach hurts."

"What has she eaten today?"

"Uh, she was at day care. I guess she ate her lunch— a cheese sandwich, carrot sticks, apple slices. And juice." Unless she'd decided to try the damn playdough.

"Probably nothing to worry about. There's been a sickness bug going round over the last few weeks, but we'll check her out, anyway."

Tabby sat quietly in a cubicle while the doctor poked and prodded, but she managed a small smile when he let her listen to his heart.

"Just let her rest today, and keep her hydrated. Best she doesn't go back to day care tomorrow either. She could still be contagious."

"Thanks for checking her over."

He looked more exhausted than Tabby when he replied, "That's what we're here for."

Out in the waiting room, Steve was fiddling with his phone, but he looked up when I took Tabby's coat from the seat next to him.

"Everything okay?"

"I might have overreacted."

"Hey, she's your kid. You're supposed to be worried."

"Ready to go?"

"Whenever you are."

Except the moment I bent to grab Tabby's lunch bag, I felt a hand on my arm.

"Ma'am? We need to have a word with you."

I forced myself to relax as the uniformed police officer looked me up and down. "Is there a problem?"

Another cop appeared behind him, his stance designed to intimidate.

"We've reason to believe you're in possession of stolen property."

Excuse me? I hadn't stolen anything. Well, apart from the car, but I'd ditched that over a week ago. "You must have me mixed up with somebody else."

The first officer's grip on my arm tightened. "A witness reported seeing you steal a wallet."

Oh, please, a wallet? Petty theft just wasn't my thing. Go big or go home, that was my motto. "Your witness must have been mistaken."

"You won't mind if we check the bag, then."

I held out my handbag. "Fine. Get on with it."

But he didn't want my knock-off Michael Kors tote.

He ignored my offering as he reached beneath the chair for Tabby's lunch bag and unzipped it. What the...?

The black leather wallet he drew out didn't belong to me, and it certainly hadn't been there when I packed Tabby's lunch that morning. So, how had it got in her bag? Steve? I swung to face him, but he looked as horrified as I did.

"I've never seen that before in my life," I said.

The cop's glower didn't change. "Sure, that's what they all say."

A third cop appeared, and the cold metal of a handcuff clicked around one wrist. As he yanked my other arm behind me, I could only protest like a bad cliché. "You've got the wrong person."

Steve's expression turned from horror to disgust, and I couldn't entirely blame him. After all, he barely knew me, and the evidence didn't look good.

"You didn't think Dobson paid you enough, so you decided to supplement your income while your own daughter was sick in hospital?" he asked.

"Of course not!"

"I saw the wallet in her bag, Farrah."

"And I've got no idea how it got there. Don't forget, it's you it's been sitting next to for the past half hour."

"Oh, so now you accuse *me* of stealing? I earn six figures, Farrah. I'm hardly going to risk that for the sake of...what? Fifty dollars?"

Tabby burst into tears at the sound of our raised voices, and one of the policemen crouched down beside her. "Don't worry, little one. We'll take care of you while we ask your mom a few questions."

"What do you mean, take care of her?"

"Child Protective Services are on hand for

situations like this."

No. No way was Tabby going into the social services system. They'd rake over our lives, and my secrets wouldn't be safe. "There's no need for that. She can stay with my sister. Steve, could you drop Tabby off with Sara? Please? None of this is her fault."

I begged him with my eyes, and for a moment I thought he'd correct my little fib. But then his shoulders dropped, and he nodded. "Fine. But after that, don't bother speaking to me again."

I could live with that. As soon as I got out of this latest mess, we'd be on our way to another new home. I took one last look at Tabby as the cops pulled me out to a waiting squad car, hating the confused expression on her face as Steve tentatively reached for her hand.

CHAPTER 8

AN HOUR LATER and I'd been fingerprinted and thrown in a cell. The fingerprinting pissed me off most. Being locked up felt oddly like coming home.

On my previous visits, I'd always managed to keep my prints out of the system. The cops wouldn't be able to connect me to any of the mayhem I'd created in the past, but to break my winning streak over something so trivial as a wallet was embarrassing.

I'd seen my file, my blessedly thin file, which had been distributed to everyone from the FBI to Interpol. Last time I checked, they'd pinned seventeen kills on me, which fell far short of my actual total, and six of the ones they'd attributed weren't even mine. If I had to guess, I'd say two of them were carried out by my biggest rival, Valkyrie, and I knew they'd given her the Canadian minister I'd bumped off during a fishing trip. But the other four? I didn't have a clue.

Valkyrie. It was a nickname, of course. I thought she was a woman, but her file was even thinner than mine. The agencies had given me a fancy moniker too— Lilith, the she-demon from Jewish mythology. That came about after a particularly tricky job a decade ago, one where I'd placed the blame squarely with Mossad.

Those had been better days. Back then, I'd been part of a loose group called the Horsemen, after the four horsemen of the apocalypse, although there had been at least a dozen of us. Not that I worked with the others. I didn't even know who they were. It was more of a classification system—the best of the best, assassins the world feared. Now look at me. I had to laugh at the irony, earning a curious glance from a woman so drunk she couldn't remember her own name.

The sound of a baton scraping along the bars made me turn my head.

"Farrah Collins?"

"That's me."

"You have a lawyer?"

Sure, on speed-dial. "No."

"You want us to appoint one? And do you want your phone call now or later?"

Later? That suggested they were expecting me to stay there, which was unacceptable.

"I'll make my call now."

The cop cuffed me again, and I stood still and let him. Without Tabby, I'd have been halfway across the country by now, but a fight at the hospital then a police chase with a sick toddler in tow? Things were so different to how they used to be.

"You get five minutes."

He shut me in a room containing a phone and nothing else.

Five minutes. If I'd been right in my assessment of character, I'd only need two, and if I'd been wrong? Well, I was fucked.

I punched in a number from memory and tapped my foot as it rang once, twice.

"Yeah?"

"Elizabeth?"

"Depends who's asking."

Was this room bugged? I had to assume so. "We met on a plane a few weeks back."

"You called to apologise to my chauffeur?"

Shit. "Sorry about that."

"Forget it. I was expecting you to do something along those lines. I had another car following out of sight, just in case."

"Oh."

"I'm sure this isn't a social call?"

"I've got a small problem."

"I knew it. People only ever call me with problems. Nobody rings because they want to catch a movie or grab brunch."

"Get me out of here, and I'll buy you fucking brunch."

"Out of where?"

"Uh...jail."

Okay, maybe two minutes had been an underestimate on my part because it took her thirty seconds to stop laughing.

"It's not funny."

"Come on, you've got to see the humorous side. You stayed in the wind for a decade and you've been here, what, three weeks? What did you do?"

How did she know so much about me? "I didn't do anything. They said I stole a wallet, but someone set me up."

"A wallet? That's bullshit. You'd hold up a convenience store or maybe a bank."

At least somebody believed me. "Can you get me out?"

"Where are you?"

"Raleigh."

"Name?"

"Farrah Collins."

"Hmmm. SatNav says two hours. I'll be there in one and a half."

The cop led me into an interview room, but I barely listened to their questions. Instead, I stayed silent as I replayed the morning's events in my head. Someone set me up, that much was obvious. But who? And why?

Steve had the opportunity, but I couldn't work out what his motive would be. The day care manager had access to Tabby's lunch bag, but why the hell would she stash a wallet in there? And who was the witness who claimed they saw me take it?

"Who called you?" I asked the cops. "Who's your witness?"

They looked at each other. "Anonymous tip," one of them said.

Interesting.

What had planting a wallet on me achieved? So far, I'd been fingerprinted and locked up. Was someone looking to link me to my earlier work? If so, why the local cops? Why not the FBI? No, they didn't know I was Lilith. If they'd had an inkling, they'd have sent a SWAT team, not three deputies.

Something else... What? They'd separated me from Tabby. But that was a fluke, right? Nobody knew I was going to take her to the hospital that day. Unless... It came to me with startling clarity. The wallet wasn't the setup. Tabby getting sick, that was the setup. The day care lady's words came back to me: "She drank her juice then she got sick." Some bastard poisoned her damn juice. And that meant my daughter was in danger, and the clock was ticking.

Fuck.

"I need to get out of here." I tried to stand, but they'd cuffed me to the metal table, and I could only straighten halfway.

"You and me both," one of the cops said, looking at his watch. "Time for our coffee break."

I was ready to kick something—someone—by the time Elizabeth turned up. Scowls were exchanged, and it was clear the captain who uncuffed me didn't like either of us very much, but I didn't hang around to find out what Elizabeth had done to piss him off.

"What's going on?" she asked as she jogged behind me to the parking lot.

"Which car?"

She pointed at a black Dodge Viper abandoned by the front steps. "I'm driving."

"Take a left onto the main road."

She didn't ask questions, just buckled up and gunned the engine out of the lot, nearly taking out a police cruiser on its way in.

"Asshole," she muttered under her breath. "Okay, where are we going in such a hurry?"

"When I got arrested, I sent Tabitha to a friend's house. But that means she's unguarded, and I think that's why they wanted me out of the way."

"Tabitha's your daughter?"

"Yes. Tabby."

"There's a gun under your seat. And put your

seatbelt on."

Elizabeth drove like a street racer on crack, and for that I was grateful. I checked the Glock semi-automatic, dropping the magazine and slamming it home again out of habit.

"Thanks."

"No problem. This friend Tabby's with, do you want to try calling her? Him?"

I thought about it for a second. "Her. No. I'd rather keep the element of surprise."

"I'll park on the next street."

I'd tucked the Glock into the back of my waistband, and I pulled my jacket over it as I walked up the path to Sara's duplex, keeping an eye out for any movement in the properties either side. Elizabeth walked next to me, her smile masking the concentration I knew simmered under the surface.

The sounds of a cartoon drifted out of Sara's open front window, and I had to jab the doorbell twice before she answered. And when she finally did open the door, her forehead creased in confusion.

"Where's Tabby?"

"They didn't tell you?"

"Tell me what?"

"Child Protective Services came and picked her up. They said they'd let you know."

Oh, fuck. I clutched at the door frame for support then felt Elizabeth's arm around my waist.

"Why did they pick her up?" I asked. "What did they say?"

"That you were a thief, and you'd been taken to jail." Sara's face clouded over as she folded her arms. "Stealing's wrong. I thought we were friends, but—"

"You mean you just handed over somebody else's child to a stranger who showed up at your door?" Elizabeth asked.

"I didn't... I mean, of course not. The lady had a business card that said she came from Child Protective Services."

"And I could get one printed up that says I'm a bona fide rodeo clown, but that doesn't mean I am one, does it?"

The colour drained out of Sara's face then her mouth set in a thin line. "I-I-I'm sorry. I thought I was doing the right thing. And you don't know for sure that the woman wasn't from CPS."

"Where's the business card? Do you still have it?"

She disappeared inside and came back a minute later with a card pinched between her thumb and forefinger as if she didn't really want to touch it. Elizabeth snatched it off her and passed it to me along with her phone.

"Go back to the car and call."

It was a US number, but when I punched in the digits, a series of clicks told me the call was being transferred elsewhere. Five seconds passed, ten, and Zacharov's arrogant voice assaulted my ears.

"You took your time. If I didn't know better, I'd say you'd lost your touch."

"Where's my daughter?"

"Tabitha's fine. Enjoying the attractions the wonderful American continent has to offer."

"I'm gonna rip your fucking throat out."

"Seven, Seven... No sense in making threats you can't carry out."

Anger turned to despair. "Why are you doing this? I

fixed your shit for nineteen damn years, and this is how you repay me? Why can't you just let me go?"

"Language, Seven. And I will let you go, after one last job. Complete it, and you get your daughter and your freedom."

One last job. This coming from the man who'd kept me locked up for the past three years? The general was as trustworthy as a rattlesnake. My fist pounded into the dashboard, but the pain barely registered. I hated this man. Hated him.

"What's the job?"

"It seems I've annoyed a few people lately."

"No fucking kidding."

"Sarcasm will get you nowhere, Seven, not when I'm holding all the cards."

I took a deep breath. "Who do you want me to kill?"

"Ah, now you're thinking along the right lines. James Harrison has been getting on my nerves lately."

It was like the air had been sucked out of the car. I couldn't speak. I couldn't even breathe.

Zacharov carried on, oblivious. "So, I suppose it's actually quite convenient that you're already in America. Saves you from making an extra trip."

"You want me to kill the president?"

"Keep up, Seven."

"Are you insane?"

He chuckled. "I prefer 'ambitious.'"

"It's a suicide mission."

"I've always had confidence in you, Seven. Even when you were a child. After you killed Pyotr, others would have taken you from that orphanage to die, but I knew you had something special. And right now, you've got an extra incentive. You don't want Tabitha to end up in the Vladivostock Home for Girls, do you?"

"You... You..." Words failed me. Just when I thought the man couldn't make my life hell anymore, he reached out from across the world and yanked me back in line. "Even if I did manage to do as you ask, how do I know you'll give Tabby back? Or that you won't renege on the freedom part either?"

"You don't, little Seven of Ten. That's a chance you'll have to take."

I stayed silent, considering my other options and coming up with only one: Go back to Base 13 and find Tabby, because I didn't believe for a second Zacharov would leave her in America, and remove his head from his shoulders while I was at it.

"Oh, and Seven? Don't be tempted to do anything rash. I'm not stupid enough to have brought Tabby back to Russia. She's far away from here, and if I stop breathing, you'll never find her."

"How can you do this?"

"Always have a backup plan, Seven. Three weeks, remember? You're on your own now, and the clock's ticking. Call me when you're done."

The line went dead, and for the first time since I scrubbed Pyotr's blood off me in the shower all those years ago, I broke down and cried.

CHAPTER 9

I SWIPED AT my eyes with my sleeve as Elizabeth opened the car door. Of all people, I didn't want her to see me weeping.

"Didn't go well, I take it?"

A strangled laugh escaped. "That's the understatement of the year."

She leaned back in the driver's seat. "Sara was as useful as a bicycle in a NASCAR race. The woman who picked Tabby up had brown hair and was aged somewhere between twenty and fifty. Sara *thinks* she was wearing glasses, maybe, and she might have been driving a car that was black, blue, or brown. So that narrows it right down."

"It doesn't matter. Zacharov's got her."

"Oh, good."

I turned to stare at her. "Good? How can that possibly be good?"

"We know where Zacharov is. At least it's not one of the multitude of other people you've pissed off over the years."

The gun at the small of my back was tempting. So tempting. "How do you know I've upset anyone else?"

"You don't get into your position without treading on a few toes."

"What do you mean 'my position?'"

Her blue eyes held mine, brown for the moment. Suddenly my contact lenses felt dry.

"Well, Lilith, I don't think either of us is under any illusion as to the nature of your job."

Fuck. No, double fuck. Triple fuck. More fucks even than that. She knew I was Lilith? How? My FBI file didn't even have a clear picture of me.

But there was no point in denying it, not with her. "How did you know?"

"I put it together over the years. A snippet here, a whisper there. It would have been lax of me not to keep an eye on the bitch trying to steal my crown. I've known you were Russian for a while, but I only got a good look at you a couple of years ago."

I barely heard her last sentence. I was still hung up on the one before. The bitch trying to steal her crown? Holy shit.

"You're Valkyrie?"

"Pleased to meet you."

She grinned, and I returned a tight smile. I was sharing air with the one person on this earth I feared more than Zacharov. Go figure.

And that raised another question.

"Why are you helping me?"

"I owe you a favour, and I always pay up."

"A favour? What favour?"

She leaned back against the headrest and closed her eyes, a brave move with me next to her. I thought I detected a groan.

"It was hardly my finest hour."

"Care to elaborate?"

"You remember a nasty little shit called Grigoriy Utkin?"

"Commander Utkin? Yes, I remember him."

And in stunning clarity, the events of my last day with the good commander came rushing back. Utkin had been a...not a friend, because Zacharov didn't have friends...an acquaintance of Zacharov. He spent time at Base 13, but for the most part, he worked elsewhere, and he facilitated the supply chain when Zacharov wanted to acquire things he wasn't supposed to have.

Yes, Utkin had been a small but important cog in Zacharov's well-oiled machine, so when rumours arose that somebody wanted Utkin out of the picture, Zacharov sent me to take care of the problem. My first job after Tabby's birth, I'd still been breastfeeding, and I'd also been furious.

Turned out the rumours were right.

Zacharov had installed me as Utkin's bodyguard, although Utkin himself wanted to use me as a plaything instead. A single threat of castration made him rethink his wandering hands. So I trailed him around, and one Sunday, he skipped church and visited a warehouse on the outskirts of Moscow to meet a potential source for some of Zacharov's weapons. And that day, the shit had hit the fan, or rather the walls, when the south end of the warehouse blew up in a ball of flame. At first, I thought there was a team attacking, but as the men around us dropped, it became apparent there was a single assassin. And she was good.

She'd have levelled the whole place, me included, if not for a rare stroke of luck. Bad for her, good for me. The rotten floor panel she fell through dropped her right at my feet.

She was dressed like the ninja she accused me of being three weeks ago, a scarf across her face, and as I held her in the sights of my customised Colt .45, Utkin had hopped around like a demented monkey yelling, "Kill her. Kill her!"

Now, any comrade of Zacharov's was an enemy of mine, and besides which, the little fucker had been irritating me all week. So I shot him instead.

"Are you badly hurt?" I'd asked.

She groaned and shook her head. "No, just winded."

She'd answered in Russian, her accent indistinct.

"I'll tell them the kill was yours."

The remains of the warehouse was filling with smoke, so I helped her outside and left her beside a rusted-out car on a vacant lot a few hundred yards away. And that was the last I saw of her. Until now.

I'd been pleased that Zacharov's empire had suffered a setback, albeit minor, and borne the brunt of his anger with a smile inside.

"You got knocked out by a falling pipe?" he yelled. "You need to keep your wits about you."

He began pacing. He always paced when he got frustrated.

"It was an accident."

"You call yourself a professional? This will not happen again."

He'd upped my gym time to four hours a day for the next two weeks, but I didn't care. The general could go fuck himself.

"That was you?" I asked Valkyrie. "In the warehouse?"

"Fucking floorboard. I had one hell of a bruise on my hip. Why didn't you kill me? I've always been curious."

"Zacharov."

She nodded, and that seemed to be enough of an answer for her.

"I got paid two million dollars for that job, and it's not like I could tell them it wasn't me. The money's yours. I figured we'd cross paths again one day, and I've been holding it in a separate account."

"Two million dollars? You got paid two million dollars?"

She shrugged. "It was a repeat customer, so I gave them a discount."

"A discount? All I got was an annual salary of fifty thousand dollars and the satisfaction of doing something for my country."

"That's the public sector for you. I bet you had twenty-five layers of bureaucracy too."

"Yes, before I started working exclusively for Zacharov. I once had to go on a job armed only with a kitchen knife, a bottle of tequila, and a cigarette lighter."

"Let me guess, he got drunk, tripped, fell on the knife, then accidentally set fire to the place?"

"That's what the police report said. How did you know?"

"It's what I would have done. So, what did Zacharov have to say about Tabby?"

What was I supposed to tell her? The truth? As someone who lied about almost everything, being honest felt a little...awkward. But my brain was mush, and I'd run out of plausible excuses.

Tap, tap, tap. Her fingernails drummed out a rhythm on the steering wheel. "Any time today is good."

"He wants me to do one last job for him, and then he'll give my daughter back."

"And you believe that?"

"Of course not. But what choice do I have?"

"Skip the job and look for Tabitha?"

"I'm an assassin, not a detective. Besides, my network is so patchy now that I wouldn't know where to start."

"You forget my network. My network's top notch."

"You're serious about helping me?"

"I wouldn't have offered otherwise. And you don't just get me, you get my team."

I couldn't believe I was even considering this. "We only have three weeks."

"Then we'd better get started. What's this job Zacharov wants done?"

Tell her? Not tell her? Tell her? Not tell her?

"He wants me to kill someone."

"No shit, Sherlock. I'd be surprised if he wanted you to bake him a cake. Although if your cooking's anywhere near as bad as mine, eating it would be as good as murder. So, who?"

Her accent was British again for the moment, but she clearly spent time in the States. Who did she work for? Where did her loyalties lie? Was she about to have a sudden attack of patriotism? I was running out of choices, and I didn't have anyone else I could trust. I had to tell her.

"James Harrison. He wants me to kill James Harrison."

The smile that spread across her face wasn't the reaction I'd been expecting.

"Why are you so happy? Did you vote for the other

guy?"

"Because you were honest with me."

"Huh? How do you even know that?"

Her grin grew wider. "You used my phone to call Zacharov. Think about it."

She'd switched from her original mousy brown hair to blonde, and she pulled a lock back behind her ear, enough for me to see the earpiece she wore.

"You bitch. You heard everything?"

"Yeah. You grew up in an orphanage?"

A lump came into my throat, and I nodded.

She laid a hand on my arm. "I'm sorry."

"It was a long time ago." I swallowed then made an effort to change the subject. "So, what now?"

"Well, killing James is out. I called him before I got back in the car. The head of the Secret Service flipped out, so James is in the White House basement right now, watching Netflix."

"James?"

"Mr. President to you."

"You're on first name terms?"

"He's an old friend."

"Really?"

"You don't believe me?" She plucked another phone from her pocket and held it out. "Speed-dial seven. Ironic, huh?"

"Does he know what you do?"

"The United States government is one of my best customers."

Fuck. I looked up at the sky, hoping for divine intervention, but all I got was a few drops of rain.

"*Blyat'. Putain de merde. Scheiße. Fasz. Pieprzyć. Mierda. Jebát'. Vraga. Fuck.*"

"You done?"

"I'm not even started. And I won't be finished until I have Zacharov's head on a stake."

"In that case, I've got some good news."

"Go on."

"James gave us the green light on Base 13."

"Us?"

"Didn't you just say you wanted Zacharov's head on a stake? It was on the cards, anyway. Why do you think I was in Russia with the inspection team?"

"I just got out of that hellhole. I don't want to go straight back in. Besides, he may be a psychopath but he isn't stupid. He'll be expecting me."

"You. Not us. He won't be expecting *us*. Look, here's the deal. You help us eliminate Base 13, and we'll help you find Tabby."

"Do you have any idea how crazy you sound? How many things could go wrong?"

Scenarios flew through my head, none of them good. Getting hauled off a plane at Domodedovo Airport. A bullet flying through my brain from a hidden sniper. One of Zacharov's stateside spies tracking me down. The general himself getting his hands on me, or worse, him punishing Tabby for my actions. Above all, I needed to keep my daughter safe.

But Elizabeth didn't share my reservations.

"Hey, it'll be Valkyrie and Lilith. What could possibly go wrong?"

"Lilith and Valkyrie, you mean."

"You're in, then?" She grinned at me again, and damned if it wasn't a tiny bit infectious.

I must have lost my mind. But she was right; there was no way I could kill the president, not within three weeks, and not with her trying to stop me. And if James Harrison was still breathing, Tabby wouldn't be.

"I'm in. Just keep away from rotten floorboards."

Chapter 10

WE PULLED AWAY from Sara's house, minus the little girl who was my whole world. The ache in my chest grew more intense with every passing mile, but I forced myself to focus on the task at hand.

"Do you have any kind of plan?" I asked Elizabeth.

"Yeah, I need dinner. I missed lunch and I'm starving."

She drove at the same breakneck speed as before, but at least that meant we'd get to our destination faster. I hadn't eaten since my aborted lunch, and it was almost nine now, but I had other things on my mind besides hunger.

"You need to eat," Elizabeth said, reading my mind. "You might not think you're hungry, but your body needs fuel. The next few weeks are gonna be tough, and straight up, you've lost your edge. You might have been snapping at my heels once, but the last few years haven't been kind, have they?"

I should have been insulted, but how could I be when she spoke the truth? While I'd been with Zacharov, my training had been non-existent, my exercise routine inadequate, and my diet ninety percent carbs. I might have been a match for Valkyrie once, but in my current state, she could have taken me blindfolded.

Still, I gritted my teeth as I replied. "No, they haven't. And a few years ago, I left you in the dust."

"Thanks for the reminder." She fell silent for a moment then her voice grew soft. "I'll help you fix things."

"Thank you," I whispered.

I still feared she'd try to double-cross me, but she was the only hope I had. Otherwise, I was as good as dead and so was my daughter. As she threw the Viper around the bends, we each withdrew into our own thoughts, mine mainly of all the ways in which I could cause Zacharov pain. Shooting was too good for him. We'd been driving for ten minutes when Elizabeth suddenly slowed.

"How did he know where to look?"

"Huh?"

"Zacharov. How did he know where to look?"

"I guess he traced your plane."

"Maybe. But we stopped in Switzerland first, so he'd have needed to send teams to both countries. And the States is huge. How the hell did he luck into finding you so soon?"

"He knows a lot of people."

"He's got more enemies than friends over here. Did you feel anyone following you? Because I sure as hell didn't."

She had a point. My mind may have been weak, but I had enough instincts left to notice a close tail. I'd spotted one man walk past outside my apartment three times last week, but when he greeted one of my neighbours with plenty of tongue, I'd figured it was a false alarm. Nothing else had pinged my radar.

"I haven't seen anybody."

So where the hell had Tabby's kidnappers come from?

"How did Zacharov track you on jobs?"

"A transponder on my belt. I think he had one in my watch too, but I left that behind in Russia."

"Ever have surgery? Even for something minor?"

"The last time was five years ago. No, six. A gunshot wound to my thigh. Wait. You think he put a tracker inside me?"

"It would explain a lot. There're some really tiny units on the market now, powered by kinetic energy. We use them quite often."

I thought back to all those times I'd woken up groggy, barely knowing where I was. "He drugged me. Every time he put me back in my cell, he'd knock me out so they could uncuff me without anybody getting hurt."

"Your cell?"

"It hasn't been a good three years."

"Shit, honey."

"He could have put a device in me then."

As we passed a derelict gas station, Elizabeth stomped on the brakes and jerked the wheel so the car came to rest next to the abandoned kiosk. The front window was broken, and an old Exxon sign creaked in the wind as rain buffeted us from all sides. The place must have been empty for years judging by the state of it.

Elizabeth reached over to the glove compartment and took out a flashlight. "If it's there, it'll be somewhere you wouldn't easily feel it. Your back, I'm guessing."

I shrugged out of my jacket and peeled off my top,

then shuddered as Elizabeth ran her cold hands over my skin.

"Sorry," she muttered.

"Just find it."

Her fingers dug into my flesh, probing, until halfway down my back, she suddenly paused.

"Got something. This could be it."

"Then take the fucking thing out."

There was no "are you sure?" and she didn't bother telling me it was going to hurt. We both knew it would. My fingernails dug into the leather seat as she took her knife to me—another Emerson CQC-6, I noticed. Evidently, she was fond of that particular model.

Twenty seconds later, she dropped an object the size of a kidney bean, dripping with my blood, onto the dash. We both stared at it.

"That bastard," I muttered.

My first instinct was to crush it, but Elizabeth reached out a hand and stopped me.

"No, we can use it. Hang on, let me stop the bleeding first. I've got a first-aid kit in the trunk."

She came back a little damp with a green bag in her hand, and I bit my tongue as antiseptic stung my back.

"I'll put gauze over it for now, but it'll need stitches later."

"I bet they're not far behind."

"No, and they're probably wondering why we've stopped in the middle of nowhere."

"They'll come along to check in a couple of minutes." I looked at my new watch, a ten-dollar digital.

"Yup."

"They'll be armed," I said.

"Yup."

"They'll be professionals."

"Yup."

"What about Tabby? If we piss off Zacharov, he could take his anger out on her."

"Fifty bucks says these guys aren't gonna turn up with beer and Twinkies. What does Zacharov expect you to do? Roll over and take it up the fuckin' ass? He'd probably be less impressed if you didn't put up a fight, and he can't hurt her, because he needs her."

She made good points there. The general himself had taught me never to back down. And these men represented the best—no, the only—lead we had.

"Are we seriously going to do this?" I asked.

"Better get the big guns out of the trunk."

I'd never liked working with a partner, mainly because I didn't trust any of them. Trust them to perform or trust them not to put a bullet through my head if it suited them. With Elizabeth, I had no such worries about her abilities. The jury was still out on the latter, but I couldn't do this alone, and she was taking a risk on me too.

I climbed out of the car, trying to ignore the pain in my back as I followed her to the rear of the car. She popped the trunk then leaned forward to remove a false bottom from the floor, revealing a slim lockbox underneath.

"Are you keeping the Glock? Or I've got a Colt M45, an AR-15, a Beretta, another Walther, or a...no, you don't want a .22 tonight."

It was a damn arsenal. "Do you always carry this stuff around?"

"I should have been a Girl Scout, huh? 'Be

prepared' and all that."

"I don't think Girl Scouts carry grenades."

"Okay, maybe not the grenades."

Elizabeth supplemented her Walther P88 with a Glock 27 in an ankle holster, plus the AR-15.

"You like the Colt?" I asked.

It was standard issue for the US armed forces, but I'd always found the standard grip a bit bulky.

"I prefer the Walther. The Colt belongs to my husband."

She was married? To who? Did her husband know what she did for a living? I'd always been terrified to tell Sam the true nature of my job or even hint at it. How the hell would that conversation have gone?

"Could you pass the butter, Zhen?"

"Sure."

"Are you working late tonight?"

"Yeah, I have to take a quick trip to Poland and help a lawyer to jump off a building."

"I'll leave dinner in the oven, then."

Nope. That confession would never have happened, and even when I started seeing Sam, I knew we had no future. But that didn't stop me from missing him every time I took a breath.

"Knife?" Elizabeth asked.

"I've still got yours from before."

"You're welcome. Here, put this earpiece in. Channel's open to me, but we're also online with the control room. Backup's on its way."

Control room. Backup. Both were foreign concepts to me.

Elizabeth threw me a grenade and clipped another onto her own belt. "Good to go?"

No, but I'd do it anyway.

"As I'll ever be."

She tugged on a balaclava to cover up her blonde hair then closed the trunk, bleeping the locks shut.

"Then let's go. Best to leave the tracker in the car. That way they'll look there first."

"I want one of them alive." I had a few questions I wanted to ask.

"Two's best. It'll give us leverage."

"Agreed."

The gas station was surrounded by woods, and over the years they'd crept closer to the cracked concrete apron surrounding the dilapidated gas pumps, the kiosk, and an old shed that could have been a bathroom. A couple of junkers were rusting into the ground at the back, half covered in creepers. Elizabeth and I headed in that direction, where we could find shelter and shadows among the foliage.

"It's been months since I was in a good gunfight," she said. "Precision kills are all very well, but nothing compares to the buzz of full-on war."

"You're crazy."

"Tell me you disagree."

I couldn't. War was full of horror, fear, and depravity, but nothing—nothing—beat the feeling of coming out on top.

The ground was slippery underfoot as we melted further into the woods. Elizabeth moved quickly and silently, and I matched her, grateful to Zacharov for training me as well as he had but hating the man at the same time.

An old oak tree gave us cover as we waited, and as the rain fell harder, Elizabeth whispered, "Showtime."

A black SUV rolled onto the forecourt, followed by another, then another. The doors opened, and four men spilled out of each, guns in their hands. Even from this distance, their confusion was apparent. Most ducked down behind their vehicles while two took cover next to the kiosk.

"Twelve against two. I almost feel sorry for them," Elizabeth whispered.

They moved gingerly, always keeping close to a car, or a wall, or a pillar. They knew I was out there somewhere, and they had to assume I was armed. What was their brief? To give me a not-so-gentle reminder from Zacharov to do my job? I'd put money on it.

Two of them approached Elizabeth's car, and a tall guy with a dark beard stepped forward to try the doors. Finding them locked, he used the butt of his assault rifle to smash the driver's window and release the locks. The second man peered into the trunk and peeled up the carpet while his colleague leaned into the cabin.

"They've found the lockbox," I whispered.

"Doesn't matter."

The first guy straightened, holding a small object between his thumb and forefinger. The tracker. His mouth opened as he realised what it was, and he swung to face the woods, gun up.

"I love that car. I really love that car," Elizabeth said softly.

A quiet sigh escaped her lips.

Then the Viper blew sky high.

CHAPTER 11

WE STARTED SHOOTING the instant the initial flash receded, firing at panicked figures silhouetted against the flames as they acted on instinct to help their colleagues. By the time they came to their senses and took cover, five more lay on the ground.

"Seven down," Elizabeth muttered, fingering the key fob-slash-remote detonator still in her hand. "Your lucky number. Fuck, I loved that car."

The flames danced high into the night, a macabre backdrop for the screams of dying men. I didn't feel any sympathy. They chose this line of work, and like the saying goes, if you can't stand the heat...

Stay cool.

I took one long breath and relaxed. This was what I used to live for. Gradually, my cluttered thoughts fell away, leaving my soul free and one single goal ahead: get them before they get us. *Us.* A new concept. Beside me, Elizabeth scanned right and left, head up, eyes sharp. Hunting.

"I'll take the right," she whispered. "I'm always right."

"Bitch."

She blew me a kiss as she disappeared into the trees, just another shadow in a world full of darkness.

I'd only got a few metres when I spotted movement

by the outhouse-slash-bathroom as a man disappeared behind it.

"One by the outhouse."

"Got it. Another on the offside of the car nearest the road."

My old instincts began to return. Heel down first, run my weight smoothly along the outside edge of my foot, and if everything was solid, place my foot flat. Stay silent. Repeat. Repeat. No sudden movements. Blend into the trees.

It didn't take me long to get a line of sight on the guy behind the outhouse. He was tight against the wall, crouched down as he glanced at the kiosk then scanned the woods, spotting nothing. I could read his thoughts.

Where is she?

Did she get to the trees?

Those were the last thoughts he ever had.

I missed with my first shot, but my second got him in the forehead, a third eye, unseeing as he dropped to the ground.

"Eight."

The rapid chatter of an automatic weapon invaded the night. Pieces of bark flew from the tree I stood behind, and I kept my arms close as chaos reigned. One of them must have seen my muzzle flash.

And Elizabeth had seen theirs.

"Nine," came through my earpiece.

A male voice startled me. "Clean-up crew's half an hour out. Try not to make too much mess."

"Tell them to bring marshmallows."

Did she ever think of anything but her stomach?

Three left. Tendrils of smoke drifted eerily around the buildings, and a loud pop made me snap my head towards the road. Just a car tyre exploding. False alarm. Or was it? A figure scuttled out from behind the vehicle, and I dropped him with two to the chest.

"Ten."

"Nice. Time to catch a couple of live ones."

"Can you see them?"

"One's on the far side of the kiosk, and I think the other's behind the cars. Not positive, though."

I was nearer to the three black SUVs than Elizabeth. "Can you get the kiosk guy?"

"Reckon I can."

"Then I'll check the cars."

"Cover me for a minute, would you?"

"Got it."

A shadow streaked through the darkness as Elizabeth broke cover. I thought she'd stop at the kiosk, but she ran right up the wall, twisting in mid-air to land on the roof in a crouch. Parkour—another love of mine before Zacharov destroyed my life. Seconds later, I heard a yell over the crackle of the fire, and Elizabeth's voice sounded in my ear.

"Eleven. Good luck."

Right, my turn. *Do not fuck this up, Seven.*

Moving further to the right, my sanctuary in the tree line let me see our remaining attacker, hunkered down behind the end car. As I watched, he moved in a crouch until he was in the gap between that vehicle and the next. Stupid move. He'd limited his field of vision and his escape routes. That meant I could backtrack then run across so only a single car stood between us, all without him noticing. I put one knee to the concrete and peered under the car, gun ready. There he was, right by the driver's door. His ankle exploded in a cloud of muscle and bone as I fired through the gap, and I was on my feet, over the car, and on top of him before he could work out what happened.

"Boo."

I threw both of his weapons out of reach then dragged him towards the kiosk by his arms as he struggled to get away. He had no chance, not with anger fuelling me. Elizabeth already had her guy cable-tied to the base of the old signpost, and I grabbed two pairs of Flex-Cuffs from her and hog-tied number twelve. Both wore the same expression—fear mixed with pain mixed with anger. But mostly fear. Two big guys who didn't look so cocky now their toys had been taken away.

Eleven spoke first. "There's two of you?"

Elizabeth grinned, but not the cheerful smirk I'd seen from her before. Now she radiated malice. "Give that boy a gold star." And her American accent was back, Southern this time.

"Who are you?"

"The person asking the questions here. I'm gonna give you a choice. We've got two of you, and we only need one. First one to talk escapes my itchy trigger finger."

She shot a round into the dirt between them for effect, and terror lit their eyes.

"What if neither of us talks?" Twelve asked.

"Then I'll shoot you both and I'm no worse off."

They looked at each other, and Eleven quickly decided, "I'll talk."

"Good." Elizabeth put a bullet between Twelve's eyes. "See, there's that rapport we built up while we were waiting for Seven here to shoot out your buddy's ankle. I knew we could be friends."

"Where's the girl?" I asked.

"I-I-I don't know. I swear."

"Who took her?"

"Krieg. He got some woman he knows to pose as a social worker."

"Who's Krieg?"

He jerked his head towards the charred corpse lying by the driver's side of the Viper. "That guy. We all worked for him."

"Johan Krieg?" Elizabeth asked.

"Yeah. You know him?"

"I know of him. Fucking cowboy. How'd he end up working for Zacharov?"

Confusion spread over Eleven's face. "Who?"

"Never mind. How did you know to come here tonight?"

"Krieg had some map on his phone. Like a tracking app."

"What app? Where did he get it?"

"I don't know that stuff. Krieg didn't share."

"He must have told you something. Y'all don't drive to a gas station in the middle of nowhere and shoot a lady for no reason."

"He said it was a custody fight. Like you...her...the lady took the kid, and she needed to be taught a lesson. We never planned to kill no one. It was supposed to be a warning. A chat, you know?"

"Real gentlemanly of ya, twelve men with all those guns coming out for a chat. Next, you'll be telling me you had a cooler full of iced tea in the trunk and you planned to share your picnic after."

"I'm sorry." He gave a couple of sniffs as he looked

around at the carnage. "It was business. Nothin' personal."

Elizabeth sighed. "Business. Well, this is our business. Back to the girl. Tell me what you know."

"Just what I already said. Krieg's girlfriend picked her up, and they took her to some other guy."

"This guy have a name?"

"Alberto."

"Surname?"

Eleven shrugged then winced. "Don't know it."

"Where did Alberto take her?"

"I figured back to her father."

"There is no father," I growled.

"Okay, okay. Don't get touchy. I think Krieg went to the airport. He was complaining about the noise."

"Which airport?"

"Like I said, he didn't share."

"What time did he meet you?" Elizabeth asked.

A siren sounded in the distance, but her expression didn't change.

"About seven. We stopped for burgers while we were waiting for...whatever this was. Look, I don't know anything else, I swear."

"What's the name of Krieg's woman?"

"Krieg's got lots of women. One for every night of the week."

"Krieg sounds like a real catch."

"He treated them right. Most of them were more trouble than they were worth."

Asshole. I fired a round from the Colt into his ugly mouth, and Elizabeth looked at me.

"Hey, I never said anything about *my* itchy trigger finger."

"Fair enough."

Half an hour later, the fire had almost burnt itself out, and a new battle was taking place at the gas station—a war of the acronyms. I'd spotted the FBI, the NSA, and the CIA, plus a whole bunch of other suits meandering around while they argued over who was responsible for what. Apparently, the local cops were stuck at the end of the road, banned from coming any further, and they weren't happy about it. Did I care? No.

"At least they came dressed for the funeral," I muttered, glancing over at the men picking their way through the mess.

"Cremation," Elizabeth said.

"Is this going to cause us a problem?"

"Not right now. We'll owe a couple of favours. See those guys over there?" She inclined her head at a small group, three men and two women, dressed more casually than the rest.

"Yes?"

"They're the cleaners. Their job is to fix shit like this. I've seen them get really creative over the years."

She whistled at them, and one of the guys wandered over.

"Javier, meet Seven. Seven, meet Javier. How's it looking?"

He seemed remarkably cheerful considering not only the situation but the time of night. "Not bad, not bad. Our first thought was a tanker explosion, but it's not as horrific as we thought. A nasty car crash should do it, with a nice blaze afterwards."

"How was the football last week?"

"Giants won. Thanks for the tickets, by the way."

"Always a pleasure."

He headed back to his colleagues as Elizabeth's phone rang. She glanced down at the screen and groaned. "Oh, shit."

I looked across sharply. "Not Zacharov?"

"Zacharov doesn't have my number—it was masked when you called him. But it's worse. My assistant."

Her assistant? I recalled her mentioning him on the plane as well. What kind of assassin had a fucking assistant?

Elizabeth answered anyway, then grimaced and held the phone six inches from her ear. I couldn't make out the words, but the screeching had to hurt.

"Bradley, would you calm down?"

More shrieking.

"No, I don't need a tow truck. I need a dumpster."

She rolled her eyes, and the person on the other end didn't let up.

"Bradley, you don't get it. It's more than a few scratches. It won't T-cut out. The car blew up, and the doors landed fifty yards away. It's still on fire now. Yes...on fire." A pause. "A new car would be good, thanks."

She hung up and sighed. "He tends to get a little emotional."

I gathered that.

Another hour and a half passed before a black SUV pulled into the melee. Elizabeth had shrugged a lot and answered a thousand questions from grey-suited clones, and after a medic had stitched up her handiwork on my back, I'd sat on a log at the edge of the lot and kept quiet. That and plotted Zacharov's demise. But when the lights on the SUV flashed, Elizabeth headed in that direction and beckoned me to do the same.

"Our ride's here."

"Where are we going?"

"Richmond. Well, close to it. It's where I live."

I took one last look at the people milling around. "Who's winning out there?"

"The NSA at the moment, but the FBI are running a close second."

The car was driven by a muscular guy with shoulder-length blonde hair. He looked like we'd got him out of bed, but in a good way. Elizabeth put her hand out for the keys, and he shook his head.

"Not tonight, darlin'. I didn't drag my ass out here to pick you up so I could have palpitations on the way back."

"Spoilsport."

"You're shotgun."

"AR-15, actually."

Between us, we collected up our pile of weapons and shoved them in the trunk. None of the suits had batted an eyelid about Elizabeth's firepower, which surprised me, but I couldn't complain.

She hopped into the passenger side while I took the backseat, and we set off past the roadblock and the motley crew of pissed-off cops.

"Can we stop for drive-thru?"

The blonde guy glanced across at her. "At eleven o'clock this morning, you said you were going out to buy a new coffee machine. What the hell happened this time? And who's your new friend?"

"Seven, meet Jed."

"Hi."

"Jed, meet Seven. Seven's also known as Lilith."

He blanched in the rearview mirror, and the car swerved briefly before he jerked the wheel back. "What, you didn't think you had enough Horsemen riding around the place without herding up another one?"

"What are you talking about?" I asked.

Elizabeth answered for him. "You know, the Horsemen? You are one, after all."

"You've met the others?"

"Not all of them."

"Which ones?"

"I'm married to Black."

Well, that explained a lot. "Could you just drop me off here?"

"He's not that bad."

"Even Zacharov's nervous of him."

"Good. He's on our side, and we'll have Red, Smoke, and Dime too. Snow's a friend, and I've met Player a few times. Black knows Pale, but he's quiet these days."

In the space of one day, I'd gone from being alone, to having a partner, to again getting involved with the deadliest collective of assassins in living history. I wasn't sure whether to relish the experience or run screaming.

Before I could make up my mind, Elizabeth's phone rang. She silenced it, then did so again, only for Jed's phone to blast out "The Star-Spangled Banner" from its cradle on the dash.

"Looks like someone wants to get hold of you, Emmy."

Emmy?

He reached over to answer, and a familiar voice filled the cabin.

"Emerson?"

"Hi, James."

"I heard a rumour you got involved in another incident tonight."

"It wasn't my fault."

"It never is." He sighed, and his voice softened. "You okay?"

"Perfect. But the Viper blew up. I loved that car."

"The car doesn't matter. I'll buy you a new car. I'm more worried about you."

The way he spoke, he didn't sound like the president. He sounded like the friend she'd claimed he was, perhaps even more.

"Honestly, I'm fine. And I've got a new friend. James, say hello to Lilith."

"As in Lilith, Lilith?"

"The one and only."

"Shit." He breathed in sharply. "Apologies. I meant, hello."

"Hi," I said. Better to be polite.

"Does this have something to do with your phone call earlier? Zacharov?"

"It's all connected," Elizabeth said. Was her name even Elizabeth? "I'll call you tomorrow with the full story, okay?"

"Make it late. I've got meetings all morning, a school visit in the afternoon, and a state dinner in the evening."

"Take care of yourself."

"That's my line."

Yes, today certainly went down as the strangest day in my life, and considering I once went undercover in a fetish club, that was saying something.

"Emerson?" I asked.

She turned to face me, looking a little sheepish. "In the interest of having an open and honest working relationship, I should probably mention that my name's not Elizabeth."

When the words "open" and "honest" left her mouth, Jed started laughing.

"So it's Emmy, then?" I asked.

"Yes. Emerson Black." The golden arches of a twenty-four-hour McDonald's up ahead caught her eye. "Stop the car. I need fries and a cheeseburger. And an apple pie. I think I've earned them."

"Make that two."

"Three."

CHAPTER 12

THE TRIP BACK to Richmond took a couple of hours, and Emmy filled Jed in on the story as we went. Three more people called to congratulate her on the mess we'd made, a girl called Sloane said she'd cleared the schedules for the next three weeks as best she could, and Bradley rang to say he was going to bed now but don't forget to drink the green smoothie for breakfast because Toby made it specially.

"Who's Toby?"

"My nutritionist. Hitler with a blender."

Great. A whole legion of people, and the idea of having to be nice to them for weeks made my chest seize. I was all right in social situations when I was playing a part, acting out a role. But stripped of my mask with my soul laid bare? I swallowed hard to keep my dinner down.

The closest I'd come to having a friend was Sam, and look how that turned out.

Finally, in the early hours, Jed slowed to a halt outside an imposing pair of wrought iron gates.

"You drive like an old woman," Emmy grumbled. "That's ten minutes of my life, lost. I'll never get it back."

"At least we got here in one piece."

"When I drive, we always get here intact. Just

faster. It's Dan who always crashes."

Mental note, don't get in a car with Dan, whoever he was.

They were still bickering as we rolled up the driveway, and I shoved a hand over my mouth to hide my gasp. What was this place? In front of us, a gothic mansion had emerged from the darkness, illuminated by enough security lights to justify their own power station.

"You live here?"

"Partly. We've got other homes as well."

Other homes? Had I side-stepped into some parallel universe where normal rules didn't apply? I'd spent the previous decade living out of a suitcase, moving from hotel to house to apartment depending on my job at the time. I'd never even owned appliances, let alone a castle.

A statue next to the door hid a retina scanner, and as Jed lined his eye up, bolts shot back with a muffled thunk.

"The door's reinforced steel," Emmy said. "All the windows are bulletproof glass, and we've got an anti-aircraft gun on the roof."

Yes, I was definitely dreaming.

I followed them through the maze to a kitchen bigger than the cell I'd lived in on Base 13. Hell, even the refrigerator was bigger than my bathroom. Emmy headed straight for it and began rummaging through the shelves, munching on a carrot she'd grabbed from the crisper drawer.

"You like pasta? Or we've got...um...ratatouille. Or a salad?"

Jed squashed beside her. "I need a beer."

I shook my head. "I'm not hungry."

At two in the morning, I needed sleep more than anything, and I'd already eaten a burger and fries.

A presence behind me made the hairs on the back of my neck prickle, and I turned to see a giant standing in the doorway. Okay, an admittedly handsome giant, but he had to be six feet six with the physique to match. For a man so big, he moved with remarkable grace as he glided over to join us.

"Seven." He held out a giant hand. "A pleasure to finally meet you."

I shook his hand, pleased when he didn't crush my fingers. "You have me at a disadvantage, because I don't know who you are."

"Black. I hear you've become acquainted with my wife."

His eyes bored into mine with uncomfortable intensity, as if they could turn me inside out and see every one of my secrets. Zacharov was right: it was all in the eyes, and Black's were dangerous.

He released my hand, and I cursed my feet as they took a step back. *Stand your ground, Seven.* I drew myself up an inch and locked onto his gaze.

"We spent the afternoon getting to know each other."

Shit, I looked away first.

Emmy stood up with an armful of plastic containers. "We even got some target practice in. At least we can cross that off the to-do list for tomorrow."

"Nice try, Diamond," Black said. "You'll be out on the range at ten, right after your workout."

"Slave driver," she muttered, but it was good-natured.

"Speaking of tomorrow..." He glanced at his watch. "Today. I've arranged a strategy meeting for noon, and Sloane's set us up in Windsor."

"Windsor?" I asked.

"It's one of the three conference rooms we have here. The others are Elsinore and Padua."

"They're locations from Shakespeare's plays," Emmy said. "Nate's a fan. You'll meet him soon."

"I thought we'd run this operation from home rather than the office," Black continued. "Seeing as some of us are likely to overstep the bounds of legality from time to time."

He may have scared me, but I kind of liked him.

"My priority is finding my daughter."

"I appreciate that, and we'll do everything we can to assist. The moment Emmy called me earlier, I put a team on the job. We've got twenty people working around the clock."

Tired though I was, I looked at the door. "I should help them."

Emmy shook her head as she fiddled with the microwave. "No, you need to rest. You're no good to anyone if you're tired."

"But the longer I leave it, the further away she could be. Hell, she could be back in Russia already."

"Like you said, you're an assassin, not a detective. Dan's an investigator, and she's leading the team."

So, Dan was a woman? Emmy was right about resting; I knew she was, but this whole "team" concept felt strange, and the idea of relying on others while I went to bed didn't come easy.

"I still feel like I should be doing something."

"And you will be. Starting tomorrow, you need to

get yourself back into decent physical and mental shape in case we need to extract Tabitha by force. Not to mention the Zacharov thing. We need the Seven of five years ago. Back then, I wouldn't have got that gun near you on the plane. You'd have noticed someone tampering with your bag in the hospital. And you sure as hell wouldn't have missed with your first shot like you did earlier."

The truth hurt. The stress that had built up over the past few hours—the past few years, if I was honest— weighed down on my shoulders as I sank to the floor.

Black crouched down at my side.

"Seven, look at me. He will not win." He took my chin between his thumb and forefinger and turned my face towards his. "He will not win."

His gaze held mine, and for the second time that day, I broke. Hot, salty tears washed down my cheeks as I cried for what I was, who I'd once been, and the person I'd never become. It barely registered when Black picked me up and carried me out of the room, Emmy following at his elbow.

Emmy's whispered, "Fuck" woke me as the sun rose over the tree line, visible through the stone balustrade of the balcony outside the bedroom window.

I rolled over and found her lying on the bed next to me. "What?"

"I fell asleep. I'm not supposed to share a bed with anyone but Black."

"He gets jealous?"

"Yes, but that's not it. I get nightmares and try to

kill people in my sleep."

"I get the nightmares, but I've never tried to kill anyone."

They'd stopped while I was with Sam, but now they were back in full force. By rights, I should have dreamed of the shooting yesterday, but after my meltdown, I'd fallen into a mercifully peaceful sleep.

She stretched her arms above her head then cursed again.

"Now what?"

"I slept in my contacts and my eyes are all fuzzy."

"Same. You wear contacts too?"

"Most of the time." She reached her hands up, peeled out the offending lenses, and dropped them onto the nightstand. "Better."

"Can I borrow a cleaning kit? I left mine back in Raleigh."

"I'll get Bradley to find you a spare. Long-sighted or short-sighted?"

"Neither. Coloured. Zacharov's number one rule—always wear my lenses. He said my eyes were cursed."

She flicked the overhead light on, and when she rolled to face me, her vivid purple eyes made me gasp. Not just because the colour was so striking, but because I'd seen those eyes before, staring back at me in the mirror every morning until the day I met Zacharov. Shaking, I reached up and pinched out my own lenses, and her look of shock matched mine.

Her voice dropped to a whisper. "Then we're both cursed."

Neither of us spoke for a full minute then curiosity got the better of me. "Your mother or your father?"

"Father. You?"

"Same."

We both had the same thought at the same time, because Emmy asked, "Who was he?" at the same moment as I asked, "Who is he?"

"No idea who mine is," she said. "Did yours ever leave Russia?"

"I doubt it. He died when I was less than a year old, so I don't remember him, but my parents were so poor they couldn't even afford heating. A plane ticket to... America? England? That wouldn't have been a priority."

"England. Well, my mother never left the country. She didn't even have a passport, mainly because she spent all her money on crack."

A coincidence, then, but a strange one.

"My mama died when I was four. Her eyes were blue. Bright blue. That's my most vivid memory of her —the way they lit up when she woke me each morning."

And it was my mama who'd taught me about the kind of love I needed to show Tabby. Yes, Mama may have worked long hours as a ballerina, with rehearsals that ran late into the evening, but when she was home, she'd doted on me. My breath hitched as I remembered how she used to braid my hair in the mornings and kiss me goodnight no matter how late she got back.

"I'm so sorry she's gone," Emmy said.

"Your mother? Is she still alive?"

"I don't know, and I don't care."

"Then I'm sorry about your childhood too."

Another couple of minutes passed before Emmy spoke. "Who knows, maybe these damned eyes give us better aim?"

"Let's hope so."

A knock on the door woke me, and I sat bolt upright. Rather than getting up, I'd gone dead to the world again. This newfound ability to sleep properly was unnerving.

Beside me, Emmy stirred and mumbled, "Fuck off. Too early."

I looked at my watch. Eight thirty. Shit! I should have been up hours ago to join the search for Tabby, and who the hell was at the door?

"Who's there?"

"Black. Have you seen Emmy?"

"She's in here."

"Are you dressed?"

"It wasn't that kind of night."

Emmy choked out a laugh beside me and flicked a tangle of hair over her shoulder.

"Don't give him ideas."

The door cracked open, and Black strode in with two mugs of coffee. Emmy held out her hands for one, and he offered the other to me. "Here. You look like you need this more than I do."

"Thanks. Is there any news?"

"Krieg was seen near a private airfield near Raleigh yesterday evening. We're tracking the planes that left, but..." He trailed off and stooped to peer at my face. "Fuck me."

"I'll have to pass."

"You've got the same eyes as Emmy."

"We've worked that one out."

The mattress squashed down as Black settled on the

edge of the bed. "Tell me more about your history."

Emmy cut him off with a kiss on the cheek. "I know what you're thinking, and we've already explored that idea. Now isn't the time to rake over Seven's childhood."

He reached out to tuck a few strands of hair behind my ear. "A difficult time?"

I nodded.

"I'm sorry."

"It's in the past. All that matters now is finding my daughter.

"We will." He rose and turned back to the door. "And you're due in the gym in half an hour."

As he left, the click of nails on wood announced more visitors, and two...well, the front one was a dog, and the other? The huge creature sure didn't move like a canine. "What the hell is that?"

Emmy disappeared beneath a mass of limbs before she came up laughing. "Which one? The dog or the cat?"

"I'm good with the dog." It looked like a Doberman. "It's the other fur-coated razor blade I was referring to."

"This is Kitty." She finally pushed the thing off her. "Kitty, say hi."

A paw the size of my hand was duly raised and waved at me.

"Kitty? You called it kitty?"

"Him, and I didn't pick the name. We're looking after him for a friend. Kitty's too big for her apartment."

No kidding. "What is he? A leopard?"

"A jaguar."

Kitty tracked me with big, yellow-hued eyes that didn't blink as I slid off the bed and walked towards the bathroom. Sleek black fur shone in the sunlight streaming in through the window.

"Is he dangerous?"

"Are you dangerous?"

"Only if the need arises."

"There's your answer. Just try not to let him lick your face—it's like being sandpapered."

Where the hell had I ended up?

CHAPTER 13

ONCE THE CAFFEINE was circulating in my veins, I felt human again. The idea of not actively hunting for Tabby left me twitchy, but the time had come to pick a side. Zacharov and his tyranny or Emmy and her equine friends. Going it alone was no longer an option.

My trust, respect, and loyalty had to be earned. Zacharov had destroyed them all, but so far Emmy was reassembling the scattered shards, piece by jagged piece. Choosing my team was the easiest decision I'd ever made.

"Can I borrow some workout gear?"

"I'll show you where my closet is, and you can take what you like. But I'll warn you now—Bradley won't pass up a shopping opportunity. Give him a couple of hours and you'll have bags of shit everywhere, and everything'll fit, and it'll all be flattering. He reads every issue of Vogue and makes notes in the margins."

She led me to the other side of the house, where her closet rivalled a small department store for choice. I headed straight for the sportswear, which was organised by type and function. Shorts, sports bra, sneakers—I soon looked the part, even if I didn't feel it.

Back in the kitchen, a lady in her fifties bustled around, stacking dishes of fruit and pastries onto a central island. I'd seen worse selections in five-star hotels.

"How many people live here?" I asked Emmy.

"Officially, just Black and me. But friends are always welcome, and when we've got a tough job on, people tend to move in for the duration."

I didn't want to eat much before we hit the gym, but as I'd only picked at dinner last night, I grabbed a banana to give me an energy boost while Emmy went for a pain au chocolat.

One mouthful in, a rainbow-coloured tornado flew through the door. When it eventually stopped moving, a small man in neon-orange skinny jeans, a pair of pink sheepskin boots, and an acid-green off-the-shoulder sweater came to a halt in front of the espresso machine. His blue hair was spiked up into a faux-hawk, and his forehead creased into a frown.

Should I laugh or run?

"Cheer up, party princess; it might never happen," Emmy said.

"It already has. The house is filled with people who shoot first then shoot again."

"Look on the bright side—we're unlikely to get burgled."

"Burglary is the least of my worries. Look at what happened last time you planned a big overseas job—your house got blown up."

Emmy turned to me with a sheepish smile. "Seven, meet Bradley, my assistant. He's a little prone to exaggeration. The house didn't blow up. There were a few bullet holes and some water damage once the sprinklers put the fire out."

Bradley jabbed Emmy in the chest. "Seven, meet Emmy, my boss. She's a little prone to bullshit."

"We've upgraded our security since then. There's more motion sensors than trees out back now."

Before the argument could continue, a second man walked in, dressed less flamboyantly in a pair of chinos and a burgundy sweater. Emmy groaned as he rummaged in the refrigerator, then glared at him when he took her pastry and replaced it with a glass of something green.

"Drink."

She took a sip and wrinkled her nose. "What is it?"

"Wheatgrass smoothie."

"This is Toby. It's his mission to make my life hell."

Toby chuckled. "Healthy, more like."

"Hell is my job." A thickly accented Russian voice came from the doorway, and a man-mountain blocked the sun as he ambled in past the window. "I spend many hours thinking up new ways to torment you."

"Alex, my personal trainer," Emmy told me. "Our personal trainer."

Oh, great. Just great. Another reminder of my homeland. I'd had a lifetime of Russian trainers, and Alex's bulging biceps told me he meant business.

"You're late," he growled.

"Did I mention his cheerful demeanour?"

"Two minutes. Hurry up."

The man made Zacharov look like a toothpick. Of all the people I'd met so far, Alex was the one who made me want to jump in front of a really big truck.

"Is he as bad as I think?" I asked when he'd gone.

"Yep."

At eleven thirty, I sagged back onto the gym mat and concentrated on breathing. There wasn't a part of me that didn't hurt.

A foot nudged my side, and I cracked one eye open to see Alex holding out a wedge of paper towels for me to wipe the blood from my nose. It hadn't been an entirely one-sided fight—the bruise spreading out over Emmy's left thigh spoke of that—but she'd definitely got the better of me today. As well as the nosebleed, I'd wrenched my shoulder, and the lump where she'd walloped my calf was swelling up nicely.

"You have room for improvement," Alex said.

Give that man a prize for the understatement of the decade. I couldn't believe how much form I'd lost. Four years ago, when I'd had a trainer as sadistic as Alex, I'd been able to hold my own against him. Today, Emmy had floored me with a right hook, and worse, I knew she was holding back.

"I know."

"Same time tomorrow, and bring your running shoes."

Toby accosted us on our way out, thrusting bottles of murky liquid into our hands. I sniffed mine—seaweed with a hint of banana. Emmy made a face and slugged hers back, and I followed suit. Anything that tasted that bad must surely be good for us.

"Okay, I give up. What was it?"

"Protein shake with sea kelp, chia seeds, and extra vitamins."

"It's worse than the wheatgrass," Emmy grumbled.

"Stop complaining. Do you want lunch served in the conference room?"

"Did you make it?"

"Tofu burgers with gluten-free crispbread and a three-bean salad."

"Why don't you skip the middleman and put it straight in the garbage disposal?"

"You'll eat it, and you'll damn well love it."

Toby stuck his nose in the air and marched out.

"Will it really be that awful?" I asked her.

"No, I just enjoy winding him up. It's like a sport."

When I got back to my room, sure enough, Bradley had invaded. The bed was covered in piles of clothes, more than I'd ever owned, and certainly more colourful. Red? He thought I'd wear red? The nightstand held a bunch of flowers, and the bathroom smelled like a tart's boudoir. I unfolded the note on my pillow and found a Mars bar underneath it. Okay, Bradley definitely had his plus points.

Gone shopping. I'll be back to sort out your hair later. B

I glanced in the mirror. What was wrong with my hair? Okay, everything. Everything was wrong with my hair. I'd only been allowed to cut it with safety scissors, and Zacharov kept a gun on me the whole time.

Five minutes in the shower, and I threw on jeans and a T-shirt and went in search of Emmy. She'd given me a map. A fucking map for a house. Worse, I needed the damn thing.

Alex was waiting outside Windsor, and when he handed me an ice pack for my leg, I resisted the urge to call him an asshole.

"Tell me if your shoulder starts to stiffen up." He cracked his knuckles. "I will fix it."

"He's good, you know," Emmy said from behind me. "Magic fingers."

Black raised an eyebrow as he walked past.

"I wasn't talking about you."

He raised the other eyebrow.

"Put your dirty mind away."

The conference room provided a sharp contrast to the period furnishings that graced the rest of the house. A round table seated twelve as equals, dark wood with a glass centre, and video screens took up one entire wall. The first thing that struck me was Tabby's face staring down at me from the top left-hand corner.

Emmy followed my gaze. "It's so we don't forget our goal."

"Where did you get the picture? I don't even have a picture."

"You remember on the plane when I said getting the Russians to pose for snapshots was easier than relying on a lapel camera?"

"Yes."

"That didn't mean I didn't have a hidden camera."

I blinked back tears—I couldn't get emotional, not in front of this crowd. "Can I get copies?"

"I'll get Bradley to make some. Actually, no, I'll ask Mack. Bradley'll print a nice photo for your wallet, but you'll also get her face printed on mugs, T-shirts, key rings, mouse mats, phone cases..."

My eyes strayed to the opposite side of the wall where Zacharov's mugshot hovered. Some joker had drawn devil horns on him, and they glowed red against a dark background.

I studied him for a second then tore myself away.

"And that's so we don't forget our target," Emmy

said.

Besides Emmy and Black, there were three others in the room. Jed, plus a curvy brunette a couple of inches shorter than me, and a guy with Zacharov's build and hair the colour of molten dark chocolate. His eyes matched.

The brunette gave me a wave from behind her laptop. "I'm Dan. Sorry about your daughter."

"I appreciate your help."

"Any friend of Emmy's is a friend of mine."

I looked at the guy.

"Xavier," he said.

Not the talkative type, then.

Emmy motioned me to take the seat next to hers. "Xav's also known as Smoke."

So, she hadn't been kidding about the Horsemen. Seemed as if we had quite a stable of talent to choose from for this mission, and we'd need it. I touched my fingers to the knife at the small of my back, just in case. Sure, Emmy had vouched for these people, but trust didn't come easily to me, especially when some of the people in question had body counts to rival mine.

The door opened one more time, and another man walked in. The newcomer looked around Black's age, late thirties to early forties, with skin the colour of café au lait.

"Nate," Emmy told me. "You know him as Red."

He took a seat beside Black, his face as stony as the gargoyles that lurked along the roofline outside. Only his eyes showed any expression as he placed a tablet on the table in front of him, tapped a few times, and dimmed the lights.

"Are we ready to begin?"

CHAPTER 14

BLACK SAT BACK, fingers steepled, and looked at Dan. "Tabitha."

"One of the maintenance workers at the airfield saw a young child being carried onto a Cessna yesterday evening. We're assuming that was Tabby, but we've yet to confirm."

"Was she okay?" I asked. "Hurt?"

"Crying, but otherwise she looked unharmed."

A blurry CCTV picture popped up onto the screen, showing a man climbing the steps to a small twin-prop. I squinted, but there was no way to tell for sure whether the child in his arms was my daughter.

"We'll get the image enhanced, but I'm not sure it'll help," Dan said.

"Where did the plane go?"

"Florida. A small airfield near the coast. We've got a team from the local office on their way there right now."

"Why Florida?" Emmy mused. "If Zacharov wanted to take Tabitha back to Russia, why that extra step? He could have had a jet waiting in Raleigh. He had the cash and the contacts."

Black leaned forward and poured himself a coffee from the carafe in the centre of the table. "He didn't take her to Russia."

"How do you know?" I asked. Sure, Zacharov had said the same thing, but he was a liar.

"Because he's anticipating your next move. You've got a deadline, and he's given you two difficult tasks: Either kill Harrison or search for your daughter. To find Tabitha, he believes you'll have to go to him first, and by putting distance between them, he minimises the chance of you finding her."

"You think she's still in Florida?"

"No, I think she's on a boat."

"And he's always right about this shit," Jed muttered.

Dan pushed her chair back and got to her feet. "I'll get teams out to the marinas. Back in a few minutes."

Nate tapped away at his tablet, and a dozen pictures popped up on the wall—tiny bundles of electronic circuitry and what looked like white pills. "I'm curious about the tracker, whether it was long or short range, and how long it lasted. Did it look like any of the ones on screen?"

I studied the devices, but I'd only seen the tiny monster Emmy cut out of my back briefly and in near-darkness.

"The one on the right's closest," Emmy said. "What scale is that?"

"About the size of a cannellini bean."

"Yeah. Except Seven's had flatter ends."

"Interesting. That's one of the newer models. Kinetic powered and works via satellite. Zacharov wouldn't have needed local receivers. He could have sat in his armchair and tracked her from Siberia."

"Any chance of a backup device?" Black asked.

I forgot to breathe, overwhelmed by the urge to

scratch my own skin off.

Nate shook his head. "No. The perimeter monitoring systems on the estate would have picked up the signal the moment Seven stepped through the gate."

"Are you sure?" I asked.

He gave me a sharp look. Clearly, Nate didn't appreciate being questioned. "I'm sure."

Black flicked his eyes to the video wall then back to Nate, carefully avoiding my gaze. "And Tabitha? I'll bet my new Bugatti that she's got a tracker in her too."

Emmy squeezed my hand under the table in a silent show of support. Had that bastard put a tracking chip in my daughter? Who was I kidding? Of course he would have. The man had the morals of a mosquito combined with the bite of a great white shark.

Nate gave a wry laugh. "No way I'm taking that bet. I'll look into the monitoring systems. If we can find out more about the chip he used, maybe we could find a way to reverse engineer it."

"What do we know? Krieg?"

Xavier cleared his throat. "The woman who picked Tabitha up was Morgan Getz, Krieg's date for Tuesdays and the occasional Sunday. He called her yesterday morning and asked for a favour, spun her the same line about a custody battle gone wrong. He dropped Morgan back at her apartment before he took Tabitha to the airfield."

"So you had a wasted trip?"

"I didn't say that. While they were in the car, Tabitha complained about being cold, and Krieg told her not to worry, because she'd be going somewhere hot soon."

"Florida? Or further afield?"

"The guy he was supposed to be meeting called a few minutes later, and Morgan remembers Krieg snapping at him to speak English, that he wasn't a fuckin' spic."

"So, there's a possible connection to South America," Black said. "Illegals come in through Florida far more often than our government would like. Maybe this time, some cargo went the other way."

The thought of my daughter being cargo made me feel sick, but I swallowed it down. Was it a good thing or a bad thing that she might be in South America rather than Russia? Despite his many, many faults, Zacharov had always kept her safe. Would her unknown captor do the same?

A buzz of chatter followed.

"I'll get Carmen to call some of her ex-colleagues."

"Eduardo's involved in all sorts of shit. I'll get him to keep an ear open. He's easier to get hold of since Nate gave him that new secure phone."

"Do we know anyone in El Salvador since Sanchez died?"

"Jorge took over."

"The Brits have a network in Belize, and they owe me a favour."

"Nate, how connected are your Cuban relatives?"

"Panama... Don't we know a police chief there?"

"Quinn kept in touch with his people in Venezuela."

"Nicaragua... Who have we got in Nicaragua?"

This was what had been missing from my life, long before Zacharov locked me up. A team. Friends. Camaraderie. These people gave me a flutter of hope I'd never felt before, and I thanked Utkin's cold, dead heart that I hadn't pulled the trigger on Emmy two and a half years ago.

Notes were jotted, phone calls were made, and after half an hour Black shushed everyone and pointed at the picture of Zacharov on the wall.

"Let's discuss our other task. We need to take care of him. We all know the background, but Seven doesn't, so I'll start with a recap." He took a sip of water then angled to face me. "For the past decade, certain items that are not supposed to be available to civilians have been finding their way onto the black market. It started off small—armour-piercing rounds, grenades, automatic weapons—but over the past few years, the problem's got worse."

"That terrorist attack where extremists took out a civilian aircraft with a missile as it took off," Nate put in.

"The explosives used to blow up a train in Belgium," Xavier said.

"And the release of a super virus at Dulles International Airport."

"Likho?" I asked.

Black nodded. "We call it Azrael, but yes."

"That's why I went to Base 13 with the weapons inspectors," Emmy said. "We prevented a tragedy last time, more by luck than anything else, but Azrael's still being advertised to the highest bidder, and we can't afford another attempt."

"There have been rumours about Zacharov for years, but it's got to the stage where the world can't ignore the problem any longer.

"Zacharov's a monster," I said.

"He is," Emmy agreed. "You gave me the location

for Likho, but we know he's got other weapons. I found one bunker myself, under the hangar at the south end of the runway."

"I can tell you of another three. One of them contains chemical weapons, so we'll need to be careful." Shit. *We'll* need to be careful. This was really happening, wasn't it? I was heading back to the one place on earth I'd never wanted to set foot inside again. "When are we going?"

Black opened up a timeline with various notes attached. Two weeks and six days until it ended, and we all knew why. My deadline to rescue Tabby.

"It's a fine balance. We need to plan enough to ensure the mission's success, but at the same time, we have a cutoff date." He used a laser to point at the nineteenth day. "We'll aim to strike then. If we take it right up to the wire, they'll be more alert. They'll know we're coming then, or we're not coming at all. Go earlier and there's a chance we'll catch them off guard. Yes, we'll plan for two days early, and that also gives us leeway."

Eighteen days to plan, and the logistics promised to be a bitch. "I can help with details of inside the base, but my external network is patchy at best now. Zacharov gives information to his operatives on a strictly need-to-know basis, which could work in our favour when we get there because many of them won't be clued into what's happening, but it doesn't help with the advance work."

"Blackwood only has a small network in Russia. We're expanding slowly, but the corruption that pervades out there makes doing business in the country difficult."

"Many of my countrymen would sell out their own flesh and blood for a few roubles. What's Blackwood?"

"The security firm we own, although this job won't be going through the books."

Emmy turned to Jed. "Can the CIA help?"

"It's not supposed to be going through our books either."

I hadn't realised Jed was CIA. What a shining example of public-private cooperation.

"I know, but when I asked James if I could borrow you for a month, he was only too happy to oblige."

"I bet he was."

Out of the corner of my eye, I caught the scowl that flashed across Black's face. What was the story there?

His face returned to its usual impassive expression before he spoke. "The Russians are also working on the basis of plausible deniability. The president has given his blessing for us to clean up the problem, but he won't provide any assistance."

"Next year's an election year," Nate muttered.

"Jed, who have you got available? We need a Russia specialist. I'm sure my wife can convince Mr. Harrison to cooperate with our needs."

"Officially, I'd have to say the current head of the Russia desk and his deputy."

"And unofficially?" Emmy asked.

"Quinn."

"Quinn as in your friend Quinn?"

"Yeah."

"The same Quinn who was sprawled on your couch when I was over a few weeks ago, reeking of whisky?"

"That's him."

"Isn't he also the Quinn who got declared persona

non grata by the Russians a couple of years back and booted out of the country? And then got declared PNG by Venezuela again just months ago?

Jed shrugged and nodded.

"Now, I know I didn't get to speak to him on account of him being unconscious, but seriously? He's the best the CIA has to offer?"

"The Russian thing was unfortunate. But in the five years he was over there, he gathered intelligence you wouldn't believe, and the bugs he planted are still bringing home the goods."

"And the Venezuela thing?"

Jed grinned. "He got caught fucking the president's niece on a balcony at an official reception."

Emmy rolled her eyes. "I see why you're friends now. What about the drinking thing?"

"He's been better these last few weeks. Chess and Lara have adopted him, kind of like a puppy. Chess has been making him dinner, and Lara's been doing his laundry."

"Hand on heart, you think he's the best man for the job?"

"I do, and I also happen to know he hates Zacharov. Something about him strangling a hooker in Moscow several years back, although Quinn hates talking about it. I think he blames himself for not stopping what happened."

I closed my eyes. I hadn't heard that story, but in all honesty, it didn't surprise me.

"And I bet you dinner Quinn's still got a network out there, and dessert that he's been keeping himself informed."

"Dinner won't be necessary," Black said.

Emmy made a face at him. "Fine. Quinn then. I'll speak to James and get him seconded to the team. Same time tomorrow, everybody?"

Those seated around the table all nodded their agreement.

"Good. Oh, and Jed?"

"Yeah?"

"Do me a favour and keep Quinn sober tonight, will you?"

CHAPTER 15

HOW COULD ONLY twenty-four hours have passed since my life got turned upside down once again? This time yesterday, my biggest worry had been how many times Mr. Dobson would try to look down my top that afternoon. And whether I could resist stapling his testicles to the boardroom table if he kept doing so.

Yet, here I was, aching all over and sharing airspace with a group of people who had, until now, only been code names in the Interpol database.

I followed Emmy out of the conference room and along a corridor dominated by a macabre tapestry that seemed more suited to Zacharov's tastes.

"What's next?"

"I was only kidding yesterday when I said we could skip shooting practice. Let's head out to the range. Any preferences on what you want to shoot?"

"Can I get the Glock back?"

"Sure."

"I should probably pick up a rifle too."

"I'll show you the weapons locker."

Emmy and Black kept enough hardware in their cellar to start World War III. Everything from a Beretta pocket pistol to a rocket launcher lay racked and ready in a room off the main basement.

"I'll get Nate to add your retina scan to the database

so you can get in here when you want."

"Aren't you worried, giving me access to all this?"

She met my eyes, violet to violet. "Should I be?"

"No."

"There's your answer. Now, what do you think of this? Looks like a cell phone but it fires .22 rounds."

A lump rose in my throat. Never before had somebody showed trust in me like that, not Zacharov, and certainly nobody else I'd worked with. There and then, I vowed not to let Team Blackwood down.

I took the tiny gun from her. "Cute. I've seen similar but nothing so realistic."

"Nate made it. If it goes bang or boom, he's your man."

We collected half a dozen guns and put them into a duffle bag with ammunition, ear protection, and wraparound glasses. Emmy grabbed one handle, I took the other, and we headed out to the back of the house where someone had set up targets along the side of a huge expanse of neatly mown grass.

"Welcome to our airstrip-slash-shooting range," Emmy said.

"You've got a plane here?"

"Two small ones. One for fun and a backup for emergencies. Do you fly?"

"I used to, but I haven't got behind the controls for at least five years."

"We'll fix that when this is over. Black's a great teacher."

That was the first time she'd spoken of the future beyond the next three weeks.

"You think I'll still be around?"

"I'm kind of hoping so. I like you."

Simple as that. She liked me.

"I like you too."

Only I started to change my mind when she completely outclassed me on the range. Fuck. I was lucky if I got on the target at a thousand yards, let alone in the centre.

"Go back to the pistol," Emmy said. "You were getting better with that. Don't stress over it."

Easy for her to say. She grouped every shot within a couple of centimetres. I picked up the Glock again, but before I could load a fresh magazine, the crack of a high-powered rifle came from behind us. I got halfway to the trees before I realised Emmy hadn't moved. Worse, she was smiling.

"Dime's here," she said.

Another Horseman, and a sniper rumoured to have shot a Mexican drug lord through the eye from two thousand yards.

"Where?"

Emmy waved a hand towards the far side of the house. "Back there in the trees, somewhere."

I picked up my rifle and peered through the scope at the thousand-yard target I'd been missing all afternoon. The centre had been obliterated, and if Emmy was right, Dime had done that from fifteen hundred yards. Looked like the rumours were true.

Emmy let out one of her piercing whistles, and a silhouette emerged from a stand of pine trees and ambled in our direction. A minute later, I got another shock when I realised Dime was a woman.

"Seven, meet Carmen. Nate's wife and our resident sharpshooter."

"Hi." I'm Seven, a socially awkward assassin.

"I'll leave you in Carmen's capable hands while I make some phone calls. Have fun, kids."

Carmen put an arm around my shoulders, a sweet gesture and not one I'd expected. "I'm so sorry to hear about your daughter. We've got a son, six years old now, and I know if something happened to him..." She hefted the Accuracy International rifle she was carrying. "The world would have one less *cabrón*. Let's carry on. I was watching from back there, and you could do with widening your stance slightly."

By dinnertime, I was getting all my shots on the target, although I still had improvements to make, and I'd gained another friend. More than that, Carmen had shown me it was possible to balance motherhood with a difficult career, and that tiny seed of hope in my chest swelled a little bigger.

Rain began to fall as we walked back to the house, and Carmen looked up at the sky. "This is set for the night. Sunshine is one of the things I miss about Mexico."

"At least it's not snowing." I didn't miss that at all.

Dinner was a communal affair. I'd seen a formal dining room as I walked through the house earlier, but everybody piled their plates high from dishes on the kitchen island and sat at the long table next to it, chatting about work, sports, politics, news, and everything in between. I took a seat next to Emmy, feeling like the new kid at school. Ugh, school. We'd had a governess at the orphanage, and I'd sat by myself at the back. The other girls used to make fun of my eyes, which meant I often got into trouble for fighting.

But this place was different.

I was contemplating a second helping of food when

an unfamiliar face appeared. A redhead, taller and thinner than me, and prettier too.

"The geek squad's arrived," Emmy said.

Okay, if the geek squad looked like a supermodel.

"I'm Mack," the redhead said, perching on Emmy's lap because all the nearby seats were occupied. "I erased your fingerprints from the police database."

"She does speeding tickets too," Emmy said. "Just saying."

"Thank you."

Mack helped herself to a piece of Emmy's sushi. "Luke couldn't make it tonight. A server crashed, and he had to take care of it."

"That's fine for now. We've already got plans of the base by spreading a little cash around, but we could do with mocking up a model."

Back in Russia, mocking up a model involved a gang of conscripts, scissors, glue, cardboard, and a lot of arguments. Not so at Blackwood. A hologram reflected up from the glass centre of the table in Windsor while Mack tweaked it by looking at blueprints, satellite photos, and the photos Emmy had taken on her visit to Base 13. Mack could tilt, enlarge, and edit it with a few clicks of her mouse. By the time we started yawning, we had something close to my memories, and we'd started adding glowing red dots to signify the hazards.

"Are you staying here tonight?" Emmy asked Mack.

She looked at the clock on the wall. It had just gone midnight.

"No, I'll head home. Luke should be keeping the

bed warm by now."

Ah, so Luke was her boyfriend. Or rather, her husband, judging by the pair of rings on her left hand. I felt another pang in my chest as I thought of Sam. Would the pain ever fade?

Emmy cut into my thoughts. "I'm having a drink before I go to bed. It helps me to sleep better. Want to join me?"

"Why not?"

The lounge we ended up in had a fully stocked wet bar tucked into one corner, and Emmy unfolded her pocket knife to slice a lemon from a bowl sitting on the polished wooden surface.

"Gin and tonic?"

I nodded and took a seat on one of the high stools, staring at a framed ink blot on the wall until Emmy pushed a glass towards me. The lighting was dim, a soft yellow glow from a pair of uplighters at either side of us.

"What do you see?" she asked, nodding at the painting.

"In the Rorschach? Do you want my actual response? Or the one psych 101 says I should give?"

"I'd rather know the real you."

"It reminds me of the first man I ever killed. Blood went all over his bed, and it looked kind of like that." I may not have remembered much about that night, but I remembered that. "How about you?"

"I think it looks like a fat woman giving birth to a dragon."

A bubble of laughter escaped as I raised the glass to my lips. Fuck. Emmy had certainly been generous with the Bombay Sapphire. "I'm definitely not having more than one of these."

"I only ever have one when we've got a heavy job on. I can't shoot straight if I'm drunk."

"It's why you were worried about this Quinn guy earlier? The drinking?"

"That and I don't know him. I trust Jed's judgement, though. If he says Quinn's good, then he is."

"Or was."

"Or was," she agreed. "But he used to have a good reputation. When I spoke to James earlier, he said that if Quinn can get back the form he once had then he's the best man to have in our corner."

A bit like you. She didn't speak the words, but I knew she was thinking them.

"It's a big 'if' though, isn't it? Especially if he hasn't even been to Russia for years."

"It is. That it is."

I swirled the drink in my glass, the clink of ice cubes the only sound in an otherwise silent room. The quiet unnerved me. Back on Base 13, the guards kept the TV on twenty-four hours a day, and I'd never had the peace to simply think.

"You don't want to go back there, do you?" Emmy asked. "To the base, I mean."

"No, but I don't have a choice. And while I don't want to set foot there again, a small part of me wants to witness it firsthand when it goes up in flames. Once it's gone, and he's gone, I can finally make a fresh start."

"What happened to you there? Or if you don't want to talk about it, feel free to tell me to butt out."

Did I want to talk about it? Not really. I didn't even want to think about it. But the words tumbled out of me as if their escape could lighten my soul. I told her about Sam, how we'd met and fallen in love. Because we had. I may never have said those words back to him, but I knew how I felt, and I hoped he did too.

"And then Zacharov killed him. He must have known I was planning to run with Sam, because he got to him before I did."

"How?"

"A gas explosion in his apartment. I got there as it was still burning and stayed until the firemen carried the body bags out. One for Sam and another for his dog. I adored that damn dog too."

Emmy gathered me up in a hug, sharing a little of her strength. "I'm so sorry."

"Then Zacharov came for me, and you know what he said?"

"Go on."

"'Seven, Sam Jessop was no good for you, anyway.'"

"Zacharov's whacked."

"You're telling me. He drugged me, and the next thing I knew I was in my cell on Base 13. I didn't get out until after Tabby was born. That bastard handcuffed me to the bars as I gave birth, and all I could think of through the pain was smashing his head in with a rock."

"Maybe you'll get your wish."

"Maybe."

As long as he died, I'd be satisfied. He himself always taught me to put the task above my feelings, that when I got emotional, I also got sloppy.

"So, how did you meet Black? Has he always known what you do?"

"He was the one who taught me to do it." She

chuckled. "I met him when I was fifteen. I stole his wallet, and when he asked for it back, I broke his nose. You know, the stuff dreams are made of."

"Fifteen. I had a three-year head start. How old are you now?"

"Officially? The world thinks I turned thirty-four last May. But my birth certificate says I'll be thirty-two in December. You?"

"The same. Thirty-one. What day in December?"

"The fifteenth."

"I'm four days older."

"Don't tell Bradley. He'll plan the mother of all joint birthday parties."

Having met him a few times, I could imagine him doing exactly that.

"I've never had a birthday party."

"I didn't until I met Bradley. The first one, he flew in a group of male revue dancers from Spain. Black was supposed to be away on a job, but he arrived back early, just in time to get hit in the face with a thong as the dudes whipped it all off. Dan was riding one of them like he was a prize stallion. Black got this odd look on his face and stormed out, so I figured I'd better apologise for the men, and the music, and the mess in the ballroom, but when I found him he was laughing so hard he couldn't even speak."

"At least he saw the funny side. Zacharov would have lined the strippers up and shot them."

"There is that." Her voice softened. "How about your mum? Didn't she do anything special when you were little?"

"She loved me, but she was never quite all there. I think her heart broke when my father died. Sure, she had good days, but other times she wouldn't even get out of bed."

Over the years, I'd done my best to block out the bad days. I preferred to remember Mama happy and smiling, twirling me around the house until I was dizzy. As a ballet dancer, she'd been so pretty and graceful on the outside but broken on the inside.

"What happened to her?"

"I found her in the bath. The neighbours heard me screaming."

I pinched my eyes shut, but that did nothing to block out the sight of my mama floating in water as red as the setting sun, her hair floating on the surface like darkened cobwebs. She had a four-year-old daughter, almost five, and she'd taken the coward's way out.

Emmy rested her chin on my shoulder as I knocked back the rest of my drink. I was tempted to pour myself another, but I knew I'd regret it in the morning. Not only because I'd have a hangover, but for the lapse in my self-control.

"We're both screwed up," Emmy said. "Where do you think we'd be if we'd had normal childhoods?"

"You'd be burning cakes instead of military bases."

"And you'd be burning out the tyres on your minivan while you drove to the grocery store to pick up Turkey Twizzlers and spaghetti hoops for your three kids."

"And it would be boring as hell."

She poured a slug of tonic water into my glass and held hers up in a toast. "Here's to being fucked in the head."

I clinked my glass against hers. "To being mean motherfuckers."

"Black's already rolling his eyes at the prospect of dealing with two of us."

Two girls, two warped personalities, two allies. I returned Emmy's hug, wrapping my arms around her waist.

"Thank you for doing all this. It's like... Seven can finally die, and I can start again. Get a little closer to the person I should have been. Not the whole minivan thing, obviously, but one day I'd like a home to share with my daughter. And a dog."

We started to the door.

"Then you'll need a new name. Or your old one back."

"Ana," I whispered. "My name was Anastasia Petrova."

CHAPTER 16

THE GYM SESSION the next morning wasn't much better. I still felt drained after my talk with Emmy, and although I willed myself to react faster, I still floundered around while she moved effortlessly.

Alex noticed my sub-par performance too. "You need to work harder. Tomorrow we start with the knives, *da*?"

Knives? Fantastic. "*Da*."

"You girls can finish up on your own."

While Emmy and I sparred on the mats, Black got into the ring with Alex. The easy grace of Black's walk transferred to his fighting style, and while he and Alex were evenly matched, Black danced while Alex was all about the power. The effect was mesmerising. So mesmerising I forgot to watch Emmy and ended up on my ass again.

"Concentrate," she said, but her eyes sparkled. "Eyes off my husband and on me."

"He's..." Uh, how did I say it?

"Hypnotic? Yes, I know. And I still pinch myself every morning I wake up next to him." She held out a hand and helped me up. "Let's call it a day. I need breakfast."

Bradley was waiting at the door with towels and protein shakes. A girl could get used to this.

"Who's the new hottie?" he asked Emmy, bouncing on his toes with excitement.

"Sorry?"

"The new hottie in the kitchen. Light brown hair, hasn't shaved in a few days, but it suits him. Abs worth licking, but desperately needs wardrobe help."

"No idea. Is he on his own?"

"He's with Jed, trying to work the new coffee machine. The one I had to go out and buy because you got distracted."

She ignored Bradley's jibe. "Must be Quinn. At least he's turned up. Does he look sober?"

"I couldn't tell from looking at his ass. You're going to tell me he's straight, aren't you?"

"I believe he is."

Bradley tossed non-existent hair over his shoulder and flounced off, muttering, "The pretty ones always are."

A delicate sniff of my armpits reminded me I needed a shower. "Meet you in the kitchen? And tell me you know how to work the coffee machine?"

"But of course. I'll see you there in fifteen."

There was no sign of Jed or Quinn when I got to the kitchen a quarter of an hour later, but Emmy had made us both cappuccinos and even sprinkled chocolate on the top.

"Are we running late?" I asked.

"Barely. You want a croissant?"

Thoughts of Tabby and the progress, or lack of it, left my stomach churning.

"I'll grab something after the meeting."

Emmy threw a Danish on a plate for herself and headed for the door. "Dan was working late last night, and she started early this morning. Hopefully, we've made some progress."

"Hopefully." The word scratched at my throat.

"Should be an interesting meeting, anyway." She paused outside the door to Windsor. "Time to see if Samuel Quinn is everything he's cracked up to be."

My knees buckled as Emmy threw the door open, and coffee scalded my legs as the mug slipped from my hands. Black grabbed me under my armpits and hauled me up while Bradley rushed forwards with paper towels, but I barely noticed.

All my attention was on the ghost sitting at the table in front of me.

I knew he was a ghost, because his face was white. The look of shock on it mirrored my own.

"Sam?" I croaked.

"Zhen?" He rose to his feet, but he didn't move any further.

"Fuck," Emmy bit out.

Time stood still as we stared at each other. Sam looked more than a few years older, especially around his eyes, but he was still Sam. My Sam.

Emmy recovered first. "Right, let's move this to another room. Everybody out."

Those seated around the table headed for the door, Sam included.

Emmy pointed at him. "Not you, you bloody idiot. Sit."

He sat.

She put her arm around my shoulders and led me

over to a chair. "I'm so sorry. I had no idea."

"How could you have?"

I'd seen the coroner loading his body into the van myself. And yet here he was, still sinfully sexy, and worse, his shocked expression had turned into a sulky glower.

Emmy squeezed my arm. "I'll be right outside if you need me."

I wanted to follow her out of the door, but my feet wouldn't move. Then we were alone.

Sam broke the silence first. "What is this? You didn't hurt me enough before, and you just couldn't resist sticking the knife in one more time?"

"No! I mean, I didn't know you were going to be here. I thought you were dead. If I'd—"

"Dead? On the inside maybe, but you did that."

"But the explosion in your apartment..."

"You knew about that? I thought you'd left town. I went to your apartment the day after you dumped me like last week's trash, but it was stripped bare. You know why I went? I was going to beg for another chance. I was that fucking stupid."

"It was empty?"

Zacharov hadn't let me go back there after he made me leave with him, so I guess it made sense. And Sam had come back for me? My heart broke apart one more time.

"Don't act like you don't know what I'm talking about. At least spare me the insult of lying to my face."

"I'm not lying."

My mind started to clear a little and process things. The man standing before me was, according to Emmy, a CIA agent called Samuel Quinn, but when I'd been with him, he was a photocopier engineer called Sam Jessop. I narrowed my eyes.

"Hang on, I'm the liar? When were you planning to tell me you were with the CIA?"

Sam crossed his arms over his chest. "That was different. My work was classified, and you were a Russian citizen."

"You fucked me every night, Sam. You lay by my side and told me we had a future together, hell, we even talked about adopting another dog. And you couldn't even tell me your name!" I was yelling by that point, but I didn't care.

"I told you my first name."

"Your first name? Because we could have built a long and lasting relationship on me knowing your first name?"

"A lot of the other stuff was true too."

"Like what?"

"Like... Wait a minute. Jed got me here because Blackwood's putting a team together to take down Zacharov, and he said there was a Russian agent involved."

"Um... Yes?"

Shit.

"Guess what, Zhen. You're the only Russian in the room."

"Oh. That."

I made a show of studying the grain of the wood on the conference room table. It was walnut, I think. Really shiny.

"Yeah, that. I'm not the only one with some explaining to do."

"Fine, I wasn't entirely honest with you either.

Happy now?"

"Deliriously."

"Please, spare me the sarcasm. At least my feelings were real."

Sam took a few steps away then whirled back to face me. "And mine weren't? Anyway, you were the one who left me."

"Not by choice. Zacharov was there that night, in the next room, listening to our conversation. If I didn't break it off, he was going to kill you there and then."

"I'm a big boy; I could have looked after myself."

The first part I knew, but the second? "Zacharov's not a man to be underestimated."

"Neither am I."

"I didn't know that."

"Well, if you'd told me the situation, I could have explained."

I sank into a chair. Sam and Zacharov hadn't been the only people in the apartment that night. It would have been two against one, and if I'd known Sam knew how to handle himself in a fight, we could have ended this nightmare before it began. But I didn't. And all this time Sam had been alive, and I'd wasted three years doing Zacharov's bidding.

"I thought you were dead," I whispered again.

"And you didn't bother to check? With your background, you should have known how easy it is to bend the truth."

"I wasn't thinking straight, okay? My hormones were all over the place."

"Wrong time of the month, was it?"

How dare he? "No, I was fucking pregnant!"

Silence. You could have heard a cockroach fart.

"Pregnant?" he asked, as if he could have somehow misheard.

I nodded.

"Was it mine?"

"What the hell, Sam? You think I was cheating?"

He shrugged. "It doesn't seem like I knew you at all."

"Well, she's yours," I snapped.

How could he even suggest I'd been with another man? I'd spent every night since I met him in his bed.

"She? A little girl?"

A crack appeared in his mask of contempt.

"Yes."

"I have a little girl?"

"*We* have a little girl."

He sat down heavily, letting out a long breath. "What's her name?"

"Tabitha. Tabby."

"Tabitha? My grandmother's name?"

"I remembered you telling me once that if you ever had a girl, you wanted to name her after your grandmother."

He tore his hands through his hair, leaving it messier than before.

"This is... I don't even know what to say." He took a deep breath, let it out. "Where is she? Can I meet her?"

What did I say? How did I tell him that the daughter he'd only just found out about had been kidnapped by a man who'd threatened to execute her in less than three weeks if I didn't do the impossible?

He mistook my silence for something else. "Look, you don't even have to tell her I'm her father. At least for the moment. I just want to see her. Please?"

"Zacharov has her."

"You left her with that monster?"

"Of course I didn't! He took her for ransom, and we have two weeks and five days to get her back. Emmy's helping me. That's what this is all about."

Sam exhaled a string of curses. "You know what? I've spent the last three years wishing I could see you again. And now I have, I wish I could turn back the clock to the day before yesterday and just tell Jed and the president that they could fix their own damn Russian mess."

Tears burned behind my eyes. "If that's how you feel, we'll manage without you."

"What, you and Emmy? You realise she's clinically insane, right? Jed told me she blew an entire army base to kingdom come on her own last year."

"Good—at least she's had some practice. And she's being supportive, unlike some people."

"I didn't say I wouldn't help. If I've got a kid out there, I owe her that much. Just because we're finished doesn't mean I'm a heartless bastard who'd abandon a child in danger."

Even though our relationship had been over for three years, his words still put a knife through my chest. And that was crazy. I knew now that our entire affair had been based on half-truths and outright lies. Who had I really loved? Sam Jessop? Because he didn't exist. I suppose I should have been thankful, because at least I had closure. No more dreaming of dancing flames, of charred bodies and silent graves. No more pining for a ghost.

And even after all the pain we'd caused each other, he was still willing to help.

"*Spa-see-ba,*" I whispered, thanking him.

There was no answering "*pa-zhal-sta.*" No "you're welcome."

Instead, "I need a few minutes."

No sooner had the door slammed behind him than Emmy cracked it open. "Do you want company?"

How should I know? I'd never had anyone to lean on before. I shrugged, and she took that to mean "yes." Crouching down in front of me, she hugged me tight, almost pulling me off my chair, and for the second time in two days, I found myself crying over Sam.

"It's all such a mess. I should be glad he's alive, but there's a part of me that wishes he was still dead, because he's not the Sam I lost my damn heart to."

"Do you want me to shoot him?" she asked, sounding kind of doubtful.

I shook my head. It was nice of her to offer, though.

"It's just a lot to take in. We don't even know each other anymore. I had to tell him about Tabby, and the look on his face when I told him Zacharov had her... He was furious."

"Probably that wasn't aimed at you."

"I don't know—he's not my biggest fan right now."

"I gathered that when he stomped off with Jed. Want me to do the 'all-men-are-arseholes' speech?"

I cracked a smile. "You have a speech for that?"

"I've had plenty of practice with Mack over the years. She used to bring home a new one every month. Dan and I took it in turns to commiserate with her when it all went horribly wrong."

"I promise it won't happen again with me. I'm off men for the rest of my life."

A pink blur rushed through the door, and Bradley

materialised in front of me with a mug in one hand and a paper carrier bag in the other. "Don't say that!"

"It's true."

"We'll find you a better one." He bustled closer and held out the mug. "Hot tea, lots of sugar."

Emmy sighed. "Bradley, we're trying to have a meeting."

"No, you're not, not with Seven so upset." He began pulling things out of the bag. "Right, here we go. Box of chocolates. Copy of *This is How You Lose Her* by Junot Diaz. iPod with 'I Will Survive' cued up on the playlist. Missoni scarf, current season. Oh, and a voodoo doll."

"Bradley also used to help with Mack," Emmy explained. "Although she's been on a good streak lately."

He grabbed my hand. "Come on, we're taking a thirty-minute girl-break."

Emmy opened her mouth to protest, but he put his hand over it. "Shut it. Half an hour."

He pulled me up, chattering away. "We'll put a face mask on, and I can do your hair while it dries. Just be careful eating the candy, because you don't want to crack the clay. Come on, I'll make you feel like a new woman."

Did I have a choice? I looked to Emmy, who shrugged. "Just go with it. Sometimes it's nice to live in Bradley's world for a little while. It's fluffy and full of rainbows."

I let him lead me upstairs, where he had an honest-to-goodness hair salon set up. Swivel chairs, one of those sinks you tip your head back into, lit-up mirror, the works. Even a pile of magazines, just in case I wanted to see which Hollywood celebrity had anorexia and which was too fat.

"Leave her hair long, Bradley," Emmy said.

Something in her tone caught my attention. "You're plotting something."

"Maybe."

Bradley put his fingers in his ears. "I don't want to know."

CHAPTER 17

DIFFERENT CONFERENCE ROOM, same shit.

The meeting had already started by the time we got downstairs. Nate, Dan, Jed, Black, and Sam's heads all swivelled around as Emmy opened the door. When I took my seat next to her, I was careful not to catch Sam's eye as I tried to ignore the queasy feeling that came with eating half a kilo of chocolates in a small amount of time.

"Who's that?" Emmy asked, nodding at the video screen.

This room, Padua, was a little smaller than Windsor, but the setup was similar. The person Emmy had enquired about was a shaven-headed man in his forties, caught in a candid shot as he boarded a boat.

"Alberto Bate," Dan answered. "The cops in Florida have suspected his involvement in a people-smuggling operation for a while, but they've never been able to pin anything on him. Our contact says his personal yacht docked in a marina near Naples last Saturday and left during the night on Monday after Tabitha got abducted."

I felt Sam's eyes boring into me, but I kept my head down. I'd failed in my most important job, which was to protect my—our—daughter. Next to me, Emmy's face betrayed no emotion at all. I used to have that face, but

I'd left it behind in Russia. At the moment, I was an open book.

Sam's voice caught as he spoke. "Are there any leads from there? What can we do next?"

"Bate's got homes in Florida, Yucatan, Limon, Puerto Cabello, and Cartagena, plus a large rental portfolio. We're checking the lot, but it's taking time because he's a secretive bastard."

"Where is he now?" Black asked.

Dan grimaced. "We haven't worked that out yet."

"I know people in Venezuela," Sam said. "I'll get them to check out Puerto Cabello."

"The president's niece?" I asked.

It just popped out, and I cursed myself. Now I sounded like the bitter ex I was.

Sam raised his eyes to the ceiling. "You were the one who ended it."

"Enough," Black said. "Quinn, call your people, and we'll contact ours."

I poured myself another coffee, willing my hands to stop shaking, and the talk turned to Zacharov. More to the point, what we were going to do about him. Sam took the lead, detailing a list of Zacharov's crimes, some of which even I didn't know about. As well as the murder of the prostitute Emmy mentioned the other day, he was suspected of killing three more women in addition to facilitating any number of war crimes.

"Oleg Zacharov," Sam said. "Sixty-one years old, six feet tall, brown hair, brown eyes. Hobbies include collecting vintage revolvers, drinking fine wines, and abusing women. Over the past decade, he's amassed an eight-figure fortune, most of which is stashed in overseas tax havens, but that's not enough for him.

He's still hawking weapons and information on the black market, approved bidders only. The guy's dirtier than Jerry Sandusky's internet search history, he's amassed enough power to start a war, and he's got the mentality to do it."

"How the hell did he get into that position?" Jed asked.

"Until he was forty or so, he rose up the ranks and kept his nose clean. Then he dropped out of sight for a while, and when he reappeared, he'd changed. Two decades ago, he moved onto Base 13 and made it his own."

"And the Russian government just let him?" Nate asked.

"Like any government, they had problems that needed to be fixed. And Zacharov was good at fixing them. As long as he got results, they left him alone."

"Until now," Emmy said.

"Until now."

"The Azrael incident took things to a whole new level. There are a lot of world leaders saying 'that could have been us,' and James is furious. He's been working behind the scenes, and he had the Russians' approval for me to go in with the inspection team, but only President Markovich and a couple of his top aides knew what I was doing."

"So this operation we're planning, it has Russian backing?" Sam asked.

"They won't get in our way, but they'll deny everything if we get caught. Publicly, Markovich will back Zacharov, but privately he knows the general's out of control."

"It's more than they've ever offered before. But still,

the job won't be easy. Apart from his escapades with ladies of the night, Zacharov's never got his own hands dirty, but he's effectively got his own private army to do his bidding. And he's a brilliant strategist."

"You're wrong," I blurted.

The anger that flashed in Sam's eyes showed he didn't like being contradicted, especially by me.

"You probably spent more time with him than anyone else," Emmy said, flicking her head towards me. "Care to share?"

Where did I start?

"I first met Zacharov when I was twelve. I was selected...no, that's the wrong word. I came to the attention of certain powers within the Russian military, and from there I ended up participating in an experimental training program. They took ten of us, all children, and developed our skills in areas that could be useful to them."

"I take it we're not talking needlepoint and playing the violin here?" Nate asked.

"No, we're talking killing, in the most lethal and efficient way possible."

In my peripheral vision, I saw Sam blanch. Well, he was going to find out sooner or later, wasn't he? And I was done with lying to him.

"Zacharov ran the program, and they brought the best they had in to train us. Marksmen, explosives guys, experts in hand-to-hand combat. They wanted us to achieve the impossible."

"And I take it you did?"

"I'm still here, aren't I?"

Emmy smiled at that.

"Not only did Zacharov run things, he took me on

as his pet project. And he did get his hands dirty. Ever watch twenty grown men cower in fear when another walks into the room? Zacharov did that to them. He taught me most of what I know, and even today, with what I am, he scares me."

"My research doesn't tally with that," Sam argued.

"Your research told you I was a receptionist."

"And you thought I was a copier repairman," he bit back.

"Children, children," Nate cut in. "This is not kindergarten. I get that you two have some personal issues, but leave them outside. We've got a two-year-old child to find and a general to eliminate. Can we get back to the task at hand?"

Sam slumped down in his chair, refusing to look at me. Well, this was going swimmingly.

Nate nodded to me and I finished up. "As I was saying, Zacharov was a fearsome soldier. We shouldn't underestimate him."

"He's got complacent, though," Emmy said. "When I was there, security wasn't what it should have been. He's been at the top too long with nobody to keep him grounded. His arrogance makes him think he's untouchable, and we can use that in our favour. Quinn, do you still have a network out there?"

He threw down his pen. He'd been doodling, harsh pen strokes that had gone through several layers of paper. "Yes. It's not what it once was, but I'm not the only person with a strong dislike of Zacharov. I've got assets who will help."

"Great. Get what you can. Nate, have you had any luck with the computers?"

"Mack's working on it, but Zacharov seems to have

employed a half-competent IT person because hacking into the system is giving her a few challenges. We'll keep you updated."

Black turned the screen dark. "Right, let's wrap this up. Same time tomorrow."

Sam shot out of the door like he had a rocket stuck up his ass, followed by Jed. My legs, on the other hand, were still like Jell-O. I slid down in my seat until my chin was level with the edge of the table, arms folded.

"What the hell do I do?" I asked Emmy.

"About Quinn?"

"No, about my outfit for Zacharov's funeral. Of course about..." Quinn. I tried the name in my head, but it didn't sound right. Sam would always be Sam to me, even if I barely recognised the person he'd now become. "About Sam."

"I'm not so good with all this relationship stuff."

"But you're married."

"Yeah, and I managed to balls that up for the first twelve years. If I tried to give you advice, it'd be like the blind leading the blind."

"You must have some idea."

"My usual tactic is to run away from the problem. It doesn't tend to work long-term, though."

In the absence of any better ideas, running seemed like the best option. "I'll get my sneakers. You coming?"

"Might as well."

CHAPTER **18**

QUINN STORMED DOWN the corridor and into the nearest empty room, slamming the heavy wooden door behind him as hard as he could.

Or at least he tried to. A high-pitched "Fuck!" sounded behind him, and Jed hopped into the room.

"You just broke my foot, asshole."

"Well you shouldn't have put it in the doorway, should you?"

While Quinn stood by one of the tall picture windows with a view over the garden, Jed hobbled over to the padded leather piano stool sitting in front of the shiny black Steinway that dominated the room. But Quinn barely saw the manicured lawn or the woods beyond. No, all he could think of was a beautiful raven-haired woman with the most unusual eyes he'd ever seen. Was she wearing contacts today? Or was that vivid violet their real colour?

In the distance, a deer meandered out of the trees, shied away from danger, real or imagined, and ran back into the dappled shade. Quinn tore himself away and flopped down on a nearby couch.

"This is Black's domain," Jed said.

"What?"

"This room. The piano belongs to Emmy's husband, and he wouldn't have thanked you if you'd taken the door off its hinges."

Ah, yes, Emmy's husband. Possibly the only person reputed to be more psychotic than Emmy herself. Quinn was glad Jed had sacrificed his foot to the greater good.

"Maybe we should go somewhere else."

"Nah, we're good. Black went out."

They sat in silence for a few minutes, until Jed broke it by tinkling away tunelessly on the keys. A horrible noise filled the room.

"What's that supposed to be?" Quinn asked.

"'Bohemian Rhapsody.'"

"I think it's safe to say you're no Freddie Mercury."

"Are you insulting my skills on the ivories?" Jed asked, clutching his hands to his chest as he feigned hurt.

"I don't think *skills* is the right word. Does Black keep anything to drink in here?"

Jed swivelled round to face him. "You're not having anything to drink. It's only two o'clock."

"People have a glass of wine with lunch."

"You're not eating lunch. And unless I'm mistaken, you're not looking for wine, either."

"Give me a break, would you? It's not every day I find out I've got a kid."

"Drinking won't help with that."

Without a bottle to turn to, Quinn punched the cushion next to him, but it didn't help to relieve the tension humming away inside. Was it too much to ask for Jed to show a little understanding?

"No need to take it out on the couch. What's it ever done to you?"

Quinn glowered at him.

"Look, buddy, it's not that bad. So your ex turned up? She's just that—an ex. I've got hundreds of them, and I don't flip out every time I accidentally bump into one."

"Your girlfriends were all disposable. What if Chess dumped you then turned up three years later? Would you act like nothing happened?"

"That's different. I love Chess."

"And I loved Zhen. At least, I loved the person I thought she was. And now I find out she's a Russian agent."

"Not just any Russian agent."

"What do you mean?"

"Nobody told you?"

"Told me what?"

Jed started laughing, and Quinn wanted to punch him rather than the cushion.

"For fuck's sake, just tell me."

"She's Lilith. Zhen, Seven, whatever her name is— she's Lilith."

Quinn froze at the mention of the woman whose name was spoken in a whisper whenever any of his Russian contacts talked about her. He'd heard more hushed tales of her savage assassinations than he wanted to think about.

"You're kidding. Tell me you're kidding."

"Nope. When we first met, Emmy introduced her as Lilith."

"Fuck. No, she can't be. They must have been playing a joke."

"They'd just killed twelve men between them, and they seemed pretty serious."

"This is... But Zhen seemed so normal. I mean, I

was dating her for a couple of months. We spent every damn night together."

"I get it. You cared about her."

"That's all in the past now." Quinn closed his eyes and grimaced. "I have screwed up *so* badly."

Lilith? *Lilith?*

"Are you sure?"

"Of course I screwed up. I invited a trained killer into my apartment. I stood next to her while she chopped carrots with an eight-inch knife in her hands. It's a miracle I'm still breathing."

"I meant are you sure it's all in the past?"

"What? Yes! Definitely."

Jed smirked and a knowing grin spread over his face. "I bet you had a good time while it lasted, though. Seven's hot as hell. Are those tits real?"

Before his brain could catch up, Quinn launched himself across the room and shoved Jed off the piano stool onto the parquet floor. Jed tried to lever himself up, but Quinn straddled him and wrapped his hands around Jed's throat.

"I...knew...you...still...cared," Jed spluttered.

"Don't talk about her that way."

Jed waved his left hand in Quinn's face, and the sunlight streaming in the window caught his wedding ring. "I'm married, remember?"

Fuck! What the hell was Quinn doing? They used to mess around like this in Ranger school, play fighting after too many beers, but this was the first time he'd genuinely been tempted to choke the life out of Jed. How old was Quinn now? Thirty-two. Far too old for this shit, and old enough that he shouldn't have let a woman get to him like this. What was it he and Jed used to say about relationships? One night only, and if the woman could still stand by the end of it, they hadn't tried hard enough. They'd lived by that rule until he went to work in Russia. In Moscow, everything had changed.

He rocked back on his knees and eased the pressure on Jed's neck.

"I don't care about Zhen anymore," Quinn said, more to himself than Jed.

"Look, I get it, man. It's difficult finding out a woman isn't what you thought. The first three months I knew Emmy, I thought she was an accountant."

"How do you get past something like that?"

"The hot, uncomplicated sex helped."

"You're so damn shallow, buddy."

"Don't knock it till you've tried it. Maybe you should? If sex with Seven is anything like sex with Emmy, it'd be worth looking past her little foibles."

"We've gone way past complicated. And how can you describe a penchant for cold-blooded killing as a little foible?"

"Suit yourself. Can you take your hands off me now?"

Quinn let go just as the door clicked open and Emmy walked in.

"Ooh, kinky. Is this a private party or can anyone join in?"

Jed turned his head towards her. "Don't you ever knock?"

"I don't tend to in my own home, no. Come on, I'm dying for an explanation here. Have you finally decided to try batting for the other team?"

"No, Quinn was just trying to strangle me."

"Do you want me to shoot him?"

Quinn felt the colour drain out of his face.

"No, we're good."

Emmy shrugged as if to say "your loss."

"So, what's going on?"

"Quinn was sharing his concerns over Seven."

"What concerns?"

"Mostly about her job. Okay, completely about her job."

Quinn gave Jed a murderous look, and he'd have put his hands around his throat again if he wasn't secretly worried that Emmy might indeed make good on her offer to put a bullet through his head.

"What about it? That she kills people? Quinn, you've killed people."

"That's different."

"Why?"

Wasn't it obvious? Quinn had only ever taken a life when absolutely necessary, when he was backed into a corner and had no choice. And even then he felt so much guilt that the lure of the bottle was often impossible to resist. Lilith, on the other hand, could assassinate a man in the morning then sit down for lunch without any qualms whatsoever, if his sources were to be believed. Had she done that when they were dating? Cut a guy's throat then tucked into those homemade beef burgers of Quinn's she claimed to love so much?

"Because my victims have all been collateral damage."

"So if you went into a warehouse to rescue say, ten teenage girls brought to the US against their will, and six snakeheads died in the process as well as two of those girls, then that's okay because they're collateral damage? But if Seven takes out the head honcho of the smuggling gang with a single, clean shot and brings down the whole damn network, then that's not okay?"

"In that scenario, I can see your point."

"You think she enjoys what she does? You think she wakes up in the morning and says to herself, 'Today's gonna be great because I get to fire a lump of lead through a man's brain?' Got news for you, Mr. Squeaky Clean. She doesn't. Neither of us do. And for the last few years, Seven was forced to do every job she did, with the choice of sacrificing her targets' lives or your daughter's. You reckon that was an easy decision for her to make? Maybe, just maybe, you could step down from your high horse and stop judging people by your own fucked-up standards."

The door slammed behind Emmy, hard, as she swept out of the room.

Jed looked up at Quinn. "Well done, buddy. Now you've managed to piss both of them off."

"Effortless it was, too. Think Emmy's on the rag?"

"Keep your voice down, would you? There are ears everywhere in this place, and if Emmy hears you say that, she really will shoot you, probably through the balls. Especially if she is."

Quinn dropped his voice to a whisper. "Well? Do you think she is?"

"No, she's usually volatile like that, and she's been worse since the drama with Black last year."

"Think I preferred my sofa."

"Too late to back out now. You might want to watch what you say near Seven too, because she and Emmy are so damn similar it's spooky. I heard Black talking to

Nate about it this morning."

"Okay, okay. I'll keep my mouth shut. So, what now?" Quinn asked.

"Are you coming to Russia with us?"

"Damn right I am. If that bastard's got my kid, I'm not leaving it to someone else to sort the problem out." Quinn sighed and got to his feet. "You know, three years ago if somebody had asked me what I wanted more than anything, I'd have had two wishes: Settle down with Zhen, maybe have a kid or two, and wipe Zacharov off the face of the earth."

"Now that's happening, at least two out of the three parts."

"Yeah. And I don't know how to feel."

"Must have been a hell of a shock, seeing her like that."

"Figured I'd been drinking too much at first. But yeah, it was a shock. And the worst part is I might never meet my kid."

Quinn had accepted Tabitha's existence, and by rights, he should have been more upset about being an unexpected father. But as the eldest of four siblings, he'd always wanted a family of his own. Fuck. A family. Zhen told him she'd grown up on the outskirts of Moscow with her parents, an older brother, and a dog named Hobo, but how did that tie in with the training program she'd spoken of? More lies. More damn lies.

"Stop thinking like that," Jed said. "You've spent the past three years moping over her and all you've got out of it is a series of hangovers. Man up and help, whether she's Zhen or Seven."

"I'm doing this for Tabitha, not her mother."

And for the girl Zacharov killed seven years ago,

soon after Quinn first arrived in Russia. There had never been anything more than friendship between him and Galya, but given time, maybe there would have been. Until he'd met Zhen, Galya was the girl who'd haunted his thoughts. She'd been studying English at Moscow State University, and like most students, she'd needed to top up her income. With her elfin looks and long, dark hair, she'd done that by hiring herself out as an escort to rich men, and one day she'd had the misfortune to end up on Zacharov's arm.

Zacharov denied everything, of course, and the police declined to do so much as interview him. Even back then, he'd had power. But Quinn knew. Galya lived in the apartment opposite his, and he'd seen her leading Zacharov inside late one evening. The next morning, she was dead.

Sam should have tried harder to get her out of that life. Should have, but he'd been so busy with work, everything else had gone to the back of the line. Well, no more.

He'd do this job for Tabitha and for Galya.

"I don't care who you're doing it for as long as you don't screw up." Jed grinned. "It'll be like old times, back in the Rangers."

Quinn couldn't help his smile. Those *had* been good days.

"I need to get out on the shooting range."

Chapter 19

WELL, THIS WASN'T awkward at all. Sam sat one end of the breakfast table while I sat the other, and although we pretended not to notice each other, I could feel his eyes on me when I wasn't looking.

"What did that pineapple ever do to you?" Emmy asked, voice low.

I forced myself to stop stabbing it with my fork. "Is he staying here?"

"Sam?"

"Of course Sam."

"He's bunking in the room next to Jed. Chess and Lara have gone on a spa weekend, and he doesn't have any food in his fridge. Besides, if he goes home, he'll probably end up on the sauce again, and then we'll have to find someone else to come to Russia."

The pineapple died again, smashed into a golden mess. "He's not coming to Russia." I turned to face her. "Tell me you're kidding?"

"Sorry. He's paired up with Jed. They were in the Army Rangers together."

Just when I thought things couldn't get any worse.

"I'm trapped in a living nightmare and I want to wake up."

"I know it's not ideal, but he speaks Russian and he knows the country. We do need him."

Sod the pineapple. I pushed the bowl away and headed for the gym. Yesterday, I'd dreaded my session with Alex, but today I relished the chance to let out some of my frustrations. For the first time since I escaped, I wondered if I'd made the right decision to leave Russia. Back there, life had been predictable, not safe exactly, but I knew what was coming. Since I left, I'd been dealt one blow after another and they just kept coming.

I'd been able to cope around Emmy and Black, but the house was fast filling up, and this morning people kept staring at me as if I was a zoo exhibit. Their curious gazes felt like snakes coiling around my limbs, waiting for the right moment to strike. And on top of it all, there was Sam.

"Early today?" Alex looked across from the weight bench where he was bench pressing...how much? I took a step closer. Shit. Four hundred pounds. The man was a machine.

"*Da*. Can't you see how enthusiastic I am?"

"We will start with the weights."

With hindsight, I should have stayed in the kitchen and taken my anger out on a watermelon. An hour and a half later, sweat seeped from my pores, and when Alex stacked another ten kilos on the leg press, I rolled off the side of the machine and crawled to the mats. Then Emmy turned up, juggling a pair of knives.

"Ready for me?"

"Do I look ready?"

She prodded me with a foot. "No rest for the wicked."

"Give me a minute."

She threw one of the knives, and it whistled past my

ear and embedded itself in the mat. Then she kicked me in the shin.

"Get up, bitch."

"What the hell?"

I grabbed the knife and flipped to my feet, brandishing it in front of me.

This time she came at me with a roundhouse. I ducked out the way and countered with a push kick, followed up with a jab from my knife. She blocked me as I'd expected her to, but I got her in the side with my knee as Alex took two hasty steps back.

And then we fought. Anything went—arms, legs, the knives, a dumbbell bar I picked up, Alex's water bottle, an electric cable Emmy ripped out the back of an exercise bike. Spit flew, blood ran, and Emmy loosened one of my teeth with a vicious right hook.

"Enough!" Black shouted.

Emmy stopped mid swing, and Alex caught my left foot before it could connect with Emmy's kidney.

Black clapped slowly as he advanced, eyes glittering. "That's more like it. You've got skills, Lilith."

Emmy smiled despite the blood seeping from her nose. "I was starting to get worried about you there."

"I wasn't in any trouble."

"No, I meant before that. Yesterday you were just going through the motions. But this...we can work with this."

I couldn't believe the way I'd snapped. Zacharov coached me to stay in control at all times, and now I'd lost it big style and injured the person who helped me when nobody else would.

"Sorry. Uh, you've got a little blood..." I pointed at her shoulder blade. "It might need stitches."

She peered back, trying to look, then gave Black a beseeching smile. "Honey, could you fix this?"

"Don't I always? How about you?" He passed me a wad of paper towels, and I pressed them to my nose. "Do you need medical attention?"

"An ice pack would be nice." Or a glacier that I could lie down on until my entire body went numb.

Sam chose that moment to walk in with Jed, and his eyes widened.

"What the hell happened? Emmy, did you do that to her?"

"Lose the attitude, would you? It was a fair fight. Mostly."

He advanced, fists balled. "You can't just—"

I cut him off. "Sam, leave it."

Black put one arm around my waist and the other around Emmy's and steered us out of the gym. "We need to get you two cleaned up."

If looks could kill, Black would have been bleeding from every orifice. Sam's eyes seared into me as we left, and when I glanced back, his jaw was clenched so tightly I was surprised he had any teeth left.

So, that went well.

After a lunch of lasagne, because it was soft and my jaw still fucking hurt, we had another fun-filled afternoon on the shooting range. Today, we stuck with the pistols and shot sitting, standing, lying on our fronts, lying on our backs, halfway up a tree, crouched behind a wall, and even swinging from a damn rope. I added a skinned knuckle to my list of injuries, but I was hitting the target, and that was all that mattered.

Sam and Jed wandered up as we were packing away our equipment, and Jed nodded at the spotting scope Emmy had set up on a stand.

"You can leave that. We're gonna have a go. You guys okay after this morning?"

"Fine. Why?" Emmy said.

"I just thought after you... It didn't look that friendly."

"We're rehearsing for war, Jed. It's not supposed to be friendly."

"Sorry I asked."

She sighed and stood on tiptoes to kiss him on the cheek. "And I'm sorry I snapped. We're all stressed at the moment."

"Forget about it."

Sam ignored us both as he got out a Colt semi-automatic, and Emmy raised an eyebrow at Jed in a silent question. He shrugged.

"We'll see you later, then."

She gave me a nudge, and we headed back to the house, carrying the bag between us again. My aches from the day's activities were starting to catch up with me, and all I wanted to do was take a handful of painkillers, wash them down with something alcoholic, and go to bed.

"You'll have to talk to him sooner or later," Emmy said.

"I don't know what to say. How on earth does anyone stay friends with an ex?"

"Easy. Look at me and Jed."

"You dated Jed?"

"'Dated' is the wrong word. I fucked Jed. And Xav.

I'm friends with them and all the other guys I've been involved with over the years. I mean, I only slept with them because I liked them, and I still like them."

"You don't think that's weird?"

"I kill people for a living, and you think it's odd I speak to my exes?"

"Okay, I guess it's not so strange. For you, maybe. But I still don't know where to start with Sam."

"Start with sleep and think about it in the morning."

CHAPTER 20

QUINN LAY AWAKE in bed that night, watching the shadows on the ceiling and regretting leaving the bottle of Jack Daniels on the bar downstairs. Jed kept reminding him to concentrate on the job, that his history with Zhen didn't matter, but he was finding that more difficult with every hour that passed.

Zhen? Seven? Were either of them her real name? Sure, she was a different person now, but she still looked the same. That pretty face, those lips, the body that made his cock stand to attention, none of it had changed. Except for the eyes. She and Emmy had this weird twin thing going on, and he'd yet to work out why. There hadn't been a good time to ask.

He'd only caught the last few minutes of their fight, but they'd held nothing back, and some of the blows made him wince. And Zhen, the girl who'd doted on his scruffy dog and taken dinner around to her elderly neighbour when the heating was broken, had scared the living hell out of him. She'd attacked with a viciousness he hadn't seen outside the underground street fights he'd snuck into as a teenager, and even then, his traitorous dick twitched.

What the hell was wrong with him?

He hadn't worked it out by morning, when he woke with a hard-on the size of the Washington Monument, and a pounding headache.

"Fuck this," he muttered as he stumbled to the en-suite bathroom. Now the damn woman was back in his dreams as well.

He took care of the first problem in the shower, but the second only got worse when he got down to the kitchen and found Zhen fiddling with the coffee machine, wearing a black running outfit that did everything for his testosterone levels and nothing for his sanity.

"Coffee?" she asked.

"Thanks."

"You still take two sugars?"

She remembered? "Yeah."

It had been their ritual every morning. She'd made the coffee in a French press while he sorted out the food. On weekdays, it had usually been toast, but at weekends when they'd had more time, he'd made pancakes or *syrniki*, the little cottage cheese dumplings so popular in Russia.

"You want pancakes?" he asked.

If she was making the effort, he figured he should too. You know, in case she got tempted to shoot him otherwise.

She looked a little surprised. "Yes, please."

He tried not to think about her standing there as he rooted through the cupboards for ingredients. Thankfully Mrs. Fairfax, the housekeeper he'd met yesterday, had stepped out or she'd probably have berated him for messing with her kitchen. Flour, eggs, milk—he found them and whipped up a batter then poured neat circles onto the griddle.

"Here," he said a few minutes later, once he'd found

a bottle of maple syrup to go with the pancakes. "I figured you could use three if you're gonna go that hard in the gym again."

"Alex is making us run this morning. But three is good."

Sitting next to her would have been weird, so he slid onto a chair opposite, thankful the table was wide enough to put a safe distance between them. Silence settled. Quinn picked at his food and vowed to sleep late the next morning to avoid the awkwardness.

Finally, Zhen spoke. "So, a copier engineer, huh?"

He shrugged. "I had contracts with offices all over Moscow. It's amazing what people let slip when they're waiting for their shit to print."

"You bugged them?"

"And anything else I could get at with a screwdriver. Did you know your boss was screwing the accounts assistant?"

"Yes. The camera I planted in his office filmed them at it on his desk."

"He died after you left. A hit and run. Drunk driver, the cops figured."

"He was ripping off Zacharov. I pushed him under a car."

Zhen took another mouthful of pancake like she hadn't just confessed to murder over breakfast.

What did Quinn even say to that?

"Don't look at me that way. I didn't have a choice. Zacharov had found out about us, and he used you as leverage to make me do it." She poured more maple syrup on her plate. "Everyone said you were good at fixing the copiers."

"I didn't know much. I watched a bunch of YouTube

videos, and I just used to take the big parts out and replace them all until the damn things started working again. The CIA subsidised the spares, so I could keep my prices lower than everyone else."

She burst out laughing. "I like that."

"It worked like a charm for five years. I always thought I'd blown my cover somehow when they tried to kill me. Is that what happened?"

"No." Zhen stared at the table. "That was because of me. I found out I was pregnant, and I wanted you to run away with me. Leave Moscow. Only Zacharov found out and got to you before I did. What did happen that night?"

A hairline crack appeared in the ice around Quinn's heart. Zhen had wanted him back? Was that the truth or another lie?

"When I got home, some fucker jumped me in my bedroom. He'd already slit Vaska's throat and rigged the apartment to blow, so I let him take my place."

If Quinn didn't know better, he'd have said Zhen's eyes got a little wet at the mention of Vaska. But Zhen was Lilith. Any sorrow would be an act.

"I'm sorry, Sam. I..." She stared beyond him then dragged her gaze back to his face. "It doesn't matter. Thanks for breakfast."

As her pert ass hurried out of the door, Quinn pushed his plate away. After that conversation, he'd lost his appetite.

"What's happening this afternoon?" Quinn asked Jed after lunch.

With the girls out running, they'd shared the gym this morning with Black, Xavier, and Logan, another Blackwood employee who'd be joining them on their trip to Russia.

"Blackwood has another training facility closer to Richmond with a state-of-the-art kill-house. We're all going to have a run through it."

Nothing would have stopped Quinn going on this mission, but his stomach hollowed out at the thought of performing a drill under the watchful eyes of Black. The guy missed nothing, and he'd already raised questions about Quinn's fitness, hence the extended training session this morning.

"Can't wait."

Two hours later, their little group assembled inside what looked like a ramshackle warehouse behind Blackwood's head office. Of course, appearances were deceptive. Inside, a series of rooms had been set up with obstacles and targets, with the aim being to get from one end of the building to the other without dying.

They'd gathered in the monitoring room, set up with video feeds from every corner. Black and Nate sat in the centre seats, swivelling the cameras to face just where they wanted them.

He cut his eyes sideways to Seven, leaning against the wall with Emmy next to the only window. Seven looked relaxed, but then their eyes met and she stiffened, just for a second, before she turned away.

Black stood and motioned to the door in the far corner. "Who's first?" His lips quirked up at one corner, and he beckoned his wife. "You'll do."

She and Seven had dressed for business, Emmy in a

skintight combination of black and dark green with a pair of thigh holsters, and Seven in looser cargo pants with a pistol on her hip and an assault rifle slung over her chest. Seemed they'd picked out their weapons of choice.

"We'll go through in pairs. As always, the simulation will throw up a few tricks," Black said.

Quinn took another look at his gun, with the laser unit fitted to the barrel for the purposes of this exercise. Back in the Rangers, they'd used real ammo, and the place reeked of cordite, but this place felt sterile, more like a house than a battlefield. At least, the bedroom, the kitchen, and the dining room did. Then the place morphed into an office building, a shopping mall, a derelict shed, a desert village, a railway carriage, and finished in a forest.

And Emmy and Seven gave a masterclass in clearing them all.

It was the first time Quinn had seen Black smile.

"The pairing is young, but it has potential. Next."

Four more pairs went through the house, starting with Evan and Isaiah, two newcomers Quinn had seen at dinner last night. Then Xav with Logan and Alex with Malachi. Quinn hadn't been surprised to learn Alex was ex-Spetsnaz, Russian special forces, and would be coming with them. Carmen took her turn with Slater, a young Californian who seemed to share her gifted aim.

Then it was his turn. He and Jed were dressed identically in black turtlenecks and combat pants, and both carried the same model of Colt. They always had acted alike, and it had been a standing joke in the Rangers, where the assholes on the team had muttered about bromance and given them the nickname "Jinn."

"Just like old times," Jed said, tapping his gun.

Only with extra nerves and a stunning lack of practice. Oh, and a whole host of Blackwood's finest watching their every move.

"Fine. Let's get it over with."

The room was pitch black when they went through the door, but the cameras watching were infrared. Two seconds, three, and Quinn's vision adjusted enough to pump two rounds into the shadow in the far corner. Lights blazed, and Jed took out a man near the sofa. Fuck, those holograms were realistic.

The next room, the kitchen, presented them with a knife-throwing demon and a guy who dressed like a college student, slumped in the corner. A hostage? Woah, no! Not with a revolver like that one.

The dining room, the office, the mall, three hostages in a hut in the village, and...holy shit...a couple at it in the bathroom of the train carriage. Humour, Blackwood-style. Then into the woods. A full moon lit the path, and a figure appeared in front of him, female with black hair like... Dammit! He'd missed the gun in her hand, and she shot him in the chest.

"Get your head out of your ass!" Jed shouted, putting one through her head.

Quinn recovered enough to take out a man who popped out from behind a tree, then the lights came up and it was over.

And from the way Seven was watching the monitors when Quinn and Jed emerged back into the control room, she'd seen his little faux pas.

Black was already standing, strapping on his own

weapons alongside Nate.

"Not bad, apart from that fuck-up at the end," Black said. He took a step forward and lowered his head and his voice so only Quinn could hear him. "I suggest you sort out your feelings for Seven before we leave for Russia."

"What? I haven't—"

But Black was gone, into the kill-house where he and Nate annihilated the opposition without hesitation.

CHAPTER 21

"WHERE'S SAM?" I asked Jed when we got back to Black's house, or Riverley, as the sign on the gatepost said.

"He said he'd stay at his place tonight. Something about needing to justify his rent payments."

"Bullshit." The word slipped out before I could stop it.

Jed shrugged. "It's what he said."

I'd seen the way Sam looked at me when he came out of the forest room. Embarrassment. Because he'd missed? Because he'd hesitated to shoot a woman who reminded him of me? Both?

I also knew Black had put her there on purpose. The way he leaned forward an inch on his chair after Sam and Jed cleared the railway carriage gave it away. Asshole. I'd told him that in the car on the way back, but he'd just laughed. "Quinn needs to learn to focus on the job," Black told me. "It's not just his life at stake if he doesn't."

And now Sam had gone.

Shit.

Emmy nudged me. "He'll get over it. Let's have dinner."

Dinner, sure. Because I really felt like eating right now.

Sam was back the next morning, but I didn't see him until we got into Windsor. He'd made his own coffee, and from the smell of it, he'd resorted to instant.

"Bate's yacht docked in Mexico the day after Tabitha was taken," Dan told us, pointing at a map on the screen. "And from there it sailed to Guatemala then Colombia. We're trying to find out what he offloaded and where, but he picks out secluded places to dock, and the satellite feeds haven't given us the information we need."

My shoulders slumped. Six days since I'd seen my daughter, and who knew how she was being treated? Did she have fresh clothes? Were they feeding her properly? Keeping her safe from the freaks who preyed on young girls like her? A tear trickled down my cheek, and I shoved my chair back, horrified. Everyone's eyes followed me as I hurried out of the room, cursing myself for having cracked once again.

"You okay?" Emmy whispered as she held the door open for me. "No, stupid question, of course you're not. Look, let's take a few minutes, okay?"

"Yeah, whatever."

I half ran around the corner, straight into a young girl with brown hair who looked from me to Emmy, confused.

"Sorry," I muttered.

"Uh, I came to see Emmy, but I guess this isn't a good time?" She fished around in her pocket and passed me a tissue.

"Tia, this is Seven. Seven, this is Tia, Luke's sister."

Ah, yes, Mack's mysterious computer hacker friend, who I hadn't met yet. "Hi."

She gave me a little wave. "Hi. What happened?"

"Seven's daughter got kidnapped, and we're looking for her."

Tia squeezed both of my hands in hers. "Don't worry. Emmy'll find her. I got kidnapped once, and she found me, no problem."

"She did?"

Emmy shrugged. "It was a team effort. What are you doing here, anyway?" she asked Tia. "I thought you were busy spending Luke's money in Paris?"

"Nick said you were short of manpower, and he called Ryan over to help for a couple of days, so I came with him." Her phone rang, and she pressed it to her ear. "Bradley? Hang on, I'll come and find you." She walked backwards towards the elevator. "See you later."

I watched her go, envious of her freedom. When I was her age, my trips to Paris involved espionage, not shopping, and I'd never have been able to pull off that skirt with those boots either.

"She's a good kid. At least, she is now. When I first met her two years ago, she was an utter brat." Emmy said. "And since she's nearly nineteen, I guess she's not really a kid anymore either."

"How did you meet her?"

A faint grimace crossed Emmy's face. "I dated her brother for a while. A short while."

"Luke?"

"I'd temporarily lost my mind, okay?"

"What about Black?"

"That's a long story, and I'll tell you all the gory details over a bottle of wine someday. But suffice to say, my sanity's returned, what little of it I had in the first place, and Mack and Luke are suited perfectly."

Intriguing, but I'd wait. Zacharov had taught me the importance of patience. "And who's Ryan?"

"Her boyfriend. At least, he is this month. They've had their ups and downs over the past year. Him being here could be useful if we need an extra person on this job."

"He works for Blackwood?"

"Yeah, in the London office mainly. His background's similar to mine in a lot of ways—he came up from the streets, and I mentored him as part of a programme run by our charitable foundation."

A charitable foundation? There were still so many things I had to learn about Emmy, but despite her occupation, it didn't surprise me to hear that she put effort into helping others.

"And Ryan is skilled?" I asked.

"I've used him on a few special projects recently. The man's got balls, but he can be headstrong on occasion."

"Like us, you mean?"

"Something like that. Come on, let's grab a coffee then go back to the meeting. Just ignore Quinn. This'll all be over soon."

Why did I get the feeling things wouldn't be quite so straightforward?

CHAPTER 22

"STOP DWELLING ON it," Jed said to Quinn as they walked into the kitchen.

But a day and a half had passed, and he still couldn't get the incident at the kill-house out of his head. A screw-up like that when the job went live could cost more than a red face. And what Black had said to him afterwards, about still having feelings for Zhen... He didn't. He couldn't. No, he needed a nice, down-to-earth girl like Chess or Lara, not a badass bitch capable of clearing a room faster than him or most of the other men they worked with.

Even if she had looked damn hot while she did it.

"Easy for you to say, buddy. You don't have to see Chess's face at work every day."

"If I did, I'd never get anything done, and for what it's worth, I'd have hesitated too."

And then the lady herself walked in, her eyes running down Quinn's sweat-covered body. Those eyes.

"Are they real?" Quinn asked before he could stop himself.

"Are what real?"

He pointed at his eyes, and she closed hers.

"Yes," she whispered.

His feet carried him over to her, and when she looked at him again, he was just inches away. "I can't believe I didn't notice before."

"I'm good at hiding things, Sam."

Quinn felt that charge in the air, the same electric sense of anticipation as when they'd first met. The urge to reach out and touch her made his fingers twitch, so he shoved his hands in his pockets instead.

"Are you still hiding, Zhen?"

Her expression didn't change, but when her lips parted slightly and her tongue slipped out to moisten them, Quinn knew she wasn't entirely unaffected by his presence.

"It's not your business anymore."

She stepped sideways, and whatever she'd come into the kitchen for, she left without it.

"What was all that about?" Jed asked.

"Truthfully? I don't know."

"Look, it's obvious you still like her."

"I..." Oh, what was the point? "She's sexy as fuck."

"Smart too."

"And that."

Seven intrigued him; that was it. Curiosity.

"It's okay to have those feelings."

"What are you now? An agony aunt? Gonna start a 'Dear Jed' column?"

"Maybe I should. Dear Jed, I had a love affair with a beautiful lady, and even though it turned out she kills people, I can't stop looking at her ass."

"I wasn't..."

"I watched your eyes track it all the way to the door. And I can't blame you for that. I mean, it's clear she doesn't skimp on the squats."

Quinn balled his fists up and resisted the urge to wrap them around Jed's throat again. "Don't. Just don't. I... I respect her, I guess. She's good at what she does, and I'm glad she's coming with us to Russia because if anybody can get at Zacharov, it's her. But I just can't reconcile her with the woman I knew."

"Does it matter who she once was? I'd say all that matters is who she is now and whether you like *that* girl. And if you do, you should tell her and stop dancing around each other."

Quinn sighed. "She already tore my heart out once. I'm not about to go back and let her do it again."

Jed tried to say something else, but Quinn held up a hand. "Do me a favour and drop it, would you? Are you up for going through the kill-house again this afternoon?"

Quinn needed to get a clean run in, more for himself than anybody else. And he needed to put Zhen and everything they'd once had firmly out of his mind.

"Hi, Jed." A female voice came from the doorway, and Quinn turned to see a young woman walk in with a brown-haired guy who had the hard look of a soldier about him.

Jed stepped in with the introductions. "Quinn, meet Ryan and Tia. Ryan works for Blackwood in London, and Tia's the sister of one of Emmy's tech gurus. Guys, this asshole is Quinn."

"Are you both here for work?" Quinn asked.

"I am," Ryan said, wrapping his arm back around Tia's shoulders once he'd shaken Quinn's hand. "Tia's here to shop."

She grinned. "My specialty. I help Bradley with decorating and stuff. We're gonna re-do the pool area with more flowers and an ice cream kiosk. Ryan, can you help us move the sun loungers this afternoon?"

"Uh, did I hear you two mention the kill-house? Any chance I could come with you? There's no such thing as too much target practice."

Tia pouted. "He'll do anything to get out of helping."

And Quinn couldn't blame him. Who wanted to spend the afternoon moving furniture? "Sure, join us. Why not?"

Chapter 23

EMMY STARED AT me over the table, looking as shattered as I felt. The black eye I'd given her four days ago was fading, but dark circles caused by lack of sleep had taken its place. We'd begun training at five—a run followed by sparring with Alex—and if I'd repeatedly punched a wall for the last hour I'd have been in better shape. But at the end, he'd promised to lighten up for a few days and stick with cardio and weights to let us both heal before we went to Russia.

And now we'd spent twelve hours straight in Windsor while the search for Tabby went on. I felt impotent as I listened to the buzz around me. Most of the conversation was in Spanish, too fast for me to follow as I'd barely had to speak the language for years.

Mrs. Fairfax brought in platters of food, but I didn't even bother taking a plate. I couldn't eat. We were at eight days now. Eight days since Tabby was taken. What if she was in a shallow grave out in the Mexican desert? Or submerged in a river with her hands and feet bound? Or—?

"I know what you're thinking," Emmy warned. "Stop it."

"I can't help it." Not the thoughts or the involuntary sniffle that escaped.

"Yes, you can. You, we, have to believe she's alive."

"But—"

"No buts." She tapped me on the head. "Fill that with something else."

Like what? As I tried to push Tabby out of my mind, memories of her father filtered in around the edges. Sam as he used to be, smiling when he came home from work. His face relaxed as he slept late on the weekends. Wearing his ridiculous comedy apron while he made dinner. One of his alleged colleagues had bought it, a half-naked man with an obvious bulge in his underwear and an arrow pointing at it with the words "Kiss This" above. Back then, I'd been only too happy to oblige. And now? We could barely manage a civil conversation.

"Not him either," Emmy said.

I threw down my pen in frustration. "How do you always know what I'm thinking?"

She shrugged. "I just do. I'm right, aren't I?"

"Dammit, I should be planning entry points, and equipment, and tactics, but it's not happening."

"It's almost midnight. Call it a day, and we can start early tomorrow."

I got up but then noticed Emmy hadn't moved. "Aren't you coming?"

"I'll just make a couple more calls," she said, but she made no move to pick up the phone.

"What's up?"

"It's nothing."

I dropped back into my seat. "Try me."

She sighed. "Black's been off lately. Like, cagey about something. We've always been able to talk about anything, but I can't shake the feeling he's keeping a secret from me."

"Have you tried asking him?"

"Not outright. I hinted, but he just skirted around the question."

"Then try asking straight. It probably is nothing, like you said."

"Okay, okay. I will."

I got to my feet again and held out a hand. "Come on, we should both get some sleep."

At the top of the stairs, I went to turn right while Emmy headed left. She slept in the west wing, far away from everybody else because of her nightmares. But before I'd made it two steps, she pulled me back into a hug.

"Thank you."

"What for?"

"For caring. This life can be lonely as hell. Sure, the house is always full of people, but sometimes I still feel alone."

"It's me who should be thanking you. If you hadn't got me out of jail, what would I be doing now?"

"Probably stalking James with a sniper rifle."

"Or dead."

"I wish we'd met sooner."

"Me too."

She gave me a tired smile. "Night, Ana."

"*Spokoynoy nochi*, Emmy."

I walked towards my room, but my mind was still churning, and I carried on along the corridor. Iron candelabras lit up the artwork on the wall, mainly glowering old men who looked as old as the house itself. An open door to my left heralded the library, a huge room full of the kind of dusty old tomes that were collected rather than actually read.

A samurai sword hung on the wall next to the door, and I reached out to touch the blade. Razor sharp. Damn thing was probably genuine. After checking the doorway, I lifted it down and swung it in a figure of eight, hearing the satisfying swish of air. How many men had lost their lives at the hands of this weapon?

The stories it could tell made me shiver, so I put it back and moved further into the room. A few couches, a desk with an old-fashioned lamp, an antique globe. I spun the globe, but it barely moved, and the clink of glass came from inside it. Ah, a secret stash.

I opened the lid and picked out a crystal tumbler from its hiding place then looked at the bottles one by one. Scotch. Gin. Vodka. Rum. No ice, but I wanted the alcohol for its numbing properties rather than its taste, so I didn't care. A generous splash of Stolichnaya would help me sleep.

Clutching my glass, I wandered over to one of the floor-to-ceiling windows that overlooked the garden. Each had a balcony outside, but it was too cold to stand out there tonight, and from the way the trees swayed, windy too.

An owl flitted across in front of me, its wings silhouetted against a backlit sky. Eyelids growing heavy, I sank onto the leather couch behind me, a high-backed monstrosity built for style rather than comfort. Although the style part was debatable too.

Clouds drifted away, revealing a three-quarter moon and its dappled surface. When I was a kid, the governess had us read a book about space, and for six months I'd wanted to be an astronaut. Then I'd changed my ambitions to qualifying for the Olympic gymnastics team, even though I could hardly do a cartwheel.

What would have happened if I'd let Pyotr rape me that night? If I'd taken the pain and kept my mouth shut?

When I left the orphanage at sixteen like all the other girls, would I have been a gymnast or an astronaut? A dancer like my mama? Or an office receptionist with manicured nails and a shitty boss like I'd pretended to be for Sam?

Maybe if I'd picked that last option, I'd still have the only man I'd ever loved.

My back stiffened as soft footsteps approached, and I slid down the seat a little so my head wasn't visible. The sound of a drink being poured told me I wasn't the only one who'd found the globe's hidden treasures.

Sam walked past me and stood at the window as I had just a few short minutes ago. The glint of amber liquid told me he'd gone for the Scotch, and he'd been considerably more generous with his measure than I had.

He must have stood there for five minutes, unmoving other than raising the glass to his lips, and I held my breath the whole time. When Zacharov taught me to swim in a near-freezing pool, he'd pushed my head under the water, his grip relentless, and I quickly learned to control my breathing and slow my heart rate until I could stay underwater for six minutes without any trouble. It was amazing how quickly my skills developed after I'd almost drowned twice.

But eventually the inevitable happened, and Sam

turned around. The glass began to slide from his grasp, but he regained his composure before it slipped from his fingers completely. Good to see he could hold his liquor.

"What are you doing here?" he asked.

I held up my glass. "Same as you."

"That wasn't what I meant."

"I know."

"Fine, be that way, *Seven*." The way he stressed my name was another reminder of my past lies.

"Just keep twisting the knife why don't you, *Quinn*?"

He knocked back the rest of his drink and headed back to the globe. "Want another?"

"I stick to one when I'm working."

"Don't judge me."

"I wasn't. I didn't mean it that..." Oh, what did it matter? He'd interpret my words in whatever way he chose.

We lapsed into silence again, and his white knuckles spoke of stress he was trying to hide. Was he thinking of Tabby too?

Sam's sigh lay heavy in the air, and he set the glass with the remains of his whisky on the low table next to the couch and walked towards the door. I thought he'd leave, but then he came back to face me.

"I'm sorry. I shouldn't have snapped."

He'd apologised? "Don't worry about it. We're both under a lot of pressure."

"It's still no excuse."

"I said it's fine."

He sat down next to me, perched on the edge of the seat as if he'd run at any second. "How is it fine, Zhen?

Our daughter's missing, and we're about to risk our lives going into Russia. I'd say things are as far from 'fine' as they could possibly get."

"Emmy said I should stay positive."

His hollow laugh echoed around the stacks of books. "Emmy's a whack job, you know that, right?"

"*She's* also my friend."

He reached over for his glass. Clearly, I'd driven him to drink again. A full minute passed before he looked back at me.

"What happened? We used to be so good together, and now..."

"You think I haven't thought about that?"

"Secrets and lies do more damage than bullets."

Wise words from Sam.

"My whole life is a lie, and it hurts," I whispered. "Fuck, it hurts."

"Ain't that the truth."

"On second thoughts, maybe I will have that drink."

I got up and fetched both bottles, my vodka and Sam's Scotch, and brought them back to the couch. He took them and poured. I knocked back a mouthful and relished the burn in my throat.

"I've got a new rule. I'm only going to lie if I'm absolutely sure the truth won't come out."

Sam rubbed his eyes with one hand. "And I'm not going to lie to the people I love."

Shit. Yeah, just keep twisting that damned knife. I forced a neutral expression as I lifted my glass. "Here's to rules."

He drank, I drank, then I drank more, and both of the moons floating outside on the horizon were beautiful.

"What was Tabitha like?" he asked, his voice a whisper.

"Don't do that."

"What? Remind you of happier times?"

"No, don't speak about Tabby in the past tense."

A tear rolled down my cheek.

"Shit, I'm sorry. I just didn't think..."

That single tear was followed by a whole flood of them, and Sam tried to pass me a handkerchief, but I shoved him back.

"Leave me alone. I've got a fucking reputation to uphold."

But he didn't let me get away with it. Three years had passed since I was last wrapped up in his arms, and damned if it didn't feel like coming home.

"Who's the real Seven?" he murmured. "The girl I knew or the bitch the world sees?"

I stayed silent as he answered his own question.

"I don't think either of them are. You've still got too many secrets."

The splash on my cheeks as Sam cried too made me clutch at his shirt and press closer until he pulled me onto his lap, and I burrowed into his chest. His heart beat against my breasts, not quite as fast as mine was racing, but Sam wasn't as calm as he appeared on the outside. And now, he pressed a kiss to my hair and made my pulse go ballistic.

"It'll be okay, Zhen. We'll fix this."

"Don't lie, Sam."

His lips brushed my temple, and another bolt of fire shot through me.

"Like I said, I'm done with that."

Chapter 24

QUINN PINCHED HIS eyes closed and rubbed his temples, willing the pounding in his head to stop. How much had he drunk last night? A beer in the kitchen with Jed. Okay, two. Then all that Scotch with...fuck, with Zhen.

Somehow, he'd still been able to walk well enough to carry her to bed, and only a burning need to use the bathroom had kept him from climbing in beside her. Thank heavens he hadn't—she'd probably have stapled his nuts to the mattress if she found him there when she woke up.

Painkillers. He needed painkillers. His muscles protested as he rolled to the side to root through the nightstand drawer. Condoms, a paperback, a few rounds of ammunition, a Taser. No Advil. He checked he was wearing a pair of boxers then stumbled next door to find Jed. At least now he'd married Chess the chances of finding him in bed with a naked woman or two had decreased markedly.

Quinn didn't bother to knock. The fact that Jed was standing stark bollock naked next to the closet didn't bother him as much as the cheerful smile on his face.

"What's so good about today?"

"Chess is coming over for lunch. You look like shit."

"I know. You got any Advil?"

Jed reached into the bathroom and tossed a packet over. Quinn didn't bother with water, just swallowed a couple dry.

"What happened?" Jed asked, then answered without waiting for Quinn to speak. "Zhen? Am I right?"

"We talked. Sort of. Well, mostly we drank."

"And?"

"And nothing." He wasn't going to tell Jed about all the tears. "Zhen hit the vodka, and Black's got good taste in Scotch, I'll give the man that."

Expensive too, Quinn bet. He'd drunk at least three figures' worth last night.

"You know we have to work today, right?" Jed asked.

Quinn leaned back against the wall and groaned. "Yeah, I know. But with all the shit that's happened, I needed something to take the edge off, okay?"

"Black's gonna give you hell if you turn up with a hangover."

"Which is why I needed the Advil."

By the time he'd had a shower and the pills had kicked in, Quinn felt vaguely human. And with him and Zhen on speaking terms again, perhaps today wouldn't be so bad?

That thought lasted until Quinn got to the kitchen. Emmy jabbed him in the chest the second he walked in the door.

"What did you to do to her?"

"What? Who?"

She pointed at Zhen, slumped over the table with a cup of coffee next to her. Toby was fussing around, shoving bananas and coconuts into a blender with a mutinous look on his face. Bradley came in with a pair of dark sunglasses and slid them onto Zhen's face.

"Anything else you need?" he asked Toby.

"Tomato juice. Raw eggs. Asparagus."

Zhen raised her head a couple of inches. "I'm not eating raw eggs."

Emmy crouched by her side. "Honey, we have to do something before Black and Nate see you like this."

Oh, hell. Zhen didn't look good. Over the last three years, Quinn had built up a tolerance to the effects of alcohol, but it seemed his ex hadn't shared his fondness for its numbing effects.

"The Russian cure is to sweat it out in the sauna," he offered.

"Does that work?"

"I used to swear by it."

Emmy clicked her fingers at Jed and Quinn. "Right, you two, get her into the sauna. Toby, bring all that shit with you."

Emmy and Black had a swimming pool complex in an annexe at the back of the house, beyond the gym. A lap pool, Jacuzzi, steam room, and sauna. The dark tiles lining the pool made the water look foreboding, a black hole that could swallow you up if you waded into its rippling depths. Maybe that was where Black hid the bodies.

With its grey stone columns, the steam room looked more like a Greek temple, and Quinn waved Jed away as he settled Zhen onto a tiled seat.

"How are you feeling?"

"Like I'm going to puke."

"Don't you drink often?"

"One drink. Never more than one drink each evening."

Emmy's phone rang with the opening bars of Pearl Jam's "Black," and they all looked at each other.

"I'll distract him," Emmy said. "You get her sobered up. And Quinn? If you pull this shit again, I'll personally cut your balls off with a blunt knife. Got it?"

Quinn nodded.

Emmy answered the phone and plastered on a smile. "Hey... Yeah, everything's fine. No, not the gym. I'll meet you in the bedroom... I've missed you... Okay, five minutes."

She dropped the phone back into her pocket and headed for the door. "You've got two hours. Fix this."

Quinn knelt to pull Zhen's tennis shoes off, then her socks. Her clothes were getting damp too, but he didn't want to strip her down to her underwear, not with Jed there and Bradley and Toby around.

"Have you taken any painkillers?" he asked.

"Paracetamol and ibuprofen."

"Just lay back and close your eyes. They'll start to kick in soon."

"I'm never drinking again."

"Probably not a bad idea."

Bradley bounced in wearing a pair of flip flops with his skinny jeans. "Right, I've got cucumber slices for her eyes, and there's a towel outside. And one of you two needs to help Nate. He wants a volunteer to test out a new body camera, and I couldn't think up an excuse."

Jed pushed away from the wall. "I'll go."

Bradley put his hands on his hips and faced Quinn. "I'm not sure I trust you to look after her, seeing as you caused this problem in the first place, but I've got the upholsterer arriving in twenty minutes. Mess this up and I'll dye your eyebrows pink in your sleep."

He flounced off, and Quinn took a seat on the bench beside Zhen and helped her to lie back so her head rested on his thigh.

"I'm sorry. I'm so sorry, beautiful."

"You didn't force the vodka into me."

"I should have stopped you."

She managed a half smile. "I'm Lilith. You think you could stop me from doing anything?"

Quinn brushed Zhen's bangs out of her eyes and trailed a fingertip down her cheek. "I doubt it. Even before, you were stubborn. Remember Klara?"

The old lady had lived three doors along from Quinn in Moscow, and her heating was always breaking. One particular cold spell, the super hadn't been too keen on fixing it, and Zhen had hammered on his door every morning at six to remind him until he gave in and got his toolbox out.

"I wonder what happened to her?"

"And all her cats."

Zhen stared into the swirling steam for a few minutes, thinking. Quinn just watched her.

"You cared, Zhen. That's how I know you're not the person everyone thinks you are. You didn't have to do that shit to help Klara or any of the others, but you still did it."

"People only remember the bad things."

"The Zhen I knew didn't do bad things." He caught her eyes and smirked. "At least outside of the bedroom."

"Sam, I can't talk about that."

He didn't want to think about it either, not with her head resting in his lap, or she'd soon know how she still affected him.

"Fine, then I'll talk about me." He held out a hand. "Samuel Quinn."

Zhen's smile trembled, and she hesitated before she placed her hand in his. "Anastasia Petrova."

"Anastasia? That's your real name?"

"Yes. Ana."

Quinn brought her hand to his lips. "Then I'm very pleased to meet you, Ana."

"Are you really from Boston?"

"Minneapolis. It's fucking cold there. Felt right at home in Moscow."

"And you're thirty-two?"

He nodded. "You too?"

"Nearly. Thirty-one."

The door to the sauna opened, and Toby placed a tray on the bench next to them and pointed to each pair of glasses in turn. "Tomato, ginger, and asparagus juice. Pineapple, banana, and coconut smoothie. Green tea. Water. Drink them all, both of you, and don't you dare pull a stunt like this again. I'm good, but I'm not a miracle worker, and your livers are screaming right now."

He stomped off without another word.

Zhen wriggled upright and wrinkled her nose at a lumpy red concoction. "This looks disgusting and smells worse."

"I'll drink it if you do."

"Fine." She grimaced then knocked the lot back.

Shit. Quinn eyed it up dubiously. "Does it taste as bad as you thought?"

"Worse."

"Brilliant." He held his nose and swallowed, and she was absolutely right. "What's wrong with a fry up and plenty of coffee?"

"Ask Toby."

"I'm tempted to go back to my apartment."

"Is it nearby?"

"In Richmond, a couple of floors below Jed."

"So, what else don't I know about you?"

"My mother really was Russian. She worked as a teacher, and my dad's retired now, but he was a detective."

"You didn't want to follow in his footsteps?"

"I thought about it, but mostly I remember him getting frustrated because of all the rules and paperwork." He shrugged. "The army was rigid, but when I joined the Rangers, we got a bit more freedom. Then Jed and I got poached by the CIA, and they didn't give a shit what we did as long as we got results."

"Until Venezuela?"

"Can we not talk about that? Kind of awkward."

Zhen grinned, and Quinn traced her lips with his thumb, resisting the temptation to dip his head and kiss them. Even now, knowing who she really was, a dangerous attraction to her simmered in his veins. Not only that, he felt the strange urge to protect a woman who a month ago, he'd have said needed his help like Bill Gates needed computer lessons. But now? He'd seen a few of the layers she kept hidden from view, and he wasn't sure she was quite as tough as her reputation suggested. Good at her job, yes, but as well as the incident in the library, every so often her guard dropped, and he glimpsed the vulnerability in her eyes.

"Why do they call you Quinn?" she asked. "Why not Sam?"

"There were three Sams in my class at school. One got called Sam, another was Samuel, and I ended up as Quinn. Mostly because I kept getting into trouble, and it was easy for the teachers to shout."

That got him a smile. "Are you an only child?"

"I've got two brothers and a sister, all younger. Scott, Sean, and Shannon. Can you spot the theme? Shannon drove us crazy, but she finally met a man we didn't want to kill and married him two years ago."

"I'm glad you've got a family."

"So have you. We'll get Tabitha back, and then you'll have your family."

What was he even saying? Sitting here with Zhen—Ana—brought his old feelings back, but every molecule of sense told him getting involved with her again would be a bad idea. A terrible idea. Being friends with her was a good plan, for Tabitha's sake, of course, but more?

No. He needed to keep his emotions under control and his dick in his pants. Look how much trouble it had caused already.

CHAPTER 25

"FEELING BETTER?" EMMY asked me the next morning. "You didn't get into another drinking contest with Quinn? Because from what I've heard, that's one competition you're never gonna win."

"My nightcap was a glass of orange juice."

"Seems as if you're getting on better, though. You're not looking at him like each step could be his last anymore."

"I think we're past that. Yesterday was...nice. Apart from the headache. And the part where I ran out of the sauna to throw up when Toby tried to make me drink that thing that smelled like haddock."

"What did Quinn do?"

"Made me coffee and told Toby to get lost."

"See? He still likes you."

"Maybe."

I turned away so she wouldn't see my smile. Because although I was pretty sure I still liked him too, I couldn't do anything about it. Not with my whole world up in the air. And even if we found Tabby and survived the visit to Russia, we were two nomads, whether he had an apartment in Richmond or not. He barely seemed to stay there. Who knew where we'd end up after Siberia? Sam hadn't mentioned his plans for the future, and I didn't dare to think about mine.

So I changed the subject instead. "What are we doing today? I want to go through the kill-house again."

"It'll have to be this afternoon. We've all got medicals this morning. Hurrah."

"That's standard?"

"Every three months, but mine's been brought forward a week. We like to know if there's anything festering that could cause us problems, keep up with vaccinations, that sort of thing."

"Okay. I haven't had a check-up in years, at least that I know of." I shuddered thinking about what they might have done to me while I was drugged. "Probably because I'd have killed the doctor if they gave me a needle."

"Dr. Stanton's sweet. Please don't maim her."

Emmy was right. Instead of being a crusty old lech like Zacharov's personal physician, Dr. Stanton was a petite Canadian in her early thirties, although she tsk-tsk-tsked when I told her my medical history, or rather, the lack of it.

"You didn't have any vaccines at all?"

"I remember having some as a teenager, but I don't know what they were."

"We'd better start again with everything. Are you travelling to Russia with Emmy?"

"Yes."

"In that case, we'll leave some of the more exotic vaccines until you get back. Best not to overload your immune system. Are you trying for a baby?"

"What? No!"

"Then you'll want the contraceptive shot as well?"

"I guess."

She stuck me with everything, and after a lunch of Toby's wild rice and halloumi cheese salad, Chess rolled up my sleeve at the kitchen table and injected me with the vaccine she'd developed herself, Apollo.

"That should protect you against Likho," she said, using a cotton ball to wipe away the spot of blood that bubbled from my arm.

"I'm not planning to get that close."

"Just a precaution," Emmy said.

"Great."

That said a lot about how she expected our trip to Base 13 to go.

I took my usual seat beside Emmy in Windsor after we'd eaten, but with Xav on his way to Guatemala to speak to a contact who hated phones, Sam took the seat on the other side of me.

"You okay?" he asked.

"I feel like a pincushion."

"Same. Did you get Apollo?"

A shudder ran through me. "Yes."

He squeezed my hand under the table. "It'll be okay."

Would it? Once I heard what Black and Nate had to say, I wasn't so sure. Mack was in the room too, and as she pressed a few keys on her laptop, the foreboding model of Base 13 rose once more from the centre of the table.

"We knew getting to the base would be difficult," Black started. "But intelligence suggests Zacharov has significant countermeasures in place. The radar tower is fully operational, the perimeter is patrolled at regular intervals, and he operates checkpoints on the only road in and out. A source close to President Markovich estimates he's got three hundred men there."

"And we've got fourteen," Sam muttered.

"Good odds," Emmy said.

I spoke up. "Yes, he has many men, and his core team is loyal. But two-thirds are conscripts, and he doesn't treat them well. They are more...disposable. If we can divide his forces, they will run rather than fight."

"You know that?" Black asked.

"Nothing is ever certain, but I heard them talking. Most of them don't like him either. They call Base 13 the Graveyard."

"Even if that's the case, we still need to reach the base first. Driving isn't possible. It's four hours from the nearest town, and electronic monitoring shows the guards at the checkpoints radio in every half hour. If we took them out as we went, the lack of contact would alert the next post, and they'd be waiting."

"So, we have to go in by air," Nate said.

"What about the radar?" Jed asked. "That'll detect an airplane a hundred miles out. We might as well paint targets on our asses."

"Well, we need to knock the radar out first."

"And how do we plan to do that?"

Black didn't say anything, just looked across at Emmy and me.

"Oh, crap," she said.

CHAPTER 26

I OVERSLEPT THE next morning, having managed to fit in an extra nightmare where I was being skinned alive while Tabby and Sam watched on without moving, and by the time I got into the kitchen Sam and Jed were talking with Xav and Logan, already dressed in combat gear.

"How was Guatemala?" I asked Xav.

"A bust. Sorry. But don't give up hope. If anyone can find her, it's Dan and Black."

He headed out, leaving me two feet away from Sam with no choice but to speak to him.

"Hi."

He motioned back to the table. "I made you toast, but it's cold now."

What did toast mean? "Thanks."

We stood there awkwardly until he moved towards the door.

"See you later, yeah?"

After our time in the sauna, I'd hoped we could stay on better terms, but the strategy planning session yesterday had ruined that idea. He hadn't been happy with Black's suggestion and even less impressed when I'd agreed to it.

Emmy sat at the breakfast bar nursing a mug of coffee. She had a second lined up behind it already.

"Didn't you sleep either?" I asked.

"Nope."

"Nightmares?"

"For once, no. Black."

"What happened? Bad news? Did he come clean about what he's been hiding?"

Emmy gave me a lopsided smile and raised her mug to take a sip. "Not exactly. I tried to ask him, but he distracted me instead."

"Distracted you? How?"

She gave a coy smile. "You really want the details?"

Er, *nyet*. "I get the picture." Shit, no, not the picture. I definitely didn't want to think about that. "I mean, no, I don't want the details."

One corner of her lips quirked up. "Anyhow, I was awake half the night, and I still don't know the answer. It's bugging me."

"Ask him again."

"I intend to. Only this time, I'm going to lock myself into a chastity belt first."

"Now?"

"I can't. He's gone to the office. Nick's been lumbered with everything, so Black's giving him a hand today seeing as we'll all be fucking off to Russia soon."

I'd learned a little more about Blackwood over the last few days. Emmy, Black, and Nate ran their global security company along with a fourth partner, Nick Goldman. It offered services ranging from personal protection to private investigation to electronic security to hostage negotiation, as well as the black ops stuff nobody talked about. And from all appearances, it made bank.

For Emmy's part, she didn't look like the part-owner of a billion-dollar company. She looked like a girl who needed to go back to bed, alone, and stay there for a week. I suspected I did too, but that wasn't an option.

"Does Nick mind looking after the company?"

"He's pissed because he's been left out, but it's not sensible for all of us to go."

"I'm worried because Nate and Carmen are both coming. What about their son?" It had been niggling at me since Black announced the teams.

"Yeah, I know, and believe me, we've had that argument many times over the years. They both insist he's an extra incentive to get the job done."

"I still feel bad about it."

"Don't."

But I did. When I'd first started playing this game, I only had myself to worry about. I gave every job my all because it didn't matter if I lived or died. But now? I had something to lose, and so did the others helping me.

"Decision's made," Emmy said. "Get some breakfast."

I crossed over to the toaster and stared at it. It had more buttons and dials than the car I learned to drive in. "How does this thing work?"

"Just press the red button on the left-hand side."

"What do all the rest do?"

"No idea. But don't worry; Bradley chose it, not Nate."

"Why does that matter?"

"If you set the muffin warmer on Nate's toaster for two minutes, you've got thirty seconds to get out of the house before it explodes."

"On second thought, I'll have granola."

"Your current speed is eight point one miles per hour."

The electronic voice spoke into my ear as I leapt over a fallen tree trunk, hot on Emmy's heels. As our plan for getting to Base 13 involved a long trek, we figured we'd better do a practice run. At least the rucksack Emmy supplied was more comfortable than anything I'd worn in Russia.

"You really think this will work?" I asked Emmy. "Going in by truck?"

"I'll tell you in ten days." She huffed out a breath. "In the time we've got, I think it's the best option. If bloody *baza trinadtsat'* wasn't so isolated, maybe another way would work."

Black's plan called for the two of us to travel in first. He and Nate had been studying live satellite feeds for the past week, watching the comings and goings from Base 13 as they listened to radio chatter and intercepted phone calls. Not Zacharov's—his paranoia meant he used an encrypted handset at all times.

The only other settlement for miles in the bleak Siberian wilderness Zacharov called home was a tank farm twenty miles to the east, set up to service the ESPO oil pipeline that ran from Tayshet to the Kozimo terminal in the Sea of Japan. Trucks travelled there from Tayshet five or six times a day with supplies, stopping to refuel before they began the four-hour journey northeast.

And in ten days' time, we'd be hitching a lift.

Needless to say, Sam hadn't been impressed with

that idea. First, he'd volunteered to go instead of me. When Black rightly pointed out that I was the only person on the team familiar with the inner workings of Base 13, Sam tried to bump Emmy from the mission and take her place. She was having none of it, and Sam ended up walking out.

"Are you sure this is a good idea?" Nate had asked Jed. "Quinn coming at all? We can't afford for him to lose his head out there."

"He'll perform. It's just...you know." Jed jerked his head towards me.

Nate sighed. "Yeah, I do. Go and talk some sense into him, would you?"

Ten minutes later, Sam came back with a new suggestion for all three of us to go, and when Black vetoed that as well, he'd lapsed into silence and kept out of everyone's way for the rest of the day.

And it didn't take a genius to see how worried he was.

"Do you think Sam will be okay?" I asked Emmy.

"He's a grown up."

Most of the time. "That's not what I meant. He was upset with me yesterday."

"He was upset with the situation. This plan gives us our best shot at rectifying things, and when we come back, you'll have the rest of your lives to make up with each other."

The electronic voice spoke again. "Your current speed is seven point nine miles per hour."

"Better get a shift on," Emmy said.

Dan was waiting for us when we got back, and her tentative smile made my heart skip.

"Did you find something?"

"Maybe. A source says Bate offloaded a girl near Progreso, and we think she's in Mérida."

I felt rather than heard Sam behind me. "Then we need to go Mexico."

Emmy turned to him, hands on hips. "No, we don't need to fly to Mexico. The most difficult part of this operation is the Russian end, and we're planning to execute that in ten days' time. You can't abandon that to go and irritate all the staff in our Yucatán office. You're doing a good enough job of that here."

"Tabitha's my daughter."

"I know that." She spoke more gently. "And we're doing everything we can to find her. Our Mexican staff are good, and if you go out there, you'll hinder rather than help them. Besides, we need your help for Russia."

He looked away, and his eyes glistened. "I just... She's my daughter. I've never even met her."

I unpeeled the fingers of one of his clenched fists and slipped my hand into his. "You will. Just let Emmy and me do our jobs." I sounded more confident than I felt, and I hated that the poker face I used so often was another thing I'd been coached on by Zacharov. "Come on, let's have lunch." I bit my lip as I turned to Dan. "You'll keep us updated?"

"You'll be the first to hear if there's any more news."

Dan's declaration wasn't quite accurate. I was the second to know, as I found out at two o'clock the next morning when my new phone buzzed beside me on the nightstand.

"Have you got any idea what time it is?" I asked Emmy.

"Unfortunately, yes. How do you fancy a little trip to South America?"

I sat bolt upright. "Have they found her?"

"Not sure. They've found the girl who was taken."

"Where? Is she okay?"

"Mérida, like we thought. A wealthy couple bought her. Nobody's managed to get a good look yet, but with the little we've seen, she seems in reasonable shape."

Her words slowly penetrated my mind. "Someone bought her? Like a fucking object? What if it was a paedophile?"

"Stay calm, honey. Kids are sometimes used as little maids, or maybe it was a woman who can't have children of her own?"

"Tabby's two. She's not much use as a fucking maid."

A beat of silence. "Right. I'll call for the plane."

I felt like a complete bitch as I threw a change of clothes and my gun into a bag and clipped a knife onto my belt, knowing that Sam was sleeping at the other end of the corridor unaware. But at two in the morning, I didn't want an argument. I wanted to find my daughter.

Emmy met me in the hallway with a bag of her own. "Carmen's on her way. She's coming with us."

More footsteps sounded on the stairs, and I whipped my head around as Bradley came into view with a small pink suitcase.

"Here, take this with you. Snacks for the journey,

clothes for you and Tabitha, spare contact lenses, a selection of wigs, and tanning lotion because you don't find many Mexicans that colour." He pointed at my admittedly pale skin.

"Thanks," Emmy said, then narrowed her eyes. "Wait a minute—how did you find out we were going?"

"Uh, lucky guess?"

"You little shit. You bugged the conference room again, didn't you?"

He took a couple of hasty steps backwards. "Otherwise I'm the last to know everything."

The crunch of tyres on the gravel outside saved Bradley from getting throttled.

"Don't think I'll forget this," Emmy told him as we walked towards the door.

"Love you too, sweet cheeks."

Emmy's jet sat ready on the runway at a nearby private airfield with the steps down to welcome us on board. A uniformed pilot looked more cheerful than he had a right to at that time in the morning.

"This is Brett. Brett, meet Seven."

He gave me a salute and a quick smile, then raised the stairs and headed for the cockpit. Carmen carried on in front of us into the cabin, dumped her bag on the floor, and slumped into a padded seat. The plane was all done out in cream leather with polished walnut accents and gold trim. Well, this sure beat military transport.

"It's too late for this. Or early. One of the two. What have we got?" Her Spanish accent seemed stronger than the other day, possibly because of where we were heading.

Emmy yawned. "Coffee first."

The plane rumbled into the air, and Emmy went to the tiny galley while I dragged myself over to the four-person table behind the cockpit. Five minutes later, Emmy brought over three cups and positioned the laptop at the end of the table so we could all see the series of surveillance photos showing a villa, two storeys and pale yellow in colour, partly hidden behind a scalloped wall. The next pictures showed a man leaving alone then returning with a woman in expensive-looking clothes, and finally, an older woman hanging washing on a line in the garden.

"José and Rosa Sanchez. He owns a building firm; she seems to spend her time shopping. The other woman's a housekeeper. We don't have a name for her yet."

"What about Tabby?"

Emmy clicked a few more times, and a blurry picture of a small silhouette behind a window came up.

"That's all we've got so far."

I squinted, but even I couldn't tell for sure whether it was her. "I don't know. I just don't know."

"It's enough of a possibility that we need to take a look, and I figured it was best we did that rather than leaving it to the Mexican team. We can hit the house tomorrow, no, this evening, and we'll only lose a day. Plus, it's sunny."

"Of course I want to be there." I bit my lip. "Sam isn't going to be happy about this."

"So, don't tell him."

It sounded so straightforward when she said it.

I thought back to the conversation we'd had. He'd finally begun to thaw towards me, and another secret could send us right back to the ice age. And then there was my own promise. What were the chances of him ever finding out about our little trip?

Should I tell him or not?

CHAPTER 27

TO TELL OR not to tell, that was the question.

Although if I were going to channel Shakespeare, something the governess in Vladivostok insisted on beating into us just because she'd been to England once, I'd be Lady Macbeth. Stained with the blood of others and unable to wash it off no matter how hard I tried.

Emmy and Carmen lay back in the reclining seats and slept, Emmy with a wrist handcuffed to the seat just in case, while I fidgeted and stared out of the window with worries about both Sam and Tabby weighing heavy on my mind.

And by the time we landed at the airport outside Mérida, just as dawn was breaking, I'd come to a decision.

"I've got to call Sam," I said to Emmy as the plane taxied to the hangar.

"You sure that's a good idea?"

"No, but if I keep hiding things from him and he finds out, then..." Any trust I'd managed to claw back would be gone. Poof. "I just need to speak to him."

She blew out a breath. "Fine. But if he jumps on a plane, you're dealing with him, not me."

"Have you got his number?"

She tossed me her phone. "Here."

My feet wanted to pace, but I forced myself to stay seated as I dialled. Richmond was an hour ahead. He should be up already.

"Emmy?"

"It's Ana," I said quietly. It felt strange using my own name after all these years.

"Where are you? I'm making breakfast for us."

"Uh..." I closed my eyes. "Mexico."

I'd expected anger, but he sounded more hurt than anything else. "You went without me?"

"It was a last-minute decision. Please, don't hate me more than you already do."

He gave a long sigh. "I don't hate you." A pause. "Just take care out there, okay? Of yourself and Tabby."

"We don't even know it's her."

"I guess I was just hoping..."

"Me too."

A shout sounded in the background. "I've got to go. We'll talk when you get back."

"Okay," I said softly, and the line went dead. At least he hadn't yelled at me.

Emmy already had my bag in her hand, and she was standing by the door as I got to my feet.

"How did it go?"

"About as well as I could have hoped."

"Good. Now, put it out of your mind because we've got work to do."

Blackwood's Yucatan office was situated in a small compound on the outskirts of Mérida. Tasteful landscaping and pastel colours blended it into the surrounding area, but underneath the facade, I could see it was a fortress. Spikes topped the ten-foot-high white stucco walls, and the beady eyes of CCTV cameras swivelled to watch us as we arrived. The solid metal security gate looked as if it could withstand the force of a truck.

"What are you thinking?" Emmy asked.

"Parachute?"

"We've got motion sensors on the roof and regular dog patrols."

"Then I'd land in the courtyard at night. Dogs can be eliminated, as can their handlers."

A man emerged from a guard house and checked underneath the car with a mirror, pausing near the offside front wheel before he nodded to a colleague, and the gate opened. Inside, we couldn't get past the door of the two-storey office building until Emmy passed a retina scan. Okay, I had to admit it—the security wasn't bad.

A dark-skinned man hurried up to us, swallowing a mouthful of whatever he'd been eating for breakfast. "Mrs. Black? Miguel Santos."

I pointed at Emmy. "She's Mrs. Black. I'm Seven."

"Seven?"

I nodded, and he shook hands with both of us then greeted Carmen with a wide smile. "And Ms. Hernandez. Good to see you again."

"You too, Mig."

Miguel led us through a door at the back of the reception area, down a long corridor, and into a conference room. "You speak Spanish?"

"Yes." Emmy answered for all of us.

"Good, good." He switched languages and continued to brief us in his mother tongue, speaking quickly in a high voice, almost too quickly for me to translate. But he had little of substance to say.

Blackwood had commandeered a room in a property opposite, and the occupants of our target house still appeared to be asleep. "But we have a video feed now."

A screen showed a peaceful residential street, the only movement a man on a bicycle pedalling slowly along, unaware he was being watched by so many eyes.

"We need to take a look in person," Emmy said.

Miguel rubbed his chin. "I thought you would. It is best to wait an hour until the street gets busier, then we'll go. And if you plan on getting out of the car, you'll need a disguise."

By eight o'clock, enough people were around that our presence wouldn't turn heads, and Emmy and I had made good use of Bradley's supplies. Emmy sported a black wig to go with her newly tanned skin, and I'd gone ten shades darker too.

"I smell funny," I muttered as I buttoned up the pale blue dress Miguel had supplied.

With over two million domestic workers in Mexico, a maid hurrying along the street early in the morning might as well be invisible. Emmy and Carmen had similar outfits, except Carmen looked like she was planning to star in an adult movie.

"Is it supposed to be that tight?" I asked.

Miguel shrugged. "Sorry. I'm not so good with the sizes."

Emmy glanced over at Carmen. "At least if she gets spotted, all the witness will remember is tits and ass."

She looked down at herself. "Maybe I'll take this home with me for Nate's viewing pleasure," she muttered.

Miguel's cheeks turned red, and he coughed into his hand. "Who wants the dog?"

Ah yes, the dog. Miguel thought if one of us borrowed the pooch, it would provide a good excuse for wandering around. I'd never worked surveillance with a canine partner before, but I'd always had a soft spot for poor Vaska.

"I'll volunteer."

A young woman walked in, holding the leash at arm's length. "*Por favor, lo llevan.*" Please, take him.

Just being polite? Or a plea?

When she handed the leash over, the beast gave a growl, teeth bared. I reached for the gun in my handbag.

Miguel laughed nervously. "Don't worry. It's just his way of greeting people."

Really? "What's he called?"

"Buffy."

I managed to keep a straight face. "You named your dog Buffy? I thought he was male?"

"My daughter named him. She was only eight at the time."

"What breed is he?"

Miguel blushed again. "His mother was an American pit bull terrier, and his father was a shitzu."

This time I gave up on trying to hold back my smirk, and Emmy doubled up beside me.

"Your dog is a bullshit?" she got out.

"My wife prefers pitzu."

I bet.

Carmen appraised the dog critically. "The shitzu was punching above his weight, wasn't he?"

Emmy shoved me towards the door. "Go. I can't take any more of this."

Whatever Buffy might have been lacking in the

personality department, he sure made up for it with his other abilities.

"This dog's great for surveillance," I whispered into the microphone built into my necklace. "He stops to sniff something or piss on it every ten seconds."

"The gardener five doors up keeps staring at me," Carmen said.

"Tits and ass." Emmy's voice came from the car parked down the block. "I told you."

By lunchtime, we'd made a few passes both on foot and by vehicle and had a selection of photos and videos to study. Buffy had displayed a remarkable ability for licking his non-existent balls and growled at every man wearing shorts. But none of us saw Tabby or any girl like her. We regrouped back at Blackwood, where Miguel's assistant pointed to the realtor's floor plan for the house spread out on the table next to a plate of cookies. I liked her more and more.

"What do you think?" Emmy asked.

"No guards, one camera above the garage," I said. "They don't look like they're expecting anyone." Which worried me, if I was honest. If I had a kidnapped kid in the house, I'd be a little more paranoid.

Emmy wrinkled her nose. "I know. Odd. I spoke to the lady who runs the store on the corner. The housekeeper comes in occasionally to buy sweets and toys, but she's been doing that for months."

"So the girl's been there for a while?"

"Seems that way."

I sagged back into one of the seats. "It's the wrong place, isn't it?"

"Where did the intelligence come from?" Emmy asked Miguel.

"The source has been proved valid in the past. I wouldn't have called you otherwise. We heard from three different people that Bate brought a young girl to Mérida the weekend before last, and the man who pinpointed the house has worked for Bate as a driver on occasion."

"Where's Bate right now?"

"Nobody's seen him."

Emmy tugged her hair behind her head in a ponytail and leaned back, eyes closed. Half a minute passed then she sat up again.

"We go in tonight."

CHAPTER 28

"READY?"

I NODDED, as did Carmen, and Emmy made short work of the back door lock with her lock picks. We'd already noted the lack of alarm, and Carmen shot out the security light that covered the garden using infrared goggles and a silenced pistol. With the shouts of late-night revellers drifting over from a nearby bar, nobody had even noticed.

Carmen stayed by the door, covering our exit as Emmy and I stole through the house. I took the first floor, she took the second, and we were back fifteen minutes later having found nothing.

"Housekeeper's asleep down there," I whispered, pointing at the end of the hallway.

"Two more sleeping in the master bedroom," she said. "No kids."

We only had the basement left. According to the realtor's plans, it was accessed by a door off the kitchen, but when we risked turning a flashlight on, there were only cupboards.

"What the...?"

"It was in the back-left corner."

I found it first, a narrow door behind a shelf of crockery that slid sideways, and my heart rate sped up as I peered into the darkness. Could my daughter be down there?

I heard the smile in Emmy's voice. "Well, I'll be damned. They've got something to hide. Looks like Mig was right. After you."

My rubber-soled shoes made no sound as I descended down the concrete steps and shone my flashlight around. The basement was done out as a playroom with a fold-out sun lounger, a bean bag seat, a toy box, and a television.

"Nice taste in furniture," Emmy said.

"They probably couldn't fit anything else through that tiny door."

The light splayed out on the wall, and a glint caught my eye. Another door, this one with a new-looking bolt on the outside. Jackpot. It slid back smoothly, well-oiled, and my hands shook as I pulled the door wide open.

"Fuck." Emmy's whispered curse came from over my shoulder.

Two girls? *Two prisoners?*

The older girl blinked in the glare from the flashlights as the smaller girl burrowed into her chest. But I'd seen enough. Neither of them was Tabby. Tears threatened as I shook my head, and Emmy swore again.

"Now what?" I asked.

"Whoever they are, I'm pretty sure they don't belong here."

The younger girl might have had dark hair like me, but the long blonde hair on the other child definitely didn't match the adults in the house above. I stepped forward and crouched to the level of the mattress they were sleeping on.

"What's your name, *nene*?" I asked her.

Her eyes darted towards the door then back to my face, and she shook her head.

"It's okay, they're all asleep. You can talk."

"Carlita," she whispered, but her accent was American.

"Is that a new name?"

She nodded then began sobbing.

"What did your mama used to call you?"

She wept harder, and I cradled her against me to try and keep her quiet. After we'd got this far, we didn't want to wake anybody upstairs.

Meanwhile, Emmy peered at the younger girl's arm, in particular, a strawberry-shaped birthmark at the top of it. "I do believe we've found Fern Fletcher."

"Who?"

"She disappeared from Boulder, Colorado three weeks ago. Her face has been all over CNN."

"And the other one?"

"I don't know, but I bet you fifty bucks the FBI do."

Carmen was hovering by the kitchen door when we came up the stairs, and her eyes widened when she saw what we were carrying.

"Tabitha?"

I shook my head.

"I'm so sorry, *cariña*. What are we doing about the couple upstairs?"

"Not a lot we can do," Emmy said. "We've broken fuck knows how many laws coming in here in the first place, so we can hardly report them to the cops."

That wasn't an answer I could accept. "They kept two children from their parents."

"I don't like it any more than you do, but we need to

leave."

My gaze landed on the knife block, and I handed Carlita, or whatever the hell her name was, to Carmen.

"Now what are you doing?" Emmy asked.

"Sending a message."

She eyed up the six-inch blade on the chef's knife and rolled her eyes. "Try not to make too much mess, okay?"

An hour later, the engines on the jet roared as the pilot raised the nose into the still-dark sky. Miguel had driven us to the airport with a promise to keep looking for Tabby.

"I'm sorry it wasn't your daughter, ma'am. But at least two little girls are going home."

I tried to take some comfort in that, but all I wanted was my daughter. Emmy gave me a hug while Carmen cuddled Fern on her lap. Carlita had stopped crying now and sat watching us.

"Am I really going home?" she asked.

Emmy gave her a friendly smile. "We'll make sure of it. Do you remember where you live?"

"Kansas," she whispered. "My new mom said my old mom didn't want me anymore."

"I'm sure that's not true."

"Then why didn't she come and get me?" She began to cry quietly again, and Emmy found a box of tissues as I stroked the girl's hair.

"Maybe she couldn't find you. Did you go outside much?"

She shook her head. "Never."

Fuck, what if Tabby was in a house somewhere, thinking the same thing? Being told a pack of lies and forced to live with a new family? I could barely hold my own tears back.

"I bet your mom still loves you, little one. What did she used to call you?"

"Summer," she sobbed, but it came out "Thummer" because her two front teeth were missing.

"Summer's a pretty name." I hugged her tighter against me. "You'll be home soon; I promise."

Emmy settled herself at the table and made a few phone calls, and an hour later she slipped back into the seat beside us.

"Summer Adams. Disappeared from a playground in Kansas six years ago."

"Six years? Shit."

"She's nine now."

Only a year older than Tabby when she disappeared. And although we hadn't found my daughter yet, the very fact that Summer was sitting beside me now gave me an important gift: hope. I'd never stop looking.

Two FBI agents met us at Silver Springs, the private airfield where Emmy and Black kept their jets. Yes, plural, because apparently they had another one kicking around somewhere. The amount of cash they had stashed away still made my eyes water.

Six a.m., and the sun was showing its face over the horizon. Up the whole night, a three-hour flight where I couldn't sleep, and all I wanted to do was crawl into bed and hold a pillow over my own face.

The taller of the two agents, a bald-headed man in an ill-fitting suit, gave his head a disbelieving shake as we climbed down the steps.

"Dare I ask?"

"Agent Stone," Emmy greeted. "No, best not to. We weren't here, and we know absolutely nothing about any of this."

"How many bodies are there?"

She looked at me.

"None."

He looked dubious. "As in actually none? Or just none that we'll be able to find."

"Really?" Emmy asked.

"Relax. I just left a note."

Pinned to the door with the knife. *Take another child, and you won't see tomorrow.* They'd take notice of that. If I'd ripped their heads off as I wanted to, it would have tipped our hand to Bate.

Emmy patted Stone on the arm. "See? Nothing to worry about. I know that's a little hard to believe."

The other agent stepped forward, an older man with the voice of a heavy smoker. "You're telling us you actually have Fern Fletcher *and* Summer Adams."

"I'm positive on Fern, maybe fifty percent on Summer. But whatever, I'm a hundred percent sure she didn't belong in a basement in Mexico, so I'm sure you'll work it out."

"If this is true, the press is going to go crazy," Stone said.

"Better get your hair done and put on your good suit, then."

"This is my good suit."

"Oh." She looked him up and down. "Tell you what, I'll get Bradley to send something over."

"I owe you one."

"You owe me at least ten, Paul. And remember, Blackwood's name stays out of the press."

"Got it."

Returning to Riverley would be bittersweet. I had the satisfaction that two girls were soon going to be reunited with their families, but at the same time, neither of those girls was Tabby and neither of those families was me and Sam.

Hang on. What was I thinking? Sam and I weren't a family, merely two screwed up individuals who knew more about firearms and explosives than trips to the park or visits to Disneyland. What a mess we'd made of everything.

In the backseat of the car, Emmy put an arm around my shoulders, and Carmen squeezed my hand.

"You okay?" Emmy asked.

"No."

"That was a dumb question, wasn't it?"

"Yes."

"We won't stop looking for Tabby. I promise."

"I know." I choked back a sob. "But I can't bear thinking of her alone out there. She's so young, and apart from her time here, she's never known anything but a prison cell. I'm her *mother*. She should be with me, and I've failed her."

Carmen pushed a few strands of hair out of my eyes. "You haven't failed her. Zacharov's *es un lunático*."

"But—"

"Don't do yourself down," Emmy said. "You did

everything you could in a hellish situation. Now, we need to think positive. We're going to find her, okay?"

"Okay."

I didn't share her conviction, but at least I wasn't alone in this anymore.

CHAPTER 29

SAM WAS WAITING in the hallway when we arrived back, and one look at my face was enough to drain the hope from his eyes.

"It wasn't her," he said.

"No."

"We found two other missing girls," Emmy told him, trying to soften the blow.

"Are you serious?"

"You've seen Fern Fletcher on the news?"

"Yeah. Fuck." He rubbed his eyes, and from the looks of him, he hadn't had much sleep either. "That's who you found? Alive?"

"She was okay, physically."

But mentally? How long would those scars take to heal? And Summer's? My heart bled for my own daughter, just like Zacharov's would when I got near him.

"I need sleep," I mumbled, heading for the stairs and leaving Sam behind.

Let the nightmares begin.

A knock at the door woke me, and I groaned as I stretched my arms over my head. "Who is it?"

"Me," Sam said.

"What do you want?"

"Can I come in?"

I'd shucked off all my clothes and fallen into bed, and now I gathered the quilt around me. Not that he hadn't seen me naked before—far from it, he'd explored every inch of me with his lips, fingers, and tongue. But now? Having him in the same room without the barrier of clothes between us felt uncomfortable. Or worse, I might be tempted to drop the damn covers altogether if he gave me a proper smile.

"Hang on."

I rolled out of bed and pulled on a pair of shorts and a T-shirt. Not one of mine—the shirt came to my knees—but I figured if it was in my closet, it was fair game.

When I opened the door, Sam was leaning against the wall opposite carrying heaven in a cup.

"You worked out how to use the coffee machine?"

"Mrs. Fairfax helped me, or you'd have been stuck with instant."

I reached out for the caffeine fix, but even after I'd taken my first sip, Sam didn't move.

"Did you want something else?"

"It's almost three p.m. Are you getting ready for the jump tonight?"

"What jump?"

"Nobody told you?"

"Clearly not, Sam. I've had other things on my mind."

He reached out and touched the top of my arm, and I stared down at his hand. What did that tiny caress mean?

"Don't stress, beautiful. Black's arranged a practice jump for the team tonight, and I just assumed you'd be joining us."

"Even though I'm going in by truck?"

His mouth set in a hard line, and I regretted reminding him.

"Emmy's still coming."

"In that case, I guess I am too." He went to walk away, but I caught his hand. "Sam?"

"Yeah?"

"Thanks for not being mad at me for going to Mexico."

"I can't pretend I was thrilled about it, but at least you told me. If I'd found out from someone else... Yeah, that would have pissed me off."

I clicked the door closed behind me and leaned back against it. I *had* made the right choice yesterday morning, then.

For once in my life, I'd made the right choice.

"Tell me again, why are we throwing ourselves out of a perfectly good plane?" I asked Emmy as we prepared our gear for the evening's excursion.

We'd commandeered the ballroom to pack our parachutes, much to Bradley's annoyance. Apparently, he wanted to measure up for new drapes.

"So I can see how the team performs under pressure. If we've got any cracks, I'd rather expose them before we're in the middle of Siberia. From that comment, I take it you're not so keen on skydiving?"

"It was never my favourite thing, but the whole

experience was tainted by my first jump."

"What happened? It can't be as bad as mine—I was sixteen, and I chickened out at five thousand feet, so Black threw me off the ramp."

Had he been taking lessons from the general?

"I was fourteen. Zacharov strapped me to an army major who smelled of cabbage and sent me out tandem. Asshole got a hard-on halfway through the flight, and he had wandering hands. He'd have lost them that day if Zacharov hadn't been watching." Even now, I still shuddered about the scratch of his beard on my neck and his cock pressing into my ass. "I only ever jumped solo after that."

Emmy made a gagging noise. "Yuck. I'm surprised Black hasn't had that idea, the horny git."

"The whole chastity belt thing didn't work out, then?"

"Nope, and he's still hiding something." She finished packing up her parachute and stood up. "You know what? I'm gonna ask him now. If I'm not back in twenty minutes, come and throw a bucket of cold water over us."

She strode out the door, and Sam chuckled beside me. "Jumping out of airplanes isn't that bad."

"You did a lot of parachuting in the Rangers?"

"I was airborne qualified before I even went to Ranger School, and while I was there, I used to make extra jumps on the weekend for fun."

"You're crazy."

He waggled his eyebrows at me. "Want to do a tandem jump, beautiful?"

I threw my sweater at him, but he caught it and held it up against himself. "Not my style."

"You're impossible."

"You like a challenge."

Twenty minutes came and went without any sign of Emmy. I used the time to mull over the conversation I'd just had with Sam. He'd been friendlier, almost flirty, and I didn't want to admit how good that felt. Back in Moscow, his lighthearted teasing had been the polar opposite of the general's cold demeanour, and my smiles had become instinctive rather than rehearsed. But now? His kindness hurt more than his anger, because Sam wasn't mine anymore.

Dammit, where was Emmy? She wasn't serious about the bucket of cold water, was she?

Sam read my mind. "Forget it. Black's probably got her naked in bed by now. I don't understand where the old bastard finds the energy. Did you know he ran a marathon while you were away then went straight into the kill-house when he got back?"

"Nice to see him leading from the front. Back in..."

I trailed off as Emmy appeared in the doorway, her face uncertain. It wasn't a look I'd seen on her before.

"What?" I mouthed.

She beckoned me over, and I shrugged at Sam. "Back in a bit."

He blew me a kiss, and I couldn't help laughing. Despite the shitstorm, he still made me smile.

"Well?" I asked when I got outside.

Bradley sashayed down the corridor carrying a bouquet of flowers, and Emmy waited until he'd rounded the corner before she spoke. "Okay, so I asked him outright, but he said it concerned you too, and he'd tell us together."

"Did he give you any clues?"

She hesitated before answering. "No."

"What is it?"

"He looked worried. Black never looks worried."

"Where is he?"

"In the music room."

As we got closer, the sounds of Beethoven grew louder. I had a CD of it once, back when I was allowed a stereo.

"Shit. He only plays when he's stressed," Emmy said, her frown deepening.

"Maybe he's nervous about tonight's jump?"

"No, that's not it."

Black played like a concert pianist, and I sat next to Emmy on the squashy leather sofa opposite the Steinway grand until he lifted his hands from the keys. Emmy was right—he didn't look happy as he took a seat in an armchair at right angles to us.

"What is it?" she asked. "Just spit it out, would you?"

He reached out and cupped her cheek in his hand. "Always so impatient, Diamond."

She folded her arms and glared at him. "Are we falling out of the sky today or tomorrow?"

Black sighed as he took a piece of paper out of his pocket and unfolded it. "I got curious."

"About what?"

"You two." He tapped the side of his head, beside his eyes. "I'm not the only person who's been thinking it. Nate's noticed the similarities too."

"That we have the same colour eyes? We already talked about that."

"Yes, you did. But it's more than that. You think the same, and you fight the same."

He smoothed the paper out and slid it over the coffee table so it lay in front of us.

I peered down and read it, just one short paragraph with Blackwood's company logo at the top of the sheet.

Results of the Autosomal comparison on samples A and B are as follows:

Total cM - 1,848.1

Largest cM -148.3

Comparison

XDNA Total cM - 108.9

Largest cM - 49.2

What was it? Some sort of lab report? "That means nothing to me."

I glanced across at Emmy, and she'd gone a couple of shades paler.

"You know what this is?" I asked her.

She pointed at the line marked *Total cM*. "The results of a centiMorgans DNA test. The person behind sample A is related to the person sample B was taken from. A result close to 1,700 indicates a reasonably close relative. A grandfather or grandmother, aunt or uncle. Maybe a half-sibling. We see this a lot in paternity disputes." She closed her eyes. "Black, tell us."

He pointed at Emmy. "You're A. Seven is B."

It took a few seconds for that to sink in. I looked at Emmy, and she looked at me, violet eyes to violet eyes.

"I don't think you're my grandmother or my aunt," I whispered.

My world quietly fell apart in that room at Riverley, with the strains of Beethoven still echoing in my ears. The last bit of who I was, my early childhood, had been a lie. All these years I'd been the daughter of Nikita and

Vasily Petrov, but now, suddenly, I wasn't. Because if Vasily never left Russia, and Emmy's mother never left England, then Vasily couldn't really be my papa, could he?

And like she had so many times over the past two weeks, Emmy mirrored my thoughts. "Who the fuck was our father?"

"I don't know." But I did know my mama was no longer the saint I'd cast her as in my mind. She'd cheated on Vasily? Had he realised? Or had she lied to him too?

Emmy clutched at my hand, and I squeezed hers back as tightly as I could. I needed her support, more now than ever.

"Are you okay?" she asked.

"No."

She hugged me fiercely, and I hugged her back, and I knew then that I might have lost a father, but I'd gained a sister. The sister I'd spent my whole damn life without and only found because of a stroke of bad luck. And whoever my father might have been, I hated him for that.

"Now what?" I whispered. "You said you didn't know whether your mother was alive. What if—"

"I'm not speaking to her."

Black knelt down beside us and rested a hand on Emmy's thigh. "Do you want me to speak to her?"

She looked up at him. "She *is* alive?"

He started to roll his eyes then stopped himself. "Rehab. Again."

Emmy scrambled to her feet. "No. Forget her. And forget our violet-eyed asshole of a father too. He didn't want to be in our lives. He left you in an orphanage and me in a drug den, so who cares about him? We've got each other, and that's more than we had two weeks ago."

She was right. If the man who donated his DNA didn't care enough to stick around, then what did he matter? "Let's go jump out of a plane."

Black leaned down to kiss Emmy on the forehead. "Are you okay to go tonight? If you want to take a few hours, I'll let the others know."

"Me, slack off? Never. You taught me better than that."

"Seven?"

"I'm good to go."

He smiled faintly, back to his usual predatory self. "If nothing else, this has been an interesting study in genetics. The merits of nature over nurture. You two shared nothing but DNA, and you still ended up in the same place."

"And we're staying in the same place," Emmy said. "Right? When this job's over, you'll come back here?"

I nodded, swallowing down the lump in my throat. "I need to find Tabby first."

"But after that?"

"I can't think of anywhere else I'd rather be."

CHAPTER 30

TWO HOURS LATER, the G-forces pushed me sideways in my seat as the C-130 transport plane banked after takeoff. And when I say seat, I mean floor. I was sprawled out next to Emmy in the cargo hold, empty except for Team Blackwood and our bags of equipment. We'd be jumping in full kit tonight. If anything was going to come loose and fall off, it was better for it to happen over Virginia so we could fix it or replace it.

Black had commandeered the plane from the US Air Force, together with two pilots and the use of the runway at Silver Springs, half an hour from Riverley. President Markovich would be providing a similar plane for the jump into Base 13, although not quite so graciously as James Harrison. In fact, Markovich had said no at first, until I heard Black and Nate discussing the problem.

"Mention the name Irina Romanova to him."

"How will that help?"

"She's the wife of one of his aides, and he's sleeping with her."

"I take it his wife doesn't know?"

"Apparently not."

But Zacharov did, and he'd told me during one of our awkward dinners. Guess I should have thanked him for that snippet of information.

Knowledge is power, right?

For that reason, Emmy and I were keeping quiet about the DNA test results. News like that, people would talk, and even though they'd mean well, it would slip out and hand someone leverage. The sort of leverage Zacharov was using against me with Tabby. Plus, Emmy said Bradley would insist on throwing some sort of party, and I had little to celebrate at the moment.

A touch of turbulence hit. We all sat tight until the plane levelled out, then Emmy got up.

"I'm going to talk to the pilot. Back in a minute."

That left me with Sam. The row of dim strip lights cast a pale yellow glow over his face, barely recognisable under the green and black war paint he'd painted on. He used a finger to smear my own paint over my cheek.

"Missed a spot."

"Thanks."

Emmy and I had done our camouflage in the truck on the way, feeling our way in the dark, because Bradley had tried to use make-up brushes on us back at the house and we'd never have lived that down.

Tonight, we'd be doing a High Altitude, High Opening jump, or HAHO in military speak. It didn't have the thrill of a HALO, where you plummeted to earth at over a hundred miles an hour and pulled your 'chute at the last possible second, but it didn't have the added danger either. We'd exit the plane at fifteen thousand feet, complete with oxygen bottles, and deploy our parachutes soon after. Then we'd drift six miles to our target, which tonight was a little-known military base in eastern Virginia.

Why HAHO for the trip to Base 13? Sure, there was a temptation to come in hard and fast, but for that, the plane had to fly right overhead, and planes made a lot of noise. Even in the dark with no radar, there was a risk that Zacharov's men would hear our approach and use us for target practice. Far better to sneak in by opening high. Fifteen thousand feet was a compromise —HAHO jumps could be done from up to forty thousand feet, but the flight time increased with height. At the lower altitude, our team would arrive at Base 13 silently and relatively quickly.

I took deep breaths and forced my mind clear. In a few minutes, I'd need to concentrate on wind speed, direction, and my jump buddy's location, as well as that of the wider team, not keep wondering whether Tabby was okay. And it took every piece of my will not to think of her.

"She'll be fine," Sam said, leaning in close and reading my damn mind. "I bet Tabby's a fighter like her mom. And her dad."

I fought the hysterical laughter that threatened to break free. What did he think got us into this mess in the first place? If we hadn't been fighters, if we'd just been the receptionist and copier engineer we'd pretended to be, we'd all have been sitting around our kitchen table in Moscow eating dinner.

Emmy bent down beside us. "Shut up, Quinn. You're upsetting her."

"Am I? How? I was just talking about Tabby."

"Don't. Talk about the weather or something instead." She paused, listening. You could almost hear the driving rain we'd taken off in hammering on the skin of the aircraft. "Actually, not the weather. Forget about the weather."

Emmy carried on along the cargo bay, checking on each man as she went. Even though Black was officially team leader tonight, that didn't stop her from caring.

Sam rested his hand on my leg, a little higher than it should have been. I flinched then tried to block out his touch.

"Sorry," he said into my ear, a fine balance between being heard over the wind noise and broadcasting his thoughts to everyone around us.

I wasn't sure what he was apologising for—startling me or mentioning Tabby—but ultimately it didn't matter. "Don't worry about it."

"But I do. Worry, I mean. Even in those years I hated you, I still worried."

"I thought about you every day. If I could turn the clock back..."

"We can't. But we can look to the future. It's still there, isn't it?"

"What? What's still there?"

He leaned in closer, his lips brushing my ear. "Whatever drew us together in the first place. Tell me you feel it too?"

Of course I did. I couldn't just turn it off. But now really wasn't the time to be having this conversation. My pulse began to race as I inclined my head to look at him properly.

"Sam, I—"

The wail of the jump alarm drowned out my words and my thoughts. We were at the right altitude, and it was almost time to bail out. The team around us leapt into action, strapping on the last of their kit, while Sam pulled me hard against him. His lips met mine in a hard, closed-mouth kiss, only for a second, but it was enough to make me forget my own damn name.

"We'll talk about this later," he yelled, struggling to be heard as the rear ramp opened.

My hands shook as I tightened up my straps and checked Emmy's kit over while she did the same for me. All good—nothing sticking out that shouldn't be. It was time. Black motioned us forwards, and we shuffled towards the yawning exit at the back of the plane.

"I like the way he lets us go first," I said to Emmy.

She gave me a wink. "Black's a gentleman. He always comes second."

Pretty much everyone heard her say that since she'd half shouted above the wind, and Black's smirk didn't escape my notice.

"Ready?" he shouted.

Emmy grabbed my hand and we jumped together, our first adventure as sisters, the sum of the two of us greater than our individual parts. And I remembered that no matter how much I hated the thought of jumping out of a plane, the thrill of actually doing it was a rush like nothing else.

"Yeeeeeah!" I yelled, then remembered I was supposed to be Lilith and remain cold and aloof at all times.

The moonlight reflected off Emmy's teeth as she grinned back, her cheeks like little hamster pouches. She reached back to the drogue, the small pilot 'chute that would catch the air and pull out the main canopy. I did the same, black silk fluttered in the air, and then we were floating rather than falling. Time to sit back and enjoy the ride.

Or not.

A body plummeted between us, clipping the edge of my canopy and causing me to spiral to the limits of control. I grabbed at my lines, desperate to re-inflate the collapsed cells on the right-hand edge. Out of the corner of my eye, I saw Emmy cut away her main chute and take off after whoever was heading rapidly for a date with the earth below us.

Oh, fuck it. In it together, right? I jettisoned my own canopy and plunged after them.

CHAPTER 31

PLEASE, DON'T LET it be Sam. That was the foremost thought in my mind as I tucked my body into the most aerodynamic form possible, arms and legs tight to my sides. Below me, Emmy did the same, her body outlined in the moonlight against the ground below. Our target had tried to open his 'chute, but something had gone wrong, because the crumpled material flapped uselessly above him. Why hadn't he cut it away and pulled his reserve?

At least it slowed his descent a little, and Emmy caught up and scissored her legs around his waist, clinging on as they fell together. A few seconds later I reached both of them and wrapped my legs over Emmy's. Who was it?

Not Sam. Evan. My moment of relief soon ended when I saw the lines wrapped around his neck, cutting off his air supply so he'd lost consciousness. His mouth lolled open as Emmy tried to untangle the mess, but that had no effect.

I held his head back with my chin and pulled the thin cords away from his neck as Emmy got out her knife and began to cut. Shit, shit, shit. The lights of the highway beneath us were getting brighter, and the altimeter strapped to my wrist told me we were more than halfway to earth. Guess this was going to be a

HALO jump after all.

The tanto blade on Emmy's knife was designed for penetration, not delicately sawing away while tumbling towards the ground ass over tit. I managed to get a flashlight out and held it in my teeth. Was Evan still breathing? The wind rushing past made checking his vital signs impossible. All we could do was try to get him down without splattering the three of us across a field or a swath of asphalt or someone's roof. Or—I glanced below us—a tree. Great. Now we were over a forest. And some of those trees were beginning to look alarmingly large.

Emmy cut through the last of the cords, and the useless 'chute flapped away into the night. I shoved away from him, and so did she, pulling on his reserve as she did so. He jerked away from us, but I didn't have time to check whether it inflated properly. I yanked on the handle for my own backup, and it flared once before I hit the ground in a small clearing. Fuck. I tested my legs. They hurt like hell from the hard landing, but nothing was broken.

"Emmy?"

"I'm in a fucking tree."

The crackle of branches on my left said she spoke the truth.

"You okay?"

"I'll live. Find Evan. He landed to the north."

Another voice came out of the darkness. "Ana?"

"Sam?"

A beam of light cut through the trees to my left, and his silhouette jogged towards me. "I saw you cut away underneath me, and I've never been so scared in my life."

"You followed?"

"I figured you could use a hand. Everyone else will be landing miles away."

"You idiot! You cut away a perfectly good parachute! You could have been killed."

"Nah. I packed the reserve myself. I knew it'd work. Are you sure you're okay?"

"Yes. Just help me find Evan."

The camouflage outfit he wore worked too well, especially with the flashlight glinting off all the wet leaves, and it took us almost five minutes to locate him, swinging in a sapling three feet off the ground. Sam held him steady while I climbed up the trunk to cut through the lines attached to his harness. He dropped like a dead weight into Sam's arms.

"Is he alive?"

"Hang on."

I shinned down as Sam lay Evan out on the ground and checked his vital signs.

"He's got a pulse, but it's faint." Sam knelt and put his cheek under Evan's nose. "And he's breathing. But he needs medical attention."

No kidding. "I broke my radio when I landed. Does yours still work?"

"I let everyone know what happened as I was landing. A car's on its way, but it'll take a few minutes to reach us."

The quiet pad of feet on the damp humus that covered the ground signalled Emmy's approach. She'd lost her balaclava somewhere and replaced it with a handful of twigs and a bunch of leaves in her hair.

"How is he? Alive?"

"Yes, alive but unconscious."

Her shoulders sagged in relief as she knelt in the mud next to me. "Evan, you prick. If you want a threesome, there are easier ways to go about it."

He groaned in response and one eye flickered open. "Nice of you to join us."

"Shit. What happened?"

"You decided to hang from your neck rather than your harness."

He tried to sit up, but Emmy held him down on the ground. "Pack that in. You almost died. Can you still move everything? Hands? Feet?"

Evan wiggled all his limbs, grimacing as he did so, and three sighs of relief settled through the forest. Thank goodness.

"What hurts?"

"My right ankle."

"Broken?"

"Hope not."

"Help's on its way," Sam told her. "I told them roughly where we landed."

She held out her own mangled radio. "I broke this, but Nate put a tracking chip in my shoe so they'll find us, no problem."

With no other imminent danger, the adrenaline began to leave my body and a chill set in from my damp clothes. I stood and yanked what was left of Evan's parachute down from the tree and tucked it around him. No sense in him catching hypothermia along with everything else. Sam put his arm around me, and I snuggled into his warmth while Emmy burrowed under the parachute to share her body heat with Evan.

"If this was the result, I'd strangle myself every day," he joked.

At least the ordeal hadn't killed off his sense of humour.

It took another twenty minutes for the rescue party to arrive, Black, Nate, Jed, and Isaiah emerging from the twisted forest complete with a stretcher and enough medical equipment to start their own hospital. The team worked together to strap Evan down, although he waved away the oxygen and the IV fluids.

"I'm good. Just a little pain in my foot. I'll be fine by Monday."

Emmy and I looked at each other. The way his ankle had swelled up, two days of rest wasn't going to improve matters significantly.

She patted his hand. "Let's just get you to the hospital."

Dr. Stanton, the Canadian lady who'd checked me over earlier in the week, picked her way through the woods, followed by a guy in a green jumpsuit.

"She works in the ER as well?" I asked Emmy.

"No, Blackwood's expanding, and we made the decision a couple of months back to hire our own doctor. She's ex-army. We were outsourcing before, but this works out more cost effective. She'll check Evan over here then go with him to the ER."

First, Dr. Stanton crouched down and examined his ankle with Nate's flashlight, the beam so bright it would have blinded anyone who looked at it directly. Evan may have claimed to be fine, but there was no mistaking the agony on his face when she touched the joint.

"Broken or badly sprained. He'll need x-rays."

Isaiah, Evan's jump buddy, was sitting over on a fallen tree trunk, head in his hands. I followed Emmy as she went over to talk to him.

"It wasn't your fault."

"We got hit by a crosswind, and he just... disappeared."

"Don't beat yourself up."

"I should have been the one to go after him. I couldn't see where he went."

"Ise, don't. We're a team, you get that? A fucking team. Today it was me and Ana who solved the problem, and next week it'll be someone else."

"But—"

"Enough. Don't go all soft, because we need you in good shape for next week."

He straightened his back and looked her in the eye. "I won't let you down."

"Good. Come on, help me retrieve my parachute from that bloody tree."

I needed to collect mine as well. At least it was on the ground.

"Sam, can I borrow your flashlight?"

He turned away from Jed and walked over. "What for?"

"I need to find my canopy to take back with us."

"I'll come with you."

He held out a hand, but I hesitated before taking it. That hand symbolised more than a peace offering. It was Sam's silent continuation of the conversation we'd started on the plane before we jumped. And my feelings were still so jumbled it would take me hours to unravel them. Yes, we still had a spark between us, but after the mess we made last time, I didn't want to rush into anything.

I could always rely on Emmy to save me. Her

whistle turned all heads, not just mine. "See you back at the truck?"

"Yes, won't be long."

When I looked back at Sam, the hand was gone, and I wasn't sure whether to be relieved or upset.

I followed Sam down through the trees, back to the clearing I'd landed in. The canopy was where I'd left it, fluttering against the wide trunk of an old oak tree, a dark wraith in the night. Sam tucked it under one arm and went to put the other around my shoulders, but then he pulled back.

"Ana? I can't work out what you're thinking."

Him and me both. "I don't know at the moment. Everything's so confusing—you, Tabby, Zacharov—and I can't deal with it all right now."

"It's not that confusing. We're going to kill Zacharov. We're going to find Tabby." He shrugged and gave me a lopsided smile. "And I still have feelings for you."

"And I still like you, Sam. But in a week, who knows what will happen? If we survive Russia, you'll go back to work, and I'll be travelling to find Tabby. Nothing's going to be easy."

He took a step towards me, then another. I moved away, but he kept coming until my back hit a tree and I couldn't go any further, and even then he didn't stop. When he dipped his head and touched his lips to mine, I didn't know whether to push him away or wrap my arms and legs around him. In the end, my body settled for a middle ground and simply kissed him back as flames roared in my belly, sparked into life by his mere touch. Sam's kisses had always been my own personal crack, and this one was no different. His tongue swept along my lips, inviting itself in, and by the time he'd finished I was ready to rip his clothes off. I pushed my hands behind me to stop myself from doing just that.

"Love conquers all," he whispered, stroking my hair back from my forehead then cupping my cheek in his palm. "Just something to think about."

Think. *Think*. What was that again?

Sam pushed back, and his smirk told me he knew what he'd done. That he knew I needed to change my underwear.

But this time when he held out his hand, I took it.

CHAPTER 32

WITH NO REAL need for silence tonight, I let my feet crunch along the detritus of twigs and leaves as I walked alongside Sam to the trucks. It felt like our relationship, such that it was, was balanced on a pinhead, with one wrong move on my part set to doom it to failure. Sam still cared about me, he'd said as much, and I'd never stop caring about him, but the prospect of a long-term future still seemed too good to be true.

There were so many barriers in front of us—the hunt for Tabby, which was bound to be filled with frustrations; the fact that we barely knew each other; and his job. What would the CIA do if they found out he was dating a Russian spy? I'd assassinated a US congressman, for fuck's sake. Emmy and the rest of Team Blackwood might not mind my heritage, but I couldn't see the folks at the Pentagon being quite so forgiving.

And that was if we both made it back from Base 13 alive.

But Sam made me happy. He'd kept my nightmares at bay and made me look forward to tomorrow for the first time in my life. Could I pass up the chance to feel that again?

Runaway thoughts threatened to overwhelm me if I

didn't get them under control. Enough. The decision would have to wait until I returned home. If I returned home.

Home.

Yes, Virginia felt like home already, not because of the place, but because of the people. I may have spent the past decade at Base 13, but I'd rather die than live there again.

"You okay?" Sam asked just before we reached the three crew cab pickups parked on a rutted track.

"Give me nine days, and I hope I will be."

Up ahead, Emmy's dulcet tones carried along on the breeze. "I'm driving."

Black held the keys up out of her reach. "You can sit in the back with Seven."

She looked over at Sam and me, and her gaze dropped to our joined hands. "Nice try. Sam's sitting next to Seven."

Black bent to whisper in her ear, and she smiled. "Okay, you can drive."

I didn't hear what was said, but from the way his hand cupped her ass, I suspected certain favours were involved.

And that left me even more frustrated.

Sam opened the back door for me, and although I could have done that myself, his unexpected chivalry felt kind of...nice. And I hadn't had a whole lot of nice lately.

"How's Evan?" I asked Emmy.

"Kira shot him full of morphine, and she's taking him back to Riverley to change before they go to the hospital. Hopping into the ER dressed like a ninja might invite questions we don't want to answer."

"Kira?"

"Dr. Stanton."

Sam helped to stow the kit in the back of the truck, then climbed in the other side and slid his hand under the parachute on my lap to hold mine. I leaned into him and lay my head on his shoulder as Black started the engine. Warm fingers rested on my inner thigh, Sam's thumb stroking over my knuckles. "Higher," my inner harlot whispered. I knew what he could do with those fingers.

"So," Black said. "Evan's out. We need a replacement."

We did, and the thought of dropping somebody into the team at this late stage didn't fill me with joy.

"Jack?" Emmy suggested. "He came to Colombia with us last year and did a damn good job."

"Not Jack. His sister's going through an IVF cycle, and his head won't be in the game. You know how close they are. Cade?"

"Not ready. Give him a year, and my answer might be different if he doesn't let those problems with his family get to him. Ryan?"

"Ryan's a possibility. Young, though."

"Still older than both of us when we started."

"How did he do in Pakistan?" Black asked.

"Not bad at all. Kept his cool under fire, but that was a hostage rescue rather than out-and-out war. Do you think he's ready?"

"It's never easy to tell, but I think it's time for him to sink or swim. What did I say to you the first time we went on a job like this?"

Emmy took a long inhale. I knew she was remembering, and it wasn't good. "The arms dealer."

Her voice sounded robotic. "You said one of us would end up dead, and if it was me rather than him, I wasn't good enough for this game."

Zacharov had said the same to me on many occasions, and I'd hated him for it. But every time I came back, every time I walked through hell and came out on the other side, I'd felt invincible, and that feeling had become my drug of choice until I met Sam.

"And yet here you are," Black said to Emmy. "Ryan's the same. This job will make him or break him, and it's up to him whether he wants to take that step."

"You'll talk to him?"

"Tomorrow. Who else is there?"

"Ronan. Maybe. He's good with a gun, but not so versatile."

"Let's sleep on it," Black said after a few moments' thought.

"You promised I wouldn't be doing much sleeping."

Sam chuckled, and his shoulder twitched under my chin. "Don't forget you've got passengers."

Black tapped his fingers on the steering wheel as he drove, no doubt planning his next move. From what I'd seen of him, he was always objective, and cold to the point of freezing. The mask he wore slipped occasionally when he was around Emmy, but most of the time I couldn't tell what he was thinking. Back in Russia, I'd studied psychology as part of Zacharov's training, and both men bore the classic hallmarks of a psychopath. Not the whack job made so popular by the movies, but the clinical signs were there. The risk taking, the manipulation, and the disturbing lack of emotion. Only Black seemed to have a heart lurking under his icy exterior. His love for Emmy surfaced behind the closed doors of Riverley, and she loved him back, no doubt about that.

And when the truck pulled up outside the front door, he stomped on the parking brake, swept her up in his arms, and disappeared into the house. She blew me a kiss as the door closed behind them.

"So," Sam said.

"So."

"About earlier."

The kiss. I could still feel his lips on mine. "Please, don't make this more difficult. There's so much going on, and I need to think."

"Promise me you won't write us off."

"I won't. I do care about you, not just the man you were, but the one you are now." I reached a hand up to his cheek, the stubble rough under my palm. "And you'll make an excellent father. But right now, I can either be Lilith or I can be Zhen, and Zhen isn't going to get our daughter back."

"It sounds like you *are* writing us off."

"Just give me some time, okay?"

He placed his lips softly onto the centre of my forehead. "I'll give you time. I'll wait forever. Three years since Moscow, and my heart never came close to loving another woman like I love you."

I couldn't say it back. I felt it—I thought—but the words stayed stubbornly in the back of my throat. Instead, what came out was, "Don't do this, Sam."

He untwined his fingers from mine and walked up the steps without looking back.

He'd bared his soul to me, and I'd hurt him.

Right then, I wished I was the cold-hearted bitch everyone thought I was, because damned if my heart wasn't burning as well.

CHAPTER 33

"I CAN'T MAKE up my mind whether they were brave or batshit crazy," Jed said to Quinn the next morning as he stacked plates onto a barbell. "According to Seven's altimeter, she pulled her 'chute thirty metres from the ground. Emmy got to thirty-one."

"Twenty-one if you count the tree she landed in."

"I thought her hair looked dodgy."

By nine o'clock, they'd been in the gym for an hour, and there was still no sign of the girls. Quinn wasn't surprised about Emmy's lack of appearance after her comments last night—Black probably kept her up until the early hours—but he was worried he hadn't seen Ana. Was she avoiding him after his comments in the truck? He couldn't blame her if she were. She'd told him she needed time, and he'd blurted out that he loved her. Stupid. Stupid!

But Quinn still felt the need to defend her. "Seven's not crazy. She knew exactly what she was doing."

Okay, maybe a little crazy. But fuck if that wasn't a turn on.

"Says the man who took off after her. Look, I'll be the first to admit she's hot, but she scares the shit out of me."

"She's not that bad. Emmy's worse. Unpredictable."

Jed was already shaking his head. "Nah, Emmy

always treats her friends right. Seven? I saw the mess at the gas station. They killed twelve men between them."

"Yes, between them. It was a team effort."

"According to Matt in the control room, Seven shot the last guy in cold blood, right between the eyes."

"And if I'd been in front of the man who took my daughter, I'd have done the same thing."

Jed grinned as he lay back on the weight bench. "You still really like her, huh?"

Quinn sank onto a leg press machine and stared out of the window across the Riverley estate. The lawn stretched for miles. Some dude probably spent his whole life cutting it. Living in an apartment had its advantages, like the lack of gardening and cheaper heating bills, but what about Tabby? When they found her—and Quinn refused to believe they wouldn't—he'd want to spend time with her, overnight if Ana would let her stay, and kids needed to run around. Should he trade up to a house?

Dammit, he was getting ahead of himself again.

"Yeah, I still like her, okay? But I don't know if she feels the same."

"What makes you say that?"

Fuck. Quinn hated talking about feelings and all that shit, but Ana confused the hell out of him. "I kissed her last night."

"Daring." Jed glanced down. "You've still got your balls attached, right?"

"She's not that scary."

"She is, buddy. What happened? She didn't kiss you back?"

"No, she did."

"Then what's the problem?"

"It was afterwards. We talked, and I told her I still had feelings for her, and she said she needed time."

"Then give her time. Like a millennium or something."

"For fuck's sake, she's not as bad as you think. Anyway, it's a bit late for that. I might have told her I was still in love with her."

The barbell wobbled in Jed's hands, and Quinn leapt up to steady it before he dropped it on his neck.

"You did what?" Jed spluttered.

"You heard. Don't judge me—it just popped out."

"And what did she say?"

"Not a lot." Quinn sighed and sagged back against the wall. "Told me to drop it."

"Ouch."

"Yeah." Four words, and they'd hurt more than any knife.

"So, now what? You gonna move on?"

He'd spent most of the night awake, thinking about that very question, and come to one conclusion. "Hell, no. Could you move on from Chess?"

Jed's voice softened. "No, never."

"And that's how I feel about Seven. I'll have to give her the time she wants, but no way am I letting her go."

With his workout done, Quinn jumped into the shower then went to look for Ana. He had to keep reminding himself to call her by her new name, or rather, her old name. He couldn't call her Seven like everyone else, not in private, anyway. That woman deserved more than just a number.

The size of the house still made his mind boggle, and it took him fifteen minutes to check the usual places she hung out with Emmy—the shooting range, the kitchen, her bedroom. Nothing. No sign of either of them.

Black walked into Windsor as Quinn was about to leave, and he had Ryan in tow.

"Have either of you seen Seven?" Quinn asked.

Black nodded. "She headed over to the other house with Emmy."

Well, that was taking avoidance to a whole new level. "Do you know when they're coming back?"

"They do their own thing." Quinn went to leave, but Black stopped him. "I need a favour from you."

"What kind of favour?" With Black, he suspected that could mean anything from fetching a cup of coffee to spilling government secrets.

"Ryan'll be joining us in Russia, and we need to get him up to speed. As he didn't make the jump last night, I want him in the air this evening."

Another skydive? Okay, that wasn't too bad. "Just me?"

"No, you, Jed, and Isaiah. I need a team leader, and after watching you in the air last night, you've got the job. Congratulations."

The man didn't even crack a smile, but that was high praise indeed coming from him. Black started to walk off, but this time it was Quinn's turn to stop him.

"How are the girls? After last night, I mean? Are they okay?"

"Of course. Why wouldn't they be?"

"It was a close call."

Black fixed Quinn with a stare, his eyes two dark

pools that had probably swallowed a thousand souls in their time.

"Those two were born to do what they do, and that won't ever change. Never forget that."

Left with Ryan, a chill ran through Quinn as he mulled over Black's words. Was that a threat? The man clearly saw Ana's future as an assassin, another tool he could sharpen and no doubt use to do his bidding, but she was so much more than that. A lover, a mother, a rough diamond who had never been allowed to shine. Everyone else only knew the cool persona she projected to the world, but Quinn saw what she hid inside.

And he needed her to see it too.

CHAPTER 34

"TELL ME AGAIN why we're here?" Emmy asked me, speaking Russian because she needed to get the practice in before we left the States.

By "here" she meant the gym at Little Riverley, the other house she shared with her husband, right next door to the gothic monstrosity.

"Tell me again why you have two houses?"

"Riverley's nice in its own way, but this was the house I always dreamed of. Somewhere without gargoyles. Those ugly little bastards give me the creeps."

Little Riverley was as bright as Riverley was gloomy. White walls, floor-to-ceiling windows, skylights, and a huge glass-roofed pool at the back designed to look like a jungle watering hole as opposed to a simple rectangular lap pool. It even had a waterfall at one end. When Emmy showed me around, I did a double take as a green bird swooped out of a palm tree, chirping angrily at the intrusion.

"Bloody parakeets," she muttered. "Bradley was supposed to have relocated those, but he must have missed one."

"Don't they get messy?"

"Yup. We started out with a pair, which wasn't so bad, but then they started breeding. He didn't think of that when he decided we needed a more tropical atmosphere."

The gym held the same state-of-the-art equipment as Riverley Hall, or Big Riverley as I thought of it, except in here the walls were pale pink, and there was a vase of fresh flowers on the water cooler.

"Bradley again," Emmy said when she caught me looking at it. "Black won't let him get away with that shit over there." She jerked her thumb towards the grey roof just visible over the trees. "And you didn't answer my question—why are we here?"

"Uh..."

"Don't bullshit a bullshitter." She switched to English briefly.

"Fine. I'm avoiding Sam, okay?"

Her eyes narrowed. "What did he do? Did he say something to upset you?"

"Yes. I mean, no. Sort of. He kissed me."

"Isn't that a good thing? It's obvious you still like him."

"I don't know. The timing's all wrong. He's pushing for more than I can offer at the moment, and I need to focus on this job."

Emmy climbed onto a treadmill, and I took the one beside her, increasing the tempo until my arms and legs were pumping. Too fast, really—I couldn't keep that speed up for long—but for a few minutes it felt good to pound my body into oblivion. Neither of us spoke until we were both dripping with sweat.

"I'll get Black to keep Sam busy for the next couple of days," Emmy said. "Okay?"

Guilt ate away at me, but I still agreed. "*Spaseeba.*"

We stayed at Little Riverley that night. Emmy ordered in pizza, Black came over to join us, and we sat in the basement movie theatre and ripped the latest Hollywood action flick to shreds.

"He shot the dude with a .22 and his head exploded. How does that work?" Emmy asked.

"Same way that asshole just fell thirty feet and walked away," Black said.

Emmy curled into Black's side, while I lay out on the other end of the sofa with one foot dangling off the edge. For any other group of friends in America, it would have been a normal Saturday night, but this was the first time since I'd left Sam behind in Moscow that I'd got a chance to relax. And even then, my mind kept drifting to things it shouldn't. In the end, I resorted to a glass of wine. Just one. Just something to take the edge off before I turned into a jittery wreck.

It didn't help much, and after the credits rolled, talk turned back to the mission.

"How are things at Riverley?" Emmy asked.

"Not bad," Black said. "Most of the gear's ready to go, and Nate's been building fucked up shit. No issues came up on the medicals."

"How's Ryan doing?"

"As he should be. Quinn was impressed with him on the jump, and he performed as expected in the kill-house."

Which was better than I'd done. All my fears surfaced again. What if it was me who let the team down? I stayed quiet, saying the bare minimum until the other two decided it was time to call it a night.

Emmy followed me up to my bedroom. Well, my temporary room. I might never sleep in it again.

"What's up?" she asked.

"Nothing."

"What did I say earlier?"

"No bullshit. Yeah, I know."

"Come on, tell me."

I walked over to the window and stared out. The moon was a little bigger today, and in a few days, I'd be looking at that same moon from the other side of the world.

"I'm scared," I whispered.

She wrapped an arm around my shoulders. "We all get nervous."

"No, this is worse." I closed my eyes, trying not to remember but unable to forget. "I fucked up. My last job, I fucked up. I wouldn't be here now if the bodyguard's gun hadn't jammed."

"But you are here. We all have moments like that— look at me and what happened with the fucking floor. Pure, dumb luck, but I'll take it every time. And then I'll laugh in the devil's face and crack open a bottle of champagne, because every time I come home I've won again. And we'll come home next Sunday. Black's a planner, but I believe in something else. Chance, destiny, kismet, fate—call it what you like. It's out there, and I doubt Zacharov's built up many karma points."

"But if the worst does happen? Or something happens to Sam?" I could kid myself that the reason I'd held back last night was conflict with Sam's job, but the truth was, it was all me. If I let him in and the Russia operation went wrong, one of us could get hurt, and that pain would be magnified the closer we got. I'd already lost him once, and it killed me inside.

Or what if I screwed up in Siberia and cost someone else their life? How would Sam get over that? And how would I live with myself?

"Ana, don't. We're ready. Henry Ford once said 'whether you think you can or you think you can't, you're right.' And I don't think we can. I *know* we can."

"I hope you *are* right."

"Like I said before—it's Valkyrie and Lilith. What could go wrong?"

"And I told you. It's Lilith and Valkyrie."

"That's more like it. Night, sister."

The smile popped onto my face of its own accord.

"*Spokoynoy nochi, sestra.*"

The next morning, we spent hours reviewing the latest satellite footage. My talk with Emmy last night helped, and I felt in a better frame of mind. I had to believe we could do this.

After a late breakfast, an acquaintance of Emmy's sent over some recent pictures of Tayshet. Vitaly worked in Blackwood's Moscow office, but he'd lived in Siberia in his teenage years, and three days ago, he'd travelled south to help us when we arrived.

"The trucks always stop to refuel at the same place," he told us over a flaky internet connection. Buffering... Buffering... "A gas station on the edge of town. It sells coffee, and the drivers usually stop off for a few minutes extra to warm up."

Tayshet ran twelve hours ahead of Richmond, and it was already dark outside the window of the apartment Vitaly had rented for the month. Cold by the looks of it too. Even inside, his breath steamed.

"So, we can get in the trucks there? Is it well lit?"

"Maintenance is not a high priority. Half the lights are out."

"Good for us."

"And it is always the same drivers. Six faces so far."

Even better. If the same men went past the checkpoints day in, day out, the soldiers manning them were likely to get complacent. As well as cold, bored, and pissed off, because being on checkpoint duty in the midst of a forest in the Siberian winter was a punishment that would have been banned under the Universal Declaration of Human Rights if Russia had signed up for it.

"Any signs of increased military presence in Tayshet?" Emmy asked.

"There are soldiers carrying out checks at Bratsk airport, and also Irkutsk."

"And the station?"

"Yes. My colleague overheard them talking. They are looking for a woman travelling alone."

Good for us, bad for Zacharov. We left Vitaly to get some sleep while we called up pictures of the trucks, trying to work out the best places to hide. Depending on the cargo, we might be able to get inside, otherwise our best bet was to tuck ourselves up inside the chassis. It promised to be an uncomfortable trip.

Packing came next on the list. Seeing as we were going in as tourists, we could hardly stick a couple of assault rifles in our bags, but that didn't matter. Two pistols each, ammunition, a pair of matching knives, encrypted comms gear, some of Nate's special charges, and enough warm clothes to survive the trip from Tayshet to Base 13—that was all we needed. The rest we could pick up on the way.

Bradley didn't understand the concept of packing light, it seemed. He'd turned one of Emmy's spare rooms into the L.L. Bean store and bought a whole array of camping meals, everything from self-heating meatballs to freeze-dried ice cream.

"It was developed by NASA," he explained as Emmy rolled her eyes.

"Bradley, you know we're flying to Tolmachevo on a private jet? And then we're going by the Trans-Siberian railway, and it's got a buffet car. We only need food for one day, and we can buy something out there."

"But you're walking through a forest. What if you get lost? What if you get stuck for days?"

"I learned how to navigate by the sky fifteen years ago, and I'm sure Seven did too."

I nodded.

But Bradley wasn't giving up. "But if you're in the middle of nowhere, you might get hungry. What will you do without snacks?"

I shrugged. "Light a campfire then shoot a moose. Or maybe a bear."

Bradley's colour dropped a few shades. "I didn't get bear spray. I need to get bear spray."

He rushed out of the room, already pressing his phone to his ear.

"We've got guns. We don't need bloody bear spray," Emmy yelled after him, but her words went unheeded. She turned to me. "Uh, how many bears are there?"

"Not that many. And they rarely eat humans."

"Rarely?"

Only one that I knew of. I remembered that day well. One of Zacharov's henchmen, a particularly sadistic meathead named Bogdan, had taken Four and me on a survival exercise in the taiga, or snow forest, and five days in, we'd had enough. Every time one of us put a foot wrong, Bogdan ceremoniously unbuckled his belt and, well, belted us with it.

That night, I'd removed the ammunition from Bogdan's gun while Four cut up the taimen he'd caught in the river earlier when Bogdan was busy tormenting me. I'd liked Four. I kind of wished I knew what happened to him. Anyway, we'd carefully arranged the fish around Bogdan's tent and waited patiently, just like the general taught us to. Fortunately, in the battle of bear versus Bogdan, there was only ever going to be one winner.

When we'd reported the bastard's sad demise to Zacharov, he'd only tutted.

"Just one death that I've heard of. As long as we've got bullets, we'll be fine."

As Bradley's footsteps faded away, I opened one of the NASA packets and sniffed the weird multicoloured brick inside. Emmy broke off a bit and stuck it in her mouth.

"Well?" I asked.

"Surprisingly edible, but don't tell Bradley I said that." She looked at her watch. "Wherever he's gone, he'd better not take too long. I need my hair done before we go, and you could do with a trim."

Great. Just what I needed—another trip to the hairdresser, even if my ends would look more at home on a scarecrow after the past week's efforts.

A scarecrow.

That reminded me of a day just after my arrival at Base 13, one which had made me realise just how much of a sick bastard Zacharov really was. Two of the conscripts had got bored with guard duty and replaced themselves in the watchtower with a couple of uniforms stuffed with rags. Zacharov shot one and made the other bury his body. Just another day in the life of Russia's number one sadist.

Early afternoon, and Dan came over to give me an update on Tabby. Or rather, to tell me there was no news. Bate still hadn't surfaced, and there were no more whispers of foreign children being traded.

"But we'll keep looking while you're gone," Dan promised, giving me a tight hug. "I'll let you know if there's any news, and Nick's gonna come with me if we need to check any leads out."

I shook my head, much as it pained me to do so. "No, don't tell me. There's nothing I can do from Russia, and I need to stay focused." I managed a half smile. "I trust you to do what's best."

And I did. Because Emmy trusted her, and I trusted Emmy.

Bradley came back an hour later with bear spray, two flare guns, and a Spotter's Guide to wildlife in the taiga of southern Siberia. This time Emmy just smiled and accepted the kit.

"It's getting late, and I don't have time to argue," she said. "We need to get some sleep."

We did. Because although a direct flight from Richmond to Base 13 would take sixteen hours, our more circuitous route would take at least three and half days, by plane, train, car, truck, and finally on foot. Maybe we could even fit in a bicycle somewhere.

Thankfully, Bradley picked up on the urgency and got his kit out. Snip, snip, snip, and an hour and a half later we admired ourselves in the bathroom mirror.

"Not bad," Emmy whispered.

I nodded, feeling my appetite for the job grow with each passing minute. My hair wasn't as short as it used to be, and I had a few fine wrinkles around my eyes, but I looked like Lilith again now. And more importantly, I felt like her.

Zacharov was mine.

CHAPTER 35

LIKE LILITH ALWAYS did, I woke after a few hours of fitful sleep with a movie reel playing through my mind. Blood, death, Zacharov's lifeless eyes staring up at me. And Sam. Sam lying still at my feet with crimson splashes on my shoes. Not what I needed when we were due to leave for Russia at nine the next morning. I tried to force the images from my head, but every time I closed my eyes, they came back.

The clock on the nightstand ticked around another ten minutes, the illuminated hand glowing in the darkness, and I rolled out of bed. Walking used to help me relax. A soft robe hung on the bathroom door, and I slipped it on before stepping out into the corridor. Emmy's room was nearby, unlike in big Riverley where she slept in a different wing, and I paused to listen. Nothing. She had Black in there with her, but it sounded like they'd got their kicks for the night and gone to sleep. Lucky them.

The occasional uplighter staved off the darkness as I roamed the house, thinking not just of death but of causing it. The route to the radar tower, the guards' patrol patterns, the bunkers we needed to get into and clear. My breathing steadied as I walked, not through the carpeted halls of Little Riverley, but the snow-covered ground of Base 13, with one goal on my mind.

Get him before he got me.

Not Sam. I absolutely didn't think of Sam. Not his soft voice. Not his panty-dropping smile. Not the way his lips whispered up my skin and set mine on fire when he got me naked in his bed. Fuck it.

Chirping made me look up, and the angry eyes of a parakeet glowed back at me, staring down from a tree.

"Sorry, *priatel'*."

He squawked again, and I had the vague idea that if I'd had my pistol, he'd have made an excellent target. *No shooting until Friday, Lilith.* Trigger finger twitching, I gave in to the lure of the water beside me instead and stuck a toe in. How long since I'd been swimming? Years. I'd gone with Sam in Moscow once, only we'd done more splashing than actual exercise. Oh, what the hell? I dropped the robe and tiptoed down the steps, making only the barest ripple as I submerged myself.

Then I swam, emptying my mind as I concentrated on my stroke, strong arms, straight legs, flip and turn at the end. Back and forth until I began to relax enough to contemplate sleep again.

"Ana?"

Oh, shit. I paused mid-stroke, and my head sank beneath the surface. Maybe I could just stay down here, safe from the charms of the man who made me lose my whole damn fucking mind? A minute passed, maybe two, but I could still see his silhouette up there, outlined against the grey sky. Strong jaw, muscular arms, nice bulge at the— *Stop it!*

I blew out one last stream of bubbles and stood, toes bouncing on the bottom of Emmy's mock-jungle pool.

"Sam, how did you get in?"

"Jed has the access codes."

"What are you doing here?"

"I wanted to speak to you." Hurt tinged his voice. "You were planning to leave without saying goodbye, weren't you?"

"It's better that way."

"How? How is it better?"

I stayed in the middle of the pool where it was safe. "Because I need to concentrate on my job. No complications, no distractions. And you, Sam, are the biggest distraction of all."

My eyes dropped below his waist as I said that, and my stomach clenched as I remembered just how big of a distraction he was.

"Ah, so if you run away to a different house, you'll forget all about me?"

"Something like that," I muttered.

"And how's that working out for you?"

Shit, he sounded angry now.

"Okay."

"Okay? So that's why you're swimming alone at midnight rather than sleeping?"

"Fine, I was thinking about you. Happy now?"

"Totally."

Eyes glittering in the moonlight, he pulled his shirt over his head, and my breath caught. He'd still been working out. I knew he had, so why did those smooth pecs and tight abs cause a gasp of surprise? Which he heard and smirked at. Asshole.

"What are you doing, Sam?"

His hands went to his belt buckle. "I'm distracted too."

I got halfway to the steps before I remembered I was naked and hesitated. Running naked from the swimming pool probably wouldn't be my best move, especially with the way my traitorous nipples had perked up at the sight of Sam's smooth chest.

That hesitation cost me. The splash from behind was followed seconds later by Sam's breath on my ear and one rough palm splayed out across my stomach.

"We can't," I tried one last time.

"Why not?"

With Sam so damn close, all the reasons I'd discussed with Emmy suddenly didn't seem to matter so much anymore. No matter how much I tried to push him out, Sam still dominated my every thought, so why not give in to the temptation and avail myself of his talents? After all, the pulse between my thighs told me I couldn't get much more *distracted* than I already was.

Hot lips fluttered over my shoulder. "A reason, Ana. Give me one good reason to stop, and I will."

My silence gave him the answer he needed. That and the way my head tilted to the side to give him better access to my neck. One hand came up to cup a breast, and the other slid lower and pressed right where I needed it.

"I've missed the taste of you," he murmured, pressing his body against me. He'd taken everything off, and his hard cock pressed against my ass, nestling between my cheeks. Fuck, I'd missed him too.

I tried to turn in his arms, but I ended up spluttering as I slipped beneath the water. Sam laughed as he towed me over to the side, one arm across my chest as he kicked with his feet. I flipped over, and with full access, I gripped the edge of the pool as I wrapped my legs around him and kissed him with all the frustration and hurt and lust and pain and love and longing I'd been storing up for the last three years. His nails raked my back, and I arched into him, offering up my breasts. It only took a second for him to dip his head and suck on a nipple, and the flash of heat that ran downwards made me moan. My other pebbled tip got the same treatment, and I dropped my hands to grip his ass and pull him tighter to where I wanted, no, needed him.

"Patience, you dirty little bitch. Can't you see I'm enjoying myself here?"

I should have slapped him for his filthy mouth, but damned if that didn't kindle the fire inside me a little more. And two could play that game. "Enough with the playing. Just fuck me."

He moved maddeningly slowly, one finger slowly stroking. "Not yet. I'm gonna tease this sweet cunt for a while first."

"You're the most irritating man I've ever met."

"You haven't seen anything yet, *moya malen'kaya gryaznaya suka.*"

"*Nechisto sobaka.*" Filthy dog.

He plunged one finger inside me, stroking in the magic spot. Then another, stretching me. Gone was the gentle Sam who I'd spent all that time with in Moscow. New Sam was an animal with a crude mouth and fingers that took what he wanted. And new Sam made my insides blaze. I wasn't sure, but I might actually have preferred that version of him.

But I still wasn't about to let him have everything his own way. I raised my arms and slithered under the water, fastening my lips around my favourite part of his anatomy. His abs went rigid as I sucked, swirling my tongue around the tip until the need for air forced me to the surface.

"Okay, I give in. Open your damn legs, woman."

I'd got one leg wrapped around his waist when he closed his eyes and cursed. "The fucking condom's in my pants pocket."

"Dr. Stanton gave me a contraceptive shot." I grinned. "Standard procedure, apparently."

I didn't need to say the words twice. Sam's cock nudged inside me before he thrust his hips and seated himself to the hilt. Back where he belonged.

Tonight, neither of us wanted sweet and steady. Sam's hips pounded against me, taking us both higher, higher, until I detonated around him. He came a second later, breathing hard as he buried his face in the crook of my neck.

"Think you took a chunk out of my shoulder with your teeth, *suka*," he said.

"Sorry."

"I'm not. Fuck, you're hot."

I smiled into the darkness. "Only for you, *sobaka*."

He slid out of me, and we floated on our backs, holding hands under the palm trees and the stars. And that damn parakeet.

My eyes were half closed when he said those three words.

"I love you."

And this time, I could finally say them back. "*Ya lyublyu tebya.*"

Sam deferred to my need for sleep and carried me upstairs, bundled in my robe. There was no question of him going back to Riverley tonight, and I curled into his side, one leg draped over his thighs as he stroked my damp hair.

"My beautiful Ana. I may not be coming to Russia in the morning, but I'll always be with you. I promise you that."

A tear threatened to escape, and I blinked it back as I placed my hand over his heart. "In here."

"Always."

He went to mirror the gesture, but his hand crept higher.

"Sam, stop being such a man."

"These are bigger than I remember," he murmured, trailing a finger over my breasts.

"After Tabby, they never quite went back to their old size."

He flipped me onto my back and kissed his way across my stomach, flat again now. Apart from a few stretch marks, faded to a pale silver, you couldn't tell I'd once carried a child.

"We'll find her," Sam said, smiling against my belly button. "That kid's gonna be a demon with two parents like us."

I ran my fingers through his thick hair. "Yes, she is."

"Now, we sleep." He gathered me up in his arms, tightly, so our hearts beat as one. "We've got one hell of a week coming up."

Hell was right. And I'd walk through it, flip the devil off, and fight my fucking way out to get back to Sam. Because I wasn't losing him again.

CHAPTER 36

QUINN STROKED ANA'S hair as she stirred against his chest. She always used to sleep like that, close, curled into his side or draped across him, and after he'd left Moscow, he never thought he'd see that beautiful sight again. He'd been watching in the dim glow from the lamp on the bedside table, just watching for half an hour, unwilling to wake her because he didn't want her flying to Russia tired.

But now she'd opened her eyes, he couldn't resist sliding her up his body so their lips met.

"Morning." He couldn't bring himself to say "Good morning" because having to say goodbye to her meant it was anything but.

"Hey."

It looked like the lioness from last night had turned into quite the pussy cat this morning. Or maybe...just the pussy. He slipped a hand under the quilt, his fingers homing in on the magic spot.

Except Ana stopped him. "Please, don't."

Quinn held back a sigh. Not this again. "I thought after last night we'd got over your reservations?" He pressed a soft kiss to her temple. "I promise I'll only distract you for a few minutes, and we don't have to do anything more. Let me give you this."

"It's not that."

She blushed, which wasn't something she did often. "What is it?"

"It wasn't so bad in the pool, but..."

"Tell me."

"I haven't done much housekeeping down there, okay? It's been kind of low on my list of priorities."

Quinn burst out laughing. "Fuck, beautiful, you think I care about that?" He lifted the covers and squinted. "I mean, as long as I remember a map so my cock can find its way out."

She shoved him in the chest and sat up, but he held onto her hips so she didn't get far. And with her in that position, his morning wood was more of a tree trunk, even if he said so himself.

"Sure I can't tempt you?" he asked.

Ana smiled, more to herself than him, it seemed, and lifted enough for him to disappear inside her. The way his cock slid in so easily, he knew exactly what she'd been dreaming about. The same thing as him.

A curtain of black hair tickled his chest as she leaned forward to kiss him, slowing her movements to a gentle rock. Neither of them spoke. What was there to say? Quinn didn't want to speak about the past, and he didn't want to think about the future. All he wanted to do was feel, in the here and now.

He stroked his hands up Ana's thighs, noticing how she'd put on muscle since Moscow, and ran his hands up her stomach, taut and toned. Not thin but strong. Beautiful. Perfect.

Ana rose and fell in time to her own thoughts, setting a rhythm that worked for both of them as she gave and took at the same time. By the time Quinn's balls began to tighten, her cheeks were flushed, and he burned that image into his mind.

There was no scream, just a quiet gasp as her muscles tightened around him, and Quinn followed her into an oblivion where the only other thing that existed was the woman he loved.

"*Ya lyublyu tebya*," she said softly.

"I love you too, Anastasia."

Breakfast was a sombre affair, at least for Quinn and Ana. Emmy and Black seemed unaffected, but Quinn figured they'd been through this plenty of times before. Did it really get easier?

Ana was still picking at her toast when Nate arrived with a bag of equipment, and Quinn watched with interest as Nate drew out two chunky laptops and laid them on the table.

"One each," Nate said.

"Bagsy the Toshiba," Emmy said.

"You realise you can't use it for more than checking your email, right? I had to take most of the insides out to make room for the charges."

Charges? Quinn resisted the urge to shuffle towards the door.

"Small, but they'll pack enough punch to take out the radar tower."

"How do we access them?"

"Like this." He flipped the Toshiba over and unclipped the battery. "They just slide out. You've got two options to detonate them—the remote, or a thirty-second timer."

"Fun. What else have we got?"

"Comms gear, although in your case I don't expect that to last for long. Video and audio. A DSLR camera for Ana. Trackers for your boots." He placed a watch on the table in front of Ana, and a belt in front of Emmy. "A few toys. Set the alarm on the watch for three minutes past noon, and you've got twenty seconds before it goes boom. Fire this hook from the side of the belt buckle, and you've got ten metres of wire that'll hold your weight."

"Somebody's been watching too much James Bond. Do we get Aston Martins as well?"

"You've already got an Aston Martin. Ask me nicely and I might build some modifications into it."

"Pretty please?"

Nate rolled his eyes. "I'll work something out. Besides, you need to thank Marvin for the belt."

"Your new assistant?"

"He's working out quite well."

Quinn's guts churned as Emmy and Ana finished packing their bags. More than anything, he wanted to carry her back upstairs and say fuck Russia, fuck Zacharov, and most importantly, fuck Ana.

But he couldn't. He knew she needed to do this, and trying to convince her otherwise would lead to the demise of their fledgling relationship and worse. Because Tabby was still missing.

Ana strapped on her new watch and glanced at the dial. "Not bad. It even tells the time."

Emmy peered over. "And it's seven o'clock. We need to get going."

Together, they walked over to Riverley for one final briefing with the whole team. Eleven men, three women, and one hope to remove a madman from the face of the earth.

"Timing is key," Black reminded them. "Thanks to Markovich calling in a favour, we'll be flying into Mongolia while Emmy and Seven are still on the train, and then we wait. As soon as we get word from them, we'll take off for Base 13, and we need to drop in as soon as possible after they hit the radar tower. The longer they're out there by themselves, the more risk there is of failure. Fourteen against three hundred gives us a good chance. Two? More difficult."

A glance across at those two showed they both wore the same hardened look. Determination, and the confidence they needed to get the job done.

Quinn rode in the back of Black's Porsche SUV with Ana as the big man drove them to Silver Springs airfield. They'd be taking his jet to London before they swapped onto a different plane for their final flight to Novosibirsk Tolmachevo airport.

He wished she'd sat close, pressed against him like she had been in bed this morning, but instead, she gripped his hand from across the empty seat between them while she stared blankly out of the window.

"You okay?" he whispered when the car pulled up next to the aircraft hangar.

She nodded stiffly, just once, then climbed out of the car.

Emmy hefted her bags out of the trunk, Black bent to kiss her on the cheek, and she walked towards the steps lowered from the side of the jet without a backwards glance.

That was it?

Black must have read his mind. "We already said our goodbyes earlier. This works better for us."

But it was new ground for him and Ana. He couldn't wave off the love of his life, one he thought he'd lost and only just found again, off into danger with the kind of gesture he normally offered his grandmother.

Black got back into the car, allowing them some space, and Quinn picked up Ana's two bags, a rucksack and a duffle, and passed them over.

"I'll miss you," he said.

Three little words. Three totally inadequate little words.

She gave him the crooked smile he adored so much, the one he'd never seen her use for anyone else. "I'll see you in a week."

"I'll have your back. I promise."

Their kiss crossed the middle ground between the fiery passion of last night's adventures in the pool and this morning's dawn sweetness. Deep and passionate, it left a hole in Quinn's chest that could never be filled until Ana was back in his arms.

Then she too climbed up the steps without looking back.

Black didn't drive off straight away, and for that Quinn was grateful. They sat, watching, until the jet rose gracefully into the sky, carrying Quinn's heart and no doubt a piece of Black's as well. Despite the man's tough reputation, it was clear he loved his wife.

Quinn snuck a look at his phone and the photo he'd taken of him and Ana while she was still asleep. His lioness. After she'd dumped him, he'd deleted all the other pictures of them together in a fit of anger, and the few he'd printed out had burned with his apartment. Today, their relationship boiled down to the precious moment he'd captured that morning. He needed more of those, and he'd do anything to get them.

Only once the plane had disappeared into the clouds did Black start the engine for the trip back to Riverley, and Quinn forced his thoughts onto the upcoming mission. Ana would do her job; he knew that. Now he needed to perform as well.

CHAPTER 37

I COULDN'T LOOK back at Sam as I walked up the steps to the plane, because otherwise I might have been tempted not to go. Having to leave behind the man I once thought I'd never see again made this trip all the more painful. We'd been given a second chance, but would we get a third that would see us both return to American soil still breathing?

Emmy was already strapped into her seat, looking out of the window that faced away from Black's car. Guess she felt the same way.

Today, we were in the larger of Black's two planes, a Bombardier Global 8000 done out in black and grey, which gave us a bedroom as well as a bathroom and a comfortable cabin. After takeoff, Emmy unbuckled her seatbelt and stretched.

"We should get some sleep. I don't know about you, but I didn't get as much as I should have last night," she said.

"A few extra hours would have been nice, but at least the nightmares stayed away." As they always did when Sam was near.

"Things happened with Sam? When I saw him at breakfast this morning, I figured you'd given in and got some."

A grin crept onto my face. "He came over last

night."

"Came over what? You, I take it?"

"Your swimming pool, if you must know."

Emmy roared with laughter. "Nice move, Quinn." She covered my hand with hers. "But seriously, I'm glad things are working out between you."

"I just hope—"

"Don't. Don't be so bloody negative." She got to her feet. "Are you sharing the bed or staying here?"

"What about your nightmares?"

"I'll be fine from here out. They always vanish on jobs. It's like my brain has some sort of override switch built in. See? War does have its advantages."

"I'd still rather be at home baking cookies or something."

"Can you bake cookies?"

"I don't know. I've never tried. But if I can build an IED out of household items, it stands to reason I should be able to follow a simple recipe."

Emmy shook her head. "It doesn't work that way. I still can't make an edible meal to save my life."

"Good thing the general isn't holding a cookery contest then, isn't it?"

"Tell me more about Boris," I said to Emmy as we climbed down to the tarmac at London's Luton airport.

She paused to salute Brett before he went back into the cockpit then wrinkled her nose.

"Boris is an acquired taste."

The Boris in question was Boris Filippov, a Russian oligarch who owed Black a favour. We'd be joining

Boris on his plane to fly into Novosibirsk Tolmachevo, where he had enough investments that his presence wouldn't raise any eyebrows.

"In what way?"

"You'll see."

She jerked her head at the red-faced man emerging from a Rolls Royce fifty metres away. His rounded belly suggested a love of rich foods, although the three blondes who followed him out of the car didn't seem to mind.

He spotted Emmy and waved, his jowls wobbling as he grinned, and when she reached him, he embraced her in a squashy hug then opened his arms to do the same to me. Pressed into his mounds of excess flesh, I tried not to suffocate.

"My dear Emerson. Such a long time since I have seen you. Who is your friend?"

"Andie." At least that's what one of my new passports said. "And she's off limits too."

"Such a shame." He looked me up and down in a way that made my skin crawl. "No matter, I have the triplets."

Up close, they looked like Bratz dolls, all big eyes and long legs. Zacharov had bought one of those for Tabby once, but she'd never been keen on it. She'd preferred her cuddly animals, and having spent my life swimming among the bottom feeders of humanity, I couldn't blame her.

Emmy rolled her eyes as we followed them onto Boris's jet, and mine widened as we reached the cabin. She'd said Boris was an acquired taste; I said he was proof money didn't buy any.

While Black's planes were done out with

understated opulence, Boris hadn't held back from flaunting his money. There was so much gold, I needed sunglasses. And really, zebra print cushions?

Doll number one popped the cork on a bottle of champagne the moment we were airborne, while her two sisters draped themselves around Boris in the manner to which he was clearly accustomed.

"Drink?" she asked as bubbles spilled over the top.

Emmy shook her head. "Just water, thanks."

Boris guffawed. "You need to relax and enjoy the finer things in life."

"Like a foursome?"

"I'd be happy to oblige."

"Looks as if you've got your hands full already."

"With these three? No, my wife is more demanding than all of them." He laughed again then swivelled noisily in his chair to face me. I wasn't sure whether he'd passed wind, or whether the trump was due to his ass squeaking on the leather. Either way, he didn't care. "So, you are a photographer?"

"That's right."

"You should be on the other side of the lens. But Russia is blessed that you've chosen our country to be the subject of your art."

"I understand there's some beautiful scenery." Today, I was American, and allegedly a first-time visitor to the country of my birth.

"Indeed. Very beautiful. And if you get tired of looking at forests and snow, Emerson has my number. I can show you both some other aspects of our magnificent country."

Emmy chuckled. "You don't give up, do you?"

"Can you blame a man for trying?"

Yes, especially when he was already married, but I bit my tongue. Being rude to our host wouldn't be a sensible move, even if he was an asshole.

Thankfully, doll number one found vodka and caviar, and the four of them retired to the bedroom at the back of the plane for the rest of the trip. What did Boris plan to do? Lick it out of their belly buttons? Personally, I'd never understood the attraction of caviar. Zacharov ate it regularly, always beluga, so I figured it was more of a power play than anything else. *Look at me; I'm rich enough to afford salty fish eggs.*

The closer the plane got to Russia, the hotter the blood in my veins boiled. I'd made the journey back to my motherland many times before, and for the past three years, it had been with a sense of relief and anticipation. Relief that I'd survived another job, and anticipation that I'd see Tabby soon. But on this day, more than two weeks since I'd last seen my daughter, I felt only anger and a burning need to get the damn job finished.

And Zacharov. I wanted to finish him too, but first I needed to convince him to tell me where Tabby was, and by convince, I meant force. By whatever means necessary. He'd spent years teaching me how to extract information from unwilling enemies, so I hoped he'd appreciate the irony that he was about to become my next subject.

As the jet descended, Boris wandered out of the bedroom, shirt untucked, followed by his trio of admirers. I noticed one of them was wearing a new diamond bracelet. Guess she sucked the hardest.

"Are you sure you girls don't want to stay at my dacha overnight?"

"Just a lift to the train station will be fine. We've already booked tickets," Emmy said.

"My car will pick us up at the plane. My assistant tells me they've implemented new security checks in the terminal recently." He tutted. "Such inconvenience."

For us? Another security threat? Or merely a bureaucratic exercise?

"But no matter," he continued. "There is always an official who will help to bypass these things for a few roubles."

Welcome to Russia.

"Thanks, Boris." Emmy gave him a smile. "And as always, we'll return the favour when you come to the US."

The Trans-Siberian Railway, just one part of the massive Russian railway network, connected Europe to the Far East. It was possible to get on a train in London or Paris and travel all the way to China, Mongolia, or even Southeast Asia. We'd only be travelling a small portion of the route, from Novosibirsk to Tayshet, a journey of some fifteen hundred kilometres.

Many trains travelled the route, some domestic, some international, and because the timetable had been kind to us, we'd opted to journey east on train number four, the Trans-Mongolian Express. It was Chinese operated rather than Russian and the most popular with tourists.

Zacharov would have watchers at the stations, maybe even on the train, but our hope was that he'd be concentrating his efforts on the closer airports. After all, I didn't have time to spare. And with the Trans-Siberian being a service where every passenger had their own sleeping berth, anyone looking for me couldn't simply wander the carriages with a photo.

Boris dropped us off outside the station, and his driver helped us to get our bags from the trunk. While Boris was occupied with the dolls on the plane, we'd dressed more appropriately for the weather in warm boots, hats, and puffy down jackets that hid the guns securely stowed in our shoulder holsters. That meant we only had one bag left each, and we slung them over our shoulders as we headed to catch our train.

"Three o'clock, by the kiosk," Emmy whispered, and I looked in the other direction.

"What's he doing?" I asked.

"Not a lot. Looks bored."

As we already had our tickets, plus a backup pair for the Russian Rossiya service in case we'd encountered any delays, we headed straight for the platform. Money was no object, so we'd booked a two-berth deluxe soft sleeper, which meant we got a bigger cabin to ourselves as well as an en-suite bathroom. After we boarded, I dumped my bag on the lower bunk and dropped into the armchair by the corner.

"A third of the way there." And things had been worryingly smooth so far, Boris's sexual habits notwithstanding.

Emmy checked her watch. "Almost five. We should get some food and catch a few more hours' sleep."

"Agreed."

While Emmy went to the restaurant car, I got my camera out and snapped pictures of the view from the train as it pulled out of the station, all the better to fit with my cover story. Soon, we'd be travelling through snowy vistas, and in an hour it would be dark.

My stomach grumbled as Emmy came back through the door with a tray. From the smell of it, some kind of stew was lurking under the foil that covered the dishes.

"They were okay with you bringing food back to the cabin?"

"I just said you weren't feeling well. Reckon Zacharov's got a man stationed by the buffet, though. Guy on his own, eyes everywhere, uptight."

"Sounds like a possibility."

"I stopped for a chat, and he said he was a soldier on leave, travelling to Vladivostok to see his family, but I didn't buy it."

"Did he seem suspicious of you?"

"He eyed me up a couple of times, but he relaxed when I stopped to talk. Even asked me if I wanted to join him for breakfast."

"Because he thought you would make good cover for him?"

"Nah, I think he was just flirting."

I was right about the stew—borscht, a thick soup with beef and beets. Not my favourite, but it was hot and filling. I'd just finished my last mouthful when a knock came at the door. Emmy looked at me, and we both raised our eyebrows. Without speaking, we both got up, and I moved to the front of the cabin behind Emmy so whoever lurked behind the net curtain covering the glass pane in the door would see one person rather than two.

"I think it's Zacharov's man," she whispered.

Fuck. Had he seen through our plan? There was

only one way to find out.

Open the door.

CHAPTER 38

"READY?" EMMY MOUTHED.

The length of paracord I always kept in my pocket now stretched taut between my hands. I nodded, stepped back into the bathroom, and pushed the door closed, leaving just a tiny gap to see through.

"Hi," Emmy said as she cracked the cabin door open. "Oh... Rolan, right? Did I drop something when I was getting dinner?"

My fists tightened around the cord, ready to loop it around his neck if the need arose. A quick glance at the window told me it would slide down far enough to drop the body out. It was dark. Nobody would notice.

"No, no. I was looking for an acquaintance. I must have got the wrong cabin. How is your friend?"

"Oh, she ate dinner, then bleurgh." Emmy mimed throwing up and pointed at the bathroom. "It isn't pretty." She opened the door wider. "But if you want to come in while you call your acquaintance...?"

"Thank you, but I will carry on looking."

I relaxed a little as Emmy stood near the door, listening as Rolan moved up the corridor. Except his name wasn't Rolan. I recognised him from Base 13, and he was called Vova, Volya, something like that.

"He's trying the same trick at the next cabin," Emmy whispered.

But it didn't matter anymore. He'd missed me.

And he'd live.

Emmy called Black on her secure phone to check all was well, and he confirmed they were on track to leave for Mongolia in a few hours. I thought about speaking to Sam, but I didn't want to stir up emotions that would cloud my thoughts or his. My mind was busy enough already and his would be too.

We took it in turns to sleep, three hours on, three hours off, until the train pulled into Tayshet. While the town was small, the station was the starting point for the Baikal-Amur mainline which branched off to the north east, and people milled around everywhere as we climbed from the train.

"Head down, eight o'clock," Emmy muttered. "Two of them... Okay, they're looking elsewhere now."

As promised, Vitaly was waiting at the front of the station, leaning against the front of an old Lada that had more rust than paint. He raised his hand in greeting as we walked towards him.

Emmy narrowed her eyes. "When I said we needed to get where we're going without standing out, I should have put more emphasis on the 'get where we're going' part."

"Are you insulting my car? She's a tough old girl." He patted the hood and one side of the fender fell off. Without missing a beat, he reattached it with a zip tie and opened the back door. "Your chariot awaits."

The engine caught on the second try, and soon we were puttering along the road.

"How are things looking?" Emmy asked.

"The military presence has definitely picked up over the past couple of days, but so far they haven't gone door-to-door."

"We'll only be here until the early morning, and they can't cover the whole town in that time, anyway."

I couldn't help smiling. "And if he's sending men out to look for me, there will be less at the base."

"Let's hope so."

Vitaly pulled up at the back of a run-down apartment building, distinguished from its neighbours by the burnt-out car outside.

"Nice place you've got here," Emmy remarked.

"It's cheap, and more importantly nobody asks questions. I've got the kit you asked for, by the way. Cost me a few roubles on the black market, but I thought you'd rather keep the purchases away from legitimate channels."

"You thought right."

Inside, we slipped our shoes off and gathered in the tiny lounge, where we tried the survival suits on for size and re-packed our bags without all the surplus crap we'd added as cover. If anyone found us on our journey tomorrow, there really wouldn't be a convincing way to explain why we were hitching a lift on a truck to the middle of nowhere, so we might as well just shoot whoever was asking. And Vitaly had come up with plenty of ammunition, too much for us to carry, so we picked what we wanted and left him the rest.

Oh, and I had two nice, sharp knives because in line with Zacharov's training, I was prepared to skin him from face to fucking foot if he refused to tell me where my daughter was.

While we packed, Vitaly worked away on his computer. "The rest of the team are in the air. No problems."

"Any movement at Base 13?" I asked.

"Satellite photos show nothing significant."

Then it was time for our last supper and sleep. Vitaly took the sofa while we got the double bed, and I lay awake listening to the sounds of Tayshet. Only twenty-four hours to go. This time tomorrow, we'd be at Base 13, and then our real test would come.

The alarm went off at four, and I showered first. Emmy bitched like hell when the water ran cold before she'd rinsed her hair, and her delightful mood continued as we headed for the breakfast table.

"Fuck this shit. Fuck that bastard and the tank he rode in on. It's too bloody early."

"Bad night?"

"I need coffee. I haven't had coffee for two days now."

Vitaly rose silently and went to the kettle. "I only have instant."

"That'll do," I told him. "Unless you've got a first-aid kit? We could give it to her by IV."

A mug sufficed. Well, two, and by the time we were ready to leave half an hour later, Emmy was almost human again.

"Sorry," she said. "I don't do well without caffeine. The withdrawal symptoms make me want to shoot someone."

"Perhaps you shouldn't have drunk any?"

"Don't worry. I can still shoot people without it. Caffeine just means I'm smiling while I pull the trigger."

Outside, the Lada coughed to life once more on an otherwise silent street, and it was time for the third and shortest part of our journey—the trip to the gas station where the trucks refuelled before making their long journey north. That, the fourth leg, promised to be the least comfortable. Ever tried peeing when you're wearing an all-in-one survival suit? Well, let me tell you it's not fun.

Vitaly dropped us off a little way up the road from our destination, the last tendrils of night lightened by a white sky as it tried to snow.

"Good luck," he said as we strapped on our bags. Each weighed ten or so kilos, the lightest we could make them and still take everything we needed.

"Thanks." Emmy waved as she melted into the surrounding forest, and I did the same.

Then we were on our own.

One hour passed, then two, then three, and I squashed against Emmy so we could share body heat.

"Where are these bloody trucks?" she whispered. "They come like clockwork every day, and now they're late?"

"Probably the snow."

Yes, the weather gods were smiling down on us. Sure, it was freezing, but the flurries dancing in the wind would obscure us nicely as we ran from our hiding place to the truck, when one finally got there. *For fuck's sake, hurry up.*

And then it arrived, our rattling saviour, an open-backed truck stacked with boxes and stinking of diesel fumes. I recognised both the driver and the vehicle from Vitaly's surveillance photos.

Emmy grinned at me. "After you."

She was my sister and my mirror image now she'd shed her blonde wig. Zacharov was expecting me, but now he was getting a double helping of his favourite assassin. Bradley had done a good job of colouring Emmy's hair.

By the time the driver finished his coffee and rumbled off up the road, he had two extra passengers, hidden behind crates of bread and vegetables bound for the kitchen at the oil terminal.

I sat back as the lights of Tayshet grew fainter behind us. The final stage of our journey had begun.

CHAPTER 39

A FLASHLIGHT BEAM played over the inside of the truck at the first checkpoint, and I kept my gun in front of me, ready to fire if the owner got the urge to investigate the contents more thoroughly. Beside me, Emmy looked relaxed as her finger covered the trigger of her Walther.

"Cigarette, *tovarisch*?" the driver asked.

"*Da*." The light disappeared. "*Spaseeba*."

"Your boss still insisting on extra security?"

"Yes. But we never find anything. What crazy person would travel out to the base by choice?"

Ah, so Zacharov had pulled his usual trick of withholding information. He liked to trickle it out, piece-by-piece, relying on orders instead of understanding to get the job done. So the soldier knew he was looking for something, but he didn't know it was me.

The faint whiff of tobacco smoke drifted into the truck. "It is the same with the terminal. There is nothing there. I would rather go home to my wife each night than work in the forest, even if the pay is good."

Their voices drifted away, and the sound of the truck door slamming signalled the driver's return. A minute later, we trundled further into the taiga.

It was the same story at the second checkpoint—an

offered cigarette, a few friendly words, and we were on our way. Twenty minutes out, Emmy held out her phone with a one-word message on the screen from Black: *Waiting.*

It seemed Zacharov had put his best men at the third and last station, closest to the base, but by the time three soldiers clambered into the back of the truck and began moving the boxes around, Emmy and I were already watching them from the forest.

"Those are the better guys," I whispered. "Part of Zacharov's core team."

"Lucky he didn't park them further out, or we'd have had a long walk."

It only took a minute for us to strip out of our survival suits and hide them among the trees. They'd soon be covered with snow, and months would pass before it melted. We'd worn dark grey camouflage to start with, but with the change in weather, we changed into white over-suits. On the base, where Zacharov kept the conscripts busy with brooms and snow plows, we could lose them again. Were we worried about footprints? Not really. Outside the base, there was nobody to see them, and the interior would be a mess of everyone else's. Only the perimeter guards presented a risk, but dead men couldn't talk.

We could, though, and now we fastened on our comms gear. To put it on earlier would have drained the batteries, and the last thing we wanted to do was stop to replace them in the middle of a gunfight. Unused to working with a team, the sound of Mack's voice in my ear filled me with a relief I'd never expected. We weren't doing this alone.

"Everything's good," came her familiar Southern

drawl. "Team two is on standby two hours out. It's your call when they take off."

"We're in the woods," Emmy told her. "It's fucking freezing, I need to pee, and we've still got twenty miles to go."

"I love the way you're always so positive. Bradley's hysterical, by the way. He said y'all forgot your bear spray."

At least when we set off on our marathon, we warmed up. It wasn't like jogging along the road—this was a hard slog through dense woodland, following animal tracks where we could to save fighting through the undergrowth. Three of four miles in, an old logging route gave us some respite from jumping over tree trunks. Siberia had a huge problem with illegal logging, mainly run by the mafia, so it was only a matter of time before the forest near the base encountered a gang of selfish bastards out to make a quick buck. They didn't take everything, just the more valuable woods like Korean pine, oak, and linden, but it was enough to destroy the ecosystem.

I remembered when the loggers turned up a few years ago, at a time when I was still on reasonable terms with Zacharov, and when he asked me to go out and fix the problem, I'd done so with pleasure. The men's bodies would be long gone now, scattered by wild animals.

It was eleven o'clock when we reached the chain link fence surrounding the base. It stretched for miles, and Zacharov kept it well maintained. Regular patrols checked the perimeter, guards manned towers near the entrance to keep an eye out for visitors, and cameras pointed at the gates, but with the base's isolation, he'd never seen the need to implement the rigid surveillance measures seen at other military facilities.

We headed northwest, following the fence from a way back in the forest. Moving slowly, we paused each time a patrol came past. There was a jeep every ten minutes, and two men on foot each half hour, sweeping flashlights from side to side. After a mile, I motioned to Emmy to stop.

"Here. When the next patrol's gone past, we'll climb over." I pointed through the darkness at a glimmer of light in the distance. "That's the main hangar. Radar tower's three hundred metres to the west."

Once inside, I knew my way around. Before Zacharov imprisoned me, I'd had the run of the place. I knew its strengths and weaknesses, its vulnerable points and its blind spots. I knew that the guards assigned to the radar room would take a cigarette break soon after shift change. And I knew that the alarm on the fire escape that led to the radar room hadn't worked for at least six years.

Ten minutes later, and two more guards strode past, cigarettes glowing in the darkness.

"She's not coming," one of them muttered.

"I know, but do you want to tell the general that?"

So those guys knew who they were waiting for. Well, I'd be introducing myself soon enough.

"Ready?" Emmy asked.

"As I'll ever be."

"Good luck," Mack said. "Satellite's still showing nothing out of the ordinary."

We threw our white suits on the barbed wire at the top of the fence so we didn't get spiked as we climbed over, then retrieved them once we got to the other side.

No sense in announcing our arrival early.

Rather than heading straight for our main target, we cut left first, brushing away the footprints close to the fence with our snow suits so our arrival wasn't obvious, and then took a tour of the base in order to leave some little surprises. I showed Emmy the best the Russian military had to offer, from the munitions store, to the barracks, to the training complex, to the warehouse that housed the trucks. Eight charges laid with two left. We were saving those for the radar tower.

"Get team two in the air," Emmy told Mack.

"Tell them yourself."

Emmy grinned in the dim light. "Mr. Black, are you there?"

"Loud and clear, Diamond."

"Come and join the party. It'll be a blast."

The radar tower loomed ahead, an ugly grey behemoth shaped like a mushroom cloud, designed for functionality rather than style. We found a spot in the shadow of a nearby storage shed and settled down to watch our target.

"Shift change is two a.m., right?" Emmy whispered.

I nodded, and we waited. An hour ticked by, and the new troops arrived by jeep for the graveyard shift. Fifteen more minutes passed, and despite the beads of sweat trickling down my back, I suppressed a shiver. Waiting was painful at the best of times, but in minus temperatures, in the dark, in hostile territory? The worst.

"Circling a hundred miles out," came Black's voice. "We've got two hours of fuel left."

They were waiting just outside radar range. No pressure.

Then hallelujah, the side door opened, and the two guards who always manned the bottom of the tower stepped outside, breath steaming under the spotlight above the door. Cigarette break, right on time. Good to see Zacharov's crackdown hadn't caused them to change the habit of a lifetime.

Neither of them noticed as we crept closer, both far more concerned with Terek Grozny's chances against Locomotiv Moscow in the Russian premiership next week. Football had always been a favourite topic of discussion among the guards, along with the bets they made on the outcome of each match.

Well, boys, tonight you lose.

Emmy broke the taller guy's neck, while I used my paracord to garrotte the other. It took a few seconds longer than Emmy's method, but over the years, I'd found it to be more reliable. His bowels let go as I dragged his body out of the way behind the shed, and I gagged at the smell.

It was time.

Emmy stayed by the shed, acting as lookout while I stole towards the tower. Outside, I paused.

"Whatever happens, I'm glad we finally found each other," I whispered into the radio.

Emmy's voice came through. "Me too."

And Sam's. "Me three."

And finally Black's. "If you keep talking so pessimistically, I'll kick your ass when I get there."

"Fine, I'm going."

Storeys one through four accommodated the stairs, the restroom, and half a dozen supply closets, with the main radar room on the fifth floor. With everything silent above, I began my jog to the top, a silenced pistol in one hand as I kept my feet light. I'd got to the fourth floor when Mr. Murphy of Murphy's law fame decided to make his appearance. You know, what can go wrong, will go wrong? A sergeant stepped out of the men's room at the exact moment I went past, and although I got my gun up and dropped him before he could take a step, he still let out a yell first.

With the base on high alert, I only just had time to shoot out the lights before footsteps thundered across the floor above. Hiding in the men's room was an option, but a bad one because there was only one way out. Instead, I heaved the guard's body over the railing and followed him myself, clinging to the edge as his body bounced all the way to the bottom. My body dangled into the dark void as the other guards ran past. Five seconds, ten, and I heaved myself back over the railing, sidestepping the pool of blood they hadn't noticed. No sense in leaving a trail of sticky red footprints behind me.

Following procedure, one guard was waiting just inside the doorway. When I entered in a crouch, he didn't have time to swing the barrel of his gun down before he lost his head.

The radar operator threw his hands up, and I shot him too. I wasn't here to take prisoners. His body hit the console and slithered to the floor as I stuck one of Nate's charges underneath the radar screen and tossed another behind a sickly looking plant on the desk opposite.

Then I ran.

A burst of static buzzed in my ear as Emmy sent me a warning. "Four more on their way up, and I dropped three before they could get through the door. Don't trip over the bodies on your way out."

I stepped back behind a filing cabinet, listening as the doors downstairs were thrown open in turn. One. Two. Three. Four. A commotion on the landing signalled their arrival on the fifth floor, frantic whispers of "You go," "No, you go."

They came through the door as one, stupid, and I hit each with a double tap to the head before they processed another thought. Obviously, Zacharov had gone for quantity rather than quality when he prepared the shift charts for this evening.

I flew down the stairs, pausing only to ask, "Clear?" when I got to the bottom.

"Wait." The quiet snick of Emmy's silenced pistol sounded over the airwaves. "Okay, clear now."

I yanked the door open and took off running as more of Zacharov's men searched a collection of storage huts nearby.

"Break left," Emmy said. "I'm behind the tank."

I sprinted the two hundred metres, zigzagging left and right until I reached relative safety next to my sister.

"Good to go?" she asked.

"Absolutely."

She already had the remote detonator in her hand, and now she pushed the button.

The explosion was a thing of beauty. The radar tower dissolved in a cloud of orange, chunks of debris hitting the tank next to us with metallic thumps. When the smoke cleared, everything above the second floor was missing, and the steel supports hung at twisted angles like mutant spaghetti.

Damn, whatever Nate put into that charge, it was

good.

Across the base, searchlights pinged on, powerful beams cutting through the darkness as Zacharov's men began their hunt for me. I think it was safe to say Zacharov knew I'd arrived.

"Ready for some fun?" Emmy asked.

"Can't wait."

CHAPTER 40

HALF AN HOUR. We had half an hour to cause chaos, confusion, and mayhem before the rest of the team landed. Emmy grinned as she pressed the button on the detonator again, and six buildings exploded simultaneously. The munitions store rose a few metres in the air, as in, the whole fucking building, before it dissolved into a fireball. I looked away to preserve my retinas, but the noise... Shit. I stuffed my fingers into my ears, but even after the initial bang, shells were going off like overachieving popcorn.

A ripple of fear ran through my soul, creeping up on me like a damn ninja. What if Tabby was here, in the middle of all this? I quickly pushed the thought away. Zacharov lied about many things, but I knew his tactics, and logic said she was far away. He needed her safe and well-hidden to use as a bargaining chip.

"Makes the radar tower look like amateur hour, doesn't it?" Emmy said into my ear.

I nodded. Where had these explosives been all my life?

Panicked shouts came from all around as Zacharov's men took cover from the hail of debris, and I swapped my silenced .22 for the more powerful Glock. Two of the general's core team ran past, men I recognised from past missions, and I dropped them both with head shots.

Emmy nudged me and pointed east, and I copied her gesture, but west. Then we ran in opposite directions.

A yell came from behind as I shot the lock off the door of an old barracks building. Once, the base had been busier, but when Zacharov took it over, he reduced the headcount to the number he needed. The number he could control. Now, the dormitories stood dusty and abandoned, the beds rows of metal skeletons glinting in the flames visible through the shattered windows. A single dark jacket hung on a coat hook. A sentry.

The click of a door told me I wasn't alone, and I slipped through the door of a communal restroom as footsteps crunched over broken glass. I peeped through a crack as two men materialised through the dormitory door, waiting, waiting, waiting until they got level with me. More of Zacharov's core team. Good at their jobs but not good enough.

A third eye opened up in the first man's forehead as the back of his skull disintegrated in a cloud of pink, and his buddy dove to the side.

"She's in the old barracks. Building D."

Those were his last words, of course, but now the cavalry would be coming.

Or would they?

A cacophony of shots sounded in the distance, and one of the dead men's radios crackled into life.

"You're wrong. She just ran past the mess hall."

Thanks, Emmy.

I ran out and picked up the radio, reattaching the earpiece before I wedged it into my own ear.

Knowledge was power, remember? Then I borrowed the man's assault rifle for good measure. Bullets were power too.

"Twenty minutes out," Mack told me.

Our game of cat and mouse continued, only there were two mice and any number of confused cats. Men rushed from building to building, on foot and in jeeps, as we showed ourselves for a few seconds at a time.

Zacharov himself came over the radio. "What the fuck are you idiots doing? She is one woman. You assholes couldn't organise an orgy in a brothel."

Maybe not, but we were still outnumbered by a hundred to one.

Sam's voice came through in my ear. "We've bailed out. Fifteen minutes."

A truck drove past the doorway I was hiding in, the two men in the back bouncing in their seats as the driver bumped over the groaning body of one of his comrades. Easy pickings. The vehicle veered left as the driver slumped over the wheel, the tyres still spinning as it hit the wall of another barracks building.

Make that ninety-seven to one.

Trained soldiers lost their heads, both literally and figuratively, and they were running everywhere by the time our people dropped from the sky. In the control room, Mack earned her money along with Luke by filtering the conversations to keep the noise to a manageable level. That meant I got an open channel to Emmy and all the important snippets of information from the others.

"A truckload was heading for the hangar. They're not now," Jed said.

He and Sam had been assigned to protect the main

hangar, and therefore our exit route. Each of the pairs had their own tasks, including Emmy and me. And with the odds evened up, it was time to complete ours.

"Ready for Zacharov?" I asked.

"Meet you by the admin building."

We'd try his office first, a corner suite with a view over the runway and decor to match his ego. Many times, I'd sat on the other side of his oversized walnut desk, watching the planes while I listened to yet another lecture.

The door to the building hung open, swinging in the breeze, and as we went through, Emmy broke left while I went right. That way, we could force our opponents into the middle of the room and kill them without hitting each other. We kept moving, flowing from room to room the way we'd practiced in the kill-house. If we stopped, we'd be sitting targets. Room after room, we worked our way through the building, adrenalin fuelling us. Few men remained—a huddle of conscripts in a downstairs break room, a lone soldier with a rifle at an upstairs window, two panicked sergeants running down a corridor. We shot them all, and tomorrow the nightmares would come.

The door to Zacharov's office was closed, and I didn't bother knocking. A couple of bullets to the lock and a swift kick got me through it, and inside we found...nothing. Nothing but an empty safe and scattered papers showing he'd left in a hurry.

"Fuck," Emmy bit out.

"His private quarters. Hurry."

I ran out of the door with her following.

Outside, Team Blackwood decimated the base. A small, well-trained force could do a surprising amount of damage to a group of men who'd grown drunk on their own power. As the years passed, Zacharov's troops had become lazy and complacent, and the burning hell they now found themselves in was the result.

Nate and Black showed no such laxity. Black's orders came over the airwaves with an air of dispassionate authority as he led from the front, all the way into one of the weapons bunkers. One gunshot after another, and he calmly dictated his body count over the airwaves.

"Holy shit," Nate said, not quite so cool. "Zacharov's got enough nerve gas in here to take out the entire planet."

Black's voice. "Destroy it. Whatever you need to do, do it."

By then, we were jogging towards the mess room, ten metres between Emmy and me, when she stiffened and dropped. A bullet hit the wall behind where her head had been as she rolled out of the way. That's what instinct will do for you.

Ahead, Isaiah didn't fare so well. His cry came over the radio as the sniper found his mark. "I'm down; I'm hit. By the gym."

Ryan, his buddy, answered immediately. "On my way. Are you hurt bad?"

"No, hold fast," Emmy told him.

Isaiah let out a groan. "I'm bleeding."

"I can get there; I'm close," Ryan said, and I heard the panic in his voice.

Not so in Emmy's. "Stay put, Ryan. That's a fucking order."

A shadow streaked across the concrete between the

mess room and the gym, and I cursed under my breath. Stupid, stupid boy. He had his gun drawn, but he was looking in the wrong direction. Up. He needed to look up. That was where the danger was. I fired at the roof line as Emmy sprinted after him, zigzagging to make herself an unpredictable target. A muzzle flash flared in the dark. Dammit, the sniper was two buildings over on top of the indoor range, ducked behind a chimney.

Emmy was fast, but the man with the rifle was faster. Ryan's head splintered as she tackled him, the momentum driving his body into the doorway of the gym where Isaiah lay.

Then silence.

It couldn't have been more than a few seconds, but it seemed like forever before Emmy's voice came over the airwaves. "Ryan's down."

"How bad?" Black asked.

"Permanent."

"He sank, then." Cold. That was cold. "Tell me what you need."

"We have a sniper problem. Roof of the shooting range."

The irony wasn't lost on me.

Xavier's voice broke in. "I can handle that."

I stayed where I was, pressed behind a low wall listening to the sounds of a distant gun battle, until a missile screamed past and the shooting range ceased to exist.

"Have we got room on the plane for a couple of those things?" Nate asked.

Forty metres, twenty, I ran as fast as I could to Emmy. Ryan's body lay in the doorway where he'd fallen, head lolling to one side, and I stepped over him as I hurried inside. The metallic tang of blood made me grit my teeth. The only person whose blood I wanted now was Zacharov's.

Isaiah sat on the floor of the gym, propped up against a weight machine, while Emmy crouched beside him with her first-aid kit. We'd brought the basics with us, and Vitaly had topped them up when we stopped in Tayshet.

"What's the damage?" I asked.

"Looks like the bullet nicked his femoral artery. Cover the door?"

"Got it."

Emmy cut away Isaiah's pants. Under the white glow of her flashlight, blood glistened on his dark skin as it oozed down his leg.

"Just leave me," he said, his voice barely audible. "You need to finish this off."

"I don't leave men in the field. You should know that by now."

"But—"

"Shut up, Ise, or this gauze is getting stuffed in your mouth."

Emmy's fingers didn't tremble as she ripped open a packet of QuikClot Combat Gauze. I'd only used it a handful of times in the past, but the stuff was magic when it came to clotting wounds. Between that and the compression bandage, we stood a good chance of controlling the bleeding enough to get him to a hospital.

While Emmy worked, I gave Black a brief update, which was met with a typically wordy response.

"Good. Hold tight. We're at the third bunker, and it's...interesting."

Interesting?

Nate's voice came next. "Guys, do any of you have experience with nukes?"

Nukes? Zacharov had nuclear fucking weapons? I knew he had polonium, because I'd used it to kill a man once, but an actual fully functioning nuclear weapon? The man was undeniably insane.

Emmy's quiet "fuck me" echoed my thoughts.

Xavier piped up, "I had some involvement with the protocols back in Israel."

"Then get your ass over here."

Black spoke again, calm as ever. "Diamond, Seven, find our primary target and neutralise him. Carmen and Slater will take over from you at the gym."

"Understood," I said, and Emmy repeated it.

By the time our backup arrived, Isaiah's bleeding had slowed, nearly stopped, and he was doped up to his eyeballs on morphine.

"Just shoot anyone who walks through the door," Emmy instructed Slater as she handed over responsibility for the patient to Carmen.

He gave her a thumbs up. "Got it."

Time to go.

Almost.

I reached a finger out and touched the top of Emmy's ear. "You're bleeding."

"The bullet grazed me."

Fuck. So damn close. Another inch and I wouldn't have had a sister any more. I hated Zacharov. I hated that man more than anything.

A white-hot fury burned through me, so far from the ice-cold killer he'd trained I barely recognised myself.

Time to go.

Zacharov's private quarters weren't far away. A decade ago, he'd adopted one of the better buildings and refitted it as his home. Oak kitchen, marble bathroom, a whole catalogue of consumer electronics, plus a handy bunker in the basement. If he'd holed up in there, getting him out could be difficult. Unless we used that nuke...

A possibility, albeit a drastic one. But first, we had to find him.

CHAPTER 41

THE SKY BURNED orange as we ran into the night. Half of the base had to be on fire by now. And Zacharov's poor treatment of his men was paying dividends, to us at least, as Alex's voice spoke in my ear.

"The men to the south have thrown down their weapons and run into the forest. Their major yelled out that Zacharov didn't pay them enough for this *govno*. We let them go."

If only all the men shared their attitude. As Emmy and I got closer to the dragon's den, a volley of automatic fire came from the building next to it. A poor, misguided soul still thought he stood a chance.

"Go," Emmy yelled. "Clock's ticking. I'll take care of it."

I left her pulling the pin on a grenade she'd picked up somewhere along the way, and as I ran up the first flight of stairs, the inevitable explosion came. *Please, let her be okay.* When the initial bang subsided, the machine gun started up again, answered by a three-shot burst from the assault rifle Emmy had borrowed from one of the Russians.

Emmy was right—I didn't have time to stop. I needed to trust that she'd deal with the problem.

The door to Zacharov's home lay ajar, the hallway

dark inside. An invitation? A trap? Or merely the sign of a hasty exit?

Rather than spend time finding out, I knocked out the remaining shards of glass in the window to the lounge and hopped over the sill, gun up. Where was the bastard?

I'd always hated this room, stuffed with trinkets from Zacharov's travels. Zulu masks decorated one wall, and another held a samurai sword reminiscent of the one at Riverley. I stepped over the head of his leopard skin rug, complete with amber glass eyes that stared back at me, unseeing.

It gave me the creeps.

Going silently from room to room, I searched downstairs and found nothing. So far, the house had escaped the damage outside, and a glowing lamp lit the second-floor landing as I climbed the stairs. The air felt still. Where the hell was Zacharov?

Had he left already?

Or fled to the bunker?

The answer was neither. I found him in his upstairs study, sitting calmly in his chair, his phone held between his steepled fingers as he leaned back in the leather seat. Arrogant to the last. Around him sat the spoils from his decades of dubious dealings. A Persian carpet, a mahogany desk, an antique globe sitting on an equally expensive-looking side table. Then there were the modern touches. The MacBook, the conference phone, the wall of video screens where he was watching his domain burn. A fire crackled in the grate opposite him, making the room seem strangely homely and a world away from the battle raging outside.

He didn't move as I pointed my pistol at him, and

that worried me more than anything.

"So, the imbeciles downstairs abandoned their post?"

That was why I'd made it up here uninterrupted. "Your men aren't as loyal as you thought."

"No, they're not. Look at you, Anastasia. I fed you, I clothed you, I taught you everything you know, and this is how you repay me?"

It hurt more than it should to hear him use my real name. "You kept me locked up here for three years, you asshole."

"It wasn't supposed to be that way. Every day I hoped you would come to your senses, but you still fought me. Markovich is weak, and James Harrison is a troublemaker. With him out of the way, we could have ruled the world."

We? "I just wanted to live my own damn life."

"And what would you have done? Moved to America and become a housewife? Bought a station wagon and a duplex with a white picket fence and spent your time baking cakes?"

"Maybe. That should have been my choice, not yours."

"You're a killer, Anastasia. It's what you do." He shook his head and tutted. "Always fighting me."

"You tried to kill my boyfriend!" I yelled.

Zacharov showed the first chink in his armour. "Tried?"

He didn't know Sam was alive, and that made me smile. "You fucked up, old man."

His face hardened. "I will have to rectify that."

"How? Look around. You don't have a lot left."

Before I could stop him, he hurled the phone he

was holding into the fire. It shattered on impact, and the acrid smell of burning plastic filled the room.

Then he started laughing?

Why?

Why was he laughing?

What had he done?

"You see that? Apart from me, that was the last link to your daughter. The receiver for her tracking chip. I know you found yours just like I know you killed twelve men single-handedly that evening. If it hadn't been so inconvenient, I might have been impressed."

Ah, so he didn't know about Emmy's actions that night either. I touched the knife in my pocket, ready to use it if necessary.

"What about Alberto Bate?" I asked. We hadn't found him yet, but we would.

He shook his head. "Bate will never talk."

"I can convince him."

"Some men would rather die. Do you want to take that chance?"

"I don't even know Tabby's still alive. You could have killed her weeks ago."

He began laughing again, and I didn't understand what was funny.

"Shut up."

But he didn't. Zacharov still had one final card to play.

"Come now, I'm not a complete monster. She's perfectly safe with an acquaintance. I'd hardly have murdered my own grandchild, would I?"

His what? Time slowed as I processed what he'd just said. His grandchild? The only way that could be true was if her mother was his daughter.

I was his daughter?

No, I couldn't be. I *couldn't* be.

"You're lying." My voice shook, and I hated myself for that.

"Am I?"

He was. A sense of relief came over me as I realised. "You have the wrong colour eyes."

"You're not the only one who wears lenses, *tigryonak*." He reached his hands up. "May I?"

I nodded dumbly, and he pinched out his contacts. Violet eyes stared back at me, as confident as mine were shocked.

As the truth sank in, I felt disconnected from the world. This man, this monster, he'd let me live in a world of half-truths my whole life as he dished out his orders and moulded me into his personal weapon. His daughter. His fucking daughter. What kind of father did that?

"You left my mama to raise me alone then I ended up in a damn orphanage. Eight years. Eight years you left me in that place!"

"You were safe there."

"A man tried to rape me!"

"Regrettable. If you hadn't dealt with him yourself, I promise you I'd have taken care of the problem. And that incident allowed me to see your...potential."

"I don't understand you."

"Your mother was a cheap whore, Anastasia. A whiner who didn't tell me she'd lapsed on her birth control and then expected me to deal with the consequences. After her pointless husband died, she used to leave you alone in her apartment while she went out to entertain men. Do you remember that?"

My mother was a prostitute? Pink satin ballet shoes kicked at my stomach, and bile rose up my throat. And the worst part? It all fitted. I knew that for once in his life, Zacharov wasn't lying.

"Maybe if you'd stepped up, she wouldn't have had to do what she did."

"You sound just like her, you know. Argumentative. *Stay with me, Oleg. Let's be a family, Oleg.* I didn't get a moment's peace until I helped her on her way."

This just got better and better. My finger tightened on the trigger of my Glock. "You killed my mama?"

"She was a difficult woman to cope with."

So numb was I, I didn't feel Emmy's presence until she marched past me. How long had she been listening at the door?

"What about *my* mother?" she asked. "She was a bigger bitch than you. You could have done me a favour there."

Zacharov's brows knitted. "What are you talking about?"

"With the way you must have been spreading it around back then, the thought didn't occur that you could have more than one daughter, daddy dearest?"

"I..."

"Because if you're Ana's father, you must be mine too. Isn't this fun? A family reunion. We even have fireworks."

"I didn't..."

"Didn't think? Didn't care? Didn't wear a condom? All of the above?"

"Who's your mother?"

"Her name's Julie. About five feet six, blonde, most likely high on drugs. Worry not, you don't need to accuse her of being a cheap whore as well. I'm already well aware of that fact."

"You're lying."

"Am I? You never travelled to England?"

He regained some of his composure. "On occasion, but I don't remember her."

"That's no great loss. I wish I didn't either."

"This is a surprise. We should talk about this, civilly, without all the guns."

"I like my gun."

He sighed. "Fine, keep the gun. But there is always room for negotiation. Even with all the mess you've created out there, I'm willing to forgive for the sake of family."

Oh, bullshit. "You never negotiate. You just tell people what to do and kill anyone who doesn't jump into line."

"A man can change."

"Tell me where my daughter is."

"Like I said, we negotiate."

Emmy shot him in the shoulder, and he howled in pain, glaring at her with undisguised fury.

She matched him glare for glare, father to daughter, then shrugged. "What do you know? Looks like an itchy trigger finger's genetic. Tell us where Tabby is."

Wasn't that the truth? Genetics had a huge part to play in this. I mean, look at us. Emmy and I had taken two completely different paths in life and still ended up here, today, in a standoff with our father. And were we really that different to him? We were all proficient killers, and the blood staining our hands was the same shade of crimson.

My gun wavered and dropped a few inches. Could I

really shoot my own father?

He blew out a thin breath. "Okay. You win. There is another receiver."

"Where?" Emmy asked.

"Over in the cabinet." He pointed at a credenza on the far wall. "Bottom shelf."

She glanced in that direction, and the split second of distraction was all he needed to grab the gun from under his desk. Seemed he hadn't lost his touch after all. *Could* I shoot my father? I was about to find out.

Three guns aimed.

Two shots echoed through the room.

Two violet eyes were no more.

CHAPTER 42

BLACK FOUND US there, kneeling on the floor hand-in-hand, staring at the lifeless body of our father. He lay crumpled next to the desk where he fell, his revolver a foot from his outstretched hand. Nate stood at the door, keeping watch, while Black strode over.

"Diamond," he said, his voice hoarse as he scooped Emmy into his arms.

"Did you hear?"

"Yes."

"We killed him."

Black glanced over at the pool of blood spreading out on the Persian rug. "I can see that."

"He was our—"

He cut her off. "No, he wasn't. A father would have been there for you growing up. A father would have heard your first words, seen you take your first steps. He'd have driven you to your first day at school and been at your birthday parties. He'd have lectured your teenage boyfriend, and when you pranged his car in your first driving lesson, he'd have yelled at you then given you a hug. He..." Black nudged Zacharov with his foot. "Was no father."

Black may have been a cold, hard-hearted son-of-a-bitch, but he spoke the truth, something Zacharov had rarely managed to do in the nineteen years I'd known him. Emmy was so damn lucky to have her husband.

She dropped her feet to the floor and reached down to pull me up too. Then we were both wrapped in his arms, and a little of his strength flowed into me too. More footsteps sounded in the corridor, and Sam rushed towards us, followed by Jed. Black released me into Sam's arms, and my gun fell to the floor as he hugged me tight.

"Ana, beautiful, I thought I'd lost you. Those gunshots... Then silence..." He leaned his forehead against mine. "I was so damn scared."

"I'm okay," I whispered, even though I was anything but.

I'd just killed my father. Black was right about him not being a good man, but he'd still raised me in his own warped way, the one constant in my life over the last two decades. And worse, my daughter was still missing.

"I just..."

Sam kissed my forehead gently. "Shh. I heard on the radio. You don't have to talk about it."

"He didn't tell us where Tabby was." I tore at my hair. "Fuck!"

"We'll find her. I promise we'll find her. And you'll learn to live with what happened today. The memories will fade with time, and we'll make good ones to take their place. You, me, and Tabby."

His lips pressed against my temple, and I knew at that moment I'd found my own Black. We'd been through hell, quite literally according to the monitor screens flickering on the wall, and there he was, still by my side. He always would be.

I didn't even glance at Zacharov as I walked from

the room.

As we left, me with Sam and Emmy with Black, Nate and Jed began to tear the place apart, looking for something, anything, that might lead us to Tabby. But they wouldn't find anything. Instinct told me that for once, Zacharov hadn't lied when he said his phone was the only receiver. That damned leverage again. The most we could hope for was evidence of his black market dealings, information that would help to stop another disaster like Likho.

We'd have to find Tabby ourselves.

Sam guided me outside where the sound of gunfire had subsided, replaced by the roar of flames as buildings burned all around. The last of Zacharov's men had either died or gone into hiding.

"The plane's waiting, beautiful."

We were borrowing one of Zacharov's transport planes, and Blackwood's team ran back and forth, carrying boxes from jeeps into the huge belly of the aircraft. I trudged up after them and Sam settled me into a canvas seat.

"Will you be okay here?" he asked. "I could do with lending a hand outside."

"I should help."

I tried to get up. What was I thinking, sitting here?

"No, you shouldn't. We're leaving soon in any case. Isaiah's stabilised, but we need to get him to a hospital."

I looked round, seeing for the first time that Isaiah was lying on a stretcher at the front of the plane with Carmen sitting next to him. What was wrong with me? I was barely aware of my surroundings. Usually, I knew everything that was going on.

The world no longer made sense. All I felt was an overwhelming sense of...nothing. Paralysis. I shrank back into my seat and drew my knees up to my chest, shielding myself from the outside world.

Emmy walked onto the plane with Black, each holding one end of a body bag. Emmy's eyes didn't sparkle anymore. Once the pair of them had lowered Ryan's body to the floor and secured it, Black gripped Emmy's waist and walked her over to me.

"You two need each other. We'll finish up outside."

Under the harsh strip lights, she looked even worse than I felt.

"Do you want to talk about it?" I asked.

She slumped back against the side of the plane. "I've got to tell Tia that Ryan's dead. I don't think it's gonna go well."

"She knew he had a dangerous job."

"You think that'll help? It won't. Once I tell her he's dead, it won't matter that he chose to do what he did. All she'll care about is that he isn't coming back to her."

"Their relationship was serious?"

"Honestly? I don't think they'd have gone the distance, but they'd been together for over a year and he was her first. Ryan helped her to make the transition from a girl into a woman. She was such a brat when I first met her, and I'm so proud of the person she's become." A tear ran down her cheek, and she swiped it away. "Fuck, I've turned into an emotional wreck over the last twelve months. So much shit's happened. I never used to get upset like this."

I rested my chin on her shoulder as I hugged her so she couldn't see my own tears falling, although I had a feeling she knew they were there, anyway. Neither of us moved while the team brought the last few crates aboard, or while the ramp lifted, or while the plane lumbered along the runway. But when we rose into the sky, Emmy and I moved to peer through the window as I left Base 13 for the final time.

As we banked towards the horizon, Nate fiddled with something in his hand. Fresh explosions left the place awash in a sea of flame, hot enough to destroy any remaining chemical and biological weapons still hidden there and bury Zacharov and his empire forever. Base 13 had taken its secrets to the grave.

"It's gone," she whispered.

But it wasn't over. Not yet. We still needed to find Tabby.

Sam sat next to us for the long trip back, and rather than trying to separate me from Emmy, he simply held my hand all the way home.

Home.

Up until I escaped Russia, I hadn't understood that home wasn't a place, it was the people who cared about you. Home was with Emmy and Sam, wherever that may be. I'd start with Virginia.

My ears popped as the plane descended into Silver Springs. Black and Nate had spent most of the trip speaking quietly on the phone, briefing, debriefing, arranging, and negotiating. A car was waiting on the tarmac, the driver standing by the door.

"Can you take Emmy back to Riverley with you?" Black asked me.

"You're not coming?"

"I've got a lot to deal with here. It's not every day we fly a Russian suitcase nuke into the United States."

Shitting hell, he'd brought the freaking bomb back with him? I shuddered. I'd been sitting on a plane with that thing.

"Don't worry. We cleared it for safety before we took off. It was a hell of a job to find the right experts with so little notice. We had biological and chemical weapons people on standby, but a nuke was something we weren't expecting to find. Even Zacharov must have had to put in some effort to get hold of that. Anyway, it was either bring it with us or set it off, and that option seemed slightly drastic."

"Well, I'm glad I didn't know before we took off."

"Emmy would have hitchhiked back with you. She's not keen on nuclear weapons either."

Was that genetic too?

"Back to my original question," Black continued. "Will you take Emmy with you? She insists she's telling Tia about Ryan personally, and it's going to end in tears for both of them."

"I'll always be there for her. Always." Even if I felt like a mess myself.

He smiled, a soft smile I suspected he didn't often use. "Good."

"I'll be there too," Sam said.

"Appreciated. Luke's going to bring Tia to Riverley. She knows something's wrong, but she doesn't know how bad it is yet."

Poor girl. I knew first-hand there was nothing worse than losing the man you loved.

Emmy's eyes were dark and hollow as she trudged up the steps to Riverley.

"Are you going to be okay?" I asked.

"No, but I want to get this over with."

She disappeared towards the back of the house while Sam steered me into the lounge to wear a groove in the carpet as I paced up and down in front of the windows. Five minutes later, Emmy came back and stood next to me, staring into space.

"How did she take it?"

"She's gone to my house to pack her stuff. She's moving in with Luke, and she never wants to see me again."

"Did you tell her the whole story? That you tried to save him?"

"She was too busy screaming at me. And what good would giving her the gory details do? It won't bring him back. She needs somebody to blame, and that someone is me. Besides, she's sort of right. I could have vetoed the decision to put him on the team."

"The final decision to disobey your direct order lay with Ryan. Do you want me to talk to her?"

"No, let her grieve. Everyone's emotions are running too high at the moment."

I'd respect Emmy's decision, but it hurt to see the pain in her eyes. Tia may have lost her boyfriend, but Emmy had lost two friends today.

And this whole mess started with me. If I'd stayed in Russia until Zacharov sent me on another twisted mission, then fucked up and died quietly, none of this would have happened.

"Don't do it," Sam warned.

"Do what?"

"I can see all those thoughts running through your head. Neither of you is to blame for today, and if we hadn't gone after Zacharov, his actions would have led to thousands more deaths. He was a monster."

"He was my father—"

"Sperm donor," Emmy corrected.

"But what does that make me?"

Sam put an arm around my shoulders, and Emmy's too. "Neither of you are monsters. The best parts of him went into you, and the worst parts died in Russia. You two may have your sharp edges, I'll be the first to admit that, but you've both got good hearts."

A minute passed, then two, before I felt able to speak again. "What now?"

"You could go with Zacharov's duplex and a white picket fence idea?" Emmy suggested.

"I've only got an apartment," Sam said, brow crinkled.

"And I'm not driving a fucking minivan."

Sam kissed my hair. "We'll work something out. But our first task is finding Tabby. Our little girl's still out there."

"Right. We find Tabby. Everything else can wait."

CHAPTER **43**

QUINN WAITED UNTIL Black got home to take care of Emmy then carried an exhausted Ana up to bed. Only a week had passed since he'd lain next to her in Little Riverley, but so much had changed since. Back then, there'd been a buzz of optimism, that they could deal with Zacharov and get Tabby back and live happily ever after.

But what happened was no fairy tale.

Zacharov was Ana's father? Quinn sure hadn't seen that one coming. Now she had to live with having killed the bastard herself, as well as the collateral damage and Ryan's death. And they still hadn't found Tabby.

Quinn pulled the drapes as Ana slumped on the bed, too tired even to undress herself. When she showed no signs of moving, he gently pulled off her combat gear and slipped one of his T-shirts over her head.

"Sleep, beautiful."

"I don't know if I can."

"Just close your eyes. I'll look after you; I promise."

It took an hour for her breathing to slow, for her to stop fidgeting and give in to her body's need for rest. And all that time, Quinn stroked her hair, both cursing Zacharov for everything he'd put Ana through and thanking the man for bringing her into the world in the first place. Quinn gritted his teeth as he recalled the conversation he'd heard over the radio. Zacharov had called Ana "consequences." An accident. Well, Tabby hadn't exactly been planned, but that didn't mean Quinn loved her any less, or the woman who made her.

No, the man was an asshole, nothing more.

And with that thought, Quinn drifted off to sleep too.

Quinn woke the next morning with Ana draped over his chest, just like he had a week before. Only today, there was no need for goodbyes or sneaky photos because neither of them was going anywhere except downstairs for breakfast. He stroked gently down her body, pausing when he got to her delectable ass. She was his, and he was hers.

His cock twitched. See? It agreed.

Ana stirred in his arms as she pressed against him, and he lifted her hair to check whether she was still asleep. Nope. Two violet eyes stared back at him.

"Busted," he said softly.

"You got me."

Ana rolled onto her back and stretched, leaving the quilt pooled beside her.

"I have, and I'm never letting you go."

Quinn paused, unsure of the etiquette for a morning like this one. One significant part of his anatomy knew what it wanted, but was sex appropriate the morning after your girlfriend shot her father?

He leaned over and tried a kiss to start with, hoping Ana would smile. Even back in Russia, she'd never been one to smile without a good reason, but when she did, she went from beautiful to so stunning he thought his heart would give out.

The moment their lips touched, she pulled him over on top of her and kissed him with a passion he'd only dreamt of, wrapping her legs around him and cupping his cheeks with both hands. Okay, it seemed like maybe a bit of naughtiness was on the menu after all.

Ana reached down and stroked his length, causing his hips to jerk, and then widened her legs enough for him to slide inside her.

"Do something nice to me. Please. This week's been so shitty, and I just want to forget it for a few minutes."

"Nice? You think this is *nice*? A walk in the park is *nice*. Dinner at an expensive restaurant is *nice*."

She rolled her eyes, something she had to have copied from Emmy, and damned if she didn't smile too. Not a grin, but definitely an improvement on her usual expression.

"Fine, Sam. Give me a shit-hot fuck."

Quinn was only too happy to oblige.

Ana was still smiling when they walked into the kitchen two hours later, but that soon faded when they saw Dan sitting at the table. She may have been wearing ripped jeans and a T-shirt, but the laptop and the look on her face were all business. Quinn fastened an arm around Ana's waist, as much to hold himself up as her.

"What's happened?" he asked.

Thankfully, Dan spared them the good news/bad news scenario and came out with it. "We found Bate two days ago. In the morgue."

The morgue?

"Where? What happened?"

"Guatemala. He drove his car off a bridge."

"Allegedly," Ana muttered.

"Allegedly," Dan repeated. "There were no witnesses, and the police investigation has been less than thorough so far. We've got our own team en-route."

"Zacharov knew." Ana got up and began pacing, a nervous habit it seemed. "He told me Bate would never talk, but I didn't realise that meant he was dead. Zacharov probably had him killed." She tore at her hair. "Now we'll never find Tabby."

Quinn caught her hand and pulled her onto his lap. "We will. Zacharov also said she was alive and safe, and that means we've got time. Like he said, he wouldn't kill his own granddaughter. I bet he had a contingency plan in place."

The bastard *always* had a plan in place.

"He tried to kill *me*."

"Because you had a gun pointed at him, and so did Emmy."

Ana looked around the kitchen. "Where is Emmy?"

"Upstairs," Dan said. "Her demons came back last night, and she attacked Black in her sleep. He had to sedate her."

Ana stiffened, and Quinn worried that one more piece of bad news would send her spiralling over the edge.

"Emmy'll be okay. She's tough."

Dan came over to comfort Ana as well. "None of this is your fault, okay? Not Zacharov, not Ryan, and definitely not Emmy. She's had these nightmares for years, and it's not the first time Black's borne the brunt of it."

"But—"

"Have some coffee, try to relax, and she'll be awake before you know it." Dan lowered her voice a little. "And about all the other stuff... Black spoke to everybody last night about your connection to Emmy and Zacharov. Nobody on the team will mention your relationship to either of them unless you want them to."

The man thought of everything, and Quinn's admiration for him went up another notch. Keeping that secret, at least for the moment, was the best move when Ana was struggling to accept her heritage for herself. Maybe in time the truth would come out, but today wasn't that day.

Ana could make the decision in her own time, and Quinn would be there to support her whenever that happened.

CHAPTER 44

A MONTH LATER, and little pieces were slowly slotting together, except there was still one great big piece missing from the middle of the jigsaw. Tabby. Instinct told me to put everything on hold and spend every waking moment searching for her, but reason said I had to make some effort at normality, as much for Sam's sake as my own.

We weren't quite back to where we'd been as Sam Jessop and Zhen, but at least I no longer had to worry about going off-script, or Sam overhearing a conversation he shouldn't, or him finding one of my many weapons stashes. No, our first joint purchase for Sam's apartment had been a larger gun safe to share, and for the first time in my life, I was free to be myself. The trouble was, I barely understood my own personality, seeing as I'd spent my whole life pretending, but Sam helped me to discover new things about my inner workings every day. I kind of liked Anastasia and the woman she was becoming.

And I more than kind of liked falling asleep next to Sam every night and waking in his arms every morning.

We'd got into a routine—shut off the alarm, do something dirty, take a shower together then eat breakfast sitting next to each other at the kitchen counter.

And this morning, I smiled to myself as I loaded the dishwasher. Just a flicker, a runner-up attempt by muscles with a lot to learn. This was normal. I loved normal.

"Ana?" Sam called. "I'm just leaving. Do you want me to pick up a pizza on my way home? Or are we going to Riverley?"

Neither option appealed, not really. I hadn't been hungry in weeks, and when I looked at myself in the mirror, my cheeks were hollow, my eyes sunken. Every other day, Toby brought fresh, pre-prepared meals and stacked them in the fridge, despite the fact I rarely touched any of them. But I had to eat, because if I didn't eat, I'd lose my strength and that wouldn't help me to find Tabby.

I forced enthusiasm into my voice. "Pizza sounds great."

We'd sort of moved into Sam's apartment. I say sort of, because we still spent half of our time at Emmy's place, and Bradley was in the process of changing the colour scheme in our new bedroom at Sam's. He'd tried to go for violet to start with, seeing as he didn't know about my history, but Emmy vetoed it, and he grudgingly agreed to do something "rustic."

I loved spending time with my sister, don't get me wrong, but back in Moscow I'd adored being squashed up with Sam in one of our tiny apartments or the other, and Riverley was just so big. Splitting our time between there and Sam's home was working out for the moment.

As was his new job. He'd offered to quit the CIA if I wanted him to, but it was obvious espionage ran in his blood just as it did in mine. His boss tried to send him on assignment to Brazil, but Black pulled some strings, and now Sam had a new boss and a job at The Farm, the CIA's training facility in Williamsburg, Virginia, three days a week to start with. He'd be training the new recruits to do exactly what he did, except minus the part where he fell in love with a foreign spy. The CIA tended to frown upon that.

I'd redeemed myself slightly in their eyes by carrying on where I left off with Hades three years ago and turning over all the information I had on Zacharov. In return, I had a shiny new American passport and a promise that the US government would leave me alone unless I got caught doing something I shouldn't.

And caught was the operative word. They'd already offered me a contract position doing their dirty work.

And fuck me if I wasn't considering it. Emmy was right. Going completely straight was boring as hell.

But before I could commit to any new projects, I needed to find my daughter. Until she was back under my roof, I couldn't rest. Hell, some days I struggled with breathing, let alone eating. But so far, we had nothing, despite the efforts of Blackwood and all of Sam's contacts too.

Sam walked through from the bedroom, straightening his tie. He didn't need to wear a suit, but he said it scared the new recruits, and I wasn't about to complain because I got to peel him out of it every night.

He paused to give me a quick kiss before he left, and that quick kiss turned into a long, slow, deep kiss, and before I knew it, I was on my knees. An escape, that's what it was. A few blessed minutes to distract myself from missing Tabby, but it never lasted long enough. Sam's fingers fisted in my hair as I sucked—

shorter hair now, a bob with bangs—and he gripped it hard as he came down my throat.

"Fuck, beautiful. I was already exhausted after rounds one and two."

"Is that a complaint?"

Strong arms pulled me up and Sam kissed me again.

"I'll never complain about making love to you." He smiled against my lips. "But I need to go to the office for a rest."

When Sam went to the office, I did too. Emmy had arranged a desk for me at Blackwood's main facility near Richmond and given me free reign to use their resources as I needed. Sam got me a gift to celebrate my first day there—a mouse mat with his grinning face on it. I pretended to groan, but secretly I loved seeing him every time I looked down. Dan helped by working on the case in every spare minute, and Mack called me at three in the morning the day before yesterday because she was searching too. And still...nothing.

Sam was putting on a brave face for my benefit, but I knew he was hurting. Was it better or worse that he'd never met Tabby? Last week, I'd caught him watching the video of us Emmy took on the plane, and there'd been no mistaking the tears gathered in his eyes.

The doorbell rang, and I let out a long sigh. I knew who it would be, and although I adored Bradley, the thought of dealing with his eternal optimism made me want to slit my wrists.

Still, I let him in and tried not to look too upset about it.

"The fabric swatches for the drapes have arrived." He marched over to the window in the lounge and began holding samples up to the light. "Do you like the stripes? Or this sort of...abstract thing?"

"Either is fine."

"And the man's coming to measure for the carpet in half an hour. Will you be here or shall I stay?"

"I'm going to the office."

"I'll stay, then." He wandered through to the kitchen. "Ugh. You've run out of the good coffee. I'd better order some."

He meant well. A good heart, Sam said, like mine. We'd given him a pass to do whatever he wanted as long as he promised not to touch the second bedroom. That was reserved for Tabby, and decorating it now would feel like a jinx. When she came home, she could pick out her own colour scheme and her own damn furniture. We'd both spoil her rotten.

At Blackwood, I spent an hour in the gym then settled down at my desk. I'd noticed many of the employees there tended to give me the same wide berth my ex-colleagues in Russia did. Must have been my cheerful demeanour or perhaps the fact that I could bench press more than most of the men.

Emmy walked into the office fifteen minutes later, cup of coffee in hand.

"Any news?" she asked.

"Nothing. You?"

"Same old. Tia's still not speaking to me. Alex put me through hell cross-country before I'd had my first espresso, and another nightmare of a request just came across my desk."

She hesitated, and I knew there was something else. "And?"

"I'm sorry. I'll apologise first and get it out the way."

"For what?"

"Uh, I might have told Bradley when your birthday is. He kept badgering me, and if I didn't tell him, he was gonna assign you a random date."

I shrugged. "So he knows my birthday. Everyone has a birthday."

"You don't get it. This is Bradley. I talked him out of the surprise party, but he's insisting on a dinner. I might be able to get it down to ten people if I threaten to confiscate his Lamborghini."

A groan escaped. "Celebrating is the last thing I feel like doing."

"Believe me, I understand. We'll just go out and eat then have an early night. I'm still sorry."

"Fine, I'll forgive you if you join me on my conference call with the Mexican cops in half an hour. My Spanish still isn't as good as yours."

"Done."

Without Emmy, the aftermath of Zacharov would have been so much more difficult. We spent hours talking, about our childhoods, the way we'd trained, and our hopes for the future. Emmy's philosophy on family made me realise I couldn't keep dwelling on Zacharov.

"You can pick your own family. I did. I've got no mother, but two men I consider fathers."

"Who?"

"Jimmy took me in when I was fourteen. I lived with him and his wife for two years, and he gave me my first job and showed me not all men were bastards. If it wasn't for him, I wouldn't be here now."

"He helped you move to America?"

"No, he taught me to box, and that meant I managed to break Black's nose, which was why he offered to train me."

Once I'd finished laughing, I asked her who the other guy was.

"Ah, yes, Eduardo. He lives in Colombia, and he's into some nasty shit, but he's never been anything but kind to me. And when I needed to pull off the most important job of my life, he dropped everything to help me, no questions asked. So, he's family."

"I like that idea."

"You can share them. They'll both love you as much as I do. I know it. I've invited Jimmy and his wife for Christmas, so you'll meet him then."

"And Eduardo?"

"He doesn't like to leave Colombia. Too many arrest warrants out. But maybe we could take a trip there one day?"

"I want to travel to South America after Christmas to look for Tabby."

"Then I'll join you for a few days. We can take a side trip to visit Eduardo."

Two hours later, I had less hope than ever. The Mexicans hadn't got any closer to finding the links in Bate's network, and as far as the Guatemalans were concerned, his death was a tragic accident. Sunlight bounced off the cream walls in the conference room, but they still seemed to close in on me.

"Tabby could be anywhere," I said, staring into my cup of hot chocolate. "*Anywhere*."

"And we'll find her."

On the surface, Emmy had bounced back from the Russian ordeal faster than me, but while I envied her ability to look to the future, the bad dreams she was getting with worrying regularity made me long to take away all the pain she kept stored up inside.

"I wish—"

Emmy's ringing phone cut me off. Luke's name lit up the screen, and she stuck it onto speaker.

"The cops just called. Tia's been arrested again."

"What for?"

"Drunk and disorderly."

Emmy sighed. "Text me the details, and I'll make some calls."

Tia was hurting; I understood that, but this made the third incident in two weeks, and I knew from Emmy's comments it was getting more and more difficult to keep making the charges disappear. Apparently, she didn't have many favours owing from the local cops, and she'd used most of them up.

"Thanks. You know how much I appreciate it." Luke sounded close to despair too. "I just don't know what to do with her anymore. She's behaving worse now than when she was sixteen, and as she's technically an adult, I haven't got the power to do anything."

"She's living in your apartment. Can't you put some ground rules in place?"

"I tried that. She threatened to move in with Lottie and Nigel."

Lottie, Tia's best friend, worked as a receptionist

downstairs. She was a sweet girl, too sweet to deal with Tia's obvious grief on her own. And Tia's antics were affecting Emmy too. Guilt gnawed away at her every waking minute.

I'd had enough of seeing my sister get hurt. Tia needed to hear a few facts, and I would be the one to tell them to her.

I turned to Emmy and plastered on a smile. "If you sort out the paperwork, I'll pick her up."

"I can get her," Luke broke in. "She's causing everyone enough inconvenience as it is."

"It's no trouble, honestly."

"Well, if you're sure."

He sounded relieved, unsurprisingly, and so did Emmy once she'd had a difficult conversation with someone at the police station.

"Thanks for doing this."

"Can I borrow your car?"

"Ah, that was your motive? You could have just asked for the keys. I wouldn't have said no."

President Harrison had kept his word, and the new Viper was a thing of beauty. Metallic black with teal leather inside, the sound of the engine made my stomach flutter in a good way.

Black hadn't been so impressed with the gift. The president came for dinner one night, complete with a full Secret Service detail and a gift box containing the keys. Being in the same room with the man I'd once been asked to kill felt a little odd, and I guessed he felt the same way from the wide berth he gave me. But judging from the way Black kept glaring at him, any threat to Harrison's life would come from a different direction.

Whatever, the car was fuckin' A. I was working on my American swearing too, can you tell? I kept to the speed limit in town because it would have been embarrassing if Emmy had to rescue *me* from jail again too, but on the stretch of open road that led from the office, I opened the car right up. One of these was definitely going on my Christmas list.

CHAPTER 45

TIA'S FACE WAS a picture when she saw me waiting for her in reception at the police station. One of those Edvard Münch ones with the dude screaming.

She walked right past me, nose in the air. "I'm not riding with you."

"You're welcome."

"I'm calling my brother."

"I already spoke to him. He's not coming."

"I'll call Lottie, then."

"She's not coming either." Okay, so I hadn't spoken to Lottie, but I was a pretty convincing liar.

Tia hesitated. "I'll call a cab."

She pulled her phone out of her pocket, and I plucked it from her grasp. All that practice disarming terrorists had finally paid off, although, ironically, I had Zacharov to thank for that.

"Give that back!"

I folded my arms. "Make me."

Okay, so it was childish, but it was also satisfying. She actually thought about it for a fraction of a second before her shoulders slumped in defeat.

"Fine, I'll go with you. But I don't have to talk."

"No, you don't. You just have to listen."

She dropped into the passenger side, clicked her seatbelt on, folded her arms, and stared out the window as I pulled out of the parking lot.

"I know you blame Emmy for Ryan's death, but you need to understand what really happened out there."

Silence.

"The only people responsible for Ryan's death were Ryan and the person who shot him."

That got a reaction.

Tia's head whipped round. "That bitch sent him out there. She knew it would be dangerous!"

"She did, but Ryan also knew it would be dangerous, and he still wanted to go. What's more, Emmy was with him every step of the way."

"Really? *Every* step?"

"Yes, *every* damn step. He disobeyed her direct order to stay where he was and ran out into danger instead. She tried to push him out of the way, and when he got shot, the bullet grazed the top of her ear. That's how close she was. He played Russian roulette with not only his own life but hers as well. If he wasn't already dead, I'd be tempted to shoot him myself for that."

Harsh, maybe, but she needed to hear the truth. Tia was looking away from me again, but this time I could see the tears streaming down her face in her reflection in the window.

"Is that true?" she whispered.

"Every word of it. There's a recording of it too, if you get the urge to listen to it." No way should she hear that final shot, but she needed to realise I was serious.

The car ate up the miles as Tia ignored me. I may have taken a small detour. She needed some thinking time.

Eventually, she turned towards the front. She was still unable to face me, but the sideways view was an improvement on her back nonetheless.

"I've been so horrible." Tia's voice cracked, and I knew the words didn't come easily. "Emmy must hate me."

"She understands why you've been like that. Ryan was her friend, and she misses him too."

"Do you think she'll ever forgive me?"

"I know she will. You just have to start acting like the sister she considers you to be again."

"But she has you now. She doesn't need me anymore."

Had our secret slipped out? "What makes you say that?"

"I heard Luke on the phone to Mack. Don't worry, I won't tell anyone."

So, not only had Tia lost Ryan, she felt pushed out by me. And rightly so—she'd known Emmy longer than I had, and I'd just walked in with genetics on my side.

"A girl can always use another sister."

More sniffles. "I need to tell her I'm sorry."

"Do you want to go and see her?"

Tia nodded, and I called Emmy to meet us back at Riverley. The office wasn't the place for that reunion. I turned the car towards home, happy that at least one branch of the family would be complete again.

A quiet birthday dinner at a restaurant, Emmy said. Instead, Bradley had booked out the whole of a local Italian place and hired a trio of opera singers to entertain us between each course. At least that meant I didn't need to talk much.

Despite saying there was nothing to celebrate, today a small ray of light had shone into my life. While hunting for Tabby, I'd accidentally found another kid, another Fern snatched away from her parents and spirited across the country. Emmy, Carmen, and I had returned in the early hours after liberating her from the hell-hole she was locked up in, and this time, I hadn't been so kind with my knife. We'd left the Venezuelans to clear up the mess, and now Agent Stone owed me a favour too.

Back home, we'd watched the little girl being reunited with her family on television, and I wasn't the only one who shed a happy tear. Four years old, and she'd sat in my lap for the plane ride back, clutching at my jacket with one small hand as she slept. A sweet moment, even if it made me miss Tabby all the more. And I couldn't deny I'd enjoyed the trip. Working with the team of girls—my team, as I was coming to think of them—was a world away from being sent out into the cold by Zacharov.

In Il Tramonto, ten people turned into fifty as the entire team from Russia arrived with their partners. I finally met Luke for the first time when he came with Mack, Bradley brought his boyfriend, and twenty other people whose names I forgot turned up too. Even Tia came with Lottie on her arm, although like me, she mostly kept out of everyone's way. Sam and I hid in a corner, our chairs squashed together.

"Sure you're okay?" he asked, nuzzling my ear.

No, not at all, but I couldn't afford to upset my new family. "I've never had a birthday party before."

"What, never?"

"Zacharov didn't go in for all that."

"Sorry."

"Don't be. That part of my life's over now, I've got you, and I've got Emmy. Things can only get better."

"I've got a little bit of good news."

"Does it involve the bedroom?"

"I can do that too." He slid my hand into his lap under the table as proof he could deliver on that promise. "But this is about our plans after Christmas. My leave got approved."

"The whole of January?"

"The whole of January."

"Now, *that's* the best birthday present."

That and the $3 million Emmy deposited in my bank account this morning. She said the extra cash was a bonus, but she was wrong. The bonus was the Viper from Black, currently parked on the drive at Riverley so I could drown my sorrows in Amaretto without getting a DUI afterwards.

Bradley leapt onto the makeshift stage and banged a knife on a glass to quiet everyone. Nobody listened, so he hit the glass harder, and it broke. Thankfully, Emmy came to his rescue and whistled loud enough that everybody covered their ears.

"A toast," Bradley yelled. "We need a toast." From the way he was swaying, he'd had one too many martinis. "Six weeks ago, Ana came into our lives, and although she's managed to insult my decorating skills and blow everything up, she's also stolen the heart of the delicious Quinn, caught several large spiders, and been brave enough to get into a car with Emmy. And today it's her birthday. Where's the cake?"

Two waiters struggled in with a platter, and I couldn't hold back my groan. Nor could Sam or anyone else in the room. Bradley clapped in glee.

"Isn't it something? I borrowed one of the satellite photos."

The runway, the radar tower, the warehouses, the mess hall—yes, it was all there. Base 13. He'd covered the whole damn thing in candles and sparklers for added effect, and some of the icing was melting in the heat.

"It certainly is something," Emmy muttered. "Fucking ugly."

"Don't be so miserable," Bradley chided. "It's chocolate with buttercream. Now, the rest of the toast." The maître d' handed him a new glass, and he held it up. "To Ana. We're glad you're sticking around because we all love you."

Yes, he was definitely drunk. I buried my head in Sam's chest as the restaurant cheered, although secretly I couldn't help smiling a tiny bit.

It was nice to finally have a family who cared.

Chapter 46

ANOTHER TWO WEEKS passed, and the festive season was in full swing. By then, I was beginning to lose hope as well as more weight. Sam was too, I could tell, but I refused to voice my fears because that would make them real. My Spanish had improved markedly, and I'd started learning Portuguese just in case we needed to spend time in Brazil. Bradley had bought me a closet full of clothes suitable for hotter weather and sent over six different kinds of anti-wrinkle cream to tackle the fine network of lines that had developed around my eyes.

I didn't give a shit about wrinkles, only finding my daughter.

With the support of Sam's bosses and the whole of Blackwood, we'd planned our South American trip, leaving on New Year's Day. I'd considered going sooner, travelling on my own, but where would I start? We still had no concrete leads, and I'd turned into a shell of a woman who had to be reminded to shower most mornings. I needed Sam with me to lean on.

Which meant I first had to survive Christmas and Bradley's New Year's Eve party, both of which promised to be carnage.

On the last Saturday before the big day, Bradley interrupted the first lazy afternoon I'd spent with Sam since we were in Moscow. Lazy but guilt-filled. Sam had insisted I needed a break from work. He'd cooked beef stroganoff for lunch, with *kompot*, a Russian drink made from berries. I helped out by chopping up the vegetables really, really quickly—a more practical use for the knife skills I'd learned as a child.

We'd just sat down to watch a movie when my phone vibrated on the coffee table.

"Leave it," Sam said.

"I can't. He'll only keep calling back."

I reached out and put the phone on speaker.

"I need your help. Quinn's too," Bradley said.

"We're busy today."

"Nonsense. Mack checked your phones, and you're both at home."

Good grief. There was a downside to working for a security company and having a friend who was a hacker.

"Maybe we're busy at home?"

"The kinky-kinky can wait. I need people who are good climbers to help with the Christmas decorations."

"What are you—"

"No time to explain—just hurry up and get over here. Merry Christmas, by the way."

He hung up before either of us could reply, and Sam got to his feet, reaching for his jacket.

"I'm intrigued now," he said. "What the hell is he doing over there?"

"I dread to think."

When we arrived at Riverley, silver wire snaked all over the lawn like giant spaghetti, and Bradley stood on an upturned crate, gesticulating at the mess while Emmy and a bunch of her Blackwood team stood around in climbing harnesses.

"So," Bradley explained. "We just have to hang the long wires from the gargoyles at the edge of the roof and attach the shorter wires crossways to form a grid. Then we need to clip all the stars to the wires. It's really quite simple."

Tia crouched beside a huge box, clutching a handful of silver stars. "Bradley, there must be hundreds of these."

"Two and a half thousand, to be precise. And they're all solar powered, so it'll be environmentally friendly."

"What about the diesel used to ship them over from China?" asked Emmy. "And the child labour that made them?"

"Be quiet and show some Christmas spirit, would you? You know these are going up, so the less time you spend moaning, the faster it'll be over and done with."

"What if it's overcast?"

"They come pre-charged, I have a remote control to turn them on and off, and the batteries are good for five days. Stop being difficult."

"Is it too late to leave?" Sam whispered to me.

Bradley turned and waved at us.

"Yes, it is," I said through gritted teeth. "Just smile and look like you're enjoying yourself."

Two hours later, I was dangling three storeys above the ground, passing plastic stars to Emmy as she clipped them onto Bradley's "vision." Good to know that a platoon-full of the best special forces operatives money could buy were doing something so worthwhile.

"Where's Black?" I asked. I hadn't seen any sign of him since we arrived.

"He cried off. Told Bradley he had an important call with the president."

"I'm guessing he didn't?"

"Oh, he called James all right. Bradley hung around to check. But as soon as he left the room, the conversation mysteriously changed from discussing America's strategy in Syria to a critique of yesterday's hockey game."

"I wish you'd warned me. I could have come up with an excuse."

"Sorry. The only people he let off are Mrs. Fairfax and Georgia, because Mrs. Fairfax is making dinner and Georgia's pregnant."

"I think I met her at my birthday party. She must be almost due."

"Two weeks. Xav's freaking out. He made Nate build him a baby monitor that'll work from space."

Before she could clip on another star, Emmy's phone rang with Jessie J's "Bang Bang." A few of the men sniggered, and Emmy turned pink as she fished around in her pocket. "Jed changed it as a joke, and I haven't got around to swapping it back, okay?" She glanced at the sky. "Please let this be some sort of emergency."

She got hold of the phone, but when she tried to juggle it with the handful of stars, it slipped from her grasp, bounced off a windowsill, and met its maker on the edge of a stone flower pot three storeys below.

"Bollocks. That could have been important."

Two seconds later, Bradley's phone rang. "It's for you," he yelled up.

"Who is it?"

"One of the guards at the front gate. You have a

visitor who isn't on the list."

"Who? I'm not expecting anyone."

Bradley muttered into the phone again then listened. "He says it's a surprise."

"I'm not fond of surprises. What does he look like?"

More mumbling, more nodding. "About sixty, suntan, smoking a cigar. He's wearing a maroon sweatsuit with white stripes, and is, I quote, 'kind of scary.'"

Emmy's eyes went big. "No way! Tell them to let him in."

"What?" I asked. "Who is it?"

"Come on!" she called, then fast-roped to the ground, landing neatly with her knees bent.

She ignored Bradley's shouts about stars and deadlines and nightfall as she sprinted off down the drive with me following, and I pretended I hadn't heard either. We'd only got around the first bend when a black SUV with tinted windows came into view and slewed to a halt in front of us. A man hopped out of the passenger seat, looking imperious despite his relaxed attire.

Emmy didn't break stride, just carried on and threw herself into his arms. He hugged her back, smiling.

"What the hell are you doing here?" she asked. "Do you know how many wanted lists you're on?"

"I was bored. I needed a vacation." He turned to look me up and down. "And now I understand I have two girls who can break me out of jail."

"Eduardo?" I asked.

"I told her all about you," Emmy said.

His smile turned to a grin as he enveloped me in his arms as well. "Most of it is only rumours."

You know what? I already liked this father better than my first one.

He drew away and held me at arm's length. "So pretty. It is good that you two have found each other. Floriana and I thought we would spend Christmas with you, if that's all right?"

"Of course it's all right. It's better than all right. I still can't believe you're here."

"I thought a visit would be so much more personal than a phone call. Besides, I've never seen your home."

"We can do the whole tour later, and the rest of Virginia too. But come in. You must be freezing in those clothes."

He waved a hand. "It makes a change from all the sun."

Emmy looped her arm through his. "Everyone'll be thrilled to see you."

"It's nice to get such a welcome. Usually, people are not so happy when I come calling."

"That's because they don't know what a soft touch you are underneath."

She gave him a squeeze.

"You are right. I could never let that become known. I have a certain reputation to uphold."

A man after my own heart.

"Shall we get something to eat?" Emmy asked. "Drink? Does Floriana need to change? You both must be tired after your trip."

"Yes to all of those." He took my hand and kissed the back of it." But first I have a gift for you. I'm not sure I got the right one, but I negotiated sale or return."

He'd brought me a gift? "Honestly, you didn't have to."

"Nonsense. It is my pleasure."

A quiet voice from behind made my hair stand on end. "Mama?"

I whirled round and saw the little girl wearing a warm-up suit identical to Eduardo's except in candy floss pink. Her hand shook as she gripped the fur coat of a tiny, dark-haired lady who I figured must be Eduardo's wife.

It couldn't be. Could it? I dropped to my knees in front of the child, and under the long fringe and nervousness, it was. My daughter. Tabby had finally come home.

She let go of Floriana and threw her tiny arms around me. "Mama."

"I missed you too, *katyonak*. I've been trying so hard to find you."

Tears streamed down my cheeks, and I wiped them away with a sleeve as I picked Tabby up. I needed to find Sam. Eduardo could wait. Everything else could wait.

The house came into view, and Sam was on the ground now talking to Black, who'd finally decided to make an appearance now most of the work was done. Sam looked up and saw me, then saw who I was carrying, and his eyes saucered. Then he broke into a run, meeting us in the middle of the lawn.

"Is this...? Is it...?"

I nodded, and I still couldn't stop bloody crying. Sam was speechless, and so was I. I hadn't dared to imagine the moment when I introduced Sam to Tabby in case it jinxed everything.

Finally, I found my tongue.

"Tabby, this is your papa."

"Papa's in heaven. You said so."

Sam thought quickly. "It's Christmas, so I came back."

He wrapped his arms around us both and pulled us tightly against his chest. Tabby took a sharp breath because she wasn't used to that.

"It's okay, sweetie," I whispered, kissing her on the forehead. "We're a family now."

Behind us, Bradley flicked a switch, and the front of the house lit up in a glittering starscape. It was magical. Bradley's ridiculous vision was kind of pretty too.

Emmy padded up behind us and rested her chin on my shoulder. "Happy Christmas, honey."

I turned to grin at her—a proper grin, free from the burdens Zacharov had placed on me for the first time since my mama died.

"Yes, it is a happy Christmas, isn't it?"

GRAY

I was missing Mr. Gray, so I thought I'd let him tell the story of what happened next in a few bonus chapters.

If you'd like to read a little more about Xav, Georgia, Ana, and Quinn, you can download GRAY for FREE from the following link:
www.elise-noble.com/gr4y

What's next?

The Blackwood Security series continues in Red Alert...

Red Alert

How does a girl get over a broken heart?

As always, Bradley has the answer, and newly single Tia Cain soon finds herself in New York with a new job, a new apartment, and a not-so-new appreciation of cocktails.

Guided by her boss, Ishmael, Tia settles into life in the Big Apple only to be flung off balance as two men appear on the scene. One has the looks, one has the voice, and both make her heart beat faster.

Which of them can't she live without?

When a ghost from the past catches up with her, friendships new and old are put to the test in a race for survival. Can love win the day, or will demons prevail?

More details here:

www.elise-noble.com/red

If you'd like to see where the Blackwood story started, you can find that in the Blackwood Security series, starting with Pitch Black.

Pitch Black

Even a Diamond can be shattered...

After the owner of a security company is murdered, his sharp-edged wife goes on the run. Forced to abandon everything she holds dear—her home, her friends, her job in special ops—she builds a new life for herself in England. As Ashlyn Hale, she meets Luke, a handsome local who makes her realise just how lonely she is.

Yet, even in the sleepy village of Lower Foxford, the dark side of life dogs Diamond's trail when the unthinkable strikes. Forced out of hiding, she races against time to save those she cares about. But is it too little, too late?

Warning
If you want sweetness and light and all things bright,
Diamond's not the girl for you.
She's got sass, she's got snark, and she's moody and dark,
As she does what a girl's got to do.

You can get Pitch Black for FREE here:

www.elise-noble.com/pitch-black

If you enjoyed Ultraviolet, please consider leaving a review.

For an author, every review is incredibly important. Not only do they make us feel warm and fuzzy inside, readers consider them when making their decision whether or not to buy a book. Even a line saying you enjoyed the book or what your favourite part was helps a lot.

Want to stalk me?

For updates on my new releases, giveaways, and other random stuff, you can sign up for my newsletter on my website:
www.elise-noble.com

Facebook: www.facebook.com/EliseNobleAuthor

Twitter: @EliseANoble

Instagram: @elise_noble

I also have a group on Facebook for my fans to hang out. They love the characters from my Blackwood and Trouble books almost as much as I do, and they're the first to find out about my new stories as well as throwing in their own ideas that sometimes make it into print!

And if you'd like to read my books for FREE, you can also find details of how to join my review team.

Would you like to join Team Blackwood?

www.elise-noble.com/team-blackwood

END OF BOOK STUFF

Emmy's past always fascinated me, because from the start, it was what drove her. How much of who we are comes from our genes, and how much is from our upbringing?

It was a horse that taught me about the power of genetics. There have only ever been two horses in my life I've genuinely disliked, and he was one of them. Kicking, rearing, biting, bucking, striking out—if you can think of a vice, he had it. And I got the dubious pleasure of taking care of him every Saturday and Sunday morning. If I was on my own at the yard, I used to call somebody right before I led him to the field.

"If I haven't called back within ten minutes, phone an ambulance, will you? I'm probably injured."

His temper always puzzled me. He'd been owned by the same man his whole life, and this guy was big on Natural Horsemanship and only ever kind to him. So one day, right after he'd kicked his owner in the knee, I asked the question.

"What happened to make him so grumpy all the time?"

The answer?

"No idea. He's always been like that, but his sire was just like him."

The horse had never even met his father, yet he'd

inherited his bad attitude. How often does this happen with humans?

So, I decided to introduce Ana—similar to Emmy in some ways, different in others. Same father, both the daughters of prostitutes. Ana with a tightly controlled childhood, Emmy left to fend for herself. Both turned into what they became by men with psychopathic tendencies. And they shared a connection unaffected by distance. Kind of a fascinating relationship to explore.

What about Black's history? Well, that's another story.

In the meantime, I felt a bit guilty for murdering Tia's boyfriend, so I figured I'd better make up for that. Her book is up next—I actually wrote that one in 2014, at the same time as Trouble in Paradise, so it's taken me a while to get it edited and published!

As always, I need to thank the people who helped with Ultraviolet. First up were my wonderful beta readers—Jeff, Renata, Terri, Harka, Stephanie, Lina, Quenby, Musi, Nikita, David, Stacia, Jemma, and Jessica. Then came the editing by Amanda and the cover by Abi. Finally, huge thanks to my proofreaders—Emma, John, and Dominique.

OTHER BOOKS BY ELISE NOBLE

The Blackwood Security Series
Pitch Black
Into the Black
Forever Black
Gold Rush
Gray is my Heart
Neon (novella)
Out of the Blue
Ultraviolet
Red Alert
White Hot
The Scarlet Affair (2018)

The Blackwood Elements Series
Oxygen
Lithium
Carbon
Rhodium (2018)

The Blackwood UK Series
Joker in the Pack
Cherry on Top (novella)
Roses are Dead
Shallow Graves (2018)

The Trouble Series
Trouble in Paradise
Nothing but Trouble
24 Hours of Trouble

Standalone
Life
Twisted (short stories)
A Very Happy Christmas (novella)

Printed in Great Britain
by Amazon